In the

Churchyard
Spilled

In the

Churchyard
Spilled

Book one of the Llangynog Murders

Janet Newton

Kindle Direct Publishing

This is a work of fiction. Names, characters, organizations, events, and incidents are either products of the author's imagination or are used fictionally.

Cover photo by Janet Newton: the churchyard at Pennant Melangell

For Craig

Thank you for always encouraging me, for making me believe in myself, and for indulging my travel whims, wherever they took us. I love you.

In the

Churchyard Spilled

Chapter One

The car skidded to a stop midway across the bridge, worn tyres propelling the Volvo sideways before gripping the wet wood beneath. Bronwyn Bagley held tight to the steering wheel and stared into the fog, wondering if the movement she'd glimpsed meant that some wandering animal now lay beneath her car or had been tossed to the edge of the pavement.

Not a cat, she thought, *nor probably a dog.* The shapeless apparition flicking across her headlamps had looked larger, perhaps a small deer or an escaped sheep. Neither would be out of place in the small Welsh village of Llangynog, where sheep and wildlife easily outnumbered humans.

There's nothing else for it, she thought. She would have to get out of the car to look, else her conscience would bother her through a sleepless night. And she got little enough sleep as it was, she thought sourly, between worrying about the demands of her job and wondering if she'd ever have a more interesting future than what seemed at the moment to be a dead-end life.

Not that she disliked working as coordinator at St. Melangell Centre. Scheduling and other paperwork, even updating the website, she found pleasurable, and she felt good about welcoming individuals who wandered in unexpectedly. It was the gearing up mentally every time she needed to welcome a larger group through the doors or to speak to the volunteers in a meeting that filled her with anxiety. She'd never enjoyed facing a sea of faces, and she knew she never would. And tonight she'd stayed late, until past dark which didn't come all that early on a May evening, all because the group holding a conference had gone overtime.

Fog swirled around her car as she forced a deep breath and opened the door, squinting into the dark. Warily, she pushed herself upright and stood beside the opened driver's door. The damp on her face felt cold, and she shivered despite her jacket.

For the space of a minute, nothing caught her eye except the ghostly mist eddying through the glare of the car's headlamps. She leaned down and peered at the front tyre on the driver's side, seeing nothing out of place. Turning her head, she squinted at the rear of the car in the darkness. Nothing there seemed amiss either. With a sigh, she turned to walk around the car to check the other side.

A low growl froze her in her tracks. She blinked, not sure whether the creature that now loomed in front of her car was a large wolfhound or something else entirely. Perhaps the effect of the headlamps on the fog made it look as spectral as it did? She reached out to grip the edge of the open car door, wondering if she could sidle into the car without alarming it further.

The animal remained still as she managed to slide into the seat. She pulled the door shut, slamming the lock down. Now that she felt safe, she took a moment to study it before sounding her horn to chase it away.

Long-legged and skeletal like a wolfhound, the beast gazed at her as if it could see her through the windscreen and the mist. Its brown-grey fur stuck up in wet tendrils, and the ruff on its back was stiff with alarm. After what seemed a long time, it turned its head, raising its muzzle as if trying to catch her scent in the air. Seeing it in profile, she caught her breath. She'd seen this creature before, and it was no dog.

This was a Cyn Annwn, a phantom wolf-like creature that Welsh mythology said would appear before a death. She had seen one several years before when she was a teenager coming home from secondary school in Llanfillyn.

Memories paralyzed her. She'd been walking from the school bus drop-off toward her parents' farm when Granny Powers had beckoned to her from the front stoop of her cottage. Granny Powers was a little gone in the head, everyone knew that. Still, Bronwyn had climbed the crumbling stone steps and bent low over the wicker rocker so she could hear her hissing whisper. "I'm passin' it all over to you, girl," Granny Powers had said, and even though Bronwyn knew she hadn't been quite all right in the head for as long as anyone could remember, still the words stuck with her.

And then she'd seen the Cyn Annwn, standing across the roadway from the little cottage. She'd run home in a panic, which her misunderstanding parents had tried to sooth. Granny Powers died before the next morning dawned.

But...oh, God! Who was it this time? *Please, not Mum or Dad! Nor Maddock either.* Her brother and his wife Mai lived nearby in a cottage with their children. *The children! Please, not Griffyn or Maegan!*

Bronwyn gulped back panic. *It must be here for someone who's stopped at the counseling centre,* she tried to sooth herself. Pennant Melangell had been a cancer-treatment centre before, and most of those who came for counseling still suffered from the disease. Surely the Cyn Annwn portended the death of someone she didn't know. Of course, it did.

But what if it didn't? Would the Cyn Annwn appear to her to announce the death of someone she didn't know? She didn't think so, and the thought made her heart race.

Shaking, Bronwyn pressed the horn, wanting the creature gone and with it, her raging thoughts. But even before the warning blared, the apparition disappeared into the darkness.

She'd thought about Granny Powers' last words to her often during the decade since her death. Not that she wanted anything Granny might wish on her. The last thing Bronwyn needed was to sit on her front porch and mumble warnings to the tourists heading for the footpath to Pennant Melangell like Granny Powers had.

"Watch for the branch that lies across your path," she'd warned a young woman dressed in L.L. Bean shorts and hiking boots, boots that came off with difficulty after she'd fallen over a log and broken her ankle.

"Beware the dark woman," she'd warned a young man who'd found himself in some trouble after his hiking partner announced her pregnancy a few months later.

Most people shrugged off Granny's abilities as coincidence or luck, but Bronwyn thought differently. Hadn't she been right, at least most of the time? Didn't they live in a "thin place," where barriers between worlds could sometimes be crossed? Didn't Bronwyn herself sometimes see things that later came to be, just as Granny did? And then there were the Twlwyth Teg, the Welsh fairies. They never spoke to Bronwyn and assumed she couldn't understand their skittering language, so they generally ignored her. But in the week before Granny Powers' death, she'd heard them say her name once, twice, thrice, and even before the Cyn Annwn appeared she'd known the portents were not in Granny's favor.

But what could she do? She fretted as she drove the small lane through Llangynog toward home. She'd learned early on that it was better not to mention the wee folk in anyone's presence, this lesson being the most useful she'd learned in the Llangynog volunteer early primary school. She had come home from school sobbing when her classmate Glynnis taunted her after she'd innocently announced to the class that she knew of a magical pool of water beneath an oak tree because the Twlwyth Teg had told her where it was to be found.

"Bronwyn thinks fairies are real!" Glynnis had shouted, and the laughter of the entire class, small as it was, had driven her six-year-old self into a corner of the room where she'd buried her face in her hands and waited for school to end so she could go home to her mum and safety.

"I do see the Twlwyth Teg!" she'd insisted between sobs as her mum held her on her lap and hugged her.

"If you do, perhaps you shouldn't say so," her mum wisely advised her, so after that she was careful not to mention the Twlwyth Teg, the Cyn Annwn, or even wise Pysgotwr the fisherman in the presence of anyone other than her mum, her dad, her big brother Maddock, or her best friend Margred, who found her friend's oddities ignorable as long as no one else knew about them. That is, she felt comfortable chatting on to her family about her unusual friends until she hit her teens and the end of her parents' indulgence. Counseling at that point taught her the wisdom of keeping her secrets even from them.

But I can't just ignore the Cyn Annwn, she thought in a panic. *Someone is meant to die!*

She turned off the lane onto the short drive to the house, letting the car slow to a crawl as she pulled up beside her brother's Ford sedan. Mondays were regular family dinner nights at the Bagley farmhouse, which meant Maddock, Mai and the children would be waiting for her late arrival along with her parents. Old Nan, her

4

sheepdog, hobbled up to meet her, and she took a moment to pat her and compose herself before going inside.

As she'd expected they would be, the whole family was standing in the bright kitchen when she walked in the door. Homey scents of roasted lamb and vegetables welcomed her along with the greetings called her way, and she allowed a smile to ease her concerns for a moment. Surely the Cyn Annwyn wasn't there for any of them?

They carried the somewhat overcooked lamb chops and bowls of potatoes, parsnips, and carrots to the table and sat to eat, passing bowls and chatting noisily.

"Sorry I'm late," she offered, feeling bad about the chops.

"Busy day?" her mum cast her an appraising look. "You look stressed out."

She shook her head, suppressing the thought of the Cyn Annwn. "Just the usual, except that the group overstayed their time. It seems to happen more often than not."

"Maybe you could devise a plan for letting them know time's up?" Mai suggested.

Bronwyn tore a piece of bread from her slice and chewed it slowly. "I think the board are reluctant to do anything that might cause groups to book elsewhere. We're not exactly in a well-populated area, so it's a stretch to convince people to make the drive here. If we start making more rules and demands, they'll just find someplace closer and more accommodating."

"But Pennant Melangell itself offers so much more than what you'd get in some ugly building in a city," Mai pointed out. "It's lovely there, and there's a peace about it that enhances the experience of going there, even if it's for a boring workshop."

Bronwyn smiled and nodded. "That's it exactly. We do get some drop-in business for the counselling centre, and plenty of scheduled clients, too. We just need to get the word out, and I know business will pick up in the conference rooms, too."

"That's your job, isn't it?"

"A big part of it. I'm always trying to think of new ideas to bring to the council, but I never know if they'll like them or not. All I can do is try." And she did. If the centre were busier, maybe they'd even spring for a raise for her, and goodness knows she could use the money. Even living at home with her parents, she could manage only a small savings toward a newer car when hers got to a point where it was beyond repair or, eventually, a deposit for a flat somewhere where she could be on her own.

"We had two lambs before dinner," six-year-old Griffyn broke in, "and I helped."

Bronwyn couldn't help laughing at the abrupt change of topic. "Did you really?"

"Aye, it's a family business," Maddock told him, "and all of us Bagley men have to do our part, don't we?"

"Want to help, too," two-year old Maegan burbled.

"You helped me in the kitchen," Mai said. "Remember?"

Maegan pouted. "But I wanted to see the lambs borned."

"Lambs are really cute, but sometimes it's not safe for a little girl to help with them," Bronwyn couldn't help warning her. What if she were kicked by a ewe? Or...

Her family – she didn't always think to appreciate them, but she should. Not everyone was so lucky. She could feel her heart pounding in her chest as she fought fear and tried to keep a smile on her face. But no place could be safer than Llangynog for a child to grow up, could it?

She and Maddock had spent their childhoods tramping the fields and nearby forest with her dad, a quiet and hard-working farmer. By the time she was five, she'd known the names of nearly all the trees, shrubs, and flowers that grew wild in the Welsh countryside. Rose-cheeked and healthy, she was familiar with the tickle of pasture grass on her bare toes, the sucking of the bogs on her boots, and even the scraping of hard rock on her knees. She knew how to nudge a herd of sheep into a pen, how to help with the shearing, how to hold tight to a bottle of formula for a hard-sucking lamb. She learned the commands used with the sheepdogs, cuddled the pups, and helped train them as they matured. Her greatest joy had been her black Welsh pony, Hobbs, on whose back she'd spent countless hours exploring, sometimes alone and sometimes in the company of Margred, who had her own pony when they were young.

Her mum hadn't been absent in her life, of course, though she saw less of her now because she'd started working afternoons in a shop in Llanrhaedr-ym-mochnant, four miles up the road. She'd encouraged Bronwyn and Maddock in other endeavors during their childhood, things she considered important to making them well-rounded individuals. Maddock hadn't been able to sit still for long, but Bronwyn showed talent from the first childish sketches she'd made with the pencils and paper her mum had provided. Lessons in nearby Oswestry had stretched both the family budget and her mother's free time, but they had allowed Bronwyn's talent to flourish. In time, she delighted in sketching not only forest creatures, but interesting patterns of foliage on trees and shrubs, the meandering river, the barns and village cottages, the waterfalls downstream at Pennant Melangell, and even the shrine itself. It was an outlet in more ways than one because in every sketch she hid a face. It was seldom that anyone noticed these as she tried to be very subtle, but she felt a secret joy in putting them in, the risk of discovery a hidden thrill in her otherwise boring life. Some of the sketches were now offered for sale in the small gift shop in the church at Pennant Melangell, bringing Bronwyn a small bit of extra income.

"They've just hired an old classmate of yours at the Tanat," Mai interrupted her thoughts, sending her into panic again. "Glynnis Newbury, only she's called Glynnis Paisley now, as she's married." Mai worked part time as barmaid at the Tanat Inn, one of two pubs in Llangynog.

"Glynnis back?" Bronwyn frowned. *I wouldn't mind if it was her the Cŷn Annwn was here for.* But that was an awful thought, a wrong way of thinking no matter the past they shared. She forced a grimace. "And married, too? Poor guy, whoever he is. I wouldn't want to be bullied by her day and night."

Mai laughed. "She probably doesn't bully him. He's a good-looking bloke."

"I'm sure that's what caught Glynnis' eye." Bronwyn pushed her lamb chop to the side of her plate absently. "Wonder what it was that brought her back?"

"I got the impression her husband was doing something with the gas pipeline," Mai said, "so she might not be here long. And you're right – she's a mean one, she is. Snapped at me right away, and it being her first day on the job I think I was in the right and not her."

"That sounds like Glynnis," Bronwyn said. She looked at the lamb chop. "Takes my appetite away knowing she's back."

"It was mostly you she bullied," Maddock put in. "She was popular with everyone else."

"Ay, you boys liked her, if that's what you mean."

"Not me," Maddock assured her. "I only had eyes for my Mai."

Mai laughed. "You'd better say that. You're stuck with me now, with these two little ones in our household. But as for Glynnis, I agree with Bronwyn. I think I'll be avoiding her as much as possible."

"Maybe I won't have to see her at all," Bronwyn said, but if what she'd inherited from Granny Powers was second sight, it gave Bronwyn no warning that her wish was in vain.

"Is that Bronwyn the Fey?" called out a voice as she walked home past the Tanat Inn the next afternoon. She'd chosen to walk home the long way, on the four-mile footpath that ran through bogs and up hillsides between Llangynog and Pennant Melangell. It being early spring yet, her boots and trousers were muddy and thistle-dotted and her cheeks ruddy with exertion, but she'd wanted the hike to give her time to think things out. Too, she'd hoped she'd overhear the whispers of the Twlwyth Teg so she'd have a clue about who was in harm's way, but in that she'd been disappointed.

Now, hearing the mocking voice, she turned. Glynnis sat on the bench outside the door of the inn, a smirk twisting her otherwise beautiful face. Glynnis had always been lovely, Bronwyn thought resentfully, blonde and blue-eyed where most people from the area had more typical brown hair and eyes. Bronwyn had always attributed Glynnis' popularity at school to her unusual looks, since her sarcastic tongue and bullying ways weren't assets, at least not to Bronwyn's way of thinking. "Hello, Glynnis," she said.

"You never left the village?" Glynnis seized immediately on an area of Bronwyn's life where she felt left behind. She regarded Bronwyn with a little smile for a moment, and then she leapt unerringly into the other topic that afforded her the opportunity for belittling she was looking for. "And not married either, I would guess?"

"No," Bronwyn admitted shortly. There hadn't really been anyone in Llangynog, and her very short time at Glyndwr University in Wrexham hadn't resulted in any serious relationships, or truthfully, even any serious dates to speak of.

Glynnis stood up. "And you...what? Oh, that's right, the same as me. Twenty-four years old and not a single man interested, I bet."

"What's that to you, Glynnis?"

"Oh, it's nothing! Just curiosity, that's all. Myself, I'm married, and happily so."

"Congratulations," Bronwyn managed despite her annoyance, "and welcome back."

"Yeah, it's great to be back in the village," Glynnis said sarcastically. Her face twisted with distaste, and Bronwyn noticed the darker roots beneath her beautifully highlighted hair. Of course, she was a natural blonde, but one who obviously preferred an even lighter tone than the golden one she'd been born with.

"Why are you here if you prefer somewhere else?"

"My husband is working on the pipeline," Glynnis smiled and sighed. "I married a civil engineer, Davyyd Paisley, from Cardiff. Wait 'til you see him. He's gorgeous."

"I wouldn't mention the pipeline too loudly if I were you," Bronwyn warned her. "It's not a popular subject here and, if we have our way, it will never pass this close to Llangynog."

"Oh, it's going through here all right," Glynnis said. "No doubt about that. But Davyyd and I will be moved on by the time the gas comes through. It's no danger to us."

"Lucky for you," Bronwyn retorted, "but it's not just the people in danger; it's the forest itself – the plants, the trees, and the animals. Can't you think of that?"

"Progress," Glynnis shrugged. "Save the planet or save the economy. There's not much choice. The plants and animals will adapt. And Davyyd's making good money off this project."

Bronwyn took a deep breath, trying to contain her dislike for this woman. "Are you staying here in Llangynog with your mum and dad?"

"No, in Oswestry," Glynnis said. "Llangynog's too small, so we commute. It's nicer there. Bigger, you know, with more going on and nice shops." She glanced at her own black trousers and soft rose-colored blouse.

Bronwyn ignored her own hiking outfit of jeans and worn yellow jumper. It was her habit to change from her work clothes before setting out on the footpath. "Does Davyyd like it here?"

"Yeah, he likes it well enough. At least it's an escape from his ex-girlfriend, and heaven knows, they need some distance between them." She smiled, a gloating smile that marred her beauty. "I stole him from her, and she's not best pleased with either of us at the moment."

"Oh, well, good for you." Bronwyn couldn't help a snide comment. "He must be quite a catch if he goes from one to another so easily."

"You're just jealous," Glynnis' voice rose, and Bronwyn noticed that Cecil Lumley, the owner of the Tanat, glanced at them through the open doorway. "I suppose you still see fairies in the woods." She shook her head and wiggled her fingers. "I can see the future, too, Bronwyn. You couldn't get a man like Davyyd to even glance your way, that's what I think, and you'll end up a crazy old woman like Granny Powers."

Bronwyn couldn't let Glynnis know how close she'd come to hitting the mark with that statement. "Guess you have nothing to fear from me, then," she murmured.

Glynnis glared at Bronwyn for a long moment and then gave in. "We won't be here long enough to worry about that."

"Ah, well, that's good," Bronwyn said, turning away. At least having Glynnis here would be temporary, she thought. The last thing she needed was for her nemesis to come back into her life when she already wondered how she was going to ever make a happier future for herself than she had at the moment.

Chapter Two

Llangynog's normal cheerful atmosphere evaporated into controversy that spring.

The trouble began when protesters filled the car park on the first Saturday of May, along with the first serious scatter of hikers and mountain bikers bent on making their way to the shrine at Pennant Melangell or the beautiful waterfalls at the head of the valley beyond. May was a bit early for the footpath to be passable, but an unseasonably warm spring drew the hopeful to try it.

The protesters were not unwelcome. Indeed, emotions were running high now that it appeared that the gas pipeline would become reality. Although Llangynog's residents were easy-going people, this topic tended to awaken some of the ire their warlike ancestors had been famous for. So far, no Welsh longbows had come out from the attics, but a definite prejudice against the engineering team on location emerged during teatime discussions both at the two pubs and in the homes near the village.

Enjoying a rare Saturday off from work, Bronwyn had taken her niece, Maegan, and nephew, Griffyn, to the play park next to the village hall to enjoy some time outdoors in a place where she could keep a close eye on them. She'd come to no decision what to do about the Cyn Annwn, and the worry gnawed at her like a cancer. She was reluctant to let any of her family out of her sight, fighting the need to appear obsessive about it. Since Mai worked during the lunch rush at the Tanat Inn, the children typically spent much of Saturday with their father and grandfather, helping them with the sheep. She'd thought to give them a break.

She and the children watched the first of the protesters unload from a dozen cars which took over most of the car park spaces, noting their picket signs and cheerful determination.

"What's going on?" a man pushing a mountain bike called to her from the street.

"Pipeline protest," she answered him. She glanced at Maegan and Griffyn and, seeing that they were occupied, she wandered over to the edge of the playground.

"I heard something about that." He nodded to two other bikers who wheeled their bicycles up to join him. All three looked fit and athletic, with the wind-tossed hair and eager look in their eyes of men who lived for outdoor exercise, but the one who had talked to her was the best-looking of the group. Sun blonde hair just a little too shaggy and ruddy complexion perfect, he grinned at her, hazel eyes alight with interest. He had an American accent and an expensive Fezzari mountain bike.

"It's a high-pressure gas line meant to run 197 miles, part of it right through the Brecon Beacons, and Llangynog is right in the middle of it," Bronwyn explained, returning his smile.

"Through the Tanat Valley?" the man protested. "Can they get away with that?"

"Apparently someone thinks so," Bronwyn said, "but there must still be hope of stopping it, because why else would we be flooded with protesters?"

He glanced at the group of protesters, now organized and handing out leaflets, and shook his head. "Wouldn't it be more effective if they protested where the actual decision is being made? No one will even know they are here."

"Oh, I'm sure they're doing that, too. But just now we have the planners here doing the preliminary part of the work, so I'm sure they'll try to disrupt that first."

"Well, good luck to them," the American said, and then he asked something unexpected. He nodded toward Maegan and Griffyn and asked, "Are they yours?"

Bronwyn laughed. "No, just my niece and nephew."

"Well, then, I don't suppose you would join me for a drink later at one of the pubs in town?"

Bronwyn, caught off-guard, felt a hot flush run up her neck and onto her face, though she felt pleased for his asking. "I don't even know your name."

He grinned at her. "Mark McGuire, from Seattle. And you?"

"Bronwyn Bagley, from right here in Llangynog."

He laughed. "That's quite a name. I like it."

"Thanks."

"Now that we've been introduced, how about that drink tonight?" His smile remained, his warm eyes fixed on her.

"Okay," she managed, heart thumping. It'd only be a drink, after all, with him off to another picturesque biking spot the next day. Maybe it'd be fun. "Where do you want to meet?"

"Which place is best?"

"The Tanat's okay," she said, her wits returning with a swiftness that astounded her. Maybe Glynnis would be on shift tonight and she could flaunt this American a bit.

"Meet you there at 7:00?"

"Okay," she agreed, and then she grinned at her own foolishness as she turned back to Maegan and Griffyn just in time to hear Maegan shrieking.

She ran to her and knelt down. "What's happened, love?"

She tried to turn Maegan's face toward her, but the little girl shook her off and pointed. "Doggie!" she shrieked again. "Doggie! Doggie!"

Bronwyn frowned and turned to look, but she saw nothing. "There's no doggie, Maegan," she soothed her.

"Ran away," Maegan sighed, and suddenly she was quiet again, cuddling into Bronwyn's arms.

A chill ran down Bronwyn's spine. "What did it look like, Maegan?"

"Big doggie. Growling, grrr, grrr." Maegan squirmed away. "Want to go on the swing again. You push me?"

"Sure, love," Bronwyn agreed, her mind elsewhere. What Maegan described sounded like the Cwn Annwn. *Surely not,* she thought. Wasn't one death in their tiny village enough for the moment? But maybe it just appeared to more than one person to announce the same death? Children, she knew, found it easier than adults to see into the otherworld. She shivered. Someone was definitely going to die. *Please don't let it be anyone I love.*

The protesters stirred tension all that day so that, by evening, the pipeline workers on site hurried to their vehicles to escape out of the village to Oswestry or Penybontfawr, places where hotels and pubs were more welcoming. As they fled the town, so did much of the tension they had brought with them. Nevertheless, the pipeline remained a topic of conversation in the two village pubs that night.

Bronwyn had arrived early for her meeting with Mark, the American mountain biker. She could hear the piano and singing from the New Inn across the street as she hesitated at the door of the Tanat. The New Inn dated to 1751, and if it was "new," the 16th century Tanat was a historic relic that nevertheless remained a social centre for the village now as it had for the past five hundred years. Either inn offered solid, homemade food, but the Tanat attracted the locals in for a pint more often than not as they discussed the price of lambs or the controversy over the pipeline while warming themselves by the fire.

Shy now, Bronwyn tugged at the door and stepped inside, pausing to look around for Mark before choosing a table on the "drinks" side of the kitchen staircase that divided the inn rather than the "diners" side. He had mentioned only a drink, so she had eaten a sandwich at home and wouldn't presume that the offer included a meal, although prices in the Tanat were reasonable enough.

It being a Saturday night, the inn was crowded with villagers, as well as the remaining protesters and tourists trying to catch a bit of local atmosphere. None of her own family was present, but she saw Glynnis' father, who was rather known for his liking of a drink, sitting at a table with a young man Bronwyn assumed was Glynnis' husband Davyyd. Glynnis herself stood behind the bar at the moment, laughing as customers called out their orders to her and bringing them cheerfully enough.

Mark arrived on time and without the two biking friends who had accompanied him earlier. Bronwyn waved at him from her table. He pushed through the crowded room and pulled out a chair, wobbling the table a bit as he sat down.

"You got here early," he accused her, his hazel eyes assessing her.

"I thought I'd better get us a table," she told him, not wanting him to think her over-eager. "It sometimes gets a bit crowded inside, and it looks like a lot of the protesters stayed for dinner."

"Have you ordered anything yet?" He nodded toward the bar. "I'll go get us whatever you want. Are you hungry, or are we not allowed food on this side of the place?"

"They'll bring you something over here if you order it. I'm not really all that hungry, but I could do with some chips. Otherwise, you can just shout out your drink order to the bar and someone will bring it straightaway."

"Maybe I'll start with some chips, too, and then have something more later," he agreed. "Will you have a Guinness, or do you want something else?"

She suppressed a smile. "Red wine, please," she said.

"Are you laughing at me?"

"No, of course not."

"Yes, you are. What's so funny that you have to try to keep that smile off your face?" His words sounded more insulted than he looked, with a half-smile tugging at the corners of his mouth.

"Tourists always order Guinness, and it's Irish," she told him, beginning to feel more comfortable. "Wales is a different country altogether."

"Is there something local I should be sampling, then?" His smile turned into a grin as he allowed his eyes to roam away from hers and down to the blouse she'd chosen for its ability to show off her curves.

She blushed. "I'm just saying…"

In the end, he ordered a local microbrew for himself and wine for her, and they sat at the table with their chips and chatted. The mountain biking trip was his reward to himself for finishing up his college degree in corporate law, he told her with obvious pride. He and his two roommates had all attended classes together and studied together through their college years. They had pledged to take time off before signing on for real jobs, but only if they all passed the bar exam together. That motivation kept them pushing each other hard, and now they were enjoying their reward.

"Is this your first ride, then?" Bronwyn asked him.

"We've spent a week in the Lake District in England, but this is our first ride in Wales," he told her.

"And what did you think?"

"Amazing scenery," he said, "and just challenging enough to be interesting."

"Did you ride past Pennant Melangell?"

"That's what brought us here," he nodded. "We saw it online when we were doing research for the trip and it looked interesting. Beauty and mystery, amazing scenery – whoever decided to advertise it for mountain biking was a genius."

She nodded happily. "It is nice, isn't it? I work up there, in the counseling centre."

He gazed at her, surprised. "Wow, that's...well, that must be interesting."

She reached for a chip. "Why do you say that?"

"I don't know. It seems mystical, kind of a Stonehenge-type place. I don't imagine ordinary people working there. It doesn't seem the place for a job somehow."

"But someone has to work there, or it would all fall to ruins."

"Guess you're right." He grinned at her. "Tell me about the saint. We rode past the church, but I don't know the story."

"You want to hear that?" Bronwyn wrinkled her nose. "Really?" He nodded, so she took a breath. "Well, it all started a long time ago, in the seventh century when Christianity was still new to Britain."

"Is this a religious story then?" Mark frowned. "I thought Wales was magic."

Bronwyn laughed, relaxing again. "Well, Melangell was a blessed saint, after all. But yes, there's a bit of magic involved, as well."

"Okay," Mark nodded. "Tell me about it then."

"I'll be sure to get the magical part in," Bronwyn assured him. "Once there was and twice there wasn't a prince of Powys named Brychwel Ysgithrog who was out hunting with his men."

"What does that mean, 'once there was and twice there wasn't'?" Mark interrupted.

"Well, I guess it means whatever you think it means." Bronwyn's forehead crinkled in thought. "It means there's one chance it's true and two that it isn't, I guess."

"Oh, okay." Mark sat back in his chair, nearly crashing into a tray of drinks Glynnis was delivering to the table behind theirs. He was oblivious. "Go on."

"His dogs took up a hare and chased it until it hid in a horrible thorny thicket of brambles where the dogs wouldn't follow, no matter what the prince did. Finally, he got off his horse and saw that there was a woman sitting beneath the brambles praying, and the hare was hidden beneath her skirts, peeking out."

"The hare was under her skirts?" Mark grinned at the thought. "Does that mean the prince had to...errr...dive under to retrieve it?"

"No, of course not," Bronwyn retorted with a stern look, although she was trying not to grin. "This is the magical part. The woman was young and beautiful, and the prince was amazed to find her all alone in such a remote place. He asked for her story, and she told him that she was a princess of Ireland who had fled the marriage her father had arranged for her."

"Yeah, they all say something like that, don't they?"

"In this case, it was true, though."

"Once there was and twice there wasn't?" Mark raised his eyebrows. "How do you know it's true?"

"Well, that's how the legend goes. Melangell had lived in Pennant all alone for fifteen years without seeing another human being because she believed God wanted her there to serve him. The prince was so impressed by her that he dedicated the lands around to the service of God, making it a sanctuary for all wild animals including the hares and a refuge for women in retreat."

"And she lived there happily all the days of her life." Mark sat back in his chair and took a sip of his beer. "Right?"

"Right," Bronwyn answered thoughtfully. "Melangell stayed there for 37 years helping women who were searching for a spiritual retreat, and the prince's descendants continued their protection of the place for centuries afterwards."

"That doesn't sound too magical to me," Mark observed.

"Oh, and the animals behaved like family pets," Bronwyn put in hastily. Then, as an afterthought, she added, "and Pennant Melangell is a thin place, which means it is a place where the barriers between our world and the otherworld can be crossed."

"Yeah, right." Mark's skepticism twisted his face into a frown. "Do you believe that, or is it the 'once there was and twice there wasn't' situation again?"

"If you go there with the right attitude and immerse yourself in the wholeness of the place, you might feel it," Bronwyn suggested. "Thin places do have a certain spiritual feel to them in my experience."

"She knows all about that, actually," a voice interrupted her, and she looked up to find Glynnis standing at their table, her drinks tray in her hand. "We call her 'Bronwyn the Fey' because she talks to the Twlwyth Teg."

"The...what?" Mark looked at Bronwyn.

"Welsh fairies," Glynnis supplied with a sidelong glance at Bronwyn. "Right, Bronwyn?"

"Leave us alone, Glynnis." Bronwyn gave her a pleading look. "Please?"

"Sure." Glynnis shrugged. She winked at Mark, though, and Bronwyn tried to ignore the way his eyes followed her as she walked to another table to deliver an order.

Embarrassed, Bronwyn glanced away from Mark, spotting Davyyd as he chatted with Glynnis' father. Glynnis' husband was good looking, she had to admit, with an open face and lively eyes that inspired trust and a wry smile that made him look guileless. His eyes followed Glynnis as she worked, as if he could hardly take them off her. Bronwyn thought she might like him, if only he weren't linked forever to Glynnis.

It was just about then that a handful of protesters who remained spotted Davyyd and marked him as a target, despite his easygoing appearance.

"Hey, you," one of them called out, "we don't want your kind here drinking with us."

Davyyd looked at them, his expression calm and unconcerned. "Just doing my job, mate. If it wasn't me, it'd be someone else doing it." Beside him, Glynnis' father glared hard at the protester, gripping his full pint with both hands.

"Yeah, well, if you guys had any conscience, you'd all refuse, and that would stop them putting that thing in, wouldn't it?" The man stood up and walked closer. "Bet you're only concerned with what they pay you, yeah? If the money's good enough, you can look the other way when our way of life is threatened? Pretty soon there'll be nothing left but cities and ruined countryside."

"Actually, the pipeline should be perfectly safe." Davyyd put out a hand to stop his father-in-law speaking.

"Tell that to the deer, those few we have left." The man shook his head.

"Yeah, Hal's right. Tell that to the people who live here after it ruptures and destroys the village," another one put in. "Hal's from the area. He has to stay here after it's all said and done."

"Just because you have a job here, it doesn't mean we have to socialize with you," yelled another. "Go on, get out. This is our pub. We don't need your kind here."

Davyyd stood up, reaching for his jacket. "I'll go, if it'll make you happy." Glynnis' father watched morosely now but made no move to stop him.

Then Davyyd paused as a tray of beers flew out of Glynnis' hands to shatter on the protesters' table, spraying them all with foamy brew. "No, Davyyd, stay where you are," she ordered him. "You have just as much right to be here as they do, or maybe more."

"What the hell?" The man called Hal grabbed a napkin and wiped beer from his face. "You did that on purpose!"

Glynnis stuck her chin in the air. "Maybe I did. What of it?"

Hal stood up, his eyes glittering with anger. "You'll be sorry for that," he muttered loudly enough to be sure everyone in the Tanat heard him.

"Yeah?" Glynnis spat. "What are you going to do? Hit me with your sign?"

Before Hal could answer, the Tanat's owner, Cecil Lumley, emerged from the kitchen and hurried down the stairs. "What's going on out here?" He looked around and saw the wet table, frowning.

"I'm kicking them out," Glynnis informed him. "Especially this guy, Hal whatever."

"We weren't causing any trouble," Hal stormed back. "At least, not enough to cost you our business. Or are you in support of the pipeline, as well?"

"Who's supporting the pipeline?" Cecil grunted. His eyes shifted toward Glynnis. "You! Are you causing problems with the customers?"

"They started it, harassing him." She pointed at Davyyd, but didn't identify him as her husband. "They told him to leave. They threatened him. They said…"

"Okay," Cecil Lumley broke in, "all of you out. As far as I can see, this bloke isn't hurting you, and even if I do support your cause, I can't support your tearing my place apart. Go on, get!"

Grumbling, the group of protesters pushed away from their table, and one of the ladies caught Hal by the arm. He resisted her pull for a long moment, glaring defiantly at Glynnis, and then he turned and walked out, kicking the door as he passed.

Cecil Lumley looked at Glynnis. "You should be done here, as well, considering what you did just now," he said.

Glynnis let out an exasperated breath. "He only got what he deserved."

"Argue with me, and you're fired," Cecil warned.

Glynnis glanced at Davyyd, and then her eyes swept the room. At least thirty people remained at the tables, but few of them looked up to meet her eyes. "All of you should be ashamed, letting that sort of thing go on. You're to blame as much as I am." With that, she flounced away, disappearing into the kitchen.

Cecil Lumley sighed and looked around the room. "Who needs what?" he asked, picking up Glynnis' tray.

"Now, that's a fiery one," Mark commented to Bronwyn.

He said it rather admiringly, Bronwyn thought. "She's that guy's wife," she pointed to Davyyd. "That's why she was acting like that."

"Oh, that explains it then," said Mark, but his admiration for Glynnis didn't seem to be deterred by Davyyd's presence. Indeed, within twenty minutes he was ignoring Bronwyn to flirt with Glynnis as she brought them another round of drinks.

Bronwyn glanced away from Glynnis and over at Davyyd, who had, by then, been deserted by Glynnis' father and sat alone at his corner table, nursing his drink and watching as Glynnis bent low over their table, her low-cut blouse revealing more than Mark had the right to see. He didn't look angry, but only sad, Bronwyn thought, distressed at the idea that this apparently very nice man was suffering at Glynnis' hands. *We have that in common,* she thought.

As Glynnis flounced away, Bronwyn watched Mark's gaze follow her. With a shrug, she pushed her chair away from the table and stood up. "I need to get home," she announced. "I have to work tomorrow."

"What?" Mark looked up at her, startled. "We just got more drinks."

"Yeah, well, you can just as well drink both of them." Bronwyn edged away.

Mark stared at her for a long moment and then smirked. "It's that barmaid, isn't it?"

Bronwyn sighed. "Yeah, it's the barmaid. You're obviously more interested in her than in me, and that's okay. I don't even know you, and I'm sure you'll be heading back to America before I could ever get to know you. I don't mind, really." She turned away before he could say anything more. Not that he would have, she thought. He didn't even try to stop her going.

She almost made her escape unnoticed. As she pushed the door open, however, Glynnis swooped by and leaned toward her to whisper, "Too bad about your American. Not interested in you so much, huh? Well, maybe one day you'll meet someone else, and I won't be there to steal him away."

"Why do you like to bully me, Glynnis?" Exasperated, Bronwyn spoke more loudly than she intended.

"Bully?" Glynnis' blue eyes widened innocently. "I can't help it if men find me more attractive than they do you."

Before she got caught up in an argument that she knew she'd lose, Bronwyn stepped out the door and slammed it behind her, closing off both noise and light. She caught back a panicked sob, struggling to control an overwhelming flood of self-pity, and glanced around to make sure no one was outside to notice.

The lane was deserted, and the sun had set at least an hour earlier, leaving the village in darkness except for the lights twinkling from the windows of cottages and the nearly full moon in the sky above. Bronwyn hadn't thought she'd be walking home alone in the dark, but Llangynog was safe enough, even if a few of the protesters were still hanging about, which she doubted. And, truthfully, the moon was bright enough that she could have hiked the trail back to Pennant Melangell by its light if she'd wanted to that night.

She walked briskly along the paved roadway, anger at herself growing. Although the American would have been a one-time date in any case, she knew that it was not her love life that Glynnis threatened, but her pride. Surely, she was attractive in her own way, wasn't she? *Maybe I should just get out of Llangynog, make a fresh start somewhere else.* Her thoughts spun wildly. *Maybe I'd be better off in someplace that's not a thin place, someplace where I can be normal.* She stopped a wail that threatened to explode from her anguished mind onto her lips. *I don't want to be like Granny Powers!* She kicked at a stone that had fallen onto the roadway.

As she passed the car park, she saw that four cars remained in their parking slots and, for some reason, this distracted her a bit. She took a deep breath and slowed her steps. A few protesters might have remained, she thought. Or perhaps the cars belonged to hikers, taking some refreshment after a long day of climbing the hills up the quarry. Or maybe someone was staying at the New Inn, which had recently begun to advertise as a bed and breakfast.

She glanced up again at the moon, and then she looked up past the cottages to where the moonlight lit the peaks of the Berwyn mountains, leaving the slopes below in dark shadow. *I can't leave,* she admitted with a sigh that bore both contentment and sadness. *I belong here.* The short time at university in Wexham had made that clear, for she'd suffered from such homesickness that she had been physically ill. It wasn't her family she missed, either. It was the

Twlwyth Teg and the others that drew her home again. Few thin places existed in the world, and, somehow, she'd been born in one of them. She knew she couldn't be happy elsewhere, but nor perhaps could she be happy in tiny Llangynog. *What is it I want from life?* She didn't know.

She jerked to a stop as a sudden rustling at the edge of the roadway interrupted her thought, startling her. She caught her breath, listening intently. Smells of spring grass and wildflowers tickled at her nose, but the stronger acrid scent of sheep made her wonder if some had escaped the stone walls.

"Hurry! Hurry!"

Ah, then, the skittering sound was the Twlwyth Teg. She let her breath escape with relief. *Finally!* She strained to see in the dark but couldn't make them out, as they were buried in the shadows of the stone walls that separated the fields from the roadway. Still, their voices continued on, a confusing babble as they spoke all at once.

They seemed to be pacing her, Bronwyn decided, so she continued on down the road to keep them in earshot as she tried to make out enough words to tell what they were chattering about.

"Danger! Dark! Protector!" she managed to pick out, making no sense of the words at all. "Thick! Thick!" *What???* "Hurry!"

Then the voices disappeared as a car's headlamps appeared in the distance, and Bronwyn was left straining to hear the nothingness in the silence that remained.

With a sigh, she glanced up to see stars materializing in the night sky. Tomorrow, she decided, if the weather held, she'd go find Pysgotwr and ask him what was going on. Although his words were usually enigmatic and puzzling, surely she could put them together with what she'd heard from the Twlwyth Teg and Granny Powers' final words and make some sense of whatever was happening in Llangynog. It had always been a mysterious place, being so close to Pennant Melangell, but all of a sudden, its mysteries seemed to be multiplying, and if they included more deaths, she had no choice but to try to find out what was happening, to see if there was a chance of preventing whatever was meant to be.

There was no peace for Bronwyn at home, though. She'd no more than walked through the door when a car pulled up and parked beside the house. Looking out the window, she saw that it was Maddox' Ford, and she steeled herself for the lecture she suspected was coming.

He didn't disappoint. "What? Are you still a pimply teenager?" he demanded, but in a harsh whisper so as not to wake their parents sleeping upstairs.

"Glynnis provoked me," she defended herself. "Am I expected to just ignore her when she says nasty things to me?"

"Adults walk away, Bron. No matter what she said, you had that option." He hesitated. "Was it that she was flirting with your date? Was that what set you off?"

She threw him a furious look. "Everything she does sets me off! She bullies me, she flaunts all the things she has that I haven't, and then she makes a point of stealing away any man who shows an interest. She's always treated me like that. I suspect she always will."

"You want me to sort him for you?"

"What? No!"

"A gentleman should not invite a lady out, only to leave her for someone else. He needs a talking to."

"Please, Madd, don't. He's gone by now anyway, and he won't be in Llangynog by tomorrow." She looked up at him, saw the teasing grin on his face, and stood up, ready to stomp upstairs to her room.

He reached out to grab her arm. "You need to learn to look the other way, Bron. The only thing you gain by fighting with Glynnis is a reputation for being as nasty as she is."

"You wouldn't understand." She glared at him. "No one ever tried to take Mai away from you, did they? No one called you names."

"All kids do that to each other, Bron. Surely you know that."

She turned away, not wanting him to see the tears that had sprung to her eyes.

"Bron? You can't let Glynnis bother you. If you ignore her, she'll eventually go away, I promise. Her husband's job isn't meant to last more than a few weeks here." He sighed. "Want a cup of tea?"

She shook her head. "I suppose Mai called you," she managed. She turned to look at him, blinking. "It was only a little argument, not important enough for you to come running."

He closed his eyes and shook his head. "Yes, it was Mai who called, but Mum and Dad have been worried about you, too."

"No! I've not done a single thing to worry them since I've been back."

"I know, I know," he shushed her, "it's more what you haven't done. You got the job and they were happy, but now they worry about other things."

"What other things?" she demanded, thinking furiously. *I've not mentioned the wee folk once, nor do I stay out late or drink too much or...*

"They just want you to be happy, Bron. They notice you're alone a lot, walking the footpath or in the forest. They think you need friends."

"Or a boyfriend." She glared at him. "What if I don't want one?"

"It's up to you. But no one is happy being alone all the time."

"I see plenty of people at work," she reminded him, "and what's it to anyone if I prefer a quiet walk home after a long day?"

"It's rather the lack of a smile on your face, I think, that makes them think you want more."

She hesitated. "I'm not crazy, Maddox."

His smile seemed forced. "I know you're not, sweetheart. You're smart, an amazing artist, too."

"I haven't said a word about the wee folk since Granny Powers died."

"I know you haven't."

"Did you know William Blake saw angels in a tree when he was four years old? And he's one of our most treasured poets. He wasn't crazy, either."

He shook his head, a rueful grin on his face. "No, I didn't know that, sweetheart. Makes a difference, that."

She shrugged, regretting telling him about the angels. *Time to change the subject.* "So, Mai called you, thinking I was being anti-social walking out on that American after he spent the evening flirting with Glynnis."

"She was worried about you after you stormed out of the Tanat. I guess Glynnis' husband left shortly after, so he couldn't have been happy with her either."

"At least that's something," Bronwyn muttered. "Maybe her marriage isn't as happy as she'd have us think."

"Poor bloke." Maddox reached out and touched her hand. "There's more going on than just Glynnis' bullying, isn't there, love? It isn't like you to get so upset over a date that didn't work out the way you wanted."

She clenched her jaw. No way could she tell him about the Cyn Annwn and how much seeing it had upset her. What could she tell him? "You're not totally wrong, Madd," she admitted at last. "I sometimes wonder where my life is going. You know? You have Mai and the children and a great life, but I feel kind of at odds. And the biggest thing is that I don't even know what it is I want. I just know something's missing."

"Llangynog isn't the best place to meet someone, if that's what you're wanting," he went back to the boyfriend refrain. "You should be living somewhere where there are more people, but you like your job here, don't you?"

"Yeah, the job is fine. I feel good about it most of the time, and I'm getting used to the responsibilities. It doesn't pay as much as I'd like, but I was lucky they had an opening. Jobs are pretty scarce here, and really, I don't want to live somewhere else."

"But maybe you do want someone to share your life with, isn't that it? A job isn't the pinnacle of happiness for most people."

"I can't leave Llangynog," she said. "I tried when I went to university, and I couldn't do it."

"Then I guess we'll work on finding you someone who'll be content to live here," he told her. He squeezed her hand. "I'll try to do my duty as a big brother to you and find some likely candidates."

She put her hand to her mouth. "God, that'd be awful, Maddox. Please don't. I'll find someone on my own if I'm meant to. But I'm not sure that's what I want."

"Then what?"

She thought for a minute. "Maybe I'm looking for a purpose to my life."

He nodded. "Then it'll come clear, Bron. Be patient."

"I will."

"And stay far away from Glynnis in the meantime. She'll not be staying here long anyway."

"I promise." She sighed. "Thanks for coming to my rescue, Maddox."

"Anytime, sweetheart. Anytime."

She made herself a cup of tea after he left and sipped it in the empty kitchen before climbing the attic stairs to her tiny bedroom, where she opened her window to let in the cool night air and turned to nudge old Nan from the centre of the bed so that she could tuck herself beneath the quilt. The other dogs slept outside, but Nan's old bones had earned her the right to stay snug inside these days, and she'd claimed Bronwyn's bed as her own, not that Bronwyn minded at all.

She laid quiet and tried to relax, but thoughts rushed around and around in her head, try as she might to still them. Granny Powers' rasping whisper and the frantic chatter of the Twlwyth Teg played over and over again in her memory, like a song that won't leave once it's been heard on the radio. She thought and thought about her evening with Mark, torturing herself as she wondered what Glynnis offered that she didn't, hurt that once again Glynnis had managed to best her. She even thought about her life as a whole, coming back to Llangynog which only had a population of a couple of hundred people, after all, and whether she was making a dead end of it all.

Why did she let Glynnis bother her so, she wondered? Perhaps if she tried harder to know her, to find something to appreciate in her, they could make a truce of sorts. No one is all bad, she told herself, and it was true that Glynnis had other friends when they were in school. In fact, even Bronwyn's best friend Margred had gone to Glynnis' birthday parties and ridden bicycles with her sometimes. Perhaps something in her family life had caused her to be such a bully? Surely it couldn't have been that she simply got a thrill from intimidating Bronwyn? No one could be born that horrible, could she?

Bronwyn closed her eyes with a sigh. She was likely to run into Glynnis again the next day, it being a Sunday and therefore another day for hikers and mountain bikers to amble into the village pubs, requiring employees to be on the premises most of the day. She would make a point of finding her and trying to have a civil conversation with her, she told herself firmly. She'd do it right after she'd talked to Pysgotwr, and then maybe she could sleep the next night, having satisfied herself that she'd done her best with at least one of the problems in her life.

Chapter Three

Bronwyn awoke stiff and aching – and late – the next morning when she heard the church bells tolling in the village. Slowly she stretched, squinting against the niggling headache behind her eyes.

"Guess I won't be making church today," she murmured to Nan, closing her eyes again. She often attended a service, not because she felt especially religious, but thinking that it made a good impression on her bosses when she did.

A patter of rain hit her window. She opened her eyes to look and simultaneously pulled the quilt higher around her face. Spring in Wales saw rain more often than not, so this weather wasn't unexpected so much as inconvenient. The truth was, though, that many hikers came prepared for it, so it was probable that she could still get in her conversation with Glynnis. And, if she dressed for it, she could still go in search of Pysgotwr. Fishing improved in the rain, she thought, so perhaps he would be out where he could be found.

The rain had become a fine damp mist by the time Bronwyn dragged herself out of the warm bed and down to the kitchen where her mother had thoughtfully kept breakfast warm for her.

"Bacon, too, or just eggs with your toast?" she asked with a smile.

"Just the eggs," Bronwyn suppressed the urge to groan at her mother's cheerfulness. "And tea, please."

"Of course, tea. I knew that. I noticed you avoided the lamb the other night." Her mother poured two eggs waiting in a bowl into a pot of boiling water. "Turning into a vegetarian, are you?"

"Maybe, yeah, I think so. It just doesn't seem right to assume we can use animals however we wish." Bronwyn sat down at the table, settling back into the comfortable old wooden chair. She breathed in the aroma of fresh-baked bread, yeasty and nutty, and watched her mother at the stove.

"That's what this farm is all about," her mother reminded her, no criticism in her voice. "We grow animals that become food down the line."

"I know," Bronwyn conceded. "I'm just exploring the idea right now, contemplating it."

"That's good then. Thinking things out is never a bad idea."

Bronwyn smiled, despite her headache. She wondered if there was ever a time when her mother wouldn't be supportive of whatever notion took a hold of her.

"How was the date with the American, love?" Her mother dipped the eggs from the pot and put them on a plate with two slices of wholemeal toast. She set the plate in front of Bronwyn and then went to pour them both a cup of tea from the pot on the counter.

"It wasn't a date," Bronwyn grumbled. "Just a drink and a bite in the pub, that's all."

"Ah, then, it didn't go well?"

"No, it didn't," Bronwyn admitted, wishing her mother weren't quite so involved in her personal life. "Glynnis saw to that."

Her mother watched her for a long moment, and then she reached out to smooth a strand of Bronwyn's hair back away from her face where it had escaped the ponytail she often wore on weekends. "Glynnis has never been a friend to you, has she?"

Bronwyn sighed. "I am going to try, Mum. Surely Glynnis can't be all bad. I thought I'd try to befriend her, and then maybe she'll give me some peace, at least for the short time her husband is working here."

"Good luck to you, then." Her mother refilled Bronwyn's half-empty tea cup, obviously having noticed her need for its fortifying caffeine. "Your father has never had much luck making peace with Glynnis' mother, after all."

Bronwyn looked up from her eggs. "Her mother?"

"Don't tell me you didn't notice that Glynnis' mum was your dad's fiercest competition every year at the sheep dog trials."

Bronwyn thought back. "Now you mention it, I guess she was."

"It has been going on for years. She's a competitive sort. But after your dad refused to sell her one of the pups from Nan's last litter a few years ago, that's when she really went after him."

"And she's won it from him, too, from time to time." Bronwyn reached for her second piece of toast. "But only after Nan was too old to compete."

"That she has," her mother agreed. "And I suppose that's where Glynnis learned it - the joy of winning, only in her case it takes the form of bullying. But it's all the same, isn't it?"

"Yeah," Bronwyn nodded. "I guess so."

"And it's driven Glynnis' poor dad to drink, so that's what it got them." Her mother stood up and walked over to the sink. "So, feel bad for Glynnis and try to understand, Bronwyn love. And remember – she isn't going to be here in Llangynog for long."

"Thank goodness," Bronwyn said with a grin. "I can't help myself, Mum. I'll try with her, but I'll never be sorry to see her backside leaving the village for good."

The hearty breakfast went a long way toward compensating for Bronwyn's lack of sleep so that her headache was nearly gone by the time she'd dressed herself in her thick woolen trousers, boots, and a hooded jacket. Although the rain had decreased to a mist, dripping leaves from overhead trees and wet brush would not make it a pleasant walk unless she was well-dressed for the weather.

Taking a blackthorn walking stick from the corner by the door, she set out down the B4391 toward the village proper. At this time of day, she might have expected a car or two bringing hikers to the village, so she tried to walk along the edge of the pavement, what little edge there was on the narrow road, just in case a distracted driver caught her unawares with her hood up and masking the sounds.

Sheep grazed in dew-sparkled green fields on both sides of the road here, and the gray mist seemed only to emphasize the luminescence of the spring colors. Early snowdrops and hazel bloomed between the road and the stone walls, and Bronwyn spotted a fat robin sitting on a tree branch watching her.

Soon enough the pasture gave way to stone cottages lining the street. Bronwyn strode past them, seeing no one else out. Some would still be at Sunday services, she thought guiltily, and others might not even be awake yet, it being a day of rest. There were only six cars in the car park and no sign of protesters. Maybe they only came out on fair weather days then.

She passed St. Cynog's church, the Tanat Inn, the New Inn, Granny Powers' house, and the bowling green. She murmured a hello to one elderly villager, Lew Richards, who was out walking his old spaniel in the rain. He tipped his damp hat in response, and she went on her way without stopping to chat.

She was about halfway through the village when she heard the tyres of a vehicle splashing noisily on the wet pavement some distance behind her. Glancing over her shoulder, she saw what appeared to be a police car entering the village on the far end of town. She turned to watch it as it slowed to a crawl. It stopped at the car park, and two uniformed men got out and walked away from it.

She frowned. A police vehicle was unusual in Llangynog. In a village that small, it wasn't difficult to keep the peace, after all. Maybe the Cyn Annwn had had its way, and someone had died in the night. If so, it wasn't any of her family, she thought with relief.

The two men stopped in the road, apparently to discuss something, and Bronwyn considered returning to ask them if she could help. Just as she was about to turn around, however, they walked up to a house – she couldn't tell at this distance which one - and after a few moments disappeared inside. Despite her curiosity, she decided to keep to her journey. There would be plenty of gossip in the village by afternoon telling her what had happened.

Once past the village she followed the Tanat River down its peaceful valley, enjoying the day despite the dampness. Although the mist continued to blanket her with moisture, she suspected it would clear off later in the afternoon to a spectacular spring day, and for now her boots and clothing kept her warm and dry. The rain had intensified the scents of earth and water and trees, spring ambrosia that had her stopping and closing her eyes in pure enjoyment every now and then as she traveled.

The river flowed quietly past sheep-filled green fields, spotted occasionally with patches of forest land which had grown sparse through the years because of the heavy logging in the area. Remains of slate quarrying and iron mining operations provided additional scars to the landscape, reflecting policies of a time before environmentalists stepped forward to do battle with industrialists.

Still, lush rain-soaked fauna had grown back to cover much of the damage, nature attempting to restore itself to a former perfection.

And now there was the matter of the pipeline, Bronwyn remembered. Would it, too, cost the valley a bit of the beauty that remained?

Coming around a little bend in the river, Bronwyn spotted a fisherman casting his line beneath a small grove of beech trees. She hurried closer, only to recognize Cecil Lumley and not Pysgotwr casting his line.

"Thought I'd get a bit of fishing in on this fine morning," he murmured to her as she came upon him, careful not to frighten the fish. Dressed in tall rubber boots and a green plaid rain coat, he seemed perfectly happy to be out in the rain. He pointed to his creel, which lay on the bank in the grass. "I already got a nice big one."

"Good job, then," Bronwyn told him, and she walked past him, disappointed.

Her disappointment was short-lived, however. Just a half-mile farther along the river she found the object of her pursuit, Pysgotwr himself. He was standing on a grassy bit of riverbank casting his line into a calm pool of water. Beside him, an ageless black and white spaniel with the unlikely name of Michelangelo watched the fly as it hit the water, alert for any resulting movement that might mean a fish on the line.

To say that Pysgotwr was unusual was an understatement. But Bronwyn had first met him as a child when she was playing in the pasture chasing the lambs, and what child notices that the man she's gazing up at doesn't look anything like others she might know? Bronwyn didn't.

Tall as a tree he seemed to her then, and he still towered over her now. A wreath of leaves – hawthorn, beech, holly, but most prominently oak – topped his merry face, and even now she wasn't sure if he wore them like a crown or if they grew there along with his hair. The leaves changed color with the seasons, being a bright spring green with a few tendrils of flowers dripping off them at the moment. As always, he wore a tunic made of birch bark; over it, a surcoat of flat leaves that somehow held together even though she supposed them to be fragile. A thick mat of hair covered his arms and legs where they were visible, and what skin peeked through looked like rough brown bark. He went barefoot in the soft grass of the riverbank. Odd he was, Bronwyn now acknowledged. He was the Green Man of Welsh mythology, and few save her ever caught a glimpse of him. He reminded her somehow of Granny Powers.

He cast his line again and looked over his shoulder at her. "Welcome, Bronwyn. Did you bring a line? The fish bite well today."

She smiled at him. "No fisherman's line for me, I fear. I come with questions instead."

"Ask then." He let his fly lie on the still water as he turned to face her.

She looked up at his great height. He must be seven feet tall, she thought, just another of his oddities. "Something's happened here in the valley," she began.

"Starting with Granny Powers' death."

"Yes," she agreed, "and she told me she was 'leaving it all to me.' I need to know what she meant, and try as I might, I cannot puzzle it out."

"There is more." Pysgotwr waited patiently.

"Yes, there is. The Twlwyth Teg seem agitated at the moment. I heard them again last night, and they were shouting about danger and…and something about thick. I don't understand."

Pysgotwr sighed, but the merry look did not leave his face. She'd never seen him any other way than content. He gazed fondly at Bronwyn, studying her intensely despite his cheerful demeanor, and when he spoke his words were strange. "An ancient presence has been stilled," he said. It sounded important when he said it, a pronouncement of some sort.

Bronwyn stared at him. "What does that mean?"

"That you must puzzle out for yourself, for my task is but to give you the words."

"But…"

"Dear Bronwyn," he went on, "I am only a simple fisherman, not a great philosopher. I can only pass on the wisdom I have been given. I cannot do more."

She clamped her mouth shut in a grimace of frustration. "What should I do, then, to figure it out?"

Pysgotwr looked up at the sky, turning his head so as to gaze around the valley. "It is beautiful, is it not?"

Impatient, Bronwyn nodded abruptly. "What does that have to do with it?"

"Nothing," Pysgotwr answered her. Then he leveled his gaze at her. "You might start by finishing your trek," he suggested.

"I was only looking for you," Bronwyn protested. "Am I to walk in this rain all the way to Pennant Melangell then?"

"It's a lovely day for a walk."

"Maybe for you," she retorted. "I just get wet and cold."

"Then return home and forget about it all, for you'll find no answers there," Pysgotwr advised her.

"You know I can't do that."

"Yes, I do," he said.

A splash in the river bed drew their attention. Pysgotwr's fishing line had been drawn downward into the water, and Michelangelo paddled intently toward it.

"Okay, I'll do the hike," Bronwyn gave in. "But if nothing is to be found there, I am going to be very angry with you."

She left the two of them pulling in the trout he had snagged and waded away through the wet grass and brambles. On a good day this walk took two hours; today it might take three, if she was lucky. It was a good thing she didn't have much else planned. Perhaps she could catch a ride back into town with the Reverend if he was heading back in after services.

She hurried as best she could through the bramble thickets and muddy bogs, grimacing as the thick mud sucked at her boots. She could feel the cold dampness through her heavy trousers from brushing against the grass. She pushed her hood back from her face and looked at the sky. There was no sign of the misting fog lifting yet.

Sometime later the Twlwyth Teg found her resting on a rock beside the river. She had taken off her boots and was straightening out her wooly socks which had slipped down on the heels and were chaffing the balls of her feet.

Silently, they surrounded her.

She looked up to find herself in the midst of a circle of the small creatures. Each unique, they varied in height from the size of a tiny wildflower to near the height of the brambles they often hid beneath. Some had pointed, sharp features, while others sported rounded faces like cherubs. All had wings, some brightly multicolored, some like pastel gauze, and some nearly transparent and pearly. They wore clothing made of leaves, flowers, and spider web.

All were staring at her.

"What is it?" she asked, and her voice trembled a little. They'd never done anything like this before.

33

They began to circle slowly around her, and where their feet tread, mushrooms sprang up to mark the path.

"Tocsin tolls!" one said in English, or at least Bronwyn presumed it was English, as it definitely didn't sound like their own language.

"Ale-wife in the sacred churchyard lies spilled." Another took up the story.

"The guardian comes," intoned a third.

"What are you telling me?" Bronwyn demanded. She looked from one to another of the circling fairies, but now they remained silent as they continued to tread their path.

"Once, twice, thrice!" Their chorus of cries shrilled in the silent valley, and in a blink of the eye they were gone, disappeared as if they had never ventured into her sight.

Bronwyn frowned. Instead of answers, their words only deepened the puzzle.

"What is 'tocsin'?" she demanded aloud. "Tell me! I know you're there!"

But only silence answered her.

She thought about what she'd heard. *Tocsin tolls. What tolls? A bell.* She sighed aloud. *Ale-wife? Ale is beer, so maybe a pub man's wife? No, that couldn't be right. Cecil Lumley had a wife, but she wasn't involved with the Tanat at all. In fact, she so disapproved of drinking and other things associated with pubs that she distanced herself totally from the whole enterprise. Mai? Glynnis?* Bronwyn shook her head in confusion and then closed her eyes, trying to recall the rest. *Sacred churchyard. That had to be the churchyard at Pennant Melangell. Or maybe all churchyards were sacred? Lies spilled. The ale-wife lies spilled.* Bronwyn suddenly sat up and tugged on her socks and boots. *Blood could be spilled!*

"No, please God, no," she whispered under her breath as she began to run alongside the river toward Pennant Melangell. She only had a half-mile or so to go, but in places she would have to slow her steps when the footing became uncertain or obstacles lay in the path. "No, please no," she whispered again, and then she fell silent as the running took her breath away.

The church of Pennant Melangell stood quiet and empty when Bronwyn burst into the clearing and ran up the pathway. Services at the church were offered only in mid-afternoon, which meant that Reverend Wickclyff would be arriving within the hour if, indeed, she needed help. The rain would have delayed any pilgrims who might otherwise have arrived early to explore the garden and the churchyard before the service began, which explained the solitude of the site on that morning.

Slowing, Bronwyn passed through the iron gates of the lych gate and into the churchyard itself. She looked from side to side as she paused to catch her breath. "Please, please, no," she murmured again as she gazed around at the ancient gravestones. Most were of slate, natural to the area, and many were so old as to be tumbled, lichen-covered, and nearly unreadable. A scent of wet moss and dampened clay filled the air. Still, the holiness of the area enveloped her as she walked up the pathway, calming as she peered carefully from side to side.

The woman lay against the church wall itself, half-hidden by a tilting gravestone. Bronwyn could see right away that it wasn't Mai who lay there, for the blonde hair fanned out behind her head in a halo on the grey stone wall behind her. The church wall had protected her from the worst of the rain, but even so her face was moist and dewy on the misty ground so that, at first, Bronwyn thought she must still be alive.

Then she fell to her knees beside Glynnis and saw the blood soaking the wall behind her and running onto the ground beneath her. She stared at her former schoolmate for a long moment, hesitating, her heart racing and her thoughts unfocused. Then she reached out to touch Glynnis' forehead with one unsteady finger, finding it cold and definitely lifeless. She snatched her finger back. Glynnis' blue eyes gazed out at nothing, filmed over.

"No, no!" Bronwyn whispered, catching a sob in her throat. True, she and Glynnis had not been friends – would never have been friends. But this…she would never have wished this for anyone.

What could have happened? She squeezed her eyes shut, fighting tears. *Glynnis must have had other enemies, but who?* Her thoughts raced as she opened her eyes again and stared at Glynnis' still body, willing her to move, knowing she couldn't. *The protester? Davyyd's ex-girlfriend? Davyyd himself? No, surely not. He seemed so nice and so sad.* But there it was – Glynnis flirting with the American Mark McGuire while Davyyd watched from across the room.

No, surely it must have been a stranger, someone who happened upon Glynnis as she left the Tanat last night. How had she gotten from the village to Pennant Melangell? Bronwyn lifted a hand to her forehead, trying to sort her thoughts. *The police vehicle she'd seen – that must have been something to do with Glynnis. The Tylwyth Teg...oh, yes, they'd known, hadn't they?*

She turned her head and looked around the churchyard. Gravestones lined up like ghosts in the misty air, leaving faint shadows behind. She gaped at them, trying to decide if someone watched her from those shadows. Nothing moved. Even the birds were still in the face of the violence that had happened there. She held her breath for long minutes, listening for the slightest noise. Nothing disturbed the silence.

Shaking, she knelt down then and pushed herself awkwardly to a sitting position with her back to the church wall. Her mind so muddled with shock that she couldn't think, she lifted Glynnis' body just enough so that she could slip her arm beneath her and shift her into her lap. Somewhere deep within she knew that she could do nothing for her childhood nemesis any longer, but irrationally, she didn't want Glynnis to feel alone in that empty churchyard. She had seen enough crime shows on the telly to know she shouldn't disturb a potential crime scene, but she couldn't seem to stop herself. She sat with her back against the church wall, holding Glynnis in her arms as tears streaked down her face and onto the stillness of Glynnis' own.

Twenty-two minutes later Reverend Wicklyff arrived to unlock the church doors and heard a faint call from the churchyard. Peering around the edge of the building, he saw what appeared to be Bronwyn sitting against the wall of the church on the still-damp grass. He hurried over to her, calling out an answer to her summons, and then stopped dead still as he saw that Bronwyn was not alone at all, but that she held another person in her arms and that the other person was limp and blood-soaked.

"What?" he stammered. "Bronwyn?" He gaped at her, his mouth open and eyes wide.

"Please, Reverend, help me," Bronwyn pleaded softly. She stared up at him, her eyes unfocused. She seemed paralyzed, unable to move beneath her burden. Her teeth were chattering and she was shivering uncontrollably.

Shocked, he knelt down and eased Bronwyn away from Glynnis' body, letting it roll gently onto the grass. He recoiled at the dark stains on her jacket and trousers, but rallied enough to ask, "What happened?"

Bronwyn didn't answer.

He peered at Glynnis, lying on the grass now with her glazed blue eyes still gazing skyward. *Beyond help,* he thought, crossing himself and murmuring a prayer in her direction.

He helped Bronwyn into the church, leaving Glynnis lying where she was. The police wouldn't want the body to be disturbed, he told himself, but he kept glancing out the window protectively, wondering whether he should be standing watch over her body instead of caring for Bronwyn. At least he could cover her? But no, he didn't think that was acceptable. Leave the scene as close to as it was as he could and focus on what he could do. Bronwyn was alive, while Glynnis was obviously not.

He sat Bronwyn down in an empty wooden pew, helping her out of the blood-stained outer clothing. Childlike, she allowed him to undress her without protest. "Will you be okay for a minute?" he asked, careful to appear much calmer than he actually felt.

She nodded, tears rolling down her cheeks. Her eyes were huge with shock, and a sudden spasm chattered her teeth.

He hurried into his tiny office to dial 999, watching Bronwyn from the open doorway as he did so. Seeing that she hadn't moved, he poured her a quick cup of tea from his flask, adding two large lumps of sugar from a canister he kept on a shelf. He grabbed his own overcoat and hurried back to where she still sat staring at nothing. He wrapped his coat around her and offered the tea, bending down to look into her eyes. She blinked and took the mug in her hands, sipping at it numbly while he sat alongside her, murmuring soothingly to her about God's will and whatever else came into his head, not worried about whether his words made sense or not.

Bronwyn thought later, when she was able to think again, that Glynnis' influence on her life might have ended with her death. She could not have imagined then that Glynnis' death would impact her even more deeply than her life had, gifting her with answers she never would have anticipated.

Chapter Four

Will Cooper had never thought himself superstitious. As a child, he had walked under many ladders on the city streets of Gloucester, seen black cats traverse his path as he ran through neighbors' gardens, and had never crossed his fingers hoping to be chosen first for sport teams in school.

But now, cheering for a brown colt named O'Malley's Gold in the third race at the Cheltenham Race Track that Sunday afternoon in May, he almost wished he had a lucky charm like the green and purple striped socks his mate Edward Smythe wore.

He'd chosen O'Malley's Gold because, as a backward colt, the odds were not in his favor for a win. That promised Will a huge payout for his ten-pound investment should the colt come in first, second, or third. Unfortunately, O'Malley's Gold had fussed around in the gate, resulting in his running last for the first half of the race. He had now moved up to catch the number five horse in a field of eight, but Will suspected he had no stamina to keep up the surge this late in the race. He would know in a few seconds anyway, and Edward would rub it in his face if his choice, King's Favorite, kept his first-place position.

His mobile phone vibrated just as the horses pounded across the finish line, and Will tucked the phone into his shoulder so that he could hear above the roar of the crowd. This proved nearly impossible as Edward shouted and pounded him on the back, while their third companion, Lesley Dunkirk, planted a firm kiss on the cheek that was not huddled into his shoulder.

"Cooper here," he said into the phone, ducking away from Edward and Lesley to protect the phone from their antics.

"Chief Superintendent Bowers," said the voice on the other end.

"What's going on, sir?" Will hated getting these calls on a weekend, for it always meant trading whatever relaxing activity he was involved in for work, and not pleasant work, either. Ever since he'd been forced off drugs and narcotics and into major crimes two years earlier, he'd found few enough moments to spend with his old friends from the department. Edward had been his partner and still worked drugs and narcotics, while Lesley was a 999 operator and his occasional date for the past couple of years. The three of them had stayed the previous night at the Hotel de la Bere, a 15th century manor house that occupied a hillside above the racecourse and offered a certain shabby classiness at affordable prices. It had given their outing a holiday feel that dissipated quickly as the chief superintendent spoke.

"Got a murder at Llangynog." Marcus Bowers was, as always, all business. "I've got you and DCI Notley on call this weekend, so you've got the case."

Will allowed himself an internal groan. Sean Notley had been a murder detective for more than twenty years and fancied himself a modern-day Sherlock Holmes, complete with cane and calabash pipe, though the pipe seldom appeared at crime scenes and witness interrogations. To make it worse, Notley considered Will his subordinate rather than his partner, no matter that Bowers had made it clear from the start that wasn't the case.

"Where's Llangynog?" Will still had trouble placing small Welsh villages whose names all looked alike on a map, even though the past two years of his career in law enforcement had been spent on the North Wales Police Force. At the time he'd signed on to drugs and alcohol in South Wales, he'd thought it a good enough escape from Gloucester and his family, using the fact that he was a good distance away in Cardiff as an excuse to avoid visits as much as possible. Now that he was even further away in Caernarfon, though, the distance had become an impediment, keeping him from visiting his niece Lark as often as he'd like to.

"In the Tanat River valley near Llanfyllin. Where are you?"

"Cheltenham." Will knew he should not have left North Wales on his on-call weekend, but had thought he could get away with a couple of days' holiday without it being noticed. Serious crime in Wales was almost unheard of, after all. But obviously he'd been wrong. "It'll take me three hours to get to Caernarfon. I can meet Sean there, and we can head out to Llangynog together."

"I'll send him on to Dolgellau. That'd be closer." Chief Superintendent Bowers' voice remained clipped and businesslike, neither friendly nor critical. "I'll give Notley the details, and he can share them with you on the way down."

"Anyone on scene now?" Generally, the local constables and the medical examiner would be the first on the scene, and the murder detectives could arrive a bit later. They'd want to see the body in situ, but their being late wouldn't hold things up. The scene of crime investigators would take hours to finish their work before the body could be moved.

Bowers answered in the affirmative before ringing off and leaving Will to inform his mates of his imminent departure.

"Boo," teased Lesley, tossing her short red curls and winking at him. "At least Edward has a whole day off now and then. You get called out every time we try to have some fun."

"You owe me, mate," Edward informed him, "so don't try to run off before paying me my winnings."

"I didn't see the end of the race," Will told him. "How did O'Malley do?"

"Fourth." Edward grinned.

"And no staying around to see if I can win it back," Will complained good-naturedly. He pulled a twenty-pound note from his pocket and handed it to Edward. "See you get Lesley home safe, right?" At least he'd had the foresight to drive his own car.

Edward grinned at him. "Oh, you can be sure of that, mate."

Will left them pouring over the racing form, choosing their horses for the following race. He found his 1996 MGF in the car park and drove north toward Tewkesbury. From there he would catch the M5 North, cutting off at Worcester in order to avoid the Birmingham traffic. On an early Sunday afternoon, traffic shouldn't be heavy on the A449. Still, he knew they'd arrive much later at the murder scene than was desirable.

He missed Edward, missed working with him. He and Edward had been a team, respected by the rest of the department for their successes particularly in their undercover work. Yes, it had been dangerous work, but damn it, he missed it nevertheless- the excitement of it, the exhilaration of a case broken, even the feeling that they were always walking a thin line between life and death.

It hadn't been his choice to be reassigned, a term that might have meant being put on minor crimes or even traffic duty had it been his own fault, but which in his case meant investigating murders now instead of going after drug-addicted lowlifes. Major crimes offered a different sort of thrill, he had to admit. Now he seldom felt himself in personal danger, and there was satisfaction in a solve that nearly equaled the thrill of a narcotics arrest...nearly, but not quite.

But if he could go back and change things? Oh, yes, in a heartbeat he would.

It had been Julia's fault. He could think of her now without the self-blame and anger that had haunted him the first year after her death. Julia had been a will-o-the-wisp, a fragile waif of a girl with wild, pale hair and too-big, light blue eyes. He couldn't think of her eyes without remembering John Lennon's song, *"Julia."* Given her pale eyes and vacant smile, *i*t always seemed to him to be a good description of her, even when she was a young girl, before the drugs got their hold on her and twisted her life into shambles. Julia had been Will's baby sister.

She had been a dreamy child who'd led a lonely existence and never seemed to mind it. Indeed, she often seemed unaware of other children, humming aloud as she played or read or even sat in a classroom. She never played with neighboring children, but could often be found poking around in the garden making daisy chains or dancing around the drawing room in her mother's dress-up clothes. Eight years younger than Will and ten years younger than their older brother, George, she grew up very like an only child – a child largely ignored by their socialite mother and workaholic father.

Later she did make friends, friends who seemed drawn to her eccentricities. In her teen years she drifted away, as Will saw it now. She stopped coming home, sometimes for a week or more at a time, he found out later. When she was home, she shut herself in her bedroom and came down only long enough to eat a few bites at dinnertime. She seldom spoke to anyone.

Will, of course, had been largely unaware of this, having left home at eighteen for university and then a career of his own. At first, he had tried to stay in touch with Julia, but as his new life consumed him, he more or less forgot about her, which accounted for some of the guilt he now felt. The other thing was, though, that he should have recognized the signs and known about the drug use before it was too late. Had he not wanted to see? Or had he been

41

too absorbed in his own newfound freedom to wonder about the sister he'd left behind?

Whichever it was, nothing could be done now to turn back the clock. When the call came from his parents about the overdose, he could only stand and watch as his world tumbled around him. He could no longer work drugs and alcohol, he was told, for his family problems would prevent him from doing his job impersonally. George, his older brother, reacted to the crisis by immigrating to Canada with his wife and two sons. His parents tried to pretend Julia had never happened, embarrassed in front of their friends now that they could no longer hide her downward spiral. Never very involved with their children, they maintained a polite distance from Will, as well, although he knew they looked forward to his visits now as they never had before because he would take Lark off their hands for an afternoon and give them both a pretense of their old life for that short time, at least.

For Lark, Julia's fatherless daughter, had become the ward of her grandparents, now in their late sixties. Will could only imagine their shock at having to take in their young granddaughter, a precocious child who had somehow managed to develop an intense curiosity about the world despite having been raised those first four years by a mother whose drug-induced stupor left her sleeping on the couch while her child watched the telly in a darkened studio flat.

He smiled, thinking of Lark. She looked only a little like Julia, for Lark's eyes were a brilliant blue, where Julia's had been pale, and Lark's hair had a reddish tint and a slight curl to the wisps that escaped her braids. And Lark was anything but dreamy and fragile, a leader of the neighborhood children in games and sports and never afraid to climb the tallest tree in the garden or face down the biggest bully in her class. He adored her.

He skirted Shrewsbury and took the turnoff for the A458, which would take him directly to Dolgellau. He checked the time on the dashboard clock: 3:45. Not bad. He should be in Dolgellau by 4:00 or earlier, and surely that would put them in Llangynog before 5:00. He swallowed hard. Beginning an investigation this late in the day was not the ideal situation, though it was not unusual either, murder being as unpredictable as it was. Still, this time the lateness lay squarely on his shoulders because he'd ignored the rules again.

He'd not done that before Julia's death. He'd played it by the book, earning himself a good reputation and several promotions. But now he let things slide, knowing they'd be overlooked by his superiors because of his situation. Chief Superintendent Bowers never called him on the small stuff, never demanded his adherence to procedures that, to him, now seemed meaningless. Perhaps one day Bowers' patience would run out, but until that happened, Will tended to take advantage of his situation whenever he felt like it. And he did, often.

Will's parents had not approved of his career choice, of course. His father had expected that one of his sons would follow in his footsteps and become a solicitor, taking over his position at the firm when the time came. George had disappointed him first by choosing a career in real estate, and when Will had told his father that he intended to enter the police force, he had not spoken to either of them beyond a formal hello on holidays in several years. Neither of them turned up regularly for visits, at least not until Lark had come to stay. Now, Will tried to get there at least once a month on a weekend when he was not on call.

The clock had just turned 3:55 when Will pulled into the car park of the Dolgellau Police Station, headquarters for the Meironnydd District which included Llangynog. Although each district had its own intelligence units and crime teams, the Force Major Incident Team would be called in from Western Division Headquarters in Caernarfon for a murder investigation. Will was now a part of this team, so this case would become his to solve, along with Sean "Sherlock" Notley. Will hoped for a quick solve. He didn't know if he could tolerate Notley for more than a day or two at a time.

Notley was waiting for him inside the two-story white building, watching for him from one of the large windows on the ground floor.

"Took you long enough, then," he complained as Will hurried through the door, his spare clothes in his hands. While he might have stretched the rules by leaving the district while on the rota, he didn't think he could get away with wearing jeans and a casual shirt to an investigation. He kept a set of appropriate clothing in his car. "Where were you, anyway?"

Will shrugged. "Cheltenham, for the races."

Notley snorted. "Cheltenham! You're supposed to stay in the district when you're on call."

"Unlike you, I do have a social life," Will replied shortly. "It'll take me five minutes to dress and we can get on the road."

"Oh, yeah, you're in a hurry now," Notley snorted. "That's right – I forgot. You're the special one who isn't expected to follow rules. Should have landed in street crimes, in my opinion."

"Fortunately, your opinion doesn't matter," Will mumbled. He pushed his way toward the restroom. In minutes he strode back out the door and headed for a patrol car, not watching to see if Notley followed.

"We're taking an unmarked, and you'll be driving." Notley spoke from behind his back.

Will took in a deep breath, but kept his silence. He stepped aside to allow Notley ahead of him and followed him to an unmarked maroon Volvo V70. He slid into the driver's seat, reaching for the keys. "Where are we going?"

"Llangynog," Notley said gruffly.

"I don't know where it is," Will told him.

"If they'd hire Welshmen to police Wales, people would know where the villages are." Notley pulled out his pipe and a bag of tobacco and began to stuff it. The tobacco had a heady, rich scent that had Will breathing in deeply in response. "Head out on A494 and follow it to the B4391 down the Tanat River Valley."

As Will pulled onto the highway and headed north, Notley began to fill him in on the case. "Young woman name of Glynnis Paisley got herself murdered sometime last night. Twenty-four years old, married to a man named Davyyd Paisley. They live in Cardiff, but he's working on the gas pipeline up there and that's apparently where she's from. Someone named Bronwyn Bagley found her this morning in the churchyard at Pennant Melangell with her head bashed and stab wounds, as well."

"Which killed her?"

"Don't know yet." Notley took a deep puff of his pipe. "My money's on the woman who found her. That's usually how it goes. Probably a romance gone bad."

"Who identified her?"

Again, Notley puffed on his pipe. "The Bagley woman. That means they knew each other; another reason she looks good for the murder."

Will ignored him. "Is the body still at the site?"

"Waiting for us," Notley frowned. "The doc should be done by now, I'd think. Probably just the constables left keeping sightseers away, unless forensics beat us there, which might be the case, as late as we are. We'll get a good look at the crime scene and then leave them to it."

Will chose to overlook the jab. "The site's secure, then?"

Notley sighed heavily, for effect Will thought. "Now it is."

Now. Will shook his head slightly. "Does that mean the Bagley woman touched the body?"

"Touched it? Yeah, you might say that." Notley took his pipe in his left hand and tapped it out the window, scattering the remaining ash and tobacco back onto the road behind them. "She sat down and held the victim in her lap."

"What?"

"Must not watch crime shows, or she'd know better." Notley shook his head. "That's how the first person on the scene found her. It's going to make it tough for us."

"I'd say so. Tough for her, too." Will thought about it. Maybe Notley was right, then, and the Bagley woman was responsible for the murder. That'd be cold, though, to stay and sit holding her after. Who could do that? You'd have to be a little crazy. Or feeling really guilty.

"Turn's coming up." Notley pointed to a road sign half-hidden behind the thick shrubbery that lined the road. "Hard to see the sign if you don't know the area."

Will signaled and took the exit, merging onto a country road that wound through farmland heading west. Will drove with caution, noting the blind corners. The roadway was dry now, although evidence of the night's rain remained in puddles in some of the pullouts. The sun had erased the haze and lit the landscape, highlighting the valley's verdant beauty.

After what seemed a long drive in silence, they emerged from between the hedges and the Tanat Valley stretched out below them on their right, a pastoral scene of grassy meadows filled with grazing sheep. The Berwyn Mountains, brilliant with sunshine and contrasting shadow, filled the horizon on the far side. Wooden fences competed with stone walls for keeping the sheep enclosed, and an occasional cottage indicated habitation. Will felt a sense of peace, a contentment coming from the quiet countryside, and he relaxed into the drive despite the grisly mission that waited ahead.

They passed by Llangynog. Will noted the two pubs, the small car park, the churches, the town hall, the play yard, and the modest country cottages, but more than anything he noticed the people standing outside talking. Word had gotten back to the village, of course, and as with any small place, it had spread quickly. That was to be expected.

They made the turn at St. Cynog's church and drove on another two miles to Pennant Melangell. Flocks of young pheasants fluttered out from the hedges on both sides of the lane, fleeing just in front of the Volvo as Will tried to avoid hitting them. *Some farmer must be breeding them,* he thought. Finally, the road opened up with the church of Pennant Melangell in front of them. The gray stone Norman chapel stood in the center of a group of ancient yews, its churchyard filled with slabs of gray stone, marking the graves of ancient inhabitants. Will noted a second building nearby, which Notley told him was a counseling centre.

The remote location gave the site a certain mystique, he thought, guessing that made it a destination for pilgrims looking for a spiritual lift. One found that in other places in Wales – ruined abbeys, for instance, and Will found himself drawn to them, even while many others passed them by without noticing.

They got out of the car, took time to pull protective overalls over their clothes and shoes, and approached the constable standing outside the yellow crime scene tape that marred the otherwise peaceful churchyard. A small group of spectators, some with mountain bikes and others dressed for hiking in boots and thick trousers, stood nearby, chatting quietly while keeping an eye on things. *Ghouls*, Will thought. There were always some at every crime scene, people hoping to catch a glimpse of the body or overheard comments that could become gossip when they returned to the village. Sometimes the murderer himself stayed to observe, as well. He eyed them, looking for anything that seemed off as they walked up to the constable guarding the lych gate.

Will and Sean Notley flashed their warrant cards and were allowed to duck beneath the tape and enter the churchyard. Will saw the victim immediately - a blue-tarped bundle lying up against the church wall beyond the gravestones. Two more constables stood watch. The ME had obviously finished his work because everyone on scene appeared to be standing at leisure, no doubt waiting for them to arrive.

"This is where she was found?" Notley asked, pulling on gloves and lifting the tarp to catch a glimpse of the victim.

One of the constables stepped forward. "Wynn Aldridge, Guv," he introduced himself and then pointed to his companion. "My partner, Helen Rees."

"Sean Notley." Notley turned to look at Aldridge. "Now that the niceties are over, you can answer my question."

Will raised his eyebrows behind Notley's back, earning him a grin from Helen Rees. Then he turned his attention to Wynn Aldridge's answer.

"Miss Bagley said she was lying half against the church wall here." He pointed to a smear of blood against the gray stone.

"What time?" Notley replaced the tarp over the body and straightened.

"What time?"

"When was she found?" Notley clarified with exaggerated patience.

Aldridge's frown relaxed. "Oh, that would be around 1:00 this afternoon, or maybe just a bit before."

"Miss Bagley came up here alone?"

Helen Rees stepped forward. "I talked to her, gov. She said she missed the service at St. Cynog's this morning so decided to come on up here. They have an afternoon service here," she went on helpfully, "with tea and cakes after."

"Tea and cakes," Notley repeated. He thought for a minute. "What time is the service?"

"The reverend says 3:00. He arrived around 1:30 and found Miss Bagley sitting against the church wall with the victim in her lap. He says she called out to him."

"Why did she arrive so early? The service wouldn't have started for another two hours," Notley observed.

"She walked up the footpath, gov." Helen Rees nodded back toward the valley. "It's further than the road and a bit of a messy path, especially this time of year. I suppose she thought it might take longer than it did, so she arrived earlier than she expected."

"You suppose?" Notley's voice rose a notch. "You did take a preliminary statement?"

"Of course, we did." Wynn Aldridge waved the report, stepping protectively between his partner and Notley. "We talked to her and got all the times and places and details. I'm sure you'll be heading right back into the village to interrogate her anyway, but we do have the notes written down for you, if you care to see before you go."

"You let her go?" Notley's eyebrows rose nearly to his hairline and he lifted his cane to shake it at them. "You let a possible suspect go?"

"She was just going back down the road to Llangynog, after all," Aldridge protested. "She'll not do a runner on us. She's a local, and anyway, why would she want to do in an old schoolmate of hers?"

Will looked up at this. "A schoolmate, you say?" He ignored Notley's outraged expression, thinking that he had played spectator to Notley's interrogation long enough.

"They grew up neighbors in Llangynog," Aldridge explained, glancing nervously at Notley. "They were in the same year."

"Friends?" Will asked.

Aldridge shook his head. "I didn't ask. I thought it pretty much a given in a village this small that everyone would be friends."

"You shouldn't make assumptions," Notley growled. "For all we know, they hated each other from childhood on." He glanced at Will. "We'll get it sorted tonight when we talk to her."

Aldridge seemed happy to be dismissed. "I'll just get some paperwork done, then, shall I, sir?" Notley waved a hand, and he scurried away.

Will squatted down, lifting the tarp with his own gloved hands. The woman had been beautiful, he thought, blonde and blue-eyed, her rose silk blouse and tan slacks suggesting fashion sense and the money to support it. He lifted her hand, turned it over to examine the underside. "No defensive wounds," he commented.

Notley squatted down beside him. "No wedding ring, either," he pointed out, "but she's wearing earrings."

Will dropped the hand and turned the woman's face to one side. "She was bashed over the head here. Looks like someone stood behind her, maybe surprised her."

"A pretty good gash," Notley observed, "but likely not enough to kill her. Maybe that's why she was stabbed, as well." He gestured toward the wounds on her chest.

Will pointed to mud that smeared the trousers. "Looks like she was dragged."

"If she wasn't killed here," Notley agreed, "it wasn't long before. There's quite a bit of blood beneath the body."

"That'll be from the stab wounds, for the most part," Will said, "maybe a little from the head wound, too. I'd guess the head wound came first, done somewhere else, and then she was brought here and finished off with a knife."

Notley nodded. "That seems reasonable, considering the evidence. We'll know more after the ME gets done."

They spent some time going over the scene, taking notes as they examined it. Besides the blood smear marring the gray stone wall, a dark pool soaked the spring grass beneath her and more stained the soil of a pathway that led from the churchyard gate to the church wall. "Killed nearby, brought here," Notley said again, tapping his cane on the dirt path. "Or killed just inside the gate and dragged to her position against the church wall. Forensics will need to check the gate and the wall for fingerprints." He examined the ground at his feet. "Footprints might be a good idea, as well, if those constables haven't trampled them all into the ground. It did rain last night, after all."

Will nodded. "How soon can we expect cause of death?"

"Soon as they get her into Caernarfon." He glanced back at the tarp-draped body. "I guess we can call for an ambulance, now we've seen the scene."

"What about the medical examiner?"

"Already been and gone." Notley's voice was smug. "There's no sense us looking at the position of the body, seeing how the Bagley woman moved her around, I suppose. We've seen the wounds. Anything else the doctor and the scene of crime technicians will tell us."

Will flinched, "I'll handle the ambulance." He'd be glad to get away from Notley's company for a few minutes. He swiped the screen of his mobile phone, noted a lack of service, and then wandered toward the church, pulling off his gloves and wondering if there was a phone inside he could use.

He produced his identification for the constable on guard at the door and stepped into a small white-washed chapel with a high wooden-beamed ceiling. Stopping just inside, he took a moment to look around. Something seemed off to him, though the church was lovely. He walked toward a screen, drawn by the bronze figure of the risen Christ above it. A plaque on the wall placed the age of the screen in the 15th century, modern when compared with St. Melangell's time, but still very old. He wandered around, looking at two medieval effigies and a series of more modern stone carvings of the hare in the legend.

"The church's reconstruction was just finished in 1990," said a voice behind him, and he turned to see a man watching him from the chancel. The man held out his hand. "I'm the Reverend Bernard Wicklyff. I'm in charge of the church here."

"Will Cooper." Will walked toward him and shook his hand. That explained the feeling he'd had of something not being quite right about the church. While it looked like an old Norman church, the musty smell of an old stone building had been missing. He wrinkled his nose. He could smell lemon oil or some kind of cleaning aid, but no mold, mildew, or other unwelcome scent.

"The actual shrine of St. Melangell is up here in the chancel." Reverend Wicklyff continued. "It dates from the 12th century. Someone dismantled it after the Reformation and used the stones in the original church, but now they've been reassembled again."

He pointed, and Will saw the stones, strangely carved. He stepped closer to examine them.

"It's a mix of Romanesque and Celtic motifs," the reverend explained. "Most unusual and very old, of course. But I suppose you'd want to get down to business, not look at our shrine."

Will smiled. "That's very considerate of you, but I'm not here to question you right now. I just need to use a phone to call for an ambulance."

"Ah, I see." Reverend Wicklyff nodded. "But the ambulance is already on its way; in fact, it should be here fairly soon. The forensics people sent for it when they were done with that part of their investigation."

"Done?" Will stammered, suddenly ashamed at the delay he'd caused.

"Done with it…the body," the reverend had to force out the words, and Will thought how hard it would be for a man of peace like this one to have come upon the scene he had earlier that day. "They would be working their way down the footpath now, trying to determine where the…the murder actually happened. I suppose they thought you'd be finished with that part of the investigation by the time the ambulance arrived." He smiled. "It takes a while for services to arrive out here."

"You found Miss Bagley holding the victim?" Will had to ask, knowing Notley would be in to interrogate the man sooner or later, but wanting to get a start without him, to ask his own questions.

"Yes, but I might not have noticed her had she not called out to me."

"What time was that?"

The reverend looked at his watch, as if it could give him the answer. "I think I arrived around 1:30, give or take a few minutes. The service would have been at 3:00, but of course that had to be cancelled."

"Did you know the victim?" Will watched the reverend carefully. He didn't expect any false information from him, but sometimes people did the unexpected.

Reverend Wicklyff looked him directly in the eye. "I didn't. My wife and I aren't from Llangynog, you see, and most of my ministry here has been after Mrs. Paisley left the village."

"Do you know when that was?" Will didn't know how that fact would be significant, but asked anyway in an effort to be thorough.

"I'd imagine she left right after secondary school. She probably went off to university or to find employment. There's not much on offer in Llangynog."

Will thought about that. Someone would have had to carry a grudge a long time if it took until the victim returned to the village before doing her in. So perhaps their investigation would have them looking elsewhere. He sighed. It was looking like something that would take some time to sort, in any case. "Do you know Miss Bagley?"

"Of course." The reverend studied him carefully with concerned eyes. "Bronwyn works here in the counseling centre. She was – is – a wonderful employee for us."

"How would you describe her demeanor when you found her in the churchyard?"

The reverend took a deep breath. "She was in shock. Her eyes were unfocused, and she could barely respond to my questions. I helped her get up and took her inside the church. I didn't think sitting with the victim on her lap was doing her any good."

"What happened then?"

"I helped her out of her bloody jacket and wrapped my own overcoat around her. She was shivering." He glanced at Will and sighed. "I gave her some sweet tea to help with the shock, but it didn't do much. I've never seen anyone in that state before. She could barely function."

Not a good sign, Will thought. He'd seen people who'd committed terrible crimes go into shock at what they'd done. "What do you think happened, sir?"

The reverend hesitated. "I hope you're not thinking of Bronwyn as a suspect."

"Everyone's a suspect until we sort things out," Will told him.

"Not Bronwyn," Reverend Wicklyff said firmly. "She'd be the last person that'd do something like this."

"I'll remember that," Will said. "Please, sir, what do you think happened?"

"I think Bronwyn arrived early and found her friend already dead."

Will ignored the reference to a 'friend.' "Why would she come two hours early for the church service?"

"She walked the footpath, which can be difficult this time of year. Maybe it didn't take as long as she'd anticipated. Or she came early to do some work at the centre before the service. She has a key. I'm sure if you ask her, there is a logical explanation."

"We will ask," Will assured him. "We have lots of questions for Miss Bagley."

"Be gentle," the reverend said. "She is a quiet soul, grew up well-protected by her parents. I don't think she would be capable of dealing with the sort of bullying questioning that you people sometimes find productive."

"I'll keep that in mind." It wasn't only Miss Bagley's parents who were protective, he thought. But he'd take the advice, try to keep Notley in order when they talked with her.

Dusk had begun to fall when he left the church, chasing the last of the spectators down the road toward Llangynog. The ambulance had to manoeuver its way around the throng who would, had they not been delayed, have traveled home along the path rather than the road. Now they wandered along the road's edge chatting about the event that had altered their plans.

Notley was standing by the churchyard gate, glaring at the forensics people still tracking blood drops down the footpath by the light of the torches they now held. They would probably be forced to work through the night, Will thought, so that evidence wouldn't disappear with the night's dew.

"It's getting late. We should head back," Will suggested, planting himself beside Notley.

Notley nodded. "We'll stop by Llangynog and question the Bagley woman and then head home to Caernarfon."

"Can't the questioning wait until tomorrow?" Will was dragging, now that the first adrenalin rush of the investigation had faded and the effects of his night in Cheltenham had taken over, and he thought that if the Bagley woman was suffering from shock, a night for her to recover might benefit them in the long run.

"Details," Notley reminded him disdainfully. "People forget the more time goes by. We need to talk to her now, while it's fresh. We'll be coming back to talk to her again, but we'll get a preliminary statement tonight before we go."

Will nodded and pulled the car keys from his pocket. He knew Notley was right, although it pained him to admit that even to himself.

They walked together to the unmarked, got in, and drove away down the road in silence. Will watched the light fade from the valley below and then from the mountaintops in the distance. He watched the roadway for escaped sheep or unwary hikers still heading for Llangynog. He watched and thought.

Not Bronwyn, the reverend had said, and his gaze had been steady and truthful. But he had to agree again with Notley, despite his reluctance to do so. First on the site was often the one to look at, after all.

Chapter Five

Darkness had fallen almost completely by the time Will and Sean Notley drove into Llangynog, although a nearly full moon was rising just above the mountains. Lights spilled from the open doors of the two inns, as well as from the windows of homes alongside the roadway and a few old-fashioned streetlights, some of which were burned out. Will slowed his speed to a crawl.

"We should have asked the reverend where Miss Bagley lives," lamented Notley as he tapped his pipe once again through his open window against the outside of the Volvo. "Guess we can stop at one of the pubs and ask."

Will acquiesced with a short nod. "You sure this interview can't wait until tomorrow? It's late, and I doubt Miss Bagley will be fleeing the village tonight."

"It's only late because you were out of your territory," Notley reminded him. He waggled his now-empty pipe toward Will. "You need to learn to follow the rules."

"Still…now that we're already late, why not wait until the morning?"

"Things will be fresher in her mind the sooner we get to her." Notley scowled and pointed. "There are two pubs across from each other on the corner there. We can stop and ask directions. You can park in the car park and we'll walk the few feet."

Will signaled and turned into the small car park, finding it half-full and lit by a dim street light. He chose an empty space near the roadway and pulled the Volvo into the spot.

They walked toward the New Inn, hearing the music blaring from the doorway. A two-story building of whitewashed stucco, it was set back a few feet from the roadside and featured a small garden room with newly-planted flower boxes hanging from the windows. Will could smell petunias and something else – he wasn't much of a gardener – hanging on the night air as they passed through the entryway. Inside, a noisy crowd competed with a piano and a chorus of locals singing accompaniment, the sounds echoing off flagstone floors and wood-beamed ceilings. If not for the paper-topped tables, rounded wood chairs, and flowered draperies on the windows, Will might have imagined himself back in time several hundred years. He stifled a smile, wishing he had time for a quick pint.

Notley pushed his way to the bar where a red-faced barman pulled pints as he kept up a lively conversation with two men seated nearby. "Excuse me," he said. He flashed his warrant card, and instantly the conversation faded as the patrons watched to see what would happen. It was obvious to Will that, although the cacophony of voices had sounded cheerful moments before, the topic of conversation must have centered on the loss of one of their own, along with speculation as to its cause. "Can you tell me where a Miss Bronwyn Bagley lives?"

The barman eyed him. He set a damp towel on the bar and turned to face them. "Just why would you be wanting to know?"

Notley lifted his chin and pointed his cane at the man. "That's none of your concern. If you could just answer my question, we'll be on our way, and you can go back to your business here." He lowered the cane and looked around the room. "All of you locals?" he called out.

Murmurs answered him, but no one spoke out.

Notley frowned and struck his cane against the bar. "Obstructing justice will get you into trouble. You don't want that, do you?" He turned back to the barman again.

The man shrugged. "She's had enough to deal with today, I think."

"Nevertheless, we'll be talking to her tonight," Notley said firmly. "She found the body and we need a statement. Where does she live?"

The barman sighed. "End of town, the stone farmhouse set back from the road on the left."

"We'll be on our way then," Notley said, and Will followed him out with a sidelong glance at the barman and an exaggerated lifting of his eyebrows. The barman smirked in response, but concern shadowed his expression as he watched them leave.

They cruised slowly through the village and pulled onto the little dirt lane that led to the farmhouse just a few dozen feet off the roadway. White dots of sheep could be seen in the moonlight that reflected off the fields to the left of the house, and Will could hear the chirp of crickets and the call of an owl as they emerged from the car and started toward the two-story stone building. Two black and white sheepdogs raced toward them from behind the house, barking furiously.

Notley lifted his cane and pointed it at the dogs. "Back!"

The dogs detoured around them, circling them and still barking, but not threatening.

Notley rapped on the door with his cane.

It opened almost immediately. A tall man stood blocking their entry. Will noted hair that had once been brown but was now dusted with gray and a pallor to the man's resigned face. The man barked out a command to the dogs and they immediately dropped back, sitting on their haunches as they watched from a few feet away. He then turned to them and held out his hand. "I'm Rees Bagley. Can I help you?"

Notley ignored the hand, but stepped up and showed his warrant card. "Does a Miss Bronwyn Bagley live here?"

The man took his time looking at the ID, staring at it as if he thought he might find it lacking somehow. Finally, he looked at Notley and replied, "Yes, she does. Bronwyn is my daughter. But she's had a terrible day, as you know. Would it be possible for you to come back tomorrow?" Even as he said the words, his face held no hope of that happening. *Lots of love there,* Will thought. *He wants to protect her. Or give her time to construct a story?*

Notley sighed, letting out his breath in an exaggerated manner, and shook his head. "I'm sorry. It's important that we talk to her right away before the details of what she experienced fade away. I'm sure you understand."

Rees Bagley studied Notley for a long moment, and Will had the feeling that the man was looking right through his partner and into his soul. *No fool, that one,* Will told himself. Then Bagley stepped back and held open the door. "Come in, then, and we'll get her."

They walked into a large, open room with low beamed ceilings and flagstones underfoot, a room that looked as if it were from the same era as the New Inn. The man pointed them to a seating area where a brown leather sofa and two flowered side chairs sat anchored by a faded rug. Then he disappeared through a doorway through which they could see a worn and scarred table and chairs and a glimpse of an Aga just beyond. Notley sat on one of the chairs, and Will took the other one. A small blaze in the stone fireplace warmed the room to an uncomfortable degree, and Will reached up to unbutton the top button of his shirt.

"Can I get you some tea?" A woman, obviously Mrs. Bagley, stood in the kitchen doorway looking at them. Slim and dark-haired, she must have been a beauty in her youth, Will thought. She had a kind look about her, a welcoming half-smile despite the circumstances.

"Please," Will responded at the same moment that Notley said, "No, thanks."

"Then I'll bring one cup," the woman concluded, and she disappeared back into the kitchen.

"Tea?" Notley gave Will a sidelong glare. "We're not here for a social call."

Will shrugged. "It sounds good at this point." Truth be told, though, he'd have preferred something a bit stronger at this hour of the day.

They waited a few long minutes in silence, Will unwilling to engage in conversation with Notley. Finally, a young woman moved into the room, flanked by the two elder Bagleys and an older version of the two sheepdogs that had greeted Will and Notley outside. She carried her own mug of tea, along with a second that she held out to Will.

Bronwyn Bagley was not the most beautiful girl Will had ever seen, but she had a presence that made him sit up and take notice. Of medium height, she was slender and moved with athletic grace that spoke of many hours' hiking in the fresh air. She was a bit pale, with luminous brown eyes that appeared nearly black in the dim light of the room – obviously, the shock of finding her dead friend had not dissipated. Her hair was chocolate with cinnamon highlights, falling to her shoulders in soft waves. She wore jeans and a cream-colored woolen jumper that probably enhanced her pallor.

Despite the signs of shock, she appeared tranquil. After handing Will his mug of tea, she settled on the leather couch between her parents, looking from Notley to Will calmly. The dog dropped down by the fire with a heavy sigh.

Notley pulled a small cassette recorder from his jacket pocket. "Do you mind if I record our conversation?" he asked. "Makes it more official, plus we don't overlook any details that way."

"She isn't being charged with anything, is she?" Rees Bagley's voice was sharp.

"No, this isn't being done under caution," Notley explained. "We just need a statement about her finding Mrs. Paisley."

"It's fine," Bronwyn murmured quietly, and Will leaned closer to hear her better.

"Okay, then, we'll start with your name and place of residence." Notley pushed a button on the recorder, holding it in his hand.

"Bronwyn Bagley. I live here in Llangynog."

"Do you have a middle name for the record, Miss Bagley? We have to be accurate," Notley reminded her.

"Bronwyn Rhianna Bagley." She took a sip from her mug, and Will saw that her hand shook as she lifted the mug to her mouth. *Maybe she wasn't as calm as she appeared then.*

Notley nodded at her. "Very Welsh. Have you always lived in Llangynog?"

"I was born here. This was my great-great grandfather's farm, so Bagleys have lived here for generations."

"That doesn't answer my question, Miss Bagley," Notley persisted, and Will glanced at him warily. Surely, he wasn't going to treat this young woman as a suspect despite his protest otherwise. Anyone could see she was in shock and needed to be treated gently, as the reverend had suggested.

Bronwyn, though, didn't seem to notice his tone. "I studied in Wrexham, Gwyndwr University, for two years. Other than that, I've lived here all my life. And, please, call me Bronwyn."

"Okay, then," Notley was all business. "Did you know the deceased, Glynnis Paisley?"

"We were schoolmates, as she grew up here in Llangynog, too. But I hadn't seen her for a long time." Bronwyn's huge dark eyes reflected the flickering of the fire, making it hard for Will to read her. He watched her, mesmerized. *No seashell eyes for her. More like doe's eyes, maybe. Gentle eyes, despite the reflection of the fire.*

"You hadn't contacted her when she came home on visits, maybe to have a chat, catch up on the gossip?"

Bronwyn hesitated, and Will blinked and focused, alert to the change in her demeanor. "No, I wasn't aware when she visited, if she did."

"Had you seen her in the past several days?" Notley fingered his cane idly, and Will saw that her father was watching him, an unhappy look on his face. "I understand from your preliminary statement that you knew Glynnis had taken a job at one of the inns in the village. Isn't that right?"

Again, Bronwyn paused, and her tea sloshed from the mug a bit as her hand shook. *Something there,* Will thought. *Something about that needed deeper questioning.* "My sister-in-law works at the Tanat Inn, and she mentioned that Glynnis had been hired as a temp worker." She started to lift her hand to brush away a strand of hair, but then put it back in her lap. "I saw Glynnis a couple of times in the past few days. The village is small, so we were bound to run into one another."

Notley leaned back and studied her. "Friendly encounters?"

She stared at him. "No, not really. Glynnis and I were never great friends."

Notley nodded, a small smile flirting with his serious demeanor, and Will fought back a sudden flare of anger. *That doesn't prove anything, Notley,* he fumed. *Get on with it.*

"What do you mean by that?"

She went quiet for a minute. When she finally spoke, it was with obvious reluctance. "Glynnis liked to bully me a bit, that's all. I didn't enjoy her company."

Will blinked at her admission. Motive? It wouldn't be the first time someone decided they'd had enough and did their tormentor serious harm.

Notley seized on the information, looking pleased. "When was this? The bullying, I mean? When you were in school together?"

Again, she hesitated, and her father turned his head to look at her, seeming to try to communicate a silent plea for her silence. She lifted her chin. "She always did it, back when we were schoolmates and again now, when I ran into her in the village."

"Can you be specific?" Notley pressed her. "You have a history with her? How deep did your hate for her run? Did you push her too far this time? Lash out after she bullied you one last time?"

"That's enough," Rhys Bagley broke in. "I think it's time we terminated this interview." His wife reached over and put her hand on his arm.

"You can't terminate the interview," Notley snapped. "She's not a minor."

"But she can stop it," her father snapped back, just as quickly. "She has the right to legal counsel before this goes too far. You're putting words in her mouth."

"Is that what you want?" Notley's chin went up and he glared at the man defiantly. "Call someone, then. We'll wait."

"It's a Sunday," Bagley pointed out, his bluster fading. "No one would come on a Sunday evening."

"Then, what?" Notley knew he'd won. "We could take her to the station and hold her while we wait for Monday morning."

Bagley closed his eyes and shook his head. His voice was quiet. "Go on, then. You give us no choice." He opened his eyes and took his daughter's hand.

"Answer the question," Notley said. "What did she do last night that you took for bullying?"

Bronwyn bit at her lower lip. "I....it's a little embarrassing," she blurted, blushing. "Can't we just say that Glynnis and I didn't get on well together? Surely that tells you what you need to know."

"Details are important," Notley insisted.

Tears sprang into her eyes and she brushed impatiently at them. "I...she was flirting with a man I was with, at the Tanat. That's all it was, but she had to make sure I knew she was doing it on purpose, gloating about it after."

"You left the pub with this man?"

She shook her head. "No. It was just a casual thing. I didn't really know him. We just shared a drink, that's all, and then we went our separate ways."

"But you were angry with her, weren't you?" Notley pressed her. "Angry enough to take revenge when you had the chance?"

She didn't answer, but her eyes showed panic. Her mother reached over and put a hand on her knee.

Stop it, Notley, Will thought. *Don't put words into her mouth that aren't true.* He shifted in his chair, glaring at his partner.

Notley threw him a glance, seeming to sense his agitation.

"You don't have to answer," Rhys Bagley interjected with a thunderous look at Notley. "No matter what he says, you don't have to answer unless they're charging you with a crime."

"Your father's right." Will couldn't hold in his disgust. "You don't have to answer any questions you don't want to." He didn't look at Notley. Was it that he worried she was vulnerable, or that he just didn't like Notley? Whichever, he was risking Notley's wrath, and he was willing to, if it kept Notley from bullying this girl.

The chair rustled as Notley sat back. "We'll come back to that later," he said, his irritation obvious. "Are you employed, Miss Bagley?"

"Call me Bronwyn, please. And yes, I am employed. I work as a coordinator at the counseling centre at Pennant Melangell." She settled back into the couch a bit. *A safe topic then,* Will thought, but then again, Bronwyn didn't know where Notley's questions would take her next.

"That's next to the church where Mrs. Paisley's body was found?"

"Yes." Bronwyn's lips trembled, and she clenched her hands in her lap.

Notley noticed. "Now, can you tell me about this morning? About finding Mrs. Paisley?"

Bronwyn looked down at her tea mug and lifted her free hand to her forehead, rubbing it just above her eyes. "I...I'm not sure what it is you want."

Will spoke without considering Notley's certain objections. "Tell it like a story if you can. Take us through it step by step." He ignored the glare Notley shot in his direction. "Try to relax. We just want to know what happened; that's all."

Bronwyn turned her head to look at him, her eyes huge in her pallid face. He smiled at her reassuringly, and she offered a wisp of a smile in return.

"I got up late yesterday morning," she began. "I had slept poorly, had nightmares all night."

"Something was bothering you?" Notley interrupted. "Perhaps something to do with Mrs. Paisley?"

Bronwyn handed her empty mug to her mother, who placed it on a side table without rising. "I can't remember what I dreamed. I only know it kept me awake."

Will nodded encouragingly. *Was it that her conscience was bothering her?* "What did you do after you awoke?"

"I ate breakfast, and then I decided to walk to Pennant Melangell for church services, as I had missed the services here in the village."

"What time was it that you set out?" Notley interjected.

She thought. "I guess it must have been eleven, half-eleven...something like that."

"You had breakfast at home?"

Bronwyn glanced at her mother. "Mum kept it warm for me, eggs and toast."

"Okay, let's go on from there. As I recall, it was raining yesterday morning. Why would you choose to walk to Pennant Melangell? I understand the pathway is something of a challenge."

"It can be challenging," Bronwyn acknowledged, "but it's also beautiful and peaceful. I love to walk, and I thought it would be relaxing, despite the rain."

Notley smirked. "So, you set out in the rain for church services?"

Bronwyn smiled a little. "I suppose it sounds crazy, but yes, I did."

"Bronwyn has always liked to be outdoors," her father broke in quietly. "She used to follow me everywhere – the pastures, the forest, alongside the river."

Will glanced at Notley to see how he was taking the interruption. Not well, to judge from his stern face. *You've got to let them be human, Notley,* Will thought. *More is gathered with honey and all that. And this kind of detail gives a clearer picture of the woman, after all.*

"Did you meet anyone on your way?" Notley deliberately turned away from Bronwyn's father and looked her full in the face.

She blanched, her face even paler than earlier. "I saw Cecil Lumley – that's the owner of the Tanat – out fishing just past the village a bit." She chewed on her lower lip for a moment. "That's all. No one else was out." Her foot began to tap a staccato beat on the floor as she fidgeted.

Will watched her. *What wasn't she saying? She didn't lie very well. Who else had she met? Who was she protecting, or was it herself?*

Notley waited a long minute, watching her, waiting to see how rattled she might be. "How long did it take you to walk to the church?"

"Maybe two hours?" Bronwyn's soft voice faltered, and her mother reached over and took her hand. "I didn't pay attention."

"Is that a typical time frame for that walk?"

She nodded warily. "It can be, depending on how fast you walk and what the conditions are."

"Are you a fast walker?" Notley persisted, and Will wondered what he was getting at.

"I walk faster in the rain," Bronwyn told him.

"So, if it took less than two hours, perhaps even an hour and a half, that would be within a normal time frame?"

"Yes, of course." Bronwyn's face flushed a little. "I didn't want to be late, after all."

Notley stopped and pulled a notepad from his pocket with his free hand. Setting the cassette recorder on the arm of his chair, he opened the notepad and jotted something down. "Okay, then, let's see if I've got this right. You left at 11:00, and services are at...what, 2:00?

"3:00," Bronwyn said shortly.

"3:00. So, you had four hours to get there, but a typical time period for that walk is two hours. Is that right? Wouldn't that put you there far earlier than you needed to be?"

"The walk can take three hours or more. I wasn't sure of the conditions."

"Ah," Notley made another note and tapped his pencil on the notepad. "Conditions being...?"

Bronwyn took a deep breath. "As you pointed out, it was raining, which meant it would be boggy. That sometimes slows a walker down. And I'd have to change my wet clothes before the service."

"I see." Notley smiled at her, a cold look that chilled more than warmed. "And you went straight into the churchyard when you arrived, is that right?" He leaned toward her, seeming to crowd her space, and Will saw her mother move closer to her protectively.

Again, Bronwyn chewed on her lower lip. *Nervous,* Will thought. *Why?* "Yes, I did."

"Why did you do that?" Notley managed to put doubt into his words, nudging Bronwyn toward a longer explanation that she otherwise might have made. Will understood what he was doing and hoped it wouldn't work. Somehow, he liked Bronwyn Bagley and wished for her to be innocent. He felt sorry for her, as well, despite the obvious comfort of loving parents and a home that had been in the family for generations.

Her explanation when it came sounded perfectly rational. "I was early," she said softly. "I often go into the churchyard or the garden if I have extra time because I find them peaceful. Ask Reverend Wicklyff. He is always telling me I'm going to catch cold with my wet shoes."

Score one for you! Will suppressed a smile.

"But it was still raining?" Notley pushed her. "Surely, you were already soaked. Why didn't you go inside where it was warm and dry?"

"I...it was locked. The church was locked." Bronwyn watched Notley guardedly.

"You work there, though. Don't you have a key?"

"For the centre, but not for the church."

"Still, wouldn't it make sense that you would go inside to dry off before church services? I can't see you wandering around the churchyard at random after hiking all that way up the footpath in the rain." Notley made another note on his pad, scribbling quickly.

She flinched, and Will saw her mother reach for her hand. "Maybe that's not important at this point," he broke in, ignoring Notley's outraged look. "We can save that question for another time." He turned to Notley, cringing at the look in his eye. "At any rate, we've probably badgered her enough after all she's been through today. Let's get on with the rest, shall we?"

Notley scowled at Will, not bothering to hide it. "Tell us about discovering the body," he muttered.

Bronwyn took a deep breath, squeezing her mother's hand, and then spoke all in a rush, surprising them all. "I went into the churchyard and walked up the path. Something seemed strange to me. The birds were quiet; everything was totally still. That's probably why I didn't stop at the centre to dry off, I think. It was eerie, and I...I was frightened. I felt that something was wrong, but I didn't know what. I very nearly turned back and might have run to the centre, but then I saw her – Glynnis – lying against the church wall."

"You knew right away it was Glynnis? How was that?" Notley's skeptical look hadn't abated with the rush of words.

Bronwyn stared at him, but her eyes were unfocused, as if she were looking inward instead of at him. Her answer came slowly. "I didn't know. I saw a blonde woman lying there. But I had to go close to her to see who it was."

"What did you do then?"

Bronwyn squeezed her eyes shut. "I knelt down and felt her face to see if she was alive."

"And?" Notley prompted her.

"And I knew she wasn't." Bronwyn's voice had grown very soft.

"How did you know that?"

Bronwyn opened her eyes. "She was cold, and she felt odd. She was staring at the sky."

Will nodded encouragingly. "That must have been hard for you to see."

"It's not a common thing to touch a dead person, you know," Notley broke in. "Most people find it off-putting. I'm surprised you were able to feel her forehead and even pick her up, considering that."

"Everyone reacts differently." Will spoke without thinking. Mrs. Bagley rewarded him with a slight smile of thanks.

Bronwyn flashed Will an enigmatic look. "I don't know quite why, but I didn't want her to feel alone there in the churchyard. I felt sorry for her, I think. I sat down and lifted her onto my lap." She peered anxiously at Notley. "I know that's the wrong thing to do, but I couldn't seem to help myself. I was frightened and confused. I wasn't thinking. I just did what felt right, without really considering the right or wrong of it."

"No damage done," Will assured her. "We'll sort it out."

"How long did you sit there like that?" Notley was not to be outdone. "An hour? More? Less?"

Bronwyn shook her head. "I don't really know. It was all so horrible, you know, and my thoughts were flying in circles, wondering who had done such a thing and why. I still can't think why I picked her up." Her nose wrinkled. "What an awful thing to do. I think I was pretty out of it until Reverend Wicklyff arrived and summoned help. I can't remember it now."

"You heard him drive up?" Notley persisted.

"I must have done," Bronwyn's eyes drifted toward the fire, unseeing. She shook her head. "I really don't remember much. I'm sorry."

"That's okay. We've probably got enough for tonight," Will broke in again, disregarding Notley's snort of disapproval. He stood up and reached to snap off the cassette recorder firmly. "We will get back to you in a day or two to see if you remember anything more. In the meantime, if you do think of anything helpful, you can give me a call." He held out a card with his name and mobile number on it.

Notley scrambled to his feet, grabbing one of his own cards from his coat pocket. "Here's mine, as well," he growled.

Bronwyn stood up. She reached out and took both cards, her hand shaking, but said nothing. A tear rolled down her cheek, and she dabbed at it with her empty hand.

"Thank you for seeing us," Will offered his hand.

She sniffled, but didn't take his hand. "I want to help," she whispered, almost to herself. "Really, I do."

"Of course. We know that." Will smiled at her reassuringly. "We'll be in touch."

As they walked out the door and into the night, Will could feel Notley's tight rage as he strode to the Volvo and jerked open the door.

He opened his own door and slid into the seat. "Look, Notley," he said without glancing at him, "she was about to collapse with shock. Let her think about it for a day or two, get over it a little. We can use the time to interview others, to see what forensics has, to review our notes from this interview, as well. Then we'll get back to her with the inconsistencies, okay?"

"It's not okay," Notley told him with a quiet fury. "You had no right to take over my interview, Cooper. That's what's wrong with you, why you'll never make it in major crimes. You do whatever you want. You blunder into the middle of things without thinking. If a pretty girl is our suspect, you make allowances, you protect her, instead of asking the hard questions. That's going to get you nowhere."

Will listened to him in silence, gripping the steering wheel. He reached down and started the engine, shifting into drive. He let the car roll toward the roadway, his foot light on the gas pedal as the two sheepdogs paced them.

Beside him Notley fumed. He pulled his pipe from his pocket, along with his packet of tobacco, and began stuffing it, shoving the tobacco into the bowl with a jabbing finger. When he had finished, he zipped the tobacco pouch shut, stuffed it back into his pocket, and flicked on his lighter. Will watched the glow of the pipe from the corner of his eye.

"You'll be off this case tomorrow," Notley seethed. "I will not work with someone who doesn't know his place."

"What place is that, Notley?" Will retorted. He turned onto the B9341. "I have every right to ask questions, too. I have the right to hand a witness my card. You are not my superior; we're equals."

"You're new to the squad. That makes me the lead on any investigation we have together," Notley thundered. "You never should have been put on major crimes. If it were me, you wouldn't even have made street crimes after what happened. You should have been terminated."

Will shook his head, sputtering with barely suppressed anger. "It wasn't my fault, what happened to my sister."

"Oh, but it was your fault," Notley insisted tightly. "You should have seen the signs, should have known. You could have saved her and put away the ones who supplied her. You could have uncovered a huge narcotics ring, but you didn't. You simply looked the other way."

"It wasn't my jurisdiction," Will mumbled. "She lived in Gloucester, not North Wales."

"And we don't cooperate on things like this? A tip wouldn't have been welcome?" Notley tapped his pipe on the car door outside his open window. "Excuses, Cooper. That's all you have. That's why no one wants to work with you. And I, for one, won't."

Will clamped his mouth shut. He pressed on the accelerator and the car increased speed despite the narrow roadway. He stared straight ahead, barely seeing the road through his rage. *Lovely fragile Julia...the waif who simply drifted out of their lives.* He swallowed heavily as guilt swamped him again. *She'd always been a pale ghost of a girl, with those nearly colorless eyes that looked empty even before the drugs. Could he have known? He probably could have, if he'd only taken the time to visit her, to be her big brother. But there it was...her so much younger and him on the fast track away from family expectations and disappointments. He simply hadn't bothered with her. And now it was too late, too late to save Julia; maybe too late to save himself, too.*

He turned onto the A494. He knew he couldn't get to Caernarfon quickly enough to suit him, but maybe Notley had said his piece and would let him drive in solitude the rest of the way.

The moon shone bright in the night sky, highlighting fields full of sheep and rocky outcroppings. An animal scurried across the road ahead, perhaps a badger, Will thought. He slowed until he was sure it had crossed safely and then pressed the accelerator again. He tried to focus on the investigation, running over their interviews with

Bronwyn Bagley and the casual conversation with Reverend Wicklyff, remembering the look of the victim in the churchyard. There had been inconsistencies in what Bronwyn had said, of that he was certain, yet so far, he didn't see her as a murderer.

By the time they pulled into the station in Dolgellau, Will's eyes ached with the strain of the previous night's holiday followed by a long and difficult day. Notley left him without a word, slamming his car door shut and marching toward his own car, his shoulders held stiff and unbending. Will sighed and watched him, glad to be rid of him at last.

He put the top down on his MG and climbed in, gliding out of the car park and onto the A470 toward Caernarfon. The chilly night air might help keep him awake for the hour's drive to his small studio apartment.

Now that he was rid of Notley, he found he could focus again on the matters at hand. First there was the investigation. He didn't really believe that he would be put off the case for ending Notley's questioning of the Bagley woman before Notley thought himself done. The poor girl was still in shock and probably should have been under a doctor's care rather than being interrogated by a bullying murder investigator, and he was sure he could make his case with Chief Superintendent Bowers, should it come to that. But he didn't think it would. Notley would cool off overnight and realize that complaining would only mark him as a thorn in the department's side.

That meant that the next day would see them back in Llangynog interviewing the family of the deceased, her employer, and everyone else who had even a distant connection with the case. They might make a trip to Cardiff eventually to sort out her life there, see if she had any enemies. Perhaps forensics would have a report for them in the morning to give them more to work with. The first few days were crucial to a murder investigation; there would be long days ahead for Will to suffer through with Notley at his side. He could only cross his fingers and hope for the right clue to lead them quickly toward the solve.

As for Julia...here Will put a block on his thoughts. What Notley had said was unpardonable, even if it had been true. It was easy to look back on things, to see what should have been done and what could have been. But life doesn't offer second chances. It was too late now to go back and change things. Pointing out what might have been was useless, and only someone like Notley would bother suggesting it. No, it was better if Will blocked out Notley's words, pushed them to a dark corner of his mind where they could be suppressed until he had forgotten them entirely. If he ever could.

If he ever could... with a determined effort, Will forced his thoughts to Bronwyn Bagley. *A pretty girl,* he mused. *Gentle somehow.* She wasn't beautiful, but something in her demeanor conveyed an inner tranquility that made her attractive. It also made him want to protect her. *But what didn't she tell us? What did she keep inside, or what did she change, even just a bit, to misdirect them or to protect herself?* He thought about it. She was so nervous, shaking really, and that wasn't just shock. She was definitely hiding something, but what?

Chapter Six

Will was right. The next morning, he checked in at western division headquarters in Caernarfon at ten minutes after nine to find Sean Notley sitting at his desk smoking his pipe and waiting for him.

"Chief Superintendent Bowers wants to meet with us at half-nine," he barked, "so we need to get ourselves in order before that." He shuffled some papers on his desk briskly, arranging them neatly in a stack.

Will nodded, noting that Notley hadn't reprimanded him for his ten-minute late arrival. "Do we have transcriptions yet of Miss Bagley's interviews?" There'd be the preliminary interview the local constables had done and then theirs. They'd want both to compare and look for inconsistencies.

"On the way."

Will grabbed a chair from a nearby cubicle and shoved it in front of Notley's desk. He sat down. "What do we have for Bowers, then?"

Notley picked up a pencil. "I've been here since before 7:00, and I've got a tentative list of potential interviews we need to get done. Husband, employer, family – you know the drill. I've been making some notes, lists of questions and things to look for. We need to talk to the medical examiner. I think that's Francis Roark on this case. We also need to get the forensics report as soon as it's available, get back and look at the crime scene again in better light, talk to everyone who'll give us the time."

"So, we're heading back to Llangynog?"

"We'll see what Bowers says." He gestured toward other officers working at nearby desks. "Maybe he'll give us some help, to speed things up."

Will pushed the chair back. "I'll make a few notes of my own before Bowers arrives," he told Notley. He walked back to his own desk and sat down.

It had been a bad night. While he'd considered the small flat in the town centre a great find when he'd rented it upon his transfer to Caernarfon, he hadn't accounted for the noise of pubs and restaurants that continued far into the night, especially on weekends. He usually slept with windows latched tightly to block out the sound, but even so he woke frequently to the singing of a drunk in the street or cheerful jeering as someone called a farewell to his mates when the din pierced the windows. Last night the flat had been stuffy with the warmth of early summer, so he'd tried leaving the windows open a crack so that some of the fresh sea air might bring in a cooling airiness. It had been a mistake. While the sea air had been refreshing, the noise outside had jolted him awake so often that he'd not drifted into a sound sleep until well after midnight.

Not that there weren't compensations. Once last summer he'd brought Lark home with him for a week's holiday away from her grandparents. Together they'd explored every inch of Caernarfon Castle, Lark's red-blonde pigtails bouncing as she'd skipped merrily ahead of him. Later he'd told her tales about Edward I and his conquest of Wales and the building of the castles after Edward's cruel defeat of Llewellyn and his son Davyyd. A bit of a history buff, he had been able to supply enough specific details about the time period to intrigue Lark, who even at her young age seemed to share his passion for it. He'd described in vivid detail how the princes of Wales were still crowned in Caernarfon Castle, just as Prince Edward's son had been in the 1200s. Lark had loved it, devouring the facts voraciously and demanding more as she lay curled on his sofa with a cup of hot chocolate at her side. Another day they'd walked the perimeter of the city walls and then taken a tourist cruise out into the quay where they could see the castle from the water side. He grinned at the thought. Lark had some tough questions for the tour guide that day and offered some facts of her own that he hoped the other tourists thought charming rather than precocious.

He'd promised to take her to Conwy Castle the next time she visited, which he'd thought would be in July or August when he had time off work, and of course they'd spend more time at the beach then, as well. He was looking forward to it.

He sighed, pushing Lark from his mind. It was time to focus on the task at hand.

He had to admit, it wasn't just the noise of the streets that had kept him staring blindly at the ceiling for hour after hour the previous night. There was something about Bronwyn Bagley that disturbed him, and the more he thought about it, the more confused he became.

He sat at his desk and stared across the room blindly, his thoughts directed inward. He'd felt he'd had to protect her the night before, yet he saw in her a strength in her that he couldn't define. She looked perfectly ordinary – nothing odd there. Other than the fact that she touched the victim's body, she seemed to react to finding it in a normal way, and certainly something like that would disturb anyone. She'd been appropriately shocked and frightened and nervous. He couldn't quite put his finger on what bothered him about her. But there was something.

He picked up a pencil and pulled a notepad close. *"Did she have foreknowledge of the death?"* he wrote. Somehow, he thought so. Why else had she gone to the churchyard? Why had she made the trip so quickly? *When did she learn of the death? And from whom?* She had apparently been home until late morning. If she'd known then of the death, surely she'd have driven to Pennant Melangell instead of taking the time to walk. Yet she did walk, and a very fast walk it was, far faster than he thought was normal. So, somehow, she must have learned of the death between the time she left home and the time she arrived at Pennant Melangell. *Who was she protecting then? She'd said she'd seen one man on her way to the churchyard.* An interview with him would be important. *And why did she pick up the body?* This was an important question, one that she'd need to explain more rationally than she had before. Unless the deceased was a loved one, it would be very rare for someone to touch it in that way. She might have thought to cover up the fact that she already had Mrs. Paisley's blood on her by doing so, in which case she was probably guilty of the murder itself.

Chief Superintendent Bowers appeared and jerked his head toward the door. "Conference room," he ordered.

Will jumped to his feet and followed Notley through the door and down the hallway, carrying his notepad and pencil in his hand.

Inside the small room, they sat facing Bowers as he picked up a dry-erase marker and wrote "Glynnis Paisley" on the top of a whiteboard that filled one wall.

"What do you have so far?" he asked.

"No forensics yet," Notley reported. "The SOCOs might still be on scene, finishing up in the daylight. Our preliminary examination of the body showed both a head injury and knife wounds. There was a lot of blood against the church wall and on the ground beneath the body, but it appeared to us that Mrs. Paisley had been disabled somewhere else and then made to enter the churchyard, either on her own two feet or dragged there by her murderer because there was also blood on the path through the churchyard and on the gate. Cause of death is unknown at this time, but we think the head wound came first, and then the knife wounds after."

"Time of death?"

"We haven't heard from the doctor yet."

Bowers wrote on the whiteboard. "You're pretty sure that she was killed in the churchyard?"

Notley consulted some papers. "Forensics agree with our preliminary findings that she was killed or at least wounded elsewhere and then brought to the scene. They were able to find a trail of blood back through the gate and onto the footpath, where it was pretty much obliterated by the rain and the footsteps of Miss Bagley as she walked up the path."

"He's assuming it's her footprints," Will put in. "They could be anyone's at this point."

Notley hesitated. "True enough."

Bowers wrote "kill spot?" on the white board, followed by "footprints." He looked at Notley. "Name, age, marital status?"

Notley consulted his notes. "Glynnis Nesta Paisley, twenty-four, married to a Davyyd Paisley who's an engineer working on the gas pipeline that's going down the Tanat Valley. She was temporarily employed at the Tanat Inn as a barmaid while her husband did his work on the pipeline planning. She and her husband live in Cardiff when he's not on a job site. She was born in Llangynog, went to school with the woman who found her."

Bowers wrote again, switching to a blue pen for the victim information. 'How long had they been married?"

"Don't know," Notley informed him. "We thought we'd talk to the husband and family today."

"Okay, then, there's a lot of background you'll be needing to get." Bowers was all business. "Tell me about the woman who found her."

Notley looked at his notes again. "Bronwyn Rhianna Bagley, also age twenty-four, from Llangynog."

"She knew the victim?"

"Yes," Notley asserted, "but not as a friend."

"She said that?" Bowers hesitated with his pen at the whiteboard, looking over his shoulder at Notley.

"She admitted they weren't friendly," Will broke in. "They hadn't kept in touch after they left for university. She said that Mrs. Paisley bullied her from childhood on."

"Including an incident last night at the local pub that involved a man," Notley broke in.

Bowers considered that. "Could be something there. You say she was found holding the victim in her lap?"

"Yes," Notley said, "which is strange, isn't it?"

"Not usual," Bowers agreed. "I'll look over her interview later, see if anything else stands out to me. We'll probably want to talk to her again."

"That's what we thought," Notley told him smugly.

Bowers let a smile flirt with the corners of his mouth. "So, you didn't speak to anyone yesterday but the woman who found her?"

"That's all we had time for," Notley acknowledged with a side glance at Will.

Will paid him no attention. "Actually, I spoke to the reverend who's in charge of Pennant Melangell for a few minutes." He felt Notley stiffen next to him. "It was just an informal chat when I went in to use the phone."

"And?" Bowers watched them, twisting the dry-erase marker in his fingers.

"He was very protective toward Miss Bagley, the woman who found the victim. He hadn't known Mrs. Paisley at all, but it was obvious that he holds Miss Bagley in high regard."

"Not very helpful, that," Notley pointed out.

"The owner of the pub said as much, too." Will wasn't about to back down.

"Sometimes the impressions of the people who are familiar with the situation are more valuable than the provable facts," Bowers commented. "We had a call from the husband Sunday morning around 8:00 reporting her missing. As she was an adult, we didn't put much stock in it, but a couple of constables did go and check it out."

"Was a report filed?"

Bowers picked up a piece of paper. "Right here. You can take it with you."

Notley reached out to take it.

"What's your impression so far?" Bowers stood poised with the pen in his fingers.

Notley stood up. "The Bagley woman is an obvious first suspect. She had to have practically raced up the footpath because she did it in what appears to be record time, she found the body, and I find it odd that she would walk that footpath in the rain and then go straight into the churchyard for no obvious reason rather than drying off in the counseling centre, which she had a key for. She had to know what she was going to find there. And then to be found actually holding the body…who in their right mind would do that? She looks guilty to me."

Bowers studied Notley for a long moment and then turned to Will. "Is that your impression, as well?"

Will swallowed hard. He hated to contradict Notley in Bowers' presence, but he also hated to let Notley prejudice the investigation almost before it had properly begun. "No, sir, I don't agree at this point. It is true there are inconsistencies in Miss Bagley's story, but there could be many reasons for that. Maybe she was protecting someone, the real murderer. Maybe she had another reason for walking that footpath that morning that she didn't feel she could reveal. Hell, maybe she was having an affair with Mrs. Paisley's husband. I don't know. But my gut feeling is that she did not commit the actual murder. At least, that's how I feel until we investigate more. There's not that much to go on at this point, and certainly not enough for a conviction. I think we need to keep an open mind so as not to miss something important."

Bowers nodded. "I would agree with that. We need to be thorough. How do you plan to proceed?"

Notley moved between Bowers and Will. "We thought we'd head back to Llangynog this morning and talk to the victim's family, her husband, her employer, and everyone else who seems connected to the case. I'd like to see the scene again in daylight, get a better feel for how it went down. Then there's the forensics report to check out and the doctor to talk with. There are a lot of questions needing answers, in my opinion. It may take us a few days to get them."

"Okay, that sounds good." Bowers set down his marker and gestured them toward the door. "Keep me informed."

"Of course, sir." Notley walked out the door, leaving Will to follow behind him like a subordinate, he thought. But Bowers raised his eyebrows at him as he passed by, nodding toward Notley who was stalking up the hallway ahead of them, and Will suppressed a smile.

They pulled out of town and were headed east on the A470 before 11:00, which would put them into Llangynog around noon. Will pulled out his cell phone and dialed the number they had for Davyyd Paisley, arranging an interview with him at half-twelve in Oswestry, where he was staying. Oswestry was a few miles further east than Llangynog, but if he pushed his speed a bit, they would make it on time.

He tapped his phone off. "Half-twelve," he informed Notley. "After that, we can go back to Pennant Melangell and look at the scene while it's full daylight and get back to her parents afterwards, if that suits you."

Notley stared ahead at the road. "Don't ever contradict me again in front of Bowers," he growled, startling Will, whose eyes snapped toward him in quick anger. "You made me look a fool, and I don't like being made to look a fool."

"He asked my opinion," Will reminded him, fighting to control his temper. "I had to be honest, didn't I?"

"Your job is to agree with my findings," Notley insisted. "Why are you so set against the Bagley woman as the perpetrator anyway? Got a thing for her or something?"

Will's hands tightened on the steering wheel and he squinted against the slight pressure he felt behind his eyes. *A headache coming on,* he thought, *and it's Notley who's responsible for it.* "I'm just trying to be neutral until we get more facts. We've got almost nothing at this point in the investigation, haven't even talked to the husband yet, and he's the guilty party as often as not. I'm not going to set my mind on the Bagley woman until we've talked to the others and gotten the forensics report, that's all."

"You've not got the feel for a murder investigator," Notley told him. "A real murder detective knows instinctively who the guilty party is. That's what comes with experience, and that experience is something you just don't have."

"I've got eight years on the force."

"Not in homicide," Notley reminded him smugly, "so I'm warning you – let me lead this investigation and we'll get a quick solve. Go behind my back, and you'll find yourself looking for another job."

Will clamped his mouth shut and forced himself to look out the windscreen. He tried to relax, rolling his shoulders slightly and consciously easing the muscles in his forehead. If he survived this investigation with Notley, it would be a miracle. How on earth did he make it as a murder investigator with such conceited notions about himself? *I'm not giving in to him,* Will promised himself. *I'll do my job and look at all the evidence. If my findings go against Notley's, I'll stand up for what I believe.* His conscience would allow him to do no less.

They arrived in Oswestry just a few minutes past 12:30 and drove around the village centre until they found the brick Georgian-style Smithfield Hotel where Davyyd and Glynnis Paisley had been staying. Will pulled into the hotel's private car park and found a space.

Davyyd Paisley was waiting for them in the lobby, sitting in an overstuffed chair and sipping on a cup of tea. He invited them into the dining room, offering to buy them lunch.

Will, quick to take advantage of a free meal and a gourmet one, at that, chose the seafood pancake, while Notley ordered the duck. *It's probably not fair to let a suspect buy us lunch,* Will thought guiltily. The Smithfield, however, had an impressive reputation for its food, so this time he was willing to battle his conscience if that was what it took to enjoy the meal.

They arranged themselves at a corner table where some privacy would be assured. Davyyd Paisley seemed to Will to be an affable man, outgoing and friendly despite the loss he had just experienced. He agreed quickly to Notley's request to record their interview, seeming at ease and eager to be of help.

"How long were you and Glynnis married?" Notley inquired after they had the preliminaries of name, age, and occupation duly recorded.

"It's only been two months," Davyyd replied softly, his ebullience dampened visibly once the real questioning began. His eyes took on a dreamy, lost look as he looked back into the past. "She had met my former girlfriend, Rhonda Morris, in a class at Cardiff University." He glanced at them, blinking, and his eyes took on better focus. "They became friends and ended by moving in together, so that's how I got to know her. You might say Glynnis stole me from Rhonda, I guess." He sighed and shrugged. "I don't know how it happened really. One day Rhonda and I were together, and the next we weren't. Glynnis just seemed to move between us."

The waitress interrupted them with their meals, and they ate in silence for a few moments before Davyyd Paisley picked up his story again.

"Rhonda wasn't happy about it all, and I never meant to hurt her. We had been together for nearly two years, and I'd thought we'd marry once we'd both finished with school and moved on. Then I graduated and started seeing less of Rhonda, and when I did see her, Glynnis was always there, watching us, flirting with me, I guess. One day I came to visit unexpectedly, and Rhonda had gone out, so…well, you can guess what happened. Like I said, I never meant for it to go that way, but Glynnis had a way about her. Once she set her mind to something, that was all there was, and you couldn't argue with her. A few weeks later she told me she was pregnant, and my whole life changed."

"Rhonda," Notley consulted his notes, "Miss Morris…how did she feel about what happened?"

Davyyd's lip trembled. "You can imagine, I think, how shocked she was. I couldn't explain it adequately, couldn't tell her that I'd not meant to hurt her. She wouldn't talk to me, nor to Glynnis, though we both tried. She said horrible things about Glynnis, that she was evil and uncaring, that she'd put some sort of spell on me. It was nonsense, of course." He shrugged, but looked uncomfortably reflective. "I made a mistake, but Glynnis wasn't evil."

"You were happy together, then?" Will prompted him.

Davyyd nodded, and then paused. "Reasonably so, I'd say. Glynnis was…protective of me, I guess you'd call it. She was jealous if anyone else came close." He smiled sadly. "I guess some might say she was controlling, but that I didn't mind being controlled. Not really." Somehow, he didn't sound entirely convincing, Will thought, making a note in the little pad he'd brought with him.

"You called to report her missing yesterday morning at about..." Notley looked at his notes, "8:00. Is that correct?"

"Yes." Davyyd picked at his salmon, tearing it apart with his fork but eating little. "I called from my in-law's house in Llangynog after checking to see if she'd spent the night with them."

"Had you expected her to do that?" Notley asked, his pencil poised.

Davyyd met his eyes. "No, I'd thought she was going to be coming back to Oswestry on the bus."

"You didn't plan to return to Oswestry together?" Notley persisted.

Davyyd looked down at his plate and set down his fork. "She was working at the Tanat Inn that night. The owner, Cecil Lumley, offered her a temp job when he learned we were going to be in the area for a month or six weeks while I worked on the pipeline. Glynnis was bored, so she took the job."

"But you were both in Llangynog earlier, even though you had the Sunday off. Is that right?" Notley watched him, waiting for the answer.

"We were both there earlier in the day. I had thought to wait for her so we could come home together in the rental car, but I...I changed my mind."

"Why did you do that?" Will asked, setting down his fork. The seafood pancakes had been very good, filled with shrimp and whitefish in a creamy sauce. He felt satisfied with the meal, more so than with the interview.

Davyyd shook his head. "It was a misunderstanding, really. Glynnis was...she was a friendly sort, you understand. She couldn't help chatting up the fellows, just being nice, you know." His eyes looked empty, sad. "I took it wrong. There was this American fellow, you see, and I thought...well, I thought she was a bit friendlier with him than was called for. The girl he was with walked out, so I wasn't alone in my thinking."

"You had a fight with her?" Notley asked.

"No, not a fight." Davyyd swallowed as tears filled his eyes. He tried to blink them away. "I just had to get away. I told her I was tired, made an excuse. She didn't argue, said she'd get the bus home." He stopped, fighting for control. "I should have waited for her. If I had..."

"It's not your fault," Will assured him. "Llangynog is a small village and safe, after all, and her family lived there. She'd grown up there. You couldn't be expected to think something would happen to her if you left and let her make her own way home."

Notley scowled at him, a look Will was becoming accustomed to. "What time was it you left for home?"

Davyyd shrugged. He lifted his hand and dabbed roughly at his eye. "I don't know. Maybe 8:00? It was dark."

"What time was her shift to be over?" Notley's voice was brisk.

"10:00, but Lemley would have let her go a bit before that so she could make the bus."

Notley made another note, and Will did the same. He was certain that his list was shorter than Notley's, but it wouldn't hurt to have something down on paper. "Anyone see you return to the hotel?"

"I'm guessing not. I didn't check at the desk or anything."

Notley nodded and wrote. "Why did you wait until morning to report her missing?"

"I thought she'd decided to stay the night at her parents' house."

"Would that be a typical thing for her to do?" Notley persisted.

"Not really." Davyyd's voice had faded to a whisper. "It was the only thing I could think of when she didn't come back to the hotel."

"Didn't you really think she'd gone off with this American?"

Will shot a look at Notley. Putting words in the man's mouth wasn't a good idea at this point. He suspected that Bowers wouldn't like it if he heard about it later. Paisley hadn't been cautioned; even if he admitted that he'd thought she'd gone off with another man, it wouldn't be admissible if they thought it had led to her murder.

"No," Davyyd insisted, to Will's relief, "that wasn't it." But he said it weakly.

If he thought she was with that American, that would be motive. Will jotted a quick question on his notepad. "Do you know the American's name?"

"No," Davyyd said. "But Glynnis knew the woman he was with. I think they were old schoolmates."

Will sat up straighter. "Bronwyn Bagley?"

"That would be her," Davyyd confirmed.

"Did you try to phone her when she didn't show up?"

"I did try to call. I tried until about midnight, then again in the morning. She never picked up."

Notley gave Will a warning look. They'd have to ask about her mobile, see if it was found. "Okay, then. One more thing, and we'll leave you alone. Did your wife have any enemies that you know of?"

Davyyd stared at him. "You're kidding, right? What is this, NCIS or something? You're really asking me that?"

Notley's face reddened. "Of course, we do. Where do you think the TV people learned it?"

Will hid a smile.

"No, Glynnis had no enemies. She wasn't always the easiest person to get along with, but there was no one who hated her enough to do something like this." Davyyd looked from one to the other of them. "You will find whoever did this, won't you?"

It was the other thing they always said on TV, Will mused. Even the guilty ones asked it, trying to throw off the investigation. "We'll do our best," he said, and Notley murmured agreement.

"Well, that was interesting," Will ventured as he steered around a group of parked cars partially blocking the lane and accelerated to beat the oncoming traffic. "I'd say he had motive, wouldn't you? Jealous and all that? And no alibi that can be verified. Then there's the ex-girlfriend. She might have wanted some revenge. Even the American could be a suspect."

Notley pulled his tobacco pouch from his pocket. "Jealousy is a strange transformer of characters."

Will glanced toward him. "What? Is that a quote?"

The top of Notley's head turned pink where the thin strands of dirty blonde hair didn't quite cover the scalp. "Sir Arthur Conan Doyle," he admitted.

Will grinned. "Then what about 'It is a capital mistake to theorize before you have all of the evidence'?"

Notley turned in his seat to look at Will. "What?"

"I can use the internet, too," Will told him, and he was gratified to see Notley raise his eyebrows and laugh.

They drove through Llangynog and down the valley to Pennant Melangell, parking the car beside the roadway because the tiny car park was already full. They could see the uniformed forensics team working in the churchyard, fanning out toward the roadway and the foot path.

They walked into the churchyard and shook hands with the constable who greeted them. A tall thin man with hollow eyes and a hungry look, he identified himself as Marcus Robb, head of the forensics team.

"We're pretty sure she was killed here in the churchyard, and probably Saturday night rather than Sunday morning," he informed them dourly, pointing at the church wall where the body had been found. "There were blood drops and footprints leading some way down the footpath as well as toward the car park, so we think she was incapacitated elsewhere and then carried or dragged here and finished off. Body temp says it was about ten to twelve hours before we were called in."

"The question is, why would she come here late at night like that?" Will wondered. "It would have been too dark to hike the footpath, and she didn't have a car to drive up the roadway."

"There was quite a bright full moon last night," Robb reminded him. "It would have been a difficult hike, but someone who was familiar with the footpath might have managed it with the moonlight and perhaps a torch to show the way. She did grow up here, after all."

"Or she was brought up here in a car," Notley put in. "You said there was blood evidence in the car park, as well?"

"Both the car park and the footpath," Robb agreed. "And why incapacitate her elsewhere and bring her into the churchyard to finish her off? It's a puzzle, isn't it?"

"Do we have a murder weapon?" Notley asked, stooping to look more closely at the wall against which the body had been found.

"We don't have a cause of death yet," Robb replied, "but we don't have a weapon either, nor an accurate time of death. I assume she was hit with a stone or a club, something like that, and then stabbed. Someone was pretty mad at her, I'd say, from looking at the wounds. But we have nothing here that looks like a weapon so far."

"So, you're saying someone drove her up here, hit her over the head, dragged her into the churchyard, stabbed her, and then went off down the footpath to dispose of the murder weapons. Does that sound right?" Will looked from Robb to Notley, waiting.

"Maybe," Notley said, "or maybe it went the other way. Maybe they walked up here in the moonlight and then she was killed. Maybe the murderer met someone else in the car park after."

"We'll need more to go on," Will told Robb, and Robb nodded. "Did you find her mobile?"

"In a purse, flung away into some taller grass near the churchyard gate."

"Tossed away, or dropped?"

"Looked like it was tossed, but it may have been lost in a scuffle. Small bag."

"What else was in it?"

"Not much. Her phone, a wallet with a few bob, her license, two credit cards. Some tissues, a comb."

"Okay, we'll have someone give it a closer look. Maybe there'll be fingerprints on the bag." He nodded at the constable. "Good work."

They spent some time then crouched down examining the bloody grass and the blood-stained wall, looking at crushed grass and footprints on the walkway, measuring distances from the pathway to the churchyard to the car park. Will would have liked to have gone into the counseling centre, but it was locked and no one was there to let them in. He did wander back into the church, finding it unlocked but unoccupied. There was blood on the floors and on one of the wooden pews where, he supposed, Bronwyn Bagley had sat after the reverend had brought her inside the church. Of course, she had been soaked with the blood from sitting and holding the body, he mused. He wondered if it had been she who had also made the bloody prints leading to the footpath or to the car park. Perhaps their theories were wrong, and Mrs. Paisley had been both attacked and killed right there.

Later they drove back into Llangynog, maneuvering around a flock of sheep that had wandered onto the B9341 midway along. *Picturesque,* Will mused. *Peaceful, too.* He wondered suddenly about the legend of Pennant Melangell. *Something to do with a hare, wasn't it? Lark would like that story.* He vowed to learn it for her before they were done with the investigation.

Glynnis' parents met them at the door of their cottage. The father was stocky, dressed in worn jeans and an ill-fitting blue shirt.

His red nose reflected either a habit for drink, Will thought, or a lot of tears at the loss of his daughter. The mother was a tall, strong woman dressed in brown trousers, yellow blouse, and tweed jacket. Wrinkles at the corners of her eyes and mouth reflected a liking for the outdoors and made her look older than she probably was. She took charge of the conversation and it quickly became apparent that she served as the head of that household.

"My daughter was a lovely girl," she said, "who had just married and had a promising future ahead of her. Her husband is an engineer, you know. He would have had the ability to provide very well for her."

"You liked him?" Will asked.

"Of course, we did." Mrs. Newbury looked at her husband. "Didn't we, Edwirt?"

He nodded, but said nothing. Will studied him carefully. He didn't seem to object to his wife taking over the interview.

"Were you aware that your daughter hadn't gone back to Oswestry that night?" Notley asked, looking at Mr. Newbury.

"I was at the pub with my son-in-law early in the evening," he answered, "but I left before he did. I assumed he was waiting for Glynnis. He didn't say otherwise, and that was the reason he was there early on."

"Why do you think he changed his mind?" Will asked, trying to keep up with Notley on the questions.

Newbury shrugged. "There was a bit of trouble with one of those protesters. I suppose he felt unwelcome after that."

"Protesters?" Notley frowned at him.

"The gas pipeline," the man explained. "There was a group here in the village protesting it. It's meant to go right down the valley, you know, and this being a fragile ecosystem, too. Llangynog is right in the middle of it."

Will jotted that down and looked back up at Newbury. "Sounds to me like you're against it, as well," he observed. "Yet your son-in-law was working on it. Opposite sides?"

Mrs. Newbury put a hand out and touched her husband's hand. "We're on Glynnis' side, if we're on a side at all," she insisted. "The gas is needed and has to be transported somehow or another. It's just a fact of modern life, isn't it, Edwirt?"

Newbury nodded. "That's right, Gwyn; that's how it is."

Notley fixed his narrowed eyes on Newbury. "Tell me about this incident at the pub."

Newbury drew a deep breath, preparing, it seemed, for a longer speech than normal. "We was just sitting having a drink, chatting a bit while Davyyd waited for Glynnis to be done with working. Then this man across the room started shouting at Davyyd, telling him he wasn't welcome there."

"Do you know who the man was?" Will asked.

"Yeah, it was Hal Corse. Lives down the valley a bit. You pass his farm on your way up the B9341 when you're heading up here."

Both Will and Notley wrote that down. "How did Davyyd react to the confrontation?" Notley asked.

Newbury snorted. "Said he'd leave then, if that's what they wanted."

"So, he left at that time? I thought it was later, after you'd gone on home," Notley reminded him.

"No, he didn't leave then. I said he offered to leave." Newbury's face had turned red, his nose a deeper maroon. "Glynnis stepped in then, she did. Told him to stay in his seat and then spilled a tray of beer on Hal Corse and his friends."

Will's eyebrows raised, and he noticed that Notley sat up in his chair, alert. "So Glynnis took things into her own hands?"

Newbury looked at him. "What else was she to do? Davyyd wasn't standing up to them, after all. There's family honor to be defended."

"Family honor," Notley repeated. Will knew what he was thinking – that Glynnis had made an enemy that night. "And Davyyd stayed around after this man left?"

"Sure, for a while anyway."

"But you didn't?"

Newbury's ashamed look told them more than his words. "I wasn't going to stay there and drink with a man who had to depend on his wife to handle things for him."

"What time did you get home?"

"It was early, maybe around half seven." He looked to his wife, who nodded.

"And you stayed in all night?"

"We watched an episode of *Midsomer Murders*," his wife told them. "It was an old one, the one where the bird watcher got killed. We didn't go out again."

Notley looked at Newbury, and the man met his eyes. "How did Glynnis and the Bagley woman get on?" Notley's abrupt change of topics startled Will.

Now Mrs. Newbury stepped in again. "They were classmates, but never friends," she told them smugly. "There was something off about that Bagley girl from the time she was a little girl. Fey, she was. Glynnis had no time for her. Looked down on her, to be truthful."

"What do you mean when you call her fey?" Will asked.

"Bewitched," Mrs. Newbury barked. "You aren't from Wales, are you?" She nodded toward Will, ignoring Notley.

"Gloucester," he answered.

"Here in Wales we have a long tradition of folklore. Tales of fairies and elves and wizards entertained our ancestors by the fireside, and most apparently believed them true back in those days. Now, of course, people tell the tales as children's stories, if at all. But there's some, and Bronwyn is one of them, who still like to believe the stories are real. She did as a child, and she probably does now. That's what we call fey. She's an odd one. Glynnis did well to stay away from her."

Notley was staring at the woman, blinking in confusion. Will noticed, so he stirred himself and stood up, snapping his notepad shut. "Thank you for your time," he said. "We're sorry for your loss."

"Got a little off track, didn't we?" Will commented to Notley as they pulled onto the B9341 and drove west toward Caernarfon and home. Dusk was falling and shadows marked the roadway where it passed by cottages and Llangynog's inns and churches.

"I found it interesting," Notley told him, pulling out his tobacco pouch. "I thought that Bagley woman was a little off when we talked to her."

Will sighed. "It sounds as if Glynnis made an enemy in the pub last night," he reminded Notley. "And there's the husband who was unwilling to defend himself, as well. He didn't mention the altercation in the pub when we talked with him today, did he?"

"No," Notley lit his pipe and puffed at it thoughtfully. "There's more here than meets the eye," he admitted at last.

"We've our work cut out for us," Will agreed.

A stop in the station revealed a message from the medical examiner, Francis Roark, to call him. Despite it being after working hours, they put the phone on speaker and made the call.

"Ah, yes, the Paisley woman," he said once they'd identified themselves. "Better if you'd been with me for the autopsy so you could see it all for yourselves."

"We had preliminary interviews that had to be done," Notley told him. Truthfully, most of their colleagues had to be dragged to an autopsy; they'd avoid it if any excuse were available.

"She had a pretty significant blow to the head, made by something smooth."

"Not a rock, then," Will observed.

"Not sure what it was, but it wouldn't have had any sharp edges. Something man-made, most likely."

"That killed her?" Notley wanted to know.

"No, that might have incapacitated her, but it wouldn't have caused her death. She also had eleven stab wounds, the most serious being straight into her heart. That was what did it for her, and death would have been fast."

"Do you have an approximate time of death?" Will asked.

"I'd put it sometime between eleven that night and one the next morning."

Will looked at Notley, who returned the look. "Then it was shortly after she got off work," he commented.

"That's for you to figure out," said the medical examiner. "I've done my part. Now it's up to you to put the pieces together."

"The timing eliminates Bronwyn Bagley," Will pointed out after they ended the call.

"It doesn't eliminate anyone," Notley retorted. "It only means she didn't do it just before she was found holding the body. She could have done it the night before and returned to the scene."

"And so could a number of other people."

"We're not done yet," Notley agreed.

Chapter Seven

Bronwyn opened her eyes, groaned, and pushed old Nan's warm body away from her own enough so that she could turn over and look at her alarm clock. 6:28 a.m. Although the alarm wouldn't go off for another two minutes, it was time she nudged herself awake enough to take a hot shower and head up to the counseling centre for her day's work.

She had taken Monday off from the centre, not having had anything scheduled that was pressing enough to force her to come in. When she'd called, she'd been told that the centre would be closed anyway that day due to the detectives crawling all over the grounds.

Her one-day respite was, however, over now. It was Tuesday, and by 10:00 she would need to be cheerfully welcoming a group from Hope Church in Bangor arriving for the retreat they had scheduled months before. If a volunteer was on site, he or she could handle any walk-in pilgrims who might come in search of individual counseling. Those few who had already scheduled counseling would be met by the resident psychologist, Janice Hatcher. Managing the large groups came under Bronwyn's list of duties at the centre, though, so this was not a day for hiding away any longer.

She had slept little Sunday night, re-living every detail of Glynnis' death and the events that had led up to it, no matter how she tried to put it out of her mind. Her mum had crept quietly around the house Monday morning in order to allow her a good sleep-in, but it had been useless, for she couldn't shake off the horror of what had happened long enough to let her mind rest.

She had finally gotten out of bed and gone down to the porridge her mum had simmering on the Aga. The two of them then spent a comforting morning chatting over tea and later watching DVDs – romantic comedies that may not have diverted her darker thoughts quite enough, but nevertheless comforted her, wrapped as she was in an ancient quilt and her mother's love.

"I got the idea that they consider me a suspect," Bronwyn confessed at one point in the morning.

"Just let them solve it, love," her mother advised, smoothing a strand of Bronwyn's hair back off her cheek. "Truth will out, as they say. You must stay away from it all. Promise me?"

"I'll try," Bronwyn whispered, unwilling to commit to something as firm as a promise until she had thought it out thoroughly.

Later she'd put on her oldest jeans, the same comfortable jumper she'd had on the night before, and her wellies, and then she'd walked out into the pastures with her dad to check on the new lambs. They'd had a ewe with twins born on Saturday, and the ewe had been slow to accept one of her babes, so he'd been keeping a special eye on that one, as well as checking on others newly born or about to be born.

Lambing season was one of the busiest times on the farm, and her dad often worked from dawn to dusk. It was fortunate that Maddock had stayed nearby to help, as he was able to fill in and take much of the pressure off as their parents aged. In addition, he brought new techniques to farming that brought about endless conversations between the two of them as they debated whether traditional or modern farming methods worked better, and which were more profitable.

As always, seeing the new lambs as they romped around the green pasture kicking and bucking brought a smile to Bronwyn's face. She bent down and picked one of the wild daisies that grew in abundance in the field, letting the sun warm her face as she stood up again and turned her nose skyward. Then she opened her eyes again and turned to note a wren twittering from the top of a gnarled apple tree that grew in the pasture, and that brought a second smile as she saw her pony Hobbs in his favorite spot cropping the grass beneath that very tree. As if he felt her eyes on him, he looked up, stared for a moment, and then started a slow amble toward her.

"Hello, Hobbs," she called, wishing she'd thought to put a carrot in her pocket. When he got close enough, she scratched him on the neck just below his ears, his favorite spot. He stretched out his neck and closed his eyes in delight, making her smile. There was nothing like a childhood friend to cheer one up when things were down.

"Ah, that's good then," her dad commented, nodding toward her. "I like to see you smiling again, Bronwyn. These past two days have been hard for you."

The smile faded with the reminder. "I can't stop thinking of it, Dad."

"It'll take time, I'm sure," her dad said. "It's been a bad business, but I'm sure the inspectors will put an end to it soon. They'll find the man responsible."

Bronwyn sighed, idly twiddling the wild daisy in her fingers. "They think it's me."

Her dad shook his head, his graying hair soft in the spring sun. "No, that's not true. It's only that you were there, so they've a lot of questions for you, that's all. It'll be fine."

"If I could find out who did it, I'd feel better."

He turned his head sharply, his eyes fearful. "Stay away from it, Bronwyn. There might be danger if you get too close to whoever it is. And," he continued, "you shouldn't be walking along the footpath or in the forest alone now, either, not until they catch this person. Okay, sweetheart? Promise me?"

"I'll drive to work for a few days," Bronwyn replied reluctantly. "I love to walk, though, especially now in the spring. This time of year, everything looks and smells fresh and new." She smiled at him. "You know how it is. You taught me to love it. I won't be able to deny myself that pleasure for long."

He smiled at that. "Just long enough for them to figure this out will be long enough, and then it'll be safe again. And I'll walk with you sometimes, if you like, when you're at home."

"I'd like that," she told him sincerely. She wondered at times whether her father, quiet and close to the earth as he was, shared her experiences with the Twlwyth Teg. If so, he never mentioned it. But then, he probably wouldn't, would he?

And now it was Tuesday and time to get back to normal.

The calm generated by her day at home with her mum and dad dissipated quickly enough as she prepared for work. The lack of sleep had left bags under her eyes, a pallor to her skin, and a headache lurking above her eyes. She sorted through her clothes and finally chose a black skirt and soft blue blouse that might not help her peeked look, but at least looked professional.

She managed a few minutes to sit with her mum and dad for tea and cranberry scones before she dashed to the Volvo and turned the key, listening to its feeble wheezing as the starter kicked it to life. She grimaced as she rolled down the short driveway and onto the B9241. Maybe her dad could fix it again, but she knew the Volvo's days were numbered. She'd better increase the pennies she put into savings so that she could buy something else when it finally died and couldn't be brought back.

The two-mile drive took her only a few minutes, and with the road deserted that early in the day, she relaxed and found herself watching the roadside as much as the roadway. Spring had arrived in the Tanat Valley. Snowy sweet woodruff bloomed in luxuriant abundance alongside the sheep fences, dotted with thick patches of taller snowdrops and hazel. A sparrowhawk launched itself from a fencepost to capture some hapless creature, most likely a mouse, from a field as Bronwyn drove past, and she thought she saw a peregrine falcon soaring far above in the cloudless sky. As always, the young pheasants scurried down the lane just ahead of her car, frantic to reach a clearing in the hedgerows. Across the valley, the Berwyn Mountains stretched, shadows still darkening patches of green down low, but tipped with golden sunshine on their craggy peaks.

She parked the Volvo in the small car park and used her key to open the counseling centre door. No one else would be about that time of day. Reverend Wicklyff or a volunteer would come in to open the church at 10:00, although services were offered only on Mondays, Thursdays, and some Fridays, along with the Sunday afternoon service. Janis Hatcher, the chief counselor, would be there around the same time.

Bronwyn hesitated in the doorway and then turned to look back outside. The sun shone brightly behind her and a wayward bit of breeze stirred the yews so that they whispered softly in their protective circle. A dove cooed from the roof above her head, and she looked up to find it sitting on the very peak of the roof. It saw her watching and fell silent, a silence that felt like an eerie stillness to Bronwyn. She looked in every direction, seeing nothing, and then stepped inside and turned the lock on the door. Perhaps it was still the shock of finding Glynnis' body in the churchyard, but suddenly Bronwyn felt a shiver of fear being here all alone.

Ignoring her jumpiness, she busied herself preparing for the group from Bangor. Someone had set up a conference room the day before, arranging tables and chairs and a podium with microphone and computer handy for their use. She checked the computer set up, turning on the projector and checking the image on the screen, making sure there would be no glitches. She set pamphlets illustrating their offerings on a table in the back of the room and opened a couple of windows to let in the scent of the outdoors. She filled pitchers with water and ice, setting one on each of the tables. Later there would be tea provided, and then later still, a simple lunch.

She checked her watch and, with nearly an hour before the group's expected arrival, she walked into her office and sat down before her own computer. Jiggling the mouse, she watched the screen come to life, connected to the internet, and went straight to Google. It had been in the back of her mind that she might try to research the words the Twlwyth Teg had used when they'd told her of Glynnis' murder. Some of it had been in English, and none of it had been in their own language, of that she was sure. As they had never talked directly to her before, their doing so now created a puzzle to be solved, and she thought now might be a good time to start.

Tocsin tolls. She remembered the words vividly. She typed in the word "tocsin," guessing at the spelling, but suspecting it would differ from its homonym "toxin." From the options that came up, she chose a dictionary offering and was pleased to find a meaning that fit the situation: "an alarm bell or warning bell." *Ah ha!* She thought. The dictionary further listed its etymology as medieval Latin. *Medieval Latin would have been used in medieval Britain,* she told herself. *Maybe the Twlwyth Teg had learned their English a long, long time ago.*

Ale wife in the sacred churchyard lies spilled. Her fingers hesitated over the keys. Surely "ale wife" was easy enough to understand. It must be an archaic term for a bar maid. That much she'd already figured out. "Spilled," though, was used awkwardly. She typed quickly and again chose the dictionary offering. She scanned through the common definitions of the word and found what she was looking for at the very bottom of the page: "Old English, "to kill, to shed blood." *That's it, then.* Her heart raced. *The Twlwyth Teg spoke in a mix of medieval and modern English.* Next time she would be better able to decipher their words, now that she knew that.

But there had been more. Their last words to her had been easy enough to understand, certainly, so she didn't need the internet for that. *The Guardian comes.* The puzzle here, though, would be harder to solve. Who was the guardian? Where was the place he was coming to, and why? She had seen no one until Reverend Wicklyff had arrived. Was he the guardian? Or perhaps it was Pysgotwr? Welsh mythology would probably make him so.

She sat back in her chair and thought. What she really needed to do was to find Pysgotwr again and hope he would answer her questions more directly. Thinking of him reminded her of Granny Powers' words. Were they connected in some way to what had happened to Glynnis? She took a deep breath. She understood her parents' concern about her wandering about alone considering what had happened to Glynnis, but alone was the only place she was going to find the answers she needed. Those must come from Pysgotwr, the pool in the woods that had gotten her into trouble at age six, or the Twlwyth Teg.

A hushed sound interrupted her thoughts, and she turned her head to listen, freezing in her chair. She held her breath, straining to hear the sound again. *Boogeymen,* she chastised herself, but just in case she eased out of her chair, trying to keep it from squeaking, and tiptoed across to the door to the entryway. Again, she tried not to breathe. She listened for a long minute and then slowly peeked around the corner to look beyond. The entryway was empty.

Heart thumping now, she reached out to grab her umbrella from where it rested in a corner by the doorjamb and crept out away from her office. Carefully she stole along the carpeted floor, pausing by the locked main door to listen and then going on past the Janis' office and the counseling room. At each she stopped, listened, and then glanced inside, but she found nothing amiss.

Then she heard the slight sound again and recognized the sound for what it was – footsteps whispering quietly in the room just ahead, the conference room. She froze, holding the umbrella up, wanting to flee, but not knowing where to go. She waited, listening, and then turned and crept back down the hallway and slipped into the empty counselling room.

Standing at an angle behind the door, she peeked back into the entryway, which remained empty. A sudden flush of foolishness made her shake her head. *It's Janis,* she reassured herself, *or Reverend Wicklyff. One of them has come in early, perhaps to catch up on something.* But why would they not have come first to her office, having seen her car in the car park? She shivered. Something seemed off. And she had left the windows open in that room.

Steeling herself, she forced her feet forward and tiptoed toward the conference room once again. Perhaps she could just peek around the corner and see who it was?

Gripping the umbrella tight in her hands, she crept toward the door, one quiet step at a time. Her heart pounded in her chest, and the lightheadedness that accompanied it threatened to take her feet out from under her. She blinked and tried to steady her breathing.

Now she could hear the footsteps again, brushing against the carpet as they grew louder. Seizing what courage she could, Bronwyn swallowed hard and stepped into the doorway, umbrella held high like a bat.

She stopped as a wave of relief nearly toppled her.

Reverend Wicklyff stood not three paces away, the startled look on his face reflecting the one she was sure she wore on her own.

"Reverend!" she exclaimed, her voice a squeak. "What are you doing here?"

He stepped back a pace. "I've come looking for you." Gesturing toward the umbrella, he raised his eyebrows. "I'm sorry if I frightened you, Bronwyn. I only wanted to be sure things were ready for today's group before I looked for you in your office."

She lowered the umbrella, blushing. "It's just with what happened here on Sunday, I am a bit nervous."

"Yes," he agreed, "I noticed the locked door." He gave her a pensive look. "I don't believe anyone here is going to harm you, Bronwyn."

"That's probably what Glynnis thought, as well," she pointed out.

"Ah, well, Glynnis…she wasn't so much a part of things here as you are," he said. "I had a bit of a chat with one of the constables after. He asked about you. He didn't say, but I'm sure he was wondering why you'd have hurried up that footpath and straight into

94

the churchyard, as if you knew what you'd find there. I told him he wasn't to consider you a suspect, that you were entirely trustworthy."

She lowered her eyes. *Don't ask about that,* she willed him. *Don't ask me how I knew Glynnis had been killed. I can't lie to you, nor can I tell you the truth. Please don't ask!*

Her message must have gotten through to him somehow. When she made no comment, he nodded a bit and went on. "I thought you might need more time off, so that's why I came in early today. I can meet the group from Bangor, if you like. I should have called you yesterday, but with all that had happened, I never thought of it until just this morning."

She managed a tremulous smile. "Thank you, but it's fine for me to be here. I need to be busy, I think, and I need to come to terms with finding Glynnis like that. It's the old story of getting back on the horse; I need to come back to Pennant Melangell and the churchyard, and I think sooner is better than later."

He reached out to touch her hand. "That's good then. I'll just unlock the church and check on a few things, and then I'll be gone home for the day."

She watched him walk toward the door and thought of calling him back. *Do you think the Twywyth Teg are real, Reverend? There is magic about this place. Is it the saint, or something even older than that?* Then he was gone, and she was alone again with her thoughts.

The Hope Church group arrived on time, and she gave them a brief tour of the centre and the church, passing through the sensory garden and the churchyard as she did so. As always, the history of the site drew her in and she found herself relaxing, feeling at one with the wholeness of things as she guided them around. The circle of yews, the shrine, the peace of the garden, and even a glimpse of the ancient gravestones as they passed them all combined to form a sacred and holy place. The pilgrims always came away with a sense of it, she knew. Tranquility came easily to one here, and she'd been right to return as soon as she had.

After the group was settled, Bronwyn wandered back to the church and stopped in at the tiny gift shop beneath the tower to chat with Caderyn Baker, the volunteer who was working there for the morning.

"You've sold two more of your sketches," Caderyn told Bronwyn, gesturing toward a wall where the sketches had hung only a few days before. "At this rate, you'll soon be giving up your other job to work full time as an artist."

Bronwyn laughed. "Hardly, Caderyn, but thank you anyway for the compliment."

"Do you have some more you're working on?" Caderyn wanted to know.

"Now that it's spring, I'll be out and about more. I'll be sure to take the time for some sketching," Bronwyn promised her.

She stopped by the shrine in the chancel on her way out. It had been more than a thousand years that this site had offered sanctuary and peace for the people, and indeed, the creatures of the area, as well, she realized as she studied the collection of hare friezes on the wall. Little wonder, then, that the tranquility of the place was so palpable. Its offer of a safe haven must have been just as welcoming in troubled times throughout history as it was to distressed people now. *Myself included,* Bronwyn reminded herself. *I need the peace of Pennant Melangell as much as anyone else does today. There's a oneness of things that this place knows.*

Once outside, she glanced through the churchyard again. The ancient gray stones stood protected by the circle of yews and even though many of the stones had faded and were crumbling on the edges, they managed to convey sacredness, as if the spirits of those who had lived and died there somehow remained to guard the sanctity of the site.

Taking a breath, she forced herself to step off the path. Her eyes flew immediately to the spot where she'd found Glynnis' body, and she saw that crime scene tape still fluttered from stakes set up to protect that area. She took another step closer and another, heart thumping and hands clammy, drawn and repelled at the same moment.

"You're not supposed to be in here," said a voice behind her, and she whirled around, startled. It was one of the inspectors, the younger one. She had no idea of his name.

"I...I just wanted to see the spot again," she stammered. She reached up a hand to push her hair back away from her face. "I didn't know it was forbidden."

The man smiled at that, a nice smile, natural. "Not forbidden, exactly, but there is a sign at the gate that's supposed to keep people out until further notice." He stepped closer. "Will Cooper. I didn't know if you'd remember me or not."

Bronwyn nodded. "Yes, of course I remember you." She offered a tentative smile. "You were the nice one."

He grinned. "I try."

"Where's your partner?" Bronwyn wanted to know.

"Just down by the footpath," he told her. "We're waiting for the forensics people. They walked the footpath from Llangynog to here, looking for a possible attack location. It seems Mrs. Paisley was already in a bad way when she was brought here to the churchyard."

She was surprised he shared that information, especially with a suspect. *No doubt they are also timing the walk to see how long it really takes,* she thought. *That won't come out in my favor.* "They think she was hurt somewhere down on the footpath?"

"They don't know yet." He shrugged, trying now to appear noncommittal. "I saw you coming into the churchyard, so I thought I'd come ask you another question or two without Notley along to interrupt. Besides, I was a little bored standing down there waiting with only him as company, as it were."

Bronwyn felt a flush of panic and tried to suppress it, squeezing her hands into fists and standing very still. Surely this man would see her distress and wonder. "What did you need to know?"

"We understand there was a bit of an upset at the pub the night she died," he said. "Something about her objecting when someone asked her husband to leave?"

"That's so." Bronwyn made herself breathe normally. Why hadn't she thought to mention it before? Surely it was nothing to make her look bad.

"Can you tell me about it?"

"It was one of the local farmers, Hal Corse. He saw Davyyd Paisley sitting at a table and told him he didn't belong, that he should leave." She glanced at the detective. "None of us want the pipeline, and Davyyd was one of the engineers working on the site plan."

"And?"

"And Davyyd didn't want to fight with him. He offered to leave. But Glynnis wasn't having it. She dumped a tray of beers on Hal's table."

"What happened then?"

"Cecil Lumley, the owner, told Hal and his group to leave, and then he threatened to fire Glynnis for what she'd done. But he didn't. She kept on working."

"How did the others react to that?"

"The other people in the pub?" She thought about it. "They mostly just went back to their drinking and chat, but her dad left. I don't know, maybe he was mad because Davyyd didn't stand up for himself."

"Or he didn't want to watch his daughter flirting with the customers while her husband watched." The detective was still watching her. "Mr. Paisley also said that you were with an American, and that you had left the pub early, as if you found Mrs. Paisley's actions with him objectionable. Is that right?"

Bronwyn shut her eyes for a moment, trying to still her breathing, and then met the detective's eyes. "I did leave early," she admitted. *What must he think of me?* "I told you about that. I felt the man I was with was more interested in Glynnis than in me." She felt her face flush hot with embarrassment.

"Do you know his name?" he persisted. "We'd need to talk with him, I think."

Bronwyn thought. Truthfully, she had nearly forgotten the American already, with all else that had been happening. "Mark was his name. Mark McGuire, I think. He said he was from Seattle and was celebrating his law school graduation with a mountain biking trip through the U.K."

"Do you know where he was going next?"

She shook her head. "I'm afraid we didn't get that far."

He nodded. "Okay, then." He hesitated and then surprised her with a more incriminating question than most of his had been. "How angry were you about Glynnis interfering with your date?"

Bronwyn looked at him as her heart skipped a beat. How could she explain? "I wasn't that interested in him anyway," she mumbled, trying to think. "In any case, he wasn't from here, and I'd never have seen him again after that night. This was the sort of thing Glynnis always did – she was always competing, for friends, for boyfriends, for whatever she wanted, and she got pleasure from winning. I was used to it, having gone to school with her."

"You weren't angry?" His eyes bored into hers.

She blushed. "I was a little upset, but like I said, it had happened before."

"Did you have words with her?"

"She saw me out the door," Bronwyn answered. "She said maybe someday I'd meet someone, and she wouldn't be there to lure him away from me."

He raised his eyebrows. "With her husband right there?"

"That was Glynnis."

"You went straight home?"

"Yes."

"Anyone there to verify that?"

Thank goodness for Maddock. "My brother came over. He'd heard about what happened at the pub and wanted to make sure I was alright."

"How long did he stay?"

"It wasn't long, just long enough to calm me down," she admitted.

"And after that? Your parents?"

"They were asleep," she answered truthfully. She shifted, uncomfortable with the topic. Was she a serious suspect? Surely, they couldn't think she would murder Glynnis over a trifle like that?

He seemed to notice her agitation. "Did you happen to notice how her husband felt about it all?"

"He was sitting at his corner table all alone with a pint." She thought about it for a moment. "He didn't look angry with her, but maybe sad, as if it confirmed something he already knew."

"Okay." The detective smiled at her, a nice smile. "I guess that covers that bit." He nodded toward the counseling centre. "So, you're back to work now?"

She nodded. "I took yesterday off and could have had more time, but I thought it better if I just came back here and faced it all."

"That seems a good idea," he said. "You aren't walking to work now, though, are you? It may be dangerous until we figure out who did this."

Bronwyn couldn't stop a grin, which she knew was wildly inappropriate, considering. "My mum and dad have already been at me about that. But look, when you go out, check in the car park. You'll see why I prefer to walk when you see what I'm driving."

"That bad, huh?" He grinned back. "We'll try to get this solved quickly then so you can get back to your preferred mode of transportation."

"I'd appreciate that." Bronwyn told him, and then she hesitated. "Must I leave the churchyard now?"

He looked over her shoulder toward the church wall. "It's a crime scene, so we shouldn't be here disturbing things until all the evidence is collected. Still, you've already been right there in the midst of things, so I guess a moment or two won't hurt, as long as you don't get too close. Here, I'll go with you." He reached out and put his hand on her elbow, guiding her away from the pathway. "There's evidence here where you'd walk, but we'll walk on the grass alongside, so that should be okay."

They walked together toward the church wall, stepping cautiously through the grass and careful to avoid the gravestones themselves. When they were a couple of feet away, he stopped, the pressure on Bronwyn's elbow halting her progress, as well. They stood somberly, the detective waiting as Bronwyn examined the stained wall and grass from where she stood. She closed her eyes after a moment. *Let Glynnis find the happiness she couldn't find in this life,* she thought. *And restore the peace to this sacred place.* She remained still, eyes closed, for a long moment, waiting for the expected tranquility to calm her again, and finally her heart slowed and the little feeling of quiet spread from her stomach up and down the length of her body.

Then she opened her eyes and glanced sideways at the detective. "I'm ready to go now."

He nodded, his face a little puzzled. Together they walked back to the churchyard gate, where he stopped to allow Bronwyn to step through first. "I bet you like working here, so peaceful and quiet."

"I love it," Bronwyn admitted. "I'd make more money somewhere else, but this place draws me in some way I can't explain. I just feel I'm meant to be here."

"Perhaps you are then," he told her. Bronwyn saw him glance toward his approaching partner, and then he gestured with his hand. "You'd better be off, or Notley will be wanting to question you again. I'll go distract him for you."

"Thank you," she whispered. She watched him walk over to meet his partner and ask a question, and then she hurried up the path to the counseling centre, where she went into her office and firmly shut the door.

Despite the peace she had managed in the churchyard, Bronwyn fretted once she was back in her office. Notwithstanding her parents' pleas, she felt that she needed to pursue the case on her own, to help it along as best she could. Why? Because she was certain that she was a suspect in the murder, for one. And two, because she had access to witnesses that no one else did. She had connections, so to speak. It seemed wrong not to use them.

But would they talk to her? The Twlwyth Teg had never done so before that Sunday morning, so she was doubtful that they would again. Pysgotwr might help, but his wisdom usually came in the form of odd pronouncements that Bronwyn would be left to figure out. Still, it was better than nothing. Perhaps the best thing she could do would be to go to the still pond in the forest and try to see something in its depths that would answer her questions. But the problem was that her parents would most certainly be keeping an eye on her. They didn't want her to wander into the forest where she could use the pool of water or along the footpath where she might meet Pysgotwr. She sat back in her chair, frustrated.

Her opportunity came more quickly than she might have thought possible. Shortly after 4:00, a knock came at her office door and Janis, the counselor, popped her head in.

"I thought you might want to go home early," she told Bronwyn, "now that your group has left for the day. I've been kept busy today, and I've still got one or two people to see. I don't mind locking up, if you want to leave."

"Bless you!" Bronwyn cried, standing up and grabbing her purse. "Thank you, Janis. I won't forget this."

"Nor should you," Janis smiled.

Her luck held. Her mum had not yet returned from her job in Lanrhadyr, nor would she return until the shop closed at 6:00. Her dad, who would usually be expected to be at home, had left a note saying he'd run into Oswestry for lamb formula and would return shortly. Even Maddock was nowhere to be seen.

Not knowing what "shortly" meant, Bronwyn hurried into her jeans and wellies and rushed out the door, heading for the path that led across the pasture and into the forest. Old Nan followed her, dashing at the sheep like a puppy instead of the old dog she was. Bronwyn laughed aloud at her antics, happy to be outdoors again in the bright spring weather.

She climbed up over the stile while Nan ducked beneath the fence, and then they hurried into the forest. As the oaks and rowan and beech trees closed out the sun in the western sky, Bronwyn shivered a bit, blaming it on the cool air. She kept a good eye out, glancing into every shadow and squinting to see through the trees. Old Nan kept to her heels now in the forest, weary of her frolicking and seeming to feel a bit of Bronwyn's apprehension.

They took the turn in the path that led toward the pool of water. The forest seemed completely ordinary. The trees rustled overhead, the shadows of their leaves dancing on the forest floor. Bronwyn crinkled her nose at the nutty scent of mushrooms growing in little colonies like tiny castles in the damp soil underfoot. Birds fluttered from branch to branch, and once Bronwyn looked up to see an owl watching them from a branch just above their heads. The decayed leaves beneath their feet muffled their steps, so they crept quietly to the pond waiting in its secret little clearing.

Worn out from their little journey, old Nan laid down on the flat rock next to where Bronwyn knelt stilling her mind and waiting to see if anything would happen. Her thoughts were hard to quiet, however. Images ran through her mind, pictures of Glynnis lying dead, the bloodstained church wall, the detective's face as he questioned her. She took a deep breath and tried to open herself to the emptiness she needed, but the pool of water remained dark and unresponsive.

After a time, Bronwyn reached over to pat old Nan. "It's not going to work for me today, old girl," she said. The dog's tail thumped in response.

Bronwyn stood and looked around at the forest. Nothing seemed amiss. More often than not in the past the pool of water had shown her nothing; it seemed that this would be one of those times.

With a sigh, Bronwyn signaled to old Nan, and they started down the path out of the forest. As she walked, Bronwyn pulled her cell phone from her pocket and checked the time. Nearly 5:30. She had sat by the pool longer than she'd thought.

She urged old Nan into a trot and managed to jog to the edge of the forest. As she emerged into the clearing where she would climb over the stile, she heard her dad's voice in the distance, calling out for her.

"I'm here!" she shouted. She waved her arms and then, seeing that he'd noticed her, climbed up and over the stile, dropping on the other side and breaking into a run.

Her dad trotted toward her, the concern on his face easy to read. "Where have you been?" he asked, stopping and clasping her to him.

"I had to get out," Bronwyn murmured, returning his hug. "I took old Nan with me, and anyway, this is our land. I'm safe enough here." She looked up and met his worried eyes.

"I asked you not to wander about until the murderer is caught," her father scolded, pushing her away at arm's length. "What were you thinking, Bronwyn? Do you want to tempt fate?"

"I'm an adult, Dad," Bronwyn defended herself, temper flaring. "I need to make my own decisions now. I know you were worried, but you can't keep telling me what to do all my life. I was careful, I promise."

He stared at her, anger and fear and relief mingling on his expressive face. Then he sighed and shook his head. "I don't mean to tell you how to run your life, Bronwyn," he said. "It's only that your mum and I worry about you after what happened to Glynnis. We want you safe."

Bronwyn felt a tear slide down her cheek. "I know, Dad, I know. I'm sorry. I'm so sorry." The tears started to fall in earnest, and she reached up to brush them away. "It's just that I don't know what's happening, that's all. It was only a puzzle at first, something to be solved like a riddle, but now it's serious, and I don't know what to do about it all."

He stared at her. "What are you talking about, sweetheart?"

She gulped, swallowing hard. Perhaps it wasn't the right moment to mention Granny Powers' final words to her, but she couldn't stop the words flowing out. "Glynnis coming back and Granny Powers dying – all of it seems connected somehow."

He reached out to enfold her in a hug. "It's too much, isn't it? You've had such a fright finding Glynnis and all…but that memory will fade once the case is solved, and then things can get back to normal. It'll be okay. You'll see. And Granny Powers was a long time ago. I thought you were past the shock of all that."

Bronwyn leaned into her dad's shoulder, wrapping her arms around him. If only she could just stay there, wrapped in his arms like a child, then she would feel secure again.

But he didn't know the whole story. She squeezed her eyes shut. He didn't know about Granny Powers' message. He didn't know what she'd overhead from the Twlwyth Teg. He didn't even know Pysgotwr existed.

I'm passin' it all over to you, girl, Granny Powers had said. And whatever it was she was passing over, Bronwyn was sure that it included keeping her eyes and ears open to the clues that would solve Glynnis' murder and not simply waiting for the detectives to do it themselves.

Chapter Eight

Will Cooper had grown quite fond of Llangynog by the middle of the week following Glynnis Paisley's death. Because he and Sean Notley were required to interview everyone even remotely connected with the woman, they found themselves eating lunches at both the Tanat Inn and the New Inn, talking with patrons and pedestrians alike, and even sitting on a bench outside the New Inn listening to gossip as people came and went. Will was enjoying the Tanat Inn's steak au poivre, and an accompanying pint of Boddington's made even Notley's company almost tolerable.

The roadway through Llangynog proved surprisingly busy for such a small village. One had to keep a sharp lookout in order not to step out in front of a vehicle passing through. Will found it difficult to drive through the village itself in the unmarked maroon Volvo considering the number of cars parked alongside the roadway in both directions, especially during the daytime hours. The small car park was nearly always full. He found himself wondering what business brought so many people into a small village that did not even boast a shop of its own alongside the main road, but the clues to that puzzle continued to evade him.

Notley had waved the question away. "Every small village has traffic," he proclaimed, unconcerned, and Will supposed that it made no difference to their investigation.

Still, he seized the opportunity to ask the man tending bar at the New Inn. "It's the pipeline," the man told him. "We get hikers and mountain bikers this time of year, but it's the pipeline people and the protesters who've put us over the top this year." He didn't seem bothered. Business was booming, as were his wages, Will surmised.

They had followed their interviews with Bronwyn Bagley, Davyyd Paisley, and Glynnis' parents with informal questioning of Mrs. Paisley's employer Cecil Lumley, the protester Hal Corse, and the Reverend Wicklyff, along with a few of the other villagers who seemed eager to give them their observations, however unhelpful. Once the primary interviews were done, Will had expected that they would work out of their office in Caernarfon or set up a temporary office in Llangynog, but Notley had insisted that they drive back and forth every day, and Will's opinions didn't seem to stand up against Notley's experience and Sherlock Holmes confidence.

Cecil Lumley had frowned and stammered at them when they'd gone into the Tanat Inn and shown him their identification on Tuesday afternoon.

"I don't know anything that'd be of any help to you," he'd protested.

"We'd like to talk to you just the same," Notley insisted, and so they'd gone upstairs past the kitchen and into a small side room that served as office and pantry. Lumley had pushed boxes of canned goods further back into the corners and offered Notley the one chair as he perched himself on a case of tinned peas. Will stood beside the doorway and pulled his notepad from his pocket.

"What can you tell us about Glynnis Paisley?" Notley began, his own pencil hovering over his notepad. The absence of the tape recorder surprised Will, but he supposed Lumley wasn't considered a suspect so any information he would provide probably wouldn't change later in court. Still, he'd consider it useful to be able to review the interview later.

Lumley sighed and looked down at his hands. Round-faced and beginning to bald, he seemed a normal middle-aged man who took pleasure from his work and filled his free time in the outdoors. Of average height and stocky build, he exuded a natural friendliness that would be an asset in a business such as the Tanat Inn.

"Glynnis," he said after a time, "was a cheeky young thing who grew up here in Llangynog. I liked her in the bar, so that's why I hired her for the few weeks she was going to be in town. She was a flirt with the fellows. I thought she'd bring them in and keep them drinking."

Notley jotted down a note. "Having a husband didn't stop her flirting?"

Lumley smiled. "Not at all. Glynnis was a girl who did what she wanted, no matter who was around. Got that from her mum, I suspect. She's much the same way."

"And her dad?" Will asked. Notley frowned in puzzlement.

"Her dad was a tad overwhelmed what with both Glynnis and her mum in the house. Spent most of his time down here at the Tanat with a pint in his hands." He looked at Will. "Not that I blame him. Anyone might feel sorry for a fellow with those two women in the house."

"Then you disapproved of Glynnis?" Notley persisted.

"Not at all. She was a great barmaid most times. Wouldn't have wanted to live in the same house, that's all."

Will and Notley considered this for a moment before Notley moved on with another topic. "Tell us about the altercation that took place here on the night Glynnis was murdered."

Lumley rubbed at his nose. "Ah, it didn't amount to much. Just a few protestors harassing Glynnis' husband and she lost her temper on them. I booted them out, and that was that."

"We heard she dumped a tray of beer on them." Will commented, watching closely now.

"Wasn't something they didn't deserve," Lumley insisted. He glared at them. "Don't approve of that pipeline myself, but you can't have people trying to start brawls in the pub now, can you?"

"So that man," Notley consulted his notes, "Hal Corse. He wasn't mad at Glynnis?"

"Course he was mad," Lumley admitted, "but not mad enough to murder her, that's for sure. It was only spilt beer, after all."

"And he left peacefully when you asked him to?" Notley studied him.

"Sure, he did, didn't he?" Lumley nodded with a shrug. "Was a losing battle for him, so why'd he want to stay longer?"

"What time does the pub close in the evenings?"

"We start to wrap up around eleven and lock the doors at midnight."

"What time did Mrs. Paisley leave?"

"She had to catch the bus, so she left a little before ten."

Will made a note. "Everyone was gone from the car park by then?"

"I'd guess so. I didn't go outside to check."

"No CCTV?"

"No reason for the expense," Lumley said. "Llangynog isn't known for its crime."

Notley launched into a new topic. "You were out fishing the morning Glynnis' body was discovered?"

Lumley blinked. "Sure…I like to fish on a morning before we open."

"It was raining, though," Notley pointed out. "Not the best of weather."

Lumley's face reddened. "Fish bite better in the rain, as everyone knows."

He's trying to figure out how we know, Will realized. *Why does that matter?* "Did you catch anything?"

"I did," he said, and then his face brightened. "Ah, it will be Bronwyn who told you she saw me out that morning when she was out walking the footpath."

"What time was that?" Notley's pencil hovered above the pad of paper.

"I was out early," Lumley said. "Don't remember when she came by."

"Can you guess?" Notley pressured him. "Can you give us an approximate time?"

Lumley fidgeted, wriggling on the case of peas. "Had to open the pub by noon, so I'd guess it was half-eleven, more or less."

"Did she seem to be in a hurry?" Notley pushed.

"Not that I noticed, but then, I was focused on the fish, wasn't I?" Lumley told them. He inclined his head toward the door. "Got to get down there at the bar soon. Thing's will be getting busy and poor Mai's all alone on the floor since Glynnis is gone."

Notley snapped his notepad shut and pushed it into his pocket. "Thanks for your time, then. We'll be in touch."

Will held out a card. "You might hear something owning a place like this," he said. "Give us a call if there's anything helpful, will you?"

Lumley stared at the card and then reached out to take it with obvious reluctance. "Sure," he said, and he motioned them out the door before following them. Will knew there wasn't a chance in a million he'd call them even if he did hear something that might affect the case.

Afterwards, Notley had been triumphant with the interview. "He's a potential witness, having seen Miss Bagley on her way to the crime scene," he told Will as he lit up his pipe.

Will grimaced. "She was on the way to the crime scene, but that doesn't mean she committed the crime," he pointed out. *What is Notley's obsession with Bronwyn all about?* he wondered. Maybe his partner's experience gave him an insight Will was lacking, but he just couldn't see it.

Their interview with the protester, Hal Corse, was not so successful. Having obtained directions to his farm from the mail clerk in the village hall, they drove back up the B9341 for three miles to where a lane ran between fields of sheep toward a white-washed cottage and barns.

They found him in the barn tending to a newborn lamb he had carried in from the adjoining field. "Its mum won't claim it," he explained, "so I'll have to substitute for her if it's to survive." He finished giving it the bottle of milk he was holding and settled it on a pile of straw next to where he was kneeling. "It'll be fine for the moment." He looked up at them and slowly stood. "Suppose you're here about that girl that was murdered. I didn't do it."

Will suppressed a grin. The man was direct, he had to give him that.

Notley tapped his cane on the barn's stone floor. "We heard you'd had a bit of a problem with her at the Tanat Inn that night."

"My misfortune that it was the same night she was killed," Corse replied, glancing at the cane with a frown. "Can't say I was happy about having a tray of ale dumped on me, but I'm not a fool. A man would have to be crazy to kill over something like that." He reached down and stroked the lamb, and then straightened. "I left the Tanat when Lumley asked me to and came directly home. Ask anyone. My car was gone out of the car park long before that woman was done with her shift."

Notley nodded. "We will ask, you can be sure. I don't suppose any of your mates came along home with you, just to give you an alibi?"

Corse swallowed. "My wife's inside, if you want to ask her when I got home. Some of the others left when I did; some stayed on after, I guess." He shrugged. "Didn't know most of them."

Notley paused, waiting for more, and then when it didn't follow, he went on. "Have you ever hiked the footpath from Llangynog to Pennant Melangell?"

Corse shook his head, seeming confused. "Who'd have time for something like that? I do enough walking just taking care of my farm." He snorted. "Only fools with too much time on their hands go out walking for fun."

"You've never done it, even as a youngster?" Notley pushed him.

"Never," said Corse firmly. "I've never been a hiker. I've no time for it."

"But you had time to join the protest?"

Corse's face turned red. "'Course. That's something that matters."

Notley let him fidget for a moment before changing topics. "Did you know Glynnis Paisley?"

Corse barked a short, humorless laugh. "No, didn't know her. We weren't schoolmates, and she apparently left the village for university as soon as she could. Don't attend church there. I doubt she'd have been hanging around the pubs when she was younger, so we'd have had no occasion to run into each other, would we?" He paused. "Did know her dad a bit from talking to him in the pub about farming and the weather and such. And I do remember her mum being someone important when it came to the sheep dog trials in September. As I recall it, that Bagley girl's dad and her were always a close match to win with their dogs, so it might be there's a history of bad feeling between the families." He shrugged. "I don't know."

Will groaned silently. *Oh, great. Here's another one pointing his finger at Bronwyn.*

"We'll need a list of the other protesters," Notley told Corse.

"Don't have one," Corse shot back. "It was just signs put up in the pubs that brought us together. Don't know who organized it at all."

"Would you have a flyer?"

"Why would I?" Corse defended himself. "Saw it and noted the time, so I went. It's a good cause, after all. The last thing we need in this valley is a gas pipeline after they've already scarred the land with the quarries and mining."

Notley sighed, gripping his cane tightly as he scratched it across the stone floor. "Okay, then. Thanks for your time."

Reverend Wicklyff had been friendlier than the others, at least. They'd met him in his small office at Pennant Melangell, where he'd welcomed them with a firm handshake and a smile.

"Bronwyn's been an ideal employee," he'd explained after they'd introduced themselves. "It'd have been a shock for her to come upon her friend's body like that, I'm sure."

"Can you tell us about that morning when you found them in the churchyard?" Will asked.

He thought for a minute. "I arrived here at the church around half-one, I think. Services start at three, but the church would be opened by two at the latest. The ladies would be here early making the scones for after the service, of course, and I like to be ready before they arrive. The occasional pilgrim comes in early and wants to talk, you see."

"You said earlier that you heard Miss Bagley call out," Notley reminded him. "Tell us about that."

"I had gotten out of my car and was walking toward the church when I heard a voice." He was quiet a moment. "I didn't recognize it as Bronwyn's voice at first. She sounded different somehow, perhaps shaky or frightened. It was the shock, of course." He paused and looked at them. "I searched for the person the voice belonged to, and when I poked my head into the churchyard, I saw them – Bronwyn sitting and holding the other woman on her lap."

"How did she seem?" Notley asked. He'd been taking copious notes as the reverend spoke.

"She didn't seem like herself at all," Reverend Wicklyff admitted. "Her eyes were wild and she was covered in blood. She acted as if she'd had a knock on the head herself, maybe. I had to persuade her to lay the body down and to come inside with me. She didn't want to leave her friend, you see. She wanted to stay in the churchyard with her."

"But you insisted that she come inside?"

"Yes, I did. I could see that there was nothing she could do for her friend. It was raining, and she was wet and in shock, so I thought it best if she were inside and away from it all." He looked at them anxiously. "If I did something wrong, I apologize. My concern was for Bronwyn. I haven't known her for long, but she is a wonderful person, an excellent employee."

Notley's pencil hovered. "You keep saying that. Can you explain why she is such a great employee?"

The reverend looked at Will as if seeking support, and Will nodded slightly. "Bronwyn has a peace about her," he said then, "a tranquility that expresses the essence of this place. Not only is she a competent organizer and efficient manager, but her whole attitude is welcoming to our pilgrims. For nearly twelve hundred years, this place has served as a refuge. Bronwyn facilitates that welcome for troubled people." He hesitated. "She grew up here in the valley, you see, and she…she seems to grasp connections between earth and spirit that most of us long for and can't find." He stopped talking and shook his head. "I often think she should be in charge here, and not me."

Notley raised his eyebrows. "Are you saying she's the saint reincarnated?" An amused smile conveyed his skepticism, and Will tensed in response.

Reverend Wicklyff's head remained high and his voice firm. "We don't understand all the secrets of the spirit," he murmured.

To Will's dismay, they'd spent most of Thursday and Friday lounging around Llangynog, sitting on the bench outside the New Inn, watching elderly men playing bowls on the green, and listening to the mums who brought their children to play at the play park, hoping to overhear some gossip.

"We've got to be available in case someone has information to report," Notley had insisted.

"Our time might be better spent interviewing the ex-girlfriend in Cardiff or pushing the forensics people to get us a report," Will had objected. He felt stifled working with Notley, having to go along with his partner's quirks and slow, methodical approach to the investigation. He wondered if there was a way they could split up, each investigating on his own rather than burdening each other with vastly different ideas of how to proceed, but he controlled his impatience and followed Notley around, feeling useless.

"Our Bronwyn is a great girl all around," one woman informed them as they watched her children play on the merry-go-round. "Course, Glynnis was a lovely girl, too."

"Going to rain again this weekend," reported one of the men on the bowling green. "It'll erase evidence, you know, if you're searching the footpath."

"I'd ask the men playing at snookers in the hall," advised another. "Stephen and Wynn are often out and about. Maybe they've seen something."

But they hadn't, when Will and Notley checked with them. It seemed no one had anything useful to say to help them solve the case.

On Friday night, Will's cell phone rang twice.

The first call was from Lark, which brought an instant smile to his face as he pictured her happy blue eyes and the red curls escaping from her braids.

"Hi, Uncle Will," she greeted him. "Grandmother said I could call you if I don't talk more than five minutes."

"Then we'll talk fast," he replied, hoping the smile was coming through the line to her. "What's up?"

"Are you coming to see us this weekend?" He could hear the hope in her voice.

"I'm on a case, love. I can't come until it's solved."

There was a silence on the other end. *She misses me,* he realized. *And I miss her.*

"Is it a woman who died?" Lark's voice trembled.

"Yes, it was," Will told her, hoping she wouldn't ask for more detail.

"Like my mum?"

He let out a breath. "No, not like your mum at all. This one was different."

She digested that for a moment. "Will you have it solved by next weekend?"

"Probably not that soon. We've been busy interviewing people, but we haven't found the right clues yet. It may take us some time, but if it does, I can still probably take a day off soon and come to see you. Is anything wrong?"

Her words came out in a rush. "Graham at school has a litter of baby bunnies, and he said I could have one. But Grandmother says no. I was going to get a white one and name it Cotton Tail. You know, Flopsie, Mopsie, Cotton Tail, and Peter. This one is a girl, so it couldn't be Peter, but Cotton Tail is a good name, too. It could live in the garden, Uncle Will. The wall goes all the way to the ground everywhere except the gate, and we could block that so it wouldn't get out. I do so want to have her!"

Ah, Peter Rabbit, her favorite stories. He should never have taken her to the Tailor's Shop in Gloucester. "Listen, love. I don't think Grandmother and Granddad are up for a pet. They never let me have one, either. But when you come to visit me here this summer, I have a place I want to take you that you're going to love. It's where my case is, so I'm learning all about it. There's a story about a princess and a hare," he improvised, vowing to learn about the legend as soon as he could.

"A hare, like in the tortoise and the hare?" Lark wondered. "That's a kind of bunny, isn't it?"

"Yeah, it's a big bunny; a wild one, I think."

"Tell me the story now," Lark pleaded. "Please?"

"You've only got five minutes, remember?" he reminded her. "That's not long enough. It's a long story." *And I don't know it yet.*

"I still want my own bunny," Lark told him.

"Of course, you do," he agreed. "I can't help you there, though. You might have to be satisfied with stories instead."

"It's not the same." Lark's disappointed voice tore the smile from his face.

"Hey, I'll get this case solved, and then we'll do something rabbity, okay?"

"You'll do it fast," she pronounced, her innocent faith in him settling like a stone around his heart. "I know you will."

The second call was from his sometime girlfriend Lesley Dunkirk, another voice that brought the smile back to his face.

"I thought by now you'd have called to make sure I got home alive," she complained after saying hello.

"Edward is entirely trustworthy," Will retorted, "although certainly not as sexy as I am."

Lesley's laugh echoed in his ear. "How's the case coming along?" she wanted to know.

"Not as well as I'd like," Will lamented. "If it keeps up the way it's going, it may be a long time before I get a day free again."

"Well, when you do, I figure you owe me a nice weekend out of town. I'm thinking the Lake District would be nice this time of year, or maybe the seaside."

He grinned. "I live at the seaside, love, so I think that could be arranged."

Then she turned serious. "I do miss you, Will."

His grin faded. "I miss you, too. It's not the same since I was reassigned. I miss you, I miss Edward, I miss it all."

"I meant it in a more romantic way," she told him. When he didn't respond, she went on, "Really, Will – are you okay with things the way they are now?"

He hesitated, his heart suddenly thumping. *Is she talking about my reassignment, or about her...us?* "You mean the case, working murder now – all of that?"

Her laugh was a delicious tickle in his ear. "Yeah, that's what I meant. What did you think?"

He ignored the last part, wondering how honest he should be about the first part. He decided to give her some of the truth, at least. "Edward and I worked together so well. We had the same ideas about how to proceed, knew what each other was thinking. We were a team in every sense of the word." He thought for a moment before going on. "Working with Notley is a frustration every minute. It's like I know what needs to be done, but he holds me back. I feel like we're wasting time when the case needs solving quickly, and it kills me."

"Do you work with him on every case?"

Will allowed himself a grimace. "It's the luck of the draw. There are five of us, so we are assigned according to who's on the schedule when the murder happens." He hesitated again. "But none of them are the same as working with Edward, even if Notley's the worst of the crew."

He waited for her response, and when it came, he could hear sincere sympathy in her voice. "I'm sorry it all happened this way, Will. Sorry about Julia, sorry about your transfer...everything."

"I know," he managed, despising himself for revealing so much. It was time to end the conversation. "I'll call when I'm free, okay?"

He rang off. Lesley was out of sight, out of mind right now. With his mind occupied with the case, he felt distracted by her banter, and not in a good way. But she was Lesley, and she was the most promising relationship he'd had in years, so he probably should sort out his priorities and quit obsessing about Notley and

Bronwyn Bagley and the whole mess. He sighed. Maybe he could ask Chief Superintendent Bowers for a weekend off once the initial investigation was done, and that would put him on a better path mentally than he was feeling on at the moment.

After the phone calls, Will's restlessness drove him outdoors. Caernarfon's city walls enclosed a tourist Mecca of pubs, restaurants, and shops. Although the sidewalks wouldn't be crowded until later in the summer when the sea warmed enough to draw swimmers and sun seekers, plenty of activity had blossomed with the spring weather to offer interesting people watching opportunities.

For a long while, Will sat on a bench outside an upstairs pub. Courting couples holding hands and singles dressed to draw notice passed him as they climbed the stairway to the open door, where American and British music blasted nearly too loud for normal conversation. Will watched them go, letting the melancholy that had followed the two phone calls to settle in the pit of his stomach. Sitting outside a pub watching people go by was the sort of thing he had done a lot of during his days in drugs and alcohol, and he found a comfort in mimicking his former assignments now, even if it was just a mindless way to pass the time.

He sat there on the bench until the cool breeze off the sea drove him away near midnight. By that time, the music had become softer and the voices louder, and Will had managed to push both Lark and Lesley to the back of his mind where they wouldn't distract him from the case.

The next morning found Will bleary-eyed and stiff as he meandered into a meeting with Notley and Chief Superintendent Bowers, both of whom had arrived earlier than he and were waiting for him beside Notley's desk. Bowers cast him a questioning look as he motioned them into the conference room, but he refrained from mentioning Will's obvious tardiness, a fact for which Will was inordinately grateful.

"Progress?" asked Bowers, picking up a dry-erase marker from the tray

"Time of death was between eleven Saturday night and one the next morning." Notley took the lead.

Bowers wrote. "That leaves it open for anyone to have done it," he observed.

"Scene of crime says she was knocked on the head somewhere else and then dragged to the churchyard. Her clothes were in tatters, and she had scrapes on her legs and lower torso. She'd have been held by the arms and pulled along, probably unconscious or nearly so."

"But she was killed in the churchyard itself?"

Notley consulted the printed report in his hand. "Stabbed several times there. A slice to the heart killed her, but other wounds were severe enough that more than one could have been fatal."

Bowers frowned. "Why not just cut her throat and be done? The perpetrator must have needed to take out some frustration in the attack."

"It speaks of intense personal involvement," Will suggested, "rage toward the victim."

"Yes," Bowers agreed. "Not a casual, impulsive thing, but driven by a strong urge to hurt her. It speaks of strong emotion. Who do we have for suspects? Anyone hate her that much?"

"We've interviewed the victim's employer and the protester she had an altercation with the night she was murdered," Notley went on. "Neither one gave us much useful information, but the employer confirmed some things that we'd learned earlier."

"Such as?" Bowers' marker touched the white board.

Notley consulted his notes. "He confirmed the incident between the victim and the protester Hal Corse and said that Mr. Corse left peacefully when asked to."

"You're eliminating him as a suspect then?" Bowers waited before writing.

"No, not at all," Notley said. "Things aren't always what they first appear. He was angry, and it's possible that he came back and took out that anger on her later in the evening."

Bowers wrote Corse's name on the board under the heading "suspects." Will found himself relaxing a bit at that; maybe Notley wasn't so set on Bronwyn Bagley as the murderer, after all.

"What else?" Bowers wanted to know.

"Two more things stand out in my mind," Notley reported. "First, he told us that he considered Mrs. Paisley a flirt, someone to draw the men into the pub and keep them there."

"He said it made no difference that she was married," Will added, needing to say something.

"And he confirmed that Bronwyn Bagley, the woman who found the body, passed by as he was fishing at about half-eleven on the morning she found the victim."

Chief Superintendent Bowers looked at them both. "But the victim was killed the night before."

"That's true," Notley agreed, "but who's to say she wasn't returning to the scene of the crime? She might have set out and made sure someone saw her to establish the time and the fact that she'd been in the village that morning and not watching over a crime scene, waiting for a time when she could claim she'd discovered a body she already knew was there."

Notley nodded. "So, you're saying you have two suspects at this time?"

Will took a breath. "We have yet to interview either the American she was flirting with at the pub or the ex-girlfriend."

Bowers straightened. "Why is that?"

Will looked at Notley. "We've been talking to the villagers in Llangynog, trying to get a feel for what might have happened. I'm not sure if anyone's managed to locate either the American or the girlfriend at this point, since we've been out of the office all week." He felt Notley's frown and ignored it.

Bowers nodded. "Check on that as soon as we're done here. What else?"

"I thought we might walk the footpath," Notley said, "to get a feel for how long it might take and to see if we can find anything that looks like an attack site."

"Forensics still doesn't know where she was first attacked?" Bowers demanded. "Did they walk the footpath themselves?"

"Yes, sir, but they weren't able to find anything. It rained on the night of the murder, and evidence was washed away."

"There's no murder weapon, then?"

Notley spoke up. "They know she was hit with something first, not a rock but something smooth and probably man-made, and then she was stabbed, but they don't have either of the weapons at this point. It was that cut to her heart that killed her, but there were plenty of other wounds."

"And you want to time the walk because...?"

"The Bagley woman seems to have made that hike in record time, as if she was hurrying through it. We think she knew about the murder before she set out on that walk."

"Or she learned about it from someone along the route," Will added, wanting to be fair.

Bowers took a deep breath, closing his eyes. "Then we have very little at this point."

"That's right," Will agreed. Somehow, he felt vindicated after spending the long week shadowing Notley, though he doubted Bowers would see it that way.

Bowers stood up. "I want you to find that American and the ex-girlfriend. Get what you can from forensics. Review the transcriptions of the earlier interviews and get back for seconds if you have questions. This case is dragging out longer than it should." He glared at them. "We have little serious crime to deal with here in North Wales. I want our reputation to stay high. Am I making myself clear?"

"We've got to pick up the pace," Notley said once they were out of Bowers' earshot. "You've been late every day, holding us back. It's been nearly a week and what have we got? Nothing." He jabbed his cane at the floor. "Not a thing."

Will rolled his eyes, making sure that Notley didn't see him do it. "I've been following your lead," he reminded him. "Maybe if we'd been hiking the footpath or consulting with our people back here in Caernarfon, we'd have been making better use of our time. We got nothing from talking to the villagers in Llangynog. It's been a waste of our time."

"I've been in touch with the forensics people," Notley informed him. "Every day."

"And what have we gotten from them?" Will couldn't keep the impatience from his voice.

"We already knew she was attacked somewhere else, but they don't know where – either the car park or somewhere along the footpath. They've been little help with that."

"We had that information the first night. There's nothing else?" Will demanded.

"They've not managed to find a weapon. Blood at the scene was all the victim's. There have been no identifiable fingerprints yet. All we know for sure," Notley said miserably, "is that she was bludgeoned over the head, taken to the churchyard from somewhere else, and then stabbed to death."

Will sighed. "What good is it for us to walk the footpath? We aren't likely to find anything they didn't find."

"We might," Notley ventured. "Maybe they missed something."

"Maybe we'd be better off finding the ex-girlfriend down in Cardiff," Will countered.

Notley stopped walking and turned to face him fully. "Okay, Monday we'll go down there. It'll be a whole day of travel and back, so you'd better be on time for a change. On Sunday we'll walk the footpath before we go to the memorial service. Agreed?"

Will shrugged. "Sure, whatever you think. We'll have to change our clothes before we go to the service. How about the American?"

"No one's located him yet."

"Are they even looking?"

Notley gave him an incredulous look. "Of course, they're looking. They're checking hotels and trying to access his Visa records. It's just not that easy to find someone who's on the move."

"Maybe he doesn't want to be found," Will suggested.

"You consider him a serious suspect?" Notley wanted to know. "What reason would he have had for killing that woman?"

"No one knew him. Maybe he's a serial killer."

Notley laughed. "Wouldn't that make it easy for us." He rubbed the handle of his cane thoughtfully. "We need a break, Cooper."

"It'll come," Will assured him, but it was a false assurance. Truthfully, he didn't think the case would be solved at all, not without something unexpected appearing to push them in the right direction.

Chapter Nine

Unfortunately, Bronwyn's contacts did not appear to want to help solve the mystery of Glynnis' death.

Not that she had a lot of opportunities to seek them out.

Spring brought with it a rush of engagements at Pennant Melangell, necessitating not only Bronwyn's presence to facilitate their use of the centre's conference room, but also a good deal of office time arranging schedules, lunches, and publicity. In the week following Glynnis' death, the centre had events scheduled every day from Tuesday through Saturday, including two church retreats, a cancer support group retreat, and a meditation group instructor conference.

Bronwyn struggled out of bed each morning by 6:30, gulped several cups of hot tea, and chugged up the roadway in her Volvo before 8:00, often finding herself alone in the car park until Reverend Wicklyff or someone else arrived more than an hour later. Uncomfortable with it but unwilling to explain her paranoia to Janis or the volunteers, she left the main door unlocked as she hurried to set up the conference room and work at her computer in the quiet of the morning. Truthfully, she didn't work as efficiently as she normally would, being ready to jump at every little noise or odd breath of air, but somehow things got done.

Despite the presence of large groups there for retreats and a steady stream of individuals seeking counseling, Bronwyn enjoyed a good deal of solitude during those first days back at work. Once she had settled her groups in the conference room, no one else sought her out with the usual questions and problems that routinely came up at the centre. She supposed that they felt she needed time to deal with what had happened, rather than being bothered with incidental problems that anyone, truth be told, could solve. And, despite the fact that she'd have preferred a more normal routine, she appreciated their efforts to make things comfortable for her.

By Thursday, she noticed that the crime scene tape was gone from the churchyard, along with the sign on the gate. Sometime later when she walked from the counseling centre to the church for her semi-weekly conference with Reverend Wicklyff she saw that the blood stain had been washed from the church wall, and she thought about who had performed that service and felt sorry for him. She had seen little sign of police presence since the activity on Tuesday, so she supposed Reverend Wicklyff had ended up doing it once given permission to do so. She wondered what the crime scene workers had found out in their walk from Llangynog to Pennant Melangell, but had no way to find out.

Because the schedule at the counseling centre was so full, Bronwyn ended by working extra hours so that by the time she arrived home in the evenings there was no time for a walk out to the pool of water or even down to the banks of the River Tanat, where Pysgotwr often fished. *The Twlwyth Teg can find me in the village,* she reminded herself, *and I first met Pysgotwr while running through the pastures with the lambs.* If they had information for her, they would seek her out, surely. Still, their invisibility frustrated her when she felt such pressure to find out what they might know.

On Thursday evening, her mobile phone rang with a call from her childhood friend Margred in Ireland.

"I heard about Glynnis," Margred explained, "so I had to call. Is it true? Is she really murdered? And you found the body?"

"It's true," Bronwyn admitted, wondering if she dared explain just how she'd known the body was in the churchyard and deciding that she didn't. Margred had ignored her peculiarities during their childhood, but now that they were adults, she might not be so quick to dismiss Bronwyn's quirks.

"Tell me all about it," Margred insisted. "How did you happen to find her? Did they catch whoever did it yet?"

"There's not much to tell," she told her friend. "I walked down the footpath to Pennant Melangell so I could go to services there that afternoon. I arrived early, so I went into the churchyard, and there she was. That's all there was to it, really."

But Margred was not to be easily satisfied. "Tell me about finding her. Do you mind? What did she look like? How was she killed?"

Bronwyn closed her eyes, clutching the cell phone tightly to her ear. "Ghoul," she accused Margred. "Why would you want to know what she looked like? She was dead. Use your imagination."

"You never liked her," Margred said in reply. "You didn't kill her yourself, did you, Bron?"

"Is that what you think?"

"No, of course not. But they haven't caught the murderer yet, have they?"

Bronwyn thought she could hear the lie in her words. "No, they haven't, but they will. Then you'll be sorry you asked me that."

Margred laughed. "Oh, Bron, don't be silly. I don't really think you did it, even if you did hate Glynnis from the time we were babies."

"There wasn't much to like."

"No, there wasn't," Margred agreed. "She picked on you most of all, but she wasn't really very nice to anyone. Win at all costs. That was Glynnis."

"Are you coming to the memorial?" Bronwyn asked. She couldn't keep the hopeful note from her voice.

"Too far to come for dear Glynnis," Margred said. "We're coming in August for a visit, though. I'll see you then."

"Sure," Bronwyn said. *If I'm not in gaol.*

After her talk with Margared, Bronwyn started seeing her solitude at work in a different light. Now when a volunteer or two came in, the glances in her direction as they turned to avoid her path seemed cautious, rather than thoughtful. Reverend Wicklyff's generosity in offering her more days off work made her wonder, as well. Perhaps he didn't feel she was to be trusted any longer, not if he suspected her of Glynnis' murder. She started watching Janis and the volunteers for signs of mistrust, feeling uneasy around them. She spent more time than usual in her office, often sitting idle at her desk when there was no work to be done.

On Friday afternoon after a long day of smiling at the centre volunteers only to see the speculation in their eyes in response, a knock came at Bronwyn's office door and she looked up to see Janis Hatcher, the chief counselor, standing just inside.

Bronwyn gave her a hopeful smile. "Hello, Janis. What can I do for you?"

Janis brushed one of her bronze curls away from her cheek. "It's more what I might do for you," she said.

Bronwyn blinked. "What is that?"

"I wondered if you needed someone to talk to," Janis offered. "I'm a counselor, after all, and you've had a horrible experience." She hesitated. "Of course, everything would be confidential, you know."

Bronwyn narrowed her eyes. "I have nothing to hide, Janis."

"Of course not." Janis smiled at her apologetically. "Then...do you want to talk? I have some time free just now."

Bronwyn thought for a moment, and then she shook her head, just once. "I'm fine, Janis. Really, I am. I'll feel better once the villain's caught, but other than that, I'm doing well."

Janis nodded. "I just thought I'd offer." She turned to go.

"Wait," Bronwyn called her back. She looked at Janis, whose warm brown eyes and natural smile invited confidences. "Do people who come here think I murdered Glynnis?"

Janis' eyes widened. "No, of course not," she assured Bronwyn, but again, Bronwyn thought she heard a lie in the words. "Why would you do that?"

"I wouldn't," Bronwyn assured her. "I didn't."

Glynnis' memorial was set for early that Sunday afternoon, scheduled by the family on a day when nearly everyone in Llangynog would be free to attend. Knowing Glynnis' mother, she would be counting heads and making note of anyone not in attendance, too, thought Bronwyn cynically as she put on a dark blue dress that she knew she'd be uncomfortable in. *It's only a few hours,* she told herself, *and surely I owe Glynnis that much.* She had, however briefly, wished the Cyn Annwn was there for her, after all, and that wish had come true.

People crowded into St. Cynog's church, many having arrived early in order to assure themselves a seat in the small building. Bronwyn sat near the rear of the church with her mother and father on either side, and Maddock and Mai seated on the aisle side of her father. Bronwyn observed a quiet hum of what she took for gossip as they filed onto the pew, an annoyance she ignored as best she could. She noticed Glynnis' husband Davyyd seated in the front pew with Glynnis' family, though she could see only the backs of their heads. She stared at him unthinkingly until her mother nudged her and shook her head, and then she blinked and looked away toward the altar where dozens of flowers testified to the shock of Glynnis' untimely demise.

The service was short, simple, and flattering to the memory of a young woman who, truthfully, had not gathered many admirers during her childhood in Llangynog. Oh, it was true that Bronwyn spotted several other former schoolmates seated together just in front of her, but they appeared to remain dry-eyed throughout the service. She noted a couple of other young women she didn't recognize and assumed they were friends Glynnis had made in Cardiff. Even Davyyd Paisley looked composed when he rose at the end of the service to walk out with the family, and it seemed only Glynnis' parents had real tears in their eyes.

Once outdoors again, the mass of people stood about in the roadway as Glynnis' family greeted them in turns. As she waited with her parents, Maddox, and Mai, Bronwyn took the time to study the crowd, which did, indeed, appear to include the entire village of 250 inhabitants, along with a few outsiders such as the young women Bronwyn had noticed earlier. She saw the two detectives standing to one side watching the crowd, and she turned away, trying to use her parents to block their view of her.

"Bronwyn," said Glynnis' mother when she turned to them at last. She reached a hand up and raked it through her short, untidy hair, but didn't offer it to any of Bronwyn's family. She seemed at a loss for words, her eyes dark with shock and the wrinkles on her cheeks standing out even more than usual with her pallor.

"We heard that you held Glynnis on your lap in the churchyard," Glynnis' father said, stepping forward. Then he rubbed at his brimming eyes and sniffed a bit, unable to go on.

"Yes," Bronwyn said quietly. "I...I didn't want her to feel alone."

Glynnis' mother's eyes filled, and she dabbed at them with a handkerchief that she held in her fist. She swallowed convulsively.

"Thank you," Glynnis' father managed. "You're a good lass, to do that for our girl." He patted Bronwyn awkwardly on the shoulder and turned away, putting his free arm around his wife's shoulders and guiding her along to another waiting group of people.

Davyyd stepped up then and took Bronwyn's hand. "Thank you for what you did for her." His voice quivered. "I know you and Glynnis were schoolmates. It must have been hard for you to find her like that."

Bronwyn squeezed his hand and then let go. "I did what anyone would have done," she murmured. "I'm so sorry for your loss."

He looked at her, and Bronwyn could see real pain in his eyes. But that wasn't all. If she wasn't mistaken, there was a certain relief there, as well. *Curious,* she thought. *It might be interesting to see what Davyyd does next, now that Glynnis is gone from his life.*

A flood of giddiness washed over Bronwyn as she and her parents left the crowd behind and walked through the village toward home. As the narrow walkways in the village centre became a choice of a dirt pathway alongside the roadway or the road itself, she had to restrain herself to keep from skipping. The tension from the morning's ordeal had fled, and unexpected relief brought a smile to her face.

As they passed beyond the cluster of cottages, Bronwyn looked out over the valley she loved. Clouds drifted across the sky, layers of dark upon light and every shade between. They cast shadows down the hillside, highlighting a patchwork of greens ranging from emerald to sage to a dark forest green where the conifers of the forest met the grassy pastureland. Barren rock dotted the hillsides, forming a stark contrast to the softness of the fields below. Far in the distance, the Berwyn Mountains formed a backdrop to the picture, stretching like a dragon's spine along the horizon. Looking at it now, Bronwyn could imagine why her ancestors had chosen the dragon as the symbol of Wales.

Once they arrived home, Bronwyn hurried to change her dress into jeans and a comfortable old blue tee shirt, wondering as she pulled on her oldest pair of trainers how she could convince her parents that it would be safe for her to go out into the forest land just as far as the pool of water.

"I'm going out for a walk," she informed them after joining them for a cup of tea and a scone. "I'll take Nan with me, and I'll keep a sharp eye out. After all," she reminded them with a smile, "I've been going out there on Hobbs since I was five years old."

"But I was close by," her dad argued. "You only went out of the pasture when I was going into the forest land, too."

"When I was five, that was true," she acknowledged, "but Margred and I used to ride out there alone by the time we were seven or so, and we were perfectly safe. The forest loves me, and it wouldn't let any harm come to me. Anyway, I'm an adult," she continued bravely, trying to assert an independence she knew it was past time for, "even if I do still live here with you, and I want to go walking this afternoon."

Her mother looked at her strangely. "The forest loves you?"

Bronwyn blushed. "It's just a figure of speech. I am safe there, Mum. Really, I am. Anyway, other girls my age are running around day and night in cities like Cardiff or London, where murders happen all the time."

"That's true," her dad allowed. He looked at her mum and shrugged. "Just keep your eyes and ears open, will you?"

"I always do," she promised.

She set out across the pasture, Nan at her heels. The ewes and lambs scattered out of her path, but Hobbs ambled toward her as she passed the apple tree, and she paused to offer him an apple she'd tucked into her rucksack.

Then it was up and over the stile, a heavy drop onto the mossy path on the other side, and she was into the forest.

Bronwyn felt the calm in the pit of her stomach as her breathing slowed and she allowed the tranquility of the forest to fill her. She stopped and turned her face skyward, opening her mind to the connectedness of the earth and all that lives on it. She felt the cool spring air on her face as it gifted her cheeks with a healthy blush. She smelled the moistness of the dirt beneath her feet, a scent fragrant with leaf mold, fungi, and conifer needles that summer sun would soon manage to subdue. She licked her lips, tasting on them the promise of berries and herbs already emerging from the winter soil into the warmth of the season. She let her eyes wander, watching the patterns of the leaves as they swayed overhead, noting the multiple shades of green leaf and brown bark and white blossom in the exuberance above her.

She stood thus for several minutes, breathing slowly and luxuriating in the harmony of nature, allowing herself to grow lazy with it. Then, with a deep cleansing breath, she set off again down the pathway toward the pool of water that lay beneath the old oak.

The little glen was peaceful on that Sunday afternoon. Bronwyn sat on the flat rock, patting it until old Nan jumped up and lay down on its warm surface beside her. She gazed into the pool, watching the still water and trying to empty her head. The earlier calm she had achieved held her in good stead – the memories that had plagued her the last time she had visited kept their distance this day. But that did not guarantee a vision in the water. She waited, watching the water and hoping, but all she saw was a dark and quiet pool of water.

After a few minutes, she sighed and turned away, disappointed. She reached for her rucksack and rummaged inside until she found her sketch pad and pencils, and then she sat back on the rock and began to draw the pool of water, with its rocky banks and the forest surrounding it.

As the features of the little glen took shape on her paper, Bronwyn felt the last of the tension leave her shoulders. She took some time drawing the oak tree with its gnarled trunk and countless knotholes, and then she started on the rocks just across from her. Here and there she put in a bit of dark color for the moss just above the water level and, in other places, she drew crooked cracks and splits with darker lines.

Old Nan sighed and shifted position, stretching out in a bit of sun that shot down through the branches of the oak. Bronwyn smiled. She probably shouldn't include old Nan in her sketch, as people either wanted a nature drawing or one with people and animals, but not both, when it came time to put down a bit of money for one of her drawings. Perhaps old Nan's face would be the one she sketched into the bark of the oak tree then? Or maybe this sketch would be one she would keep just for herself. This drawing had been done in a place she didn't want to share, after all, a place sacred to her.

Glancing out into the pool again, she caught her breath. *What's that?* She leaned closer, staring into the water, afraid to blink. The image formed slowly – Glynnis it was, unmistakable with her bright hair even in the darkness of the pool. She was walking, peering anxiously ahead of herself and visibly annoyed about something. Glynnis was not alone; someone walked behind her, talking to her and seeming to try to calm her. Glynnis shook her head vigorously, her anger apparent. Then the vision faded.

Bronwyn sat back, thinking hard and ignoring the slight dizziness that had come with the vision. She took a calming breath. *Was that Glynnis just before her death? Who was the other person with her? Her murderer? And where were they?* It had seemed to be a dark place, perhaps a footpath, for there had been brush alongside instead of pavement or buildings. *But why show me that?* She hadn't seen enough to determine who the other person with Glynnis might be or even where they were.

Beside her old Nan woke with a start and lifted her head, staring at a spot behind Bronwyn. Heart pounding, Bronwyn turned slowly, pushing herself around on the rock while still in her seated position, raising fearful eyes to see what had disturbed the old dog.

The Twlwyth Teg surrounded her, circling slowly and silently. Where their feet tread, mushrooms sprang amongst the dead leaves and mud and even in the cracks in the flat rock as they stepped between her and the pool of water. They watched her, their eyes sharp and wise and accusing. Big and small, delicate and sturdy, young and old, they studied her as they passed, each in his turn.

"What do you want?" she croaked, reaching out to sooth Old Nan with a shaking hand. "Will you tell me what you know?"

"Ale wife walks between lynchett and stirk," intoned an inches-high creature with a mane of black hair and a pointed nose. It narrowed its eyes as it spoke, enunciating the words carefully as if speaking a foreign tongue.

"Cantir strikes," chimed a second creature, its voice melodious and pure. This one was taller and had wings of gossamer silk, like palest rose petals.

"Rash boon fails," lamented a third creature, this one very small and frail with twig-like arms and legs.

Bronwyn waited, silent, as they continued to circle her, stepping deliberately as if their footprints mattered somehow.

"Thick!" blurted a tiny voice in their own odd language, and suddenly there was a cacophony of sound as they all began to shout, "Thick! Thick!"

"What does that mean?" Bronwyn cried out as Old Nan began to bark sharply beside her.

Then they stopped moving and stood shock still, with not a twitch or blink among them. From somewhere outside the circle a voice called out, "Once! Twice! Thrice!"

129

"No!" she shouted, but too late. They had disappeared.

Oh, God! Oh, God! Bronwyn thought as her thoughts swirled. *I have to remember. It's the ale wife again – that's Glynnis.* She stood up shakily, stuffed her sketch pad and pencils into her bag, and gestured to old Nan to follow her as she hurried back up the overgrown footpath. *Ale wife walks between...what is it? Lynchett?* She'd never heard that word before. *Between lynchett and stirk?* Oh, dear – she didn't know what any of it meant. She began to run, heedless of her surroundings. *Cantir strikes...wasn't cantir something to do with music? Maybe not. But could it be a bell again?*

Bronwyn reached the edge of the forest and launched herself up the steps of the stile, leaping down on the other side and setting off at a trot across the field. *What was the last part? Something fails...what was it? Rash...something rash.* She grimaced. *Murder was rash, that was certain. But it wasn't just rash, it was rash....rash boon. Yes, rash boon.* But that was no help because Bronwyn had no idea what a rash boon was.

"Hey, Bron!" called a voice, and she turned her head to see her dad and Maddock standing just off to her right. Maddock was holding a lamb in his arms, and she could see that her dad held a syringe in his hand, ready to administer an inoculation. She waved at them and continued on toward the house.

Thick, she reminded herself. They had said that before, when she'd found them beside the road that night. They said that word differently than they said the rest, said it in their own tongue and in a chorus. *What does that mean? Am I not meant to understand that part?*

Reaching the house, she pushed Old Nan onto the dog bed that lay strategically just inside the door, told her to stay, pulled off her muddy wellies, and hung her coat on a hook. Grabbing her bag, she hurried through the kitchen and across the great room to the staircase and bounded upstairs.

She grabbed a pen and notepad from the desk drawer in her bedroom and scribbled down the Twlwyth Teg's words before she had a chance to forget them. *Ale wife walks between lynchett and stirk. Cantir strikes. Rash boom fails.* She paused, wondering about her spelling, and then added the last part. *Thick.* That at least she could spell correctly in English, translated from the fairies' language, of course.

She glanced at her mobile phone to check the time. It was nearly suppertime, so too late to drive up to Pennant Melangell where she could use the computer in her office to try to decipher the words. She sighed ruefully. She could use her phone, but it would take forever to scroll through the dictionary entries on the tiny screen. The computer would be so much easier.

She tore the piece of paper from the notepad and stuffed it into her trousers pocket, and then she ambled back down the stairway and into the kitchen where she found a note informing her that a shepherd's pie waited in the refrigerator to be warmed for dinner at 6:30. She turned on the Aga and eased the casserole out and into the oven. At a low temp, it would heat perfectly within the hour it would take her mum to arrive home, and she could leave right after supper for Pennant Melangell with the excuse of a fictional last-minute booking to arrange. With luck, she could figure out the Twlwyth Teg's words before the night was over.

To Bronwyn's delight, her mum arrived home earlier than expected, and the shepherd's pie was ready to be devoured. Maddock left for his own supper, and Bronwyn gulped her meal with the excuse that she had to get to her office as quickly as possible so as to be home before dark.

The B4391 was deserted when she pulled out in her Volvo and only once did she have to pull into a lay-by to let another vehicle go by as she drove the two miles to Pennant Melangell. She supposed the residents of Llangynog had no reason to drive up there on a Sunday evening, and by that time of day, Reverend Wicklyff and the other staff would have returned home with the Sunday service completed and the church cleaned up and locked tight. Hikers and mountain bikers might be found on the footpath on a pleasant spring evening such as this one, but it was doubtful that she would encounter them on the road, although some might still be found on the church grounds.

Indeed, there were several journeyers to be found in the sensory garden and the churchyard, although the church itself was locked up and unavailable. Bronwyn parked the Volvo in the small car park and strode past them to the counseling centre, where she used her key to let herself in and then locked the door behind her.

In her office, she sat down and jiggled the mouse to wake her computer. This she did with a bit of guilt, having been instructed that it would be better to shut the computer down when she was not working and especially on weekends. Her mind had not been on task these past few days, she told herself, and she thought she could be forgiven a lapse of protocol as innocent as that. No harm, no foul anyway, since no one else would know.

She brought up Google, pulled the sheet of paper from her pocket, and began her search. She tried several spellings for "lynchett" before abandoning the effort in frustration. It seemed to be a family name or the name of an estate, but that appeared to make no sense in the context it was used. With a sigh, she typed in "stirk," hoping for better luck. Again, several spellings were required before she found a definition that seemed promising – young cow or bullock. Sitting back in her chair, she pondered that for a few minutes. There was a pasture for young cattle alongside the footpath not far from Pennant Melangell.

"Cantir" brought her the expected musical associations, never mind whether she spelled it with an "or" or an "ir." For the life of her, she could think of no link between cattle and music. *This is a lot harder than it was the first time,* she lamented. And then she had a sudden inspiration.

Going back to the Google search, she typed in "medieval words" and was both dismayed and encouraged to find over 500,000 hits. Surely one of those sites would give her some definitions that would make sense, although it might take days to find them. *I'd might as well get it started,* she told herself firmly. *It's not as if I have a lot of other options.*

It took her fourteen sites before she struck gold. "Lynchett – a small dirt bank or unplowed strip serving as a boundary between fields." Although many farmers now used barbed wire or other modern fencing, others kept to the old ways, dividing fields with hedges or stone walls or dirt banks, and all of these could be found in the area near Llangynog and Pennant Melangell.

Encouraged, she scrolled down and found "stirk" on the same site: "a pasture for young cattle." She grinned with satisfaction. *Ale wife walks between lynchett and stirk.* Now it seemed easy, because she knew a place that fit the description exactly, and it was only a few minutes' walk from Pennant Melangell – near the old farmyard at Pwll Iago Farm, just off the footpath.

It took a search of three more sites before she hit on "rash boon," a term whose medieval meaning was "a rash promise leading to unexpected consequences." Sitting back, she considered the definition in light of what she knew. *Glynnis must have made a promise to someone that led somehow to her death, or perhaps it was the other way around – someone made Glynnis a promise and then murdered her. Either way, it provides a clue that careful questioning might uncover,* she thought.

She searched the internet for another half hour before finally discovering a suitable meaning for "cantir." Although it had musical definitions that fit the time period of the other expressions the Twlwyth Teg had used, it was a different meaning of "pouring vessel for drinks such as wine, ale, or cider" that Bronwyn thought made the most sense. *Cantir strikes. Someone hit Glynnis with a beer pitcher or a wine bottle before stabbing her,"* she mused. *He'd have made her a promise of some sort and then taken her along the footpath to a certain place where the cow pasture was before striking her on the head with the pitcher or bottle. After that, he must have dragged her back into the churchyard to finish the job. Why? Why not leave her near the footpath instead of taking all the effort to put her in the churchyard?* There must have been a reason.

Bronwyn checked the time and found to her dismay that her search had taken her nearly two hours. Dusk was falling fast, and it seemed that she would not have the time to walk the footpath to where lynchett met stirk before dark. She looked out the small window in her office, trying to gather her courage and finding that she could not. It would be foolhardy to walk that footpath in the dark, considering what had happened to Glynnis. She was tempted, but it could wait until morning when she could drive to Pennant Melangell early and walk the footpath before her workday began.

Sleep came easily to her that night, her mind relaxed after having solved the puzzle of the Twlwyth Teg's words. When she woke at 6:00 the next morning, she felt refreshed for the first time in a week and eager to pursue the clues that had been given to her. She hurried through a bowl of porridge and a mug of tea before throwing a change of clothes in the car and driving the empty road to Pennant Melangell.

Once there, she sat in the car and pulled on her wellies, shrugged into a jacket, and set off down the footpath that would lead back to Llangynog, leaving a change of clothing in the car for after her walk.

She kept a sharp eye out as she walked, alert to any change in the background noise of birds and insects and breeze. She glanced often over her shoulder to watch for someone following on the path and stared ahead of her, watching for approaching foot traffic. It wouldn't be unheard of for others to be walking or biking the path this early in the morning, but it would be unusual, and Bronwyn didn't want to take any chances this far away from potential rescuers should the need arise.

Layers of cloud blocked the sun on this early May morning, casting a gloom that promised rain before noon. Dew weighed down the spring grass, bending it across the path so that Bronwyn's wellies and trousers were soon damp with it. An owl swooped from an abandoned fence post alongside the path for several feet before swerving off and diving upon its prey.

It didn't take long for Bronwyn to reach the edge of the cattle pasture, the stirk. She turned off the footpath, ducking under a wire fence that confined the cattle away from the path. There it was – an earthen wall alongside the pasture built up to enclose the pasture on the northern side.

Cautious now, she crept alongside the earthen wall, the lynchett. A glance back over her shoulder showed her something she hadn't noticed before – an opening in the fence where the wire had been cut away and the hedge flattened to allow passage onto the footpath. It hadn't been visible from the path; she wouldn't have found it without the Twlwyth Teg's clues. *Someone could drag a body through there,* she realized. She shivered and wrapped her arms around herself, forcing her feet to keep moving. It couldn't be far.

She came to a place where the pasture grass had been flattened and matted down, the mud churned up beneath. A dark stain marred the bright spring green of the grass. Kneeling, she picked up a handful of dark dirt and brought it to her nose, sniffing and then drawing away sharply. She had never smelled blood before, but the mud had a metallic odor that didn't belong to the earth.

Taking a moment for a good look in every direction, she tried to still her racing heart. At the least she had found the spot where the murder of Glynnis had begun, she knew. Still kneeling, she lowered herself to her hands and knees and began to poke around in the grass, seeing nothing. She crawled to the edges of the matted spot, pushing the grass aside to look for an object that might be hidden behind or beneath it. After only moments, she spotted a shade of green that didn't match the bright grass and crawled closer to it, reaching out to push it into the clear so she could see. It was a wine bottle – an empty green bottle that had once held a Glyndwr sparkling wine.

She took a deep breath and stood up. *I shouldn't have touched it,* she chided herself. *Too late now, though.*

Voices on the footpath brought her head around quickly. A couple who looked to be in their twenties were hiking the path, stout walking sticks striking the ground as they ambled along. She relaxed and offered them a wave, and they waved in return as they passed by the field and continued on up the path.

What should she do now with what she had found? She knew, of course, that notifying the detectives was the right choice, and the sooner she did it, the better. But she hesitated. So far, she hadn't found anything that would ease their suspicions regarding her own involvement, that is, unless the wine bottle proved to have identifiable fingerprints that would point to someone other than herself. Perhaps she should wait a few days to see if the Twlwyth Teg or Pysgotwr had any more information for her?

As she considered, the thought came to her that, no matter which choice she made, there were dangers for her involved. If she led the detectives to this site, she'd cast suspicion back on herself. If she didn't, they would eventually find it anyway, and there it was – her fingerprints were on the wine bottle. In any case, if she continued to pursue an investigation on her own, there would almost certainly be danger for her from a murderer who would want to remain undiscovered.

She'd wanted change in her life, to figure out who she was meant to be, and finding Glynnis in the churchyard had shaken things up for certain. She winced as a desire to turn back the clock and erase the events of the past days flooded her. But it was too late now for that, wasn't it? The tranquility she'd thought she'd had seemed threatened now, and she wasn't sure she could get it back without knowing who'd murdered Glynnis. She would just have to face up to whatever came next and hope it led to some greater good, somehow or other.

Chapter Ten

Neither the memorial service nor the hike from Llangynog to Pennant Melangell proved to be worth the effort, Will thought sourly by the middle of the second week after the murder. What was more, their progress was slow and he had spent twelve days in a row in close quarters with Notley, feeling frustrated at every step. His instincts told him they were going about the investigation all wrong, but Notley insisted they follow his idea of procedure, so Will seethed inside and plodded along behind him.

"No joy," he'd told Chief Superintendent Bowers after the memorial service. He and Notley had stood in the back of the church listening to a eulogy that did not match in the least the picture they had formed of Glynnis Paisley. Her parents had wiped tears from their eyes, but her husband seemed unable to take in that he was a widower at such a youthful age. After the service, the two detectives watched from a distance as the villagers gathered in the street outside St. Cynog's to offer their condolences. No one seemed out of place. Hal Corse did not show up, and neither did the American mountain biker. If the ex-girlfriend was there, she mingled successfully with the rest of the crowd.

In the end, they decided to wait until after the memorial service to hike the footpath from Llangynog to Pennant Melangell, a decision for which they were thankful by the time they had finished.

Although Will considered himself in good physical condition, the first part of the hike left him panting as they passed between the two inns, crossed the bridge, and climbed up through the old quarry to a renovated cottage, where they paused to catch their breath.

"Quite a view," Notley observed, pulling his pipe from his side jacket pocket.

Will eyed the pipe with some impatience. Surely Notley wasn't going to take the time for a smoke?

Notley caught Will's disgusted glance. "Okay, you're right. We'll want to keep up a good pace if we're to get an accurate idea how long the hike takes." He put the pipe back into his pocket and gestured at the scrap of paper Will was consulting. "Where do we go from here?"

"Uphill," Will grunted. But on the beautiful spring afternoon, with the sun shining between the clouds and the hillside green with new growth, his foul mood evaporated. As they climbed, the view of Cwm Pennant and Craig Rhiwarth opened up into an ever-changing panorama as shadows drifted across the peaks. Perhaps it wasn't so hard, after all, to imagine the attraction of that footpath, especially if you'd grown up with a love of hiking and the outdoors as Bronwyn Bagley had.

They followed a fence past sheep pens and continued into a fir wood, consulting the instructions copied from a crude map at the car park, and then they found themselves slowed by a rougher path through the moorland. They crossed fences, passed what the directions described as a prehistoric chambered burial site, and emerged into an upland bog that threatened to bring about a return of Will's earlier temper as the mud sucked at his trainers.

"No sane person would walk this path on the way to church services," Notley pointed out, holding his cane high so as not to get it muddy.

"Better use that to advantage," Will grunted, gesturing at the cane. "That's what it's for, after all."

"Have you any idea how much I paid for this cane?" Notley retorted, lifting it as he stumbled. "I'll not ruin it in this bog. No investigation's worth that."

Will smiled to himself. They struggled on through the boggy land and at last emerged onto firmer ground where the path led from the woods to a stile. Looking downward, they could just glimpse a picturesque footbridge below in Cwm Llech. They rested a few minutes in silence and then hiked on past ruined sheep pens to where the path joined a wider forest road which allowed them to make better time.

When they finally entered the churchyard at Pennant Melangell, nearly four hours had passed since they'd set out on their journey, and dusk was falling quickly as the clouds thickened and threatened rain.

"Now what?" Will asked, his feet sloshing and cold in his wet trainers. He reached down to pick a thorn from his trousers just below the knee. The socks would be ruined and have to be thrown away, but perhaps the shoes could be saved, he thought.

Notley gestured toward the car park. "Let's see if we can hitch a ride back with someone." His trouser legs drug wetly on the ground, stretched too long by the damp and mud. "At least we've found that an hour and a half is not a reasonable time for hiking that path," he pointed out.

"I didn't notice anything that looked like blood along the path. Did you?" Will grimaced as another thorn scratched at his ankle.

"I guess if the forensics people didn't see anything, we had little hope of bettering them," Notley admitted grudgingly. "I think it's time we scheduled another meeting with Miss Bagley."

"After we go to Cardiff to interview the ex-girlfriend," Will reminded him. "It's been more than a week, and she hasn't returned our calls. Maybe she's avoiding us."

Notley blinked at him. "Yes, after that," he agreed. "It's time we looked her up."

To Will's surprise, Notley agreed to spend a day catching up at their office in Caernarfon before scheduling the excursion to Cardiff for the Tuesday after the memorial service.

Working independently at his desk, Will accessed Google and searched for blogs recording hiking times for the footpath and facts regarding the gas pipeline while Notley spent his time attempting to find a current address or phone number for Rhonda Morris, Glynnis' ex-roommate and Davyyd Paisley's ex-girlfriend.

They scheduled meetings with the medical examiner and the forensics team, learning little that was new from either. As they'd been told, cause of death had been the wound to the heart, the victim having been incapacitated beforehand with a blow to the head. A trail of blood led from the churchyard gate to the wall where the victim had been found, and there was less obvious evidence of blood leading from there to both the footpath and the car park. In both cases, the blood found had been scarce drops, not amounting to a great deal, which lead to the conclusion that the head wound and subsequent blood loss from it had occurred somewhere else, with the stabbing taking place where she was found because the blood pooled beneath the body amounted to quite a lot more. Footprints and fingerprints were many, but the freshest belonged to Bronwyn Bagley, which didn't really mean anything since the woman had admitted being in the churchyard with the victim until she was found. They did learn one thing that seemed of interest: Mrs. Paisley's wedding ring was missing, although she was found wearing other jewelry that included an expensive watch, earrings, and a diamond-studded locket.

A young constable named Daniel Quigley had been put in charge of tracing the whereabouts of the American Mark McGuire. He reported that the American's Visa card had last been used in Afan Forest Park and that the local constables had been contacted about locating him for questioning.

"We'll want to question him ourselves," Notley told the young constable, and Will sighed at the thought of yet another full day in Notley's company traveling to Afan Forest Park in South Wales.

"Have you looked at her mobile?"

Quigley nodded, sorting through a stack of paper and pulling one out. "It's all pretty standard stuff. Normal apps for a person of her age: Facebook, Snapchat, Instagram, What's App. Call logs show her husband calling her that night...let's see..." he consulted the paper, "that'll be six calls between 11:30 and midnight, and then another eight calls the following morning."

"He said he called, wanting to find out why she hadn't come back to the hotel," Will remembered. "He might have made the calls to give himself an alibi, though. They don't prove anything, really."

"Computer?" Notley asked.

"Nothing here locally," Quigley told him. "She had one at the home in Cardiff, but she didn't bring it along on the trip. They'll check it out down there, give us a report."

"So that's it, then. Doesn't tell us much," Will said.

"I did a little research beyond that," Quigley confessed quickly. "It never hurts to check backgrounds to see if any of your suspects have form."

Of course, it didn't. Standard procedure. Will had just assumed Notley would have taken care of it.

"What did you find?" Notley beat him to the question.

Quigley shrugged. "Nothing for Davyyd Paisley, Rhonda Morris, or Bronwyn Bagley. They're all so squeaky clean they don't even have one traffic citation among them."

"But?" Will sensed more.

"Hal Corse had quite the time when he was younger. Starting in his teens and continuing on for a dozen years, he had arrests for shoplifting, theft, breaking and entering, and once for a brawl where he broke another bloke's nose."

"Okay," Will dragged out the word, thinking. That might move him up on their list.

"His record is clean for the past ten years," Quigley added. "Seems he grew up and took over the family farm. The responsibility keeps him on the straight and narrow."

"That doesn't eliminate the others. There's a first time for everything," Notley pointed out. "Just because someone's followed the law throughout their life, it doesn't mean something wouldn't push them into murder one day, especially if it was a spur of the moment thing. We all have a breaking point."

It was that afternoon as Will sat at his desk staring at his computer screen and wondering if he could make an early departure for home that their first break came in the form of a call to his mobile.

"Will Cooper here," he mumbled as he answered it, noting an unfamiliar number on the caller ID.

"This is Bronwyn Bagley," whispered a voice on the other end, and Will sat up straighter in his chair, gripping the phone.

"Miss Bagley," he murmured, forcing warmth into his voice, a feat that he didn't find as difficult as he'd feared. "Have you thought of something relating to the case?" He glanced at Notley working just a few feet away.

There was a silence that seemed to drag on until Will wondered if the connection had been broken. "I...I'd like to meet with you," she said, her voice very quiet. "There's something I've found that I need to show you, up at Pennant Melangell." She seemed hesitant. *Why? What is it that she knows?*

"Sure," he concentrated on keeping his voice easy and reasonable, while his mind stormed with the questions of when and where and what she might know. "We can do that."

"Not your partner," she warned, "just you, if that's okay. He makes me feel uncomfortable."

Me, too, Will lamented internally. Another glance told him that Notley had taken notice of the call after all. He was doodling with a pencil, not watching Will but obviously straining to listen to the Will's side of the conversation. He lowered his voice. "It'll have to be in an evening then. I could meet you on Wednesday evening, if you'd like."

"Not too late," she warned him. "It can't be dark."

No, Will reflected, *I wouldn't want to be meeting you in the dark anyway. You're a suspect in a murder investigation, even if I do want to think you innocent.* "I could try to get there by half-five," he offered, wondering if he could make an excuse to leave the office early on Wednesday. Or would that be the day Notley wanted to schedule a second interview with Bronwyn? If so, he would have to make an excuse to put him off.

"Yes, that'll be okay," she agreed, to his relief. Again, though, she hesitated, the silence on the other end of the line stretching out so that Will found himself searching for something to fill it.

"Shall we meet at the Tanat?"

"No," Bronwyn said, "at the counseling centre. But not inside. I'll be waiting for you in the garden."

"Okay." She obviously planned it out. "I'll see you at half-five then, in the garden."

As she rang off, he thought about the call. She'd called him, not Notley, when she was ready to talk. He couldn't help a bit of pride. Of course, he should let Notley know that she'd called, he realized. Of course, he should.

"Who was that?" Notley, as if sensing his thoughts, leaned toward him.

Will forced an easy grin. "A girlfriend, mate. Feeling neglected, she is, what with all the time we're spending on this case."

Eager to get the trip to Cardiff over and done with, Will arrived early at the station the next morning. He had the Volvo out and idling in the car park, windows rolled down and fresh sea air rolling in, when Notley drove in at precisely 7:30. The call from Bronwyn had energized him. *She knows more than she admitted earlier,* he told himself. *I know this is the break we've been waiting for, and it came to me. To me, not to Notley.* He couldn't help a grin as Notley fumbled with his cane opening the door. "Here, let me help." He reached across to pull the door handle.

Notley stared at him suspiciously. "You're cheerful this morning." He pushed his cane into the front seat on the left side away from the window and slid into the car. "What's happened?"

"Not a thing," Will responded. He shifted into drive and pulled out of the parking lot.

"You were early," Notley observed. "You're never early."

"Just ready to get this excursion finished so I don't have to listen to your witty banter."

Notley frowned. "Witty banter?"

"The game is afoot," Will informed him. "I have a good feeling about today's interview."

Notley shook his head. "If you're going to quote history's greatest detective, at least pick something appropriate." He thought for a moment. "Here's one for you: the mere sight of an official-looking person seals men's lips."

Will laughed. "It's a good thing we're interviewing a woman then."

His buoyant spirits faded a bit as they settled into the four-hour drive. Notley had not managed to reach Rhonda Morris with the phone number he'd found for her, so they were heading toward what might well prove to be a wasted trip. But wasted days were nothing new to Will. He'd followed many an unproductive lead during his days in drugs and alcohol, waiting for the rare solid tip to materialize. He knew that it was all a part of the job, and even if Rhonda Morris eluded them, there might be a new roommate or family members to interview.

The high clouds of the preceding day had thickened during the night, and a light rain began to fall as they merged onto the A470 some twenty miles south of Caernarfon. Although Caernarfon was on the north coast of Wales and Cardiff in the south, their path would take them directly across the country with little need to negotiate through small village congestion, so the next fifty miles or so would be easy driving.

Will relaxed behind the wheel and let his mind wander. *What are you up to, Bronwyn?* She'd seemed so secretive. *Why?* True, Notley seemed to grate on people and not just on Will, but surely if she had information for them, she'd expect that both of them would need to be shown whatever it was. Was he endangering himself, meeting her in what was truthfully a remote location at a time when dusk would not be far off? Should he tell Notley, after all?

As if he were listening to Will's thoughts, Notley broke in. "What's her name, Cooper?"

Will glanced at him in confusion. "Excuse me?"

Notley sighed and pulled his pipe from his pocket. "The woman you're meeting tomorrow after work." He made no effort to hide the fact that he'd eavesdropped on the phone conversation.

"I don't see where that's any of your concern." Will gripped the steering wheel and increased his speed.

Notley gave a little laugh and shook his head. "Why so secretive? Something else you're not doing by the book, Cooper?"

Will took a breath. "Lesley," he said shortly, shooting a hope toward his sometime girlfriend that she'd forgive him the lie. "Someone I knew before, when I was working drugs and alcohol."

"Oh, a lowlife, then," Notley surmised.

"What?" Will glanced at him. "Oh, no, Lesley works on the force, too. She's definitely not involved with the drug world."

Notley tapped his pipe tobacco with his fingers. "I'm glad to hear that, at least. You've been seeing her awhile?"

Will searched his mind for a way out of the conversation. "Just casually," he said. "You married, Notley?"

Notley paused to light the pipe and then his free hand swept down to flick open the passenger window. "This isn't a good job for a married man," he observed. "You're never home on time, working weekends, can't talk about the cases...not many of us manage a relationship."

Divorced then, Will surmised.

"I still like the Bagley woman as our suspect," Notley put in. "She was at the scene, she was covered in the victim's blood, her fingerprints are on the gate, and there's no way she walked that footpath unless she ran most of the way on that Sunday morning."

"All true," Will acknowledged. "But she has an explanation for everything."

"If you believe it all," Notley said. "I think we should make a trip back to Llangynog tomorrow and question her again. It's been long enough now she's got over the shock and we can push her more."

Will pondered that, taking his time. "Let's wait and see what Miss Morris has to say," he suggested. "And there's the American, as well. Quigley was hot on his trail yesterday; I bet he'll be located by tomorrow."

Notley looked at him. "What is it with you and that Bagley woman?"

"What do you mean?"

"You really don't want to see her as a suspect, do you?"

"I just don't want to jump to conclusions. It taints the investigation if we already have a suspect in mind."

Notley snorted. "Taints the investigation! Listen, Cooper, if you only knew how many times a detective's intuition paid off, you'd know why I always try to have a suspect in mind."

"Your hero Holmes never did that. He kept an open mind until things became clear to him," Will reminded him.

"Holmes is fiction," Notley retorted. He shook his head, gazing out the passenger window for a long moment. "Bowers says you'll work out, that we need to be patient with you and you'll come along. I say you don't have what it takes, no matter how patient we are."

Will eased off the accelerator and looked at Notley. "Bowers says what?" A flash of something – fear? anger? – ran from his face down through his body. He felt the sweat break out on his forehead and ignored it.

Notley shrugged, still looking out the window away from Will. "He says you were a decent enough detective down in Cardiff, and you'll come along again eventually."

Will found it hard to breathe. *God, Julia, what have you done to me?* He cracked open his window, gulping in the fresh air. "I'm good now, Notley," he said finally.

"Yeah, well, we'll see, won't we?" Notley tapped his pipe on the outside of the car and rolled the window up. "Like I said, follow my lead on this case, and maybe you'll learn something. I'm telling you, stay in the background and don't get in my way. I'll solve the case soon enough, and I'll even share the kudos with you when it's done if you don't aggravate me too much."

Will gritted his teeth and watched the road ahead. *I'll solve this case myself, Notley, and it won't be thanks to you. I'll solve it in spite of you.*

Cardiff's traffic and maze of freeways couldn't come soon enough for Will after that, but finally they plunged into the congestion of the city and found the exit that would lead them to the flat Rhonda Morris had listed as her address. Notley tried her mobile phone one more time as Will eased the Volvo down a narrow street lined with parked cars, but there was no answer.

They found the building that matched the address they had near Cardiff University in an area of former glory now filled with a mix of small but neat homes and larger places converted into flats for students. Four stories high, the building was all brick and faded plaster, a turn-of-the-century home that had known better days. Now subdivided into flats, it featured a small entrance hall lined with mailboxes, each marked with a flat number but no name.

"Which one is it?" Will asked, peering at the mailboxes.

Notley squinted at the sheet of paper. "I've no idea." He glanced around. "Let's go up and start knocking. Maybe someone can tell us which one it is we're looking for."

They tried three doors before one opened a crack to reveal a girl with black hair streaked pink and a glittery faux-diamond nose stud. Her flimsy low-cut blouse and short skirt had Will wondering how she was financing her education.

At their inquiry, she waved toward a staircase at the end of the hall. "Upstairs and the second door on the left," she said, eying them with curiosity. "Is it to do with her ex-flatmate being murdered?"

Notley seized the moment. "Did you know Mrs. Paisley?"

The girl chewed on a wad of gum. "She was Glynnis Newbury then," she allowed as an answer.

"I wasn't aware that she and Miss Morris lived here in this building when they were flatmates," Notley continued, unperturbed.

"Flats are hard to find," the girl went on. "Rhonda was here before she met Glynnis, then they shared it for a while, and after Glynnis ran off with Davyyd, she got another flatmate and stayed." It was a long speech, and the girl moistened her lips and snapped her gum.

"How did Rhonda feel about Glynnis stealing Davyyd away from her?" Will asked, stepping forward. He ignored Notley's angry intake of breath beside him.

"What do you think? She was crushed, cried for days and days. She hated Glynnis after that, and I don't think she cared at all that she was dead." The girl cocked her head to the side, studying them. "You think she murdered Glynnis? Is that why you're here?"

Notley shouldered Will aside. "We're just following up on every possibility."

The girl's eyes rounded in surprise. She giggled. "Wait 'til I tell everyone. They won't believe me at all. Do you have a card so I can prove I talked to you?"

Notley pulled a card from his pocket. "Listen, if you happen to hear anything that might help the case, call me, okay?"

"Sure," the girl agreed, and then she paused as a thought came to her. "Hey, you won't find Rhonda at home."

"Why's that?"

"Because she went to Glynnis' memorial on the weekend, and no one's heard from her since."

Notley blinked at her. "Her phone's a mobile. Why doesn't she answer?"

"Oh, that's easy," the girl said. "She doesn't take any calls from numbers she doesn't recognize. Telemarketers and all that…"

Notley reached up to scratch his head, his fingers playing over the bald spot. "Do you know where she was on the night Glynnis was murdered?"

The girl chewed her gum and thought. "That was on the Saturday before last, wasn't it?"

Notley nodded.

"Saturdays we pretty much all go out somewhere, but not together," the girl said after a while. "I don't remember seeing her, but I usually wouldn't on a weekend."

Notley smiled. "Thanks for your time."

Surprisingly enough, they found Rhonda Morris' flatmate at home. A tall girl with long, straight dark hair and unremarkable hazel eyes, she opened the door to the flat and invited them in. "I'm Emma Smith," she told them after they'd introduced themselves. "Rhonda and I have been flatmates for about two months now." She gestured toward a pair of chairs that nearly filled the small but clean room. "Please sit down. Can I bring you some tea?"

Thinking of the return trip to Caernarfon, they both declined.

She pulled a bright decorative pillow from beneath a small table. "Extra seating," she explained, lowering herself onto it. Then she looked at them expectantly.

"How long have you known Miss Morris?" Notley began, pulling his notepad from his shirt pocket.

"I only met her after Glynnis moved out," Emma explained. "She was short of money and needed a flatmate, so she put a notice up and I saw it."

Notley jotted that down. "So, you never met Glynnis?"

"No, never." Emma glanced around the room. "She had gotten married and moved out by the time I met Rhonda. There were some hard feelings involved, so she never came around after that." She hesitated. "I gathered that Rhonda thought Glynnis cheated her out of Davyyd. Apparently, she told him she was pregnant, and that was the deal breaker. From what Rhonda said, Davyyd wasn't the sort to dodge the consequences of his actions and so there was no changing what had happened. Rhonda had to accept that she'd lost him. But it was hard on her. I almost never see her happy."

"Did Miss Morris ever talk about Glynnis?"

Emma thought for a moment. "Not directly. But sometimes she'd go off on a tantrum, mad at the world, and I knew it was because of what happened with Davyyd."

"Did she talk about Davyyd?"

"All the time." Emma rolled her eyes. "You'd have thought she was still in love with him, the way she went on."

Notley wrote that down. "Did she try to contact him?"

"Not that I knew," Emma said, biting her lip with her front teeth. It made her look as if she had an overbite. "She had her pride, you know."

"But she went to the memorial," Notley pressed her. "Surely she talked to him there."

"Oh, I would imagine she would." Emma brightened. "They were together for a long time, and of course she'd want to let him know she cared about him still, despite what he'd done. Anyone would do that, surely?" She peered uncertainly at Notley.

"You haven't heard from her since the memorial?" Will asked.

Emma shook her head. "It hit her hard, I think. She wasn't the same at all that week between when Glynnis died and the service. I think she was trying to decide what to do about Davyyd, whether to call him or go see him, or what. It had her all jittery. I think she wondered if they might get back together, after all."

Notley leaned toward her. "Was she here with you on the Saturday of the murder?"

Emma stared at him. "Surely you don't think....? But..."

"We don't think anything, Miss Smith. We're just trying to be thorough, that's all."

"Oh, of course." She opened her mouth and then closed it again. She took a breath. "You shocked me, is all. I wasn't here on that Saturday, I'm afraid. I often spend weekends at home with my mum. She's a widow, you see, and I like to give her a bit of company. But I'm sure Rhonda was here."

"You'll call and ask her to get in touch with us?" Will coaxed.

"Yeah, sure, I can do that," Emma promised.

"I wonder which one she was?" Notley speculated the next morning as they sat at their desks conversing in the short distance between. "At the memorial, I mean. Which one was she?"

Will thought back. The flatmate hadn't given them much to go on ("No, I don't have a photo, I'm afraid. We're not that close. A description? Average height, I guess, or maybe a bit on the tall side. Blonde hair. Not sure about her eyes."). The other girl had not bothered to open her door a second time. "I guess it could be any of them," Will responded finally. "There weren't that many young ladies there, maybe four or five. I can't remember one of them standing alone. They all seemed part of the crowd."

"We'll put Quigley on tracking the family, get a photo," Notley decided. "Maybe she's just gone home to stay awhile, thinking about her options."

Back at the station the next morning, Will read the record of their interview with Bronwyn three times, pondering over each of her answers. Truthfully, there were a lot of unanswered questions there. In particular, there was the question of her swift hike from Llangynog to Pennant Melangell. Having accomplished the trek himself in four hours and having found supporting blogs on the internet for that approximate hiking time, he knew something was very off about her explanations. He could think of three possibilities why she would have lied to them about it. It was a fair conclusion that she must have already known about Glynnis' murder before she set out. Therefore, she either learned about the murder before she left home that morning, or she learned about it on her way up the footpath, or she, herself, was the murderer. If she'd learned about the murder from someone else, why hadn't she said? And why hike the footpath rather than drive if she knew about the murder before she left home, or even if she were the murderer? He sighed. Maybe he could coax some answers from her when he met her that afternoon if he was careful in his approach.

Sometime after their lunch break, the direct phone line to Notley's desk rang. The resulting conversation gave them new information, but opened up more questions than it answered.

"Glynnis never meant to take the bus to Oswestry," the unidentified caller informed Notley. "I saw her after it left. She was outside the Tanat chatting up a man."

"Can you describe him?" Notley had asked.

"Taller than her, with light hair," the caller said. "Not a local, or I'd have recognized him."

"Did you see her go off with him?" Notley persisted.

"Didn't pay that much attention," the caller replied. "There's people in and out of the pubs all night long on a Saturday, after all. Wouldn't notice much about her, would I? I was on my own way home. Didn't know it would end up being important."

The caller refused to give his name. "Want to remain anonymous, I do," he insisted. "It wouldn't do if word got around that I was calling."

Not an hour later, the same line rang again with a different voice on the other end.

"I wanted to report something about that murder," the caller began hesitantly. He paused, and for a moment Notley feared that he had changed his mind and hung up.

"What is it you know?" he tried.

"It's about Glynnis Paisley."

"Yes?"

The caller cleared his throat, coughing into the phone. "I saw her after she left the pub Saturday night."

"How was it you noticed her?" Notley encouraged him.

"Aw, she was a looker, she was," the caller stammered. "A girl you'd notice anyway, even if you did know she was married."

Notley nodded to himself. "What did you see, then?"

The caller lowered his voice. "I saw her heading for the car park."

"And what time was that, approximately?"

The caller fell silent again for a long moment. "Must have been after ten because the last bus had left."

"Was she alone?" Notley wanted to know.

"No," the caller said, and Notley sat up straighter. "She was with someone, but I couldn't see who."

"Man or woman?"

"I couldn't tell," the caller apologized. "It was dark, but I did try to see." He hesitated again. "I was curious about who had managed to get her out of the pub off on his own. It's not like any of us would think we had a real chance, after all."

"Long hair or short?"

"That's the thing," the caller explained. "The person had a hoodie on, even though it wasn't raining."

"Tall or short?" Notley pressured him.

"That's the other thing. Medium height, I'd say, but taller than Glynnis."

"And you've no idea who it might have been?" Notley persisted.

"Sorry," the caller said. "I know it's not much help."

He also refused to give his name, hanging up rather quickly when Notley attempted to get it from him.

"Well, there we are," he told Will after relaying the information from the second call. "That complicates things, doesn't it?"

"There's no way to know how reliable that information is without the callers identifying themselves," Will agreed. "Can we trace the calls?"

"I'll put Quigley on it." Notley paused in thought, absently scratching his balding head.

"Neither one of them thought she'd meant to catch the bus."

"The light-haired stranger could be the American," Will pointed out.

Notley nodded. "Quigley's on that, too. He should be able to track him down today or tomorrow. Then we can talk to him."

Greatly cheered by the idea that the callers had deflected suspicion away from Bronwyn, Will found Notley's attempts to work with him the rest of the afternoon almost bearable. But, at half-three, Chief Superintendent Bowers poked his head in the door and asked if he could meet with them in the conference room, and Will found it difficult to meet his eyes after his conversation with Notley on the drive to Cardiff the previous day.

Is it true? Will couldn't help wondering, despite his efforts to forget Notley's taunts of the day before. *Did Bowers really tell Notley I needed to be coddled?* He couldn't imagine Bowers, as professional as he was, saying something like that to a detective working beneath him on the squad. Yet Notley's threats to get Will fired had ceased rather suddenly, which might indicate that a conversation had taken place between Notley and Bowers about him at some point early in the investigation.

He kept his eyes on Bowers, ignoring his own discomfort and answering his questions crisply and professionally. At one point he caught sight of Notley watching him from the corner of his eye and a twinge of anger ran through him. Notley smirked, seeing that Will had noticed.

After they filled him in on the two phone calls and their conversations with Rhonda Morris' roommate and neighbor, Bowers nodded, seemingly satisfied with their progress. "The department budget being what it is, I can't afford for you two to work overtime this weekend as well," he informed them. "You're on weekdays only from now on, unless there's something that comes up that can't wait."

Will tried to keep the smile from his face. "We're not on the rota, then?"

Bowers studied him. "You've had your turn. We'll arrange the schedule for someone else to be available this weekend if a new case opens up. But don't go far, in case there's a development in this case you need to follow up on. No more trips to Cheltenham."

"No, sir," Will agreed. "I'll stay nearby."

After that, the rest of the afternoon flew by as Will pretended to study his computer screen and contemplated the possibilities for the weekend.

He could drive down to Gloucester and spend Saturday night there, giving him two half-days to spend with Lark. Maybe he could take her to Butts Farm to ride the ponies and play with the other farm animals. Maybe they would even have rabbits? Or he could take her away early Sunday morning for the drive to Warwick Castle, which he was sure she would find as fascinating as she had Caernarfon Castle last summer. Or there was always Gloucester Cathedral, where parts of *Harry Potter* had been filmed. Was she too young for *Harry Potter?* More importantly, could he get away with driving that far when he'd been specifically instructed to stay in the area? Probably not.

Then there was Lesley. He had promised her a holiday by the sea. She could leave on Friday afternoon and be to Caernarfon in time for a late dinner. They could walk the city walls and take a picnic down to the beach. He frowned. Yesterday's drizzle had turned into a steady rain overnight, and there was as yet no sign of it letting up. Perhaps he should put Lesley off until the weather cleared? Or was he just making excuses not to see her? He ignored that thought, shoving it firmly to the back of his mind. No matter what Notley had said, he knew a few cops at least who were married, apparently happily so. And Lesley, a 999 operator, worked every third weekend, so she was not always free either. Not that he was that serious about their relationship, he told himself firmly. She was an occasional date, not a steady girlfriend.

He hummed as he worked, feeling inexplicably content. This meeting with Bronwyn Bagley had him intrigued. Indeed, he was looking forward to meeting with her more than he'd looked forward to anything for the past few weeks.

This will be the break in the case, he told himself. *This meeting with Bronwyn could change everything.* He smiled, and then amended his thought as Notley glanced toward him suspiciously. *Everything pertaining to the case, that is.*

Chapter Eleven

Must be my lucky day, Will mused as he cruised along at speed on the M470 east toward Llangynog. Perhaps because of the heavy rain pounding against his windscreen, traffic was unusually light that Wednesday afternoon so he was making good time. He'd managed to get out of Caernarfon earlier than he'd hoped, shutting down his computer at 3:20 and simply walking out. He'd heard Notley call out his name, but had pretended not to. He shouldn't have to answer to Notley, after all, and if he felt like slipping out early after twelve days of steady work, he thought he had the right.

As he drove, he thought about the case. He found the disappearance of Rhonda Morris suspicious, and the American Mark McGuire seemed to be keeping just beneath their radar. Nor had he been totally satisfied with the interview with Hal Corse. The man had been confrontational and defiant, and there was the matter of his past infractions with the law. His protestations seemed just a little too adamant, raising more suspicions than they deflected. Unfortunately, he had to acknowledge that Bronwyn Bagley also remained a suspect since her story didn't add up any better than Corse's had.

And just why is that unfortunate? Will smiled and shook his head at his own folly. That feeling of protectiveness toward Bronwyn had not dissipated as the investigation continued. Although he had only caught glimpses of her from a distance since he'd encountered her in the churchyard, her image had occupied a spot in his mind that made her much more prominent than she should be. *Those deep brown eyes,* he thought, *and that inner tranquility...* that inner peace had been apparent despite her obvious nervousness about being questioned. But was that inner calm covering a cold, unfeeling killer? He just couldn't believe it. No, there had to be someone else responsible for this crime.

He pulled into the little car park at Pennant Melangell at 5:10, twenty minutes early for his meeting with Bronwyn. *Enough time to check the gift shop for something rabbity for Lark,* he decided. He reached for his jacket lying on the passenger seat, struggled into it, and then made a dash for the church.

The gift shop, located under the church tower, was very small, but to his delight Will found several hare-related items that he hoped would satisfy Lark's current passion for rabbits. He browsed through statuettes of St. Melangell with the hare peeking from beneath her skirts, small ceramic rabbits, and necklaces featuring rabbits, finally settling on a mid-size pottery rabbit meant for garden use and a picture book explaining the legend of Pennant Melangell.

He reached for his wallet, meaning to put the payment in the honesty box, and then he noticed the matted sketches for sale on a rack near the box. He was no expert, but they seemed well-done. He plucked one from the rack and looked closer, noting the fine detail that conveyed more than just the forest setting of a section of what he assumed to be the Tanat River. He flipped it over and found a sticker on the back. "Local artist Bronwyn Bagley."

He took a moment to flip through the others, choosing one on impulse to add to his small stack of items, and dropped the payment in the box.

Bronwyn was waiting on a cement garden bench beneath a small rowan tree when he'd put his purchases back into the car and strolled over to the garden. She was dressed in heavy trousers, a hooded jacket, and wellies, and the rowan's newly-leafed out branches managed to keep the worst of the downpour off her. A strong odor of damp dirt and rain hung heavy in the air, though, and no bird song interrupted the patter of rain.

"Bit of a wet day, isn't it?" he called out in greeting, trying for a casual tone in the hope that it would create some trust between them.

"Oh, dear," she said, looking up at him. "I didn't tell you we'd have to hike a bit, did I?"

Will glanced down at his oxfords, already damp from the walk to and from the church. "I've a pair of muddy trainers in the boot of the car," he said. "I guess I should have realized when you said you had something to show me up here that it meant something out of doors."

"But you've no hood on your jacket," she pointed out. She thought for a moment and then said reluctantly, "There are extra brollies in the counseling centre for people to use in the garden. I'll just tuck in and get you one while you change your shoes."

"That's really not necessary." Will would have liked an umbrella, but wasn't oblivious to her hesitation in getting him one. He held out a hand to help her up off the bench.

She took it, her hand light in his. "No, it would be silly not to use one when they're right there. I'll just be a minute."

As she hurried off toward the front doors of the centre, Will turned the other way toward the car park. He fetched the muddy trainers from the boot and then unlocked the door to sit on the driver's seat while he put them on. Still wet from the hike earlier that week, they dampened his socks almost immediately, but there was nothing he could do about that. There was no need to destroy another pair of shoes just to keep his socks dry.

She came to meet him in the car park, handing him a plain black umbrella already unfurled and damp. He took it in hand and followed her across the car park toward the footpath.

"Where are we going?" he asked, trying to catch up and walk beside her.

She stopped and waited for him. "It's just a small way down the footpath. Not far."

"What is it you have to show me?" The rain dripped off the edges of his umbrella, making it hard for him to see her clearly.

She brushed water from her own face, the hood not proving very successful in fending it off. "It's....something relating to the murder, I guess you'd say. At least, I think it is. You'll have to see it yourself."

She walked quickly, wellies sloshing noisily in the mud. He could tell at once that she was an experienced hiker as she strode down the narrow lane, head up and confident. She'd tucked her hair back beneath the hood of the jacket, but strands of it escaped to tickle at her face so that she reached up now and then to push it back beneath.

Will realized that the rain pounding on his umbrella made it hard for him to attempt any conversation with Bronwyn, so he settled for walking beside her, trying unobtrusively to hold the umbrella so that it protected her from the drizzle as well. He had to stretch his legs to keep up as they walked a mile down the lane and then turned onto another tarred lane that eventually led to a farmyard.

"This is Pwll Iago," Bronwyn called to him, gesturing toward a very green pasture filled with sheep. "What we want is just beyond, where the cattle are."

The farm had a modern farmhouse with ancient stone outbuildings strewn about it. No one seemed to be about, and Bronwyn walked past a short distance to where an earthen wall had been built up to separate one pasture from another.

The rain seemed to let up a bit as Bronwyn pointed to something Will hadn't spotted at first - a break in the fencing between the lane and the field. Will stepped closer. The overgrown hedge that separated field from path was broken and flattened, not obviously so, but once he looked closely, he could see the broken twigs littering the pathway and the dip where the hedge was disturbed.

He glanced at Bronwyn, who was watching him with a look on her face he couldn't interpret. *Wariness maybe,* he thought. *She isn't sure whether she should be showing this to me or not. She doesn't trust me yet.* "Is this it?"

She shook her head. "There's more." She brushed past him and struggled over the hedge, branches crackling as they snapped beneath her weight. Once over, she straightened and waited for him to follow, which he did even more awkwardly despite handing her the umbrella before he attempted it.

"Over here," she instructed him. "Mind the muck. The cattle have been here."

He walked over carefully and knelt down where she indicated, seeing a circle of flattened grass perhaps six feet in diameter. He couldn't be sure, but he thought he caught a slight metallic scent to the wet earth when he got close enough. He brushed at the rain streaking down his cheeks with an open hand. He looked up at Bronwyn. "Maybe a cow laid down here?"

"No," she argued, "it wasn't a cow. There was blood before the rain came. I saw it." She glanced toward the sky and gave a little laugh. "It's going to clear now," she added, nodding toward the sunset sky where a bit of light edged the gray clouds layered overhead. She closed the umbrella and set it down beside the hedge.

Will's eyes flicked toward the western sky. "About time," he muttered, and then he returned to the business at hand. "So, you think this is where Glynnis was attacked?"

Bronwyn swallowed, her eyes wary. "Yes, I'm pretty sure it was."

He studied her, noting the steadiness of her eyes. She believed what she was saying. "How do you know?"

She broke the glance and gestured toward some taller grass. "I found something else."

Slowly he stood and walked over to where the grass, or perhaps some unsavory weed since the cattle hadn't eaten it, grew. Having grown up in the city, his knowledge of botany was limited. "Where?"

She reached down and picked up a short stick from the broken hedge. Walking close enough to stand side by side with Will, she reached down and pushed at something hidden in the rain-flattened grass. "I found this hidden here."

He stared at the green wine bottle lying in the mud. Glynnis had been knocked on the head with some unidentified object, and this bottle might be just the sort of object that had been used. He'd need to get it back to the lab where they could test it and compare it with the wounds. He glanced over at Bronwyn. "Anyone could have thrown this out when they were walking the footpath," he objected, just to see her reaction.

Her eyes, when she turned them on him again, were dark. "She was lured here by someone and then hit on the head with this bottle," she said firmly. "Then they dragged her out of the field over the hedge, and that's why most of the broken twigs are on the footpath side."

He swallowed and nodded. "That does seem possible." He searched in his pocket for a discarded baggie or tissue, something with which to pick up the bottle.

"Here," she said, holding out a plastic Tesco bag. "I brought it along, thinking it might be handy."

He took the bag and the stick from her hands and used them to maneuver the bottle into the bag, spearing the twig into the mouth of the bottle and lifting it carefully. "Glyndwr sparkling wine," he muttered, and behind him he heard Bronwyn's nervous giggle. "Is that a good one?"

"Local," she answered. "I shouldn't have laughed. That was irreverent, considering."

"Do they carry this one at the pubs in the village?"

She eyed the bottle as he dropped it into the bag. "I think they serve it at the Tanat and probably at the New Inn, as well."

He nodded. "Convenient, that." The rain had definitely begun to let up, although Will felt himself soaked through. "When did you find this?" He nodded toward the flattened grass.

"Tuesday morning before the rain started," Bronwyn answered. The wet tendrils of hair had escaped her hood again, but she didn't seem to notice any longer. "I'd come early to work and hiked down here for a bit of fresh air."

He considered that, although he didn't believe it for a moment. "You hiked before you started work? Why not at lunch or on a break?"

She lifted her chin defiantly. "I find it's a peaceful way to start to the day, and I'm told it's inadvisable to hike the footpath all the way from Llangynog by myself until the murderer is caught."

She's lying, he realized. "And you just happened to walk down here and find this?" *The logical turning around spot would be the farm itself,* he thought. *Why go on past it just this far?*

"I keep my eyes and ears more open than most," she informed him. "I see things and hear things that others miss."

He remembered what Glynnis' mother had said about Bronwyn. *She's a fey one, bewitched.* There did seem something off about her; but bewitched? "Why did you wait a day to call someone? If you'd called before the rain, we might have found more here to help the case along."

Her defiance melted as quickly as it had come. "I was trying to make something of it on my own first, that's all."

They climbed back over the hedge, Will grabbed up the umbrella, and they set off back up the lane toward Pennant Melangell. Again, Bronwyn hiked at a challenging pace, and Will struggled to keep up without losing his breath. *Out of shape, Cooper,* he chided himself. Maybe it wasn't so out of line, after all, that Bronwyn hiked this in an hour and half the morning she discovered the body. His heels chafed on the trainers from the wet socks, and he knew he'd have blisters by the time they were done. He wondered whether he should be truthful about where the wine bottle had come from when he turned it in. Surely, Bronwyn would have realized that he'd have to reveal her role in locating it?

They emerged into the nearly deserted car park, their own two vehicles seeming quite lonely sitting at opposite ends with the empty spaces between. Will eyed the counseling centre, considering. "I might have some dry kit in the boot," he told Bronwyn. "Would it be possible for me to go inside and change?" Although he'd not relish the thought of driving all the way back to Caernarfon in his sopping clothing, what he really wanted was a chance to talk to her some more. Nothing in her story really added up, and he wondered how much more he could get from her if he had the chance. She'd called him, after all. Maybe she would talk if they got out of the rain.

She'd stopped beside her car, parked near the door to the centre. "It's after hours," she murmured.

"I think you mentioned once having a key," he reminded her. "I've a long drive back to Caernarfon in wet clothing otherwise."

She sighed, giving in. "Okay, then, but we shouldn't be long."

"No, not at all," he assured her, and he hurried to the MGF to search its boot for something dry to change into.

With a dry tee shirt and a pair of workout sweats in hand, he followed her through the doorway into the centre. "Come this way," she told him, and she led him to a small office, which she unlocked with her key. "My office," she said. "It's not much, but it should do as a changing room."

"Thanks," he smiled back at her. He closed the door and slipped quickly into the dry clothing, removing his sopping socks and shoving his feet barefoot into the oxfords. When he was done, he took a moment to look around before emerging back into the hallway.

The room was tiny, its only furnishings a small desk, chair, and file cabinet. The desk was overcrowded with a sleeping computer and an array of papers, pencils, pens, and other paraphernalia, all neatly organized and in place. Two framed sketches decorated the wall above the computer, one a panoramic view of Llangynog as seen from the footpath above and the other a smaller sketch of a forest glen, featuring a small pool of water, a flat rock, and a surrounding of trees.

He opened the door and stuck his head out into the hallway. "Hey, where'd you go?"

She popped her head into the hallway from another room. "Just drying off, as well." Indeed, he saw that she now wore a dark blue skirt with a creamy jumper. "These are dress clothes I keep here for when I need them," she explained.

He leaned against the doorway of her office, trying to put her at ease. "Why'd you call me then, Bronwyn?" he tried.

Alarm filled her eyes despite his attempt at a calming tone. "What do you mean?"

"You might have left all that alone and the hedge would have re-grown itself and no one would have ever known," he said. "Instead, you led me to it. I have to wonder why?"

She frowned. "I want to help solve the murder, of course. Isn't that what concerned citizens are meant to do?"

He hesitated. "Surely you must realize there's some question of your involvement," he explained carefully, "what with you being found holding the victim's body and your fingerprints all over."

She stared at him. "I told you how that happened," she reminded him, and then her eyes widened with a memory. "I forgot to say that I touched the wine bottle, as well."

He looked up at that. "Why, for heaven's sake? Didn't you think not to do it?"

She bowed her head, crossing her arms across her chest and clasping them together. "I saw it and just picked it up," she admitted. "But surely there will be other fingerprints on it?"

He shook his head. "That's not going to do you much good if yours are there, too. You are a suspect, you know."

"Can't you wipe it off?" She watched him.

"Not if I want to keep my job."

She was quiet for a moment. "They haven't asked for my fingerprints so far. Maybe they won't."

"It's only a matter of time," Will told her. "Now that they are getting a possible murder weapon with prints on it, we'll be getting them from everyone who's connected with the case."

She shrugged, obviously distressed. "Then I guess you'll have to tell them I found it and gave it to you. If they know I did it voluntarily, then they can't think I used it to bash Glynnis over the head myself. If I had, why would I have shown it to you? That makes no sense."

"Not to you, perhaps. But what if yours are the only prints on it? What if the actual murderer wiped it before tossing it away?"

Her eyes filled with tears. "I just didn't think about it," she repeated furiously, obviously trying to master her emotions. "I guess I'm just digging myself in deeper by trying to help. Maybe next time I shouldn't call you if I learn something I think is useful."

I can play that game, Bronwyn. "We appreciate any and all tips, but you'd be better off to let us solve the crime. You may be putting yourself in danger otherwise."

She closed her eyes and took a breath. "But if I hear something?"

He smiled. "I know, you hear things and see things other people don't."

She glared at him. "Well, I do. Don't you want to know if I learn something?"

He sighed. "Yes, of course we do. But don't go looking, is all I'm saying. I want you to stay safe."

"And how safe will I be if I'm arrested for Glynnis' murder?" she mumbled. She uncrossed her arms. "It's time we left. I'm late for home, and mum will wonder what's kept me."

"My partner plans to question you again," Will told her, making a last-minute decision not to press her about how and when she'd really learned of Glynnis' murder.

"Dad said he would," she replied with resignation.

Will waited for Bronwyn to start her Volvo and pull out of the car park before following her down the narrow lane. *I'll not leave you here and vulnerable in the dusk,* he thought as a premonition of danger ran down his spine. He shook it off. *It's just the wet clothes and the cold car that's got me feeling spooked.* But if she kept pursuing clues to the murder and then hiking down deserted footpaths and lingering in empty churchyards after hours, he wouldn't bet three pence on her chances of staying safe should the real killer find out.

Will sat up late that night, his mind flitting from one thought to another as if he had no control over its wild eccentricities. He opened the windows of the flat wide, letting in the sea air along with the street noise. The rain had stopped, but a fine mist hung on yet, giving the air an opaque quality that muffled sound and might have chilled him except that he welcomed its ability to keep him alert. He warmed a tin of soup to ward off the effects of hiking in damp clothing and then poured himself a small measure of Famous Grouse to sip as he sat in his leather chair with his feet propped on a hassock. Although he'd tried to distance himself entirely from his father's lifestyle, the Famous Grouse was the one habit he'd be willing to credit him for – the only one, he assured himself firmly.

He unpacked his purchases from the gift shop at Pennant Melangell, propping the framed sketch on the floor beneath a window and across from his chair where it would be readily visible. He wrapped the pottery rabbit in a towel to protect it and settled in with the little book, reading it in twenty minutes. *Lark will love it,* he mused. *No wonder the place has such a feeling of peace about it, even if the story is pure fantasy.* Although he'd never considered himself religious or spiritual, he acknowledged that certain places had a mystique that could not be rationally explained. Apparently, Pennant Melangell was one of them.

Once done with his reading, he relaxed with his whiskey and tried to organize his thoughts.

He'd have to get the wine bottle to forensics, he knew. Perhaps he could claim that an unknown informant had instructed him where to find it? That wouldn't be far from the truth, and maybe it would deflect Notley's suspicions about Bronwyn. But that wouldn't explain her prints on the bottle. *Why did she have to touch it?* Of course, he probably should be honest about her contact with him, but some stubbornness in him prompted him to evasion where Bronwyn was concerned. *Notley's so sure she's our suspect,* he told himself. *Not telling him will force him to keep an open mind about her.* If in the future he had to reveal the truth, he could justify his omission to their superiors, couldn't he? Perhaps not, but did he really care?

Notley had left a message on his mobile while he'd been hiking with Bronwyn informing him that the American, Mark McGuire, had been located in Coed y Brenin, amazingly only a few miles out of Dolgellau. He was to meet them the next morning at 10:00 at station headquarters in Dolgellau. *That'll save me spending another long day in the car with Notley,* Will thought with relief.

Will had been adamant that they find the American and interview him, but now that it was time to do so, he had to ask himself what he hoped they'd find. So what if the American had flirted with a barmaid earlier in the evening she'd been killed? He could hardly be expected to just up and admit he'd killed her. Still, Will liked him as a suspect, maybe because their list was short and he tended to like anyone who wasn't Bronwyn Bagley, he admitted to himself. But an American – they were always killing each other over in America, weren't they? And this guy was a solicitor...no, they called themselves lawyers over there. Maybe he thought he was above the law?

Admittedly others seemed to have better reason to be angry with Glynnis Paisley than the American did, though. Hal Corse had seen himself insulted and booted out of the pub on her account. Add that to the tension over the gas pipeline, and there might have been enough anger there to bring it about, especially if he'd hung around after to confront her again. Or there was the flatmate, Rhonda Morris. She'd been cheated of a marriage to a man she'd thought loved her, and all due to Glynnis. And Davyyd Paisley, as well – he hadn't seemed so mad as much as bewildered by Glynnis' actions, but oftentimes it was the spouse who was at fault. Who knew what really went on in a marriage? And he hadn't waited for her at the pub that night, had he? Or maybe he had, after all.

And Bronwyn...could a childhood bullying fester into adulthood murder over something as simple as another stolen boyfriend? It might. It just might.

But there was the question of another absolutely unidentified person, as well, Will realized suddenly. Who was Bronwyn's source? When she said she saw and heard things that others didn't, who was she seeing, and what did she hear from whomever it was? There was an unknown element in this murder investigation, and Will wasn't ready to commit to a suspect until he found out how Bronwyn knew what she did. Somehow, he needed to gain her trust. He needed her to confide in him.

And that meant separating from Notley. Will pondered that thought. Throughout the investigation Notley had kept him at his side, deciding when and where and how they would proceed at every turn. It was standard procedure that two detectives would work in thrall, Will knew, but he couldn't help feeling smothered by that expectation in this case.

Not that he and Edward hadn't worked side by side much of the time back in the day. But that was different. He and Edward had often shared the same thoughts, had worked together like two halves of the same brain much of the time. Sure, there were times when they disagreed. No team ever agreed all of the time. But there was mutual respect between him and Edward, and they could talk out their differences without feeling that one or the other of them was in the wrong and the other right. He'd always felt that he could present his case with Edward, and Edward would listen with logical objectivity. It had been the same when Edward's ideas had differed from his, as well. They were a true team. They trusted each other.

I could suggest that we'd cover more ground if we went in different directions, Will thought. But then there was the matter of the interview with the American. Both should be present for that, as well as for a meeting with Rhonda Morris when she was located. And he could hardly allow Notley to re-interview Bronwyn alone. Will took the last sip of his whiskey. It seemed there was no way out, then. He'd just have to endure Notley for however long it took until the case was either solved or shelved as unsolvable.

They left for Dolgellau at nine the next morning, Notley tapping his cane impatiently beside the unmarked Volvo when Will walked out of headquarters, having deposited the Tesco bag and its contents with the forensics team. His explanations to them had been vague and probably unsatisfactory, but his actions were behind him now, too late to change.

The rain and mist had lifted during the night, leaving a day sparkling with clear azure skies and dew-sparkled hillsides. Spring had begun to drift into early summer as May eased toward June, with trees maturely leafed out and grasses tall and lush. They left the coast and drove inland and south on the A470, mountains rising on their left and masses of foxglove blooming alongside the roadway.

They drove across the stone bridge leading into the village and maneuvered around parked cars that lined one side of the street, two-story slate buildings occupying the other side with their doors opening very close to the roadway. As in many villages in Wales, the roadways had been constructed originally for wagons and horse traffic, with no idea that one day enough room would be required between buildings for a two-lane roadway with parking alongside. Will coasted through the village centre, searching for a parking slot while watching for oncoming traffic and pedestrians. He finally saw another car pulling out at some distance from the police station and took that spot.

The American, Mark McGuire, was waiting for them in an interview room when they arrived. He'd been there early, the constable on duty informed them. He'd been given coffee and a bacon roll and asked to wait for their arrival.

They opened the door to find a young man in his late twenties with casually-tossed blonde hair and wide hazel eyes. His healthy tan and muscular build spoke of time spent outdoors in athletic pursuits.

They introduced themselves and brought him another cup of coffee. "Black," he instructed them. "And that's all or I won't make it through the ride this afternoon."

"Mountain biking?" Will inquired, although he already knew the answer. Easing into a conversation might allow him to get McGuire talking.

"Yeah," McGuire rewarded him with an easy grin, "my reward for passing the bar exams at home. We're making a tour."

"You're traveling with some mates?"

"Yeah," McGuire said, "my roommates in college. We all passed the bars together, and we'd made a pledge to take this trip afterward."

Will nodded. "I understand it's a good place for biking here. Where have you been?"

McGuire took a sip of his coffee. "Hot," he observed, setting it down. "We started in the Lake District, and then on to the Tanat Valley." Here he paused, shooting them an alert look. "I know that's why I'm here, because of what happened that night after our ride. I didn't know the barmaid had been killed until the local police found me here."

"Where did you go after the Tanat Valley?" Will asked.

McGuire looked surprised at the question, but continued readily enough. "We went to South Wales for a few days and then came back up here. But the rain kept us inside yesterday, so we were going to do the ride today."

"So back and forth across the country?" Will verified.

"Yeah, I guess so. We've been going wherever sounds good at the moment." McGuire took another sip of the coffee, grimacing. Will hoped the bacon roll had been of better quality than he knew the coffee to be. "We meet people who tell us about a ride somewhere else, and if it checks out and looks good, we go. We've found some good rides that way."

"Let's get to your time in Llangynog," Notley interjected, taking over. "When did you arrive in the village?"

"We got there that Saturday morning, I'd say around nine o'clock."

"So, you weren't actually staying in Llangynog?"

"There's not much in Llangynog for lodging, is there?" McGuire waited for an answer. "Most of what was listed on the internet was in other villages or already booked up, except for the caravan park."

"Where did you stay then?" Notley ignored his long explanation. "Oswestry?"

"Llangollen," McGuire said. "We stayed there because we thought it'd be close enough, and there's more there – restaurants and shops – than in Llangynog."

Notley paused, looking at him. "How much time did you spend in Llangynog then?"

"Not much," McGuire admitted. "We got there that Saturday morning, did the ride, and then hung around for a while that evening in the pub."

"All of you together?" Notley persisted.

McGuire hesitated and then explained. "We all did the ride together, but my friends left me later. I'd met one of the local girls and invited her for a drink. They had a few drinks themselves and then took the bus back to Llangollen." His cheeks reddened. "I didn't know exactly when I'd be heading back, so they left me the rental car."

"With the bikes?" Will asked.

McGuire nodded affirmatively. "They were on a rack on the back."

"And what time did you actually get back to Llangollen?"

"It was after midnight."

"How long after midnight?"

McGuire nodded, as if to himself. "Probably nearer one in the morning," he admitted. "I'm not familiar with the roads, and they're so narrow, and I'd been drinking. It wouldn't do to pick up an arrest for drunk driving just before starting my career in law, would it?"

Will smiled, still trying to encourage the man to talk. "Can anyone verify the time you got in?"

"I shared a room with one of my friends, Jeremiah Williams, but he was asleep when I got in, so I don't suppose he can verify much for me."

"Okay, then," Notley jotted a note on his pad and changed topics, "tell us about the girl you'd met."

"Truthfully, I don't even remember her name," McGuire admitted sheepishly. "It started with a "B," some Welsh name I didn't recognize. Her last name was "Baggie" something."

166

Will hid a smile. "Could it have been Bronwyn Bagley?"

"That's it," the American said, with another grin. "You know how it is. I just wanted a pretty girl to spend an evening with, that's all. It's not like I was going to stay there."

"No, I'm sure you had other plans," Notley assured him. "Where did you meet Miss Bagley?"

"In the village centre. She was at the playground with a couple of little kids, her niece and nephew, she said. I stopped to ask her about the protestors, and then I just asked her if she'd meet me for a drink later."

"And she agreed, just like that?"

"Yeah," McGuire said, his cheeks reddening again.

Notley waited a moment before continuing, letting the American squirm, Will thought. "I understand it didn't go so well for you later in the pub."

"What do you mean?" McGuire hesitated. "We got along fine, had a few drinks together."

"And then she left rather abruptly, didn't she?" Notley persisted.

"She was a little oversensitive," McGuire defended himself. "I mean, I just mentioned that I admired that barmaid. She was spunky, and I liked the way she stood up to that man who was harassing the engineer. It wasn't like I was dumping her or anything. But she just got up and stormed out, like I'd done something to insult her." He shook his head. "I didn't get it, but it wasn't like I planned on seeing her again anyway. I just let it go."

"How much longer did you stay at the pub after that?"

McGuire shrugged. "Maybe an hour? I didn't keep track of time. I had a couple more drinks and then I left."

"What were you drinking?" Will interrupted, holding out a hand to stop Notley's reprimand.

"Beer, but not Guinness. Boddington's," McGuire said, his face puzzled. "I understand that Guinness is a tourist drink."

Will grinned. "It is and it isn't. It depends on who's ordering it."

Notley glared at him, obviously annoyed. "Did you interact with the barmaid, Glynnis Paisley, during that time?"

The American met his eyes. "Like I said, I didn't know she'd been killed until yesterday when the police found me at the hotel."

"That doesn't answer my question."

McGuire watched him for a moment and then his shoulders drooped. "I flirted with her. That's why the other girl left, like I told you. She flirted back, too."

"Did you leave the Tanat Inn before or after Mrs. Paisley left?"

McGuire paused, blinking. He seemed to consider his answer before it came, perhaps thinking that it would be easily verifiable. "It was about the same time, I guess."

"You guess?" Notley pushed him. "Either you did or you didn't."

"Okay," the American conceded, "I left right behind her. I thought maybe we could connect, you know? She was obviously having fun flirting with me. Her husband had walked out. Why not give it a try? I might have gotten lucky."

"Did you?" Notley raised his eyebrows.

"Did I what?"

"Did you get lucky?"

McGuire snorted. "She barely gave me a glance once we were outside. I tried to talk to her, but then someone called her from the parking lot and she just walked away."

"Who was that?"

"I don't have any idea. I didn't know she was going to be murdered, so I really didn't pay attention."

"You just gave up?"

McGuire glared at him. "Yes, I did. You try it and, if there's no spark, then you give it up and go home."

"The person in the car park, was it a man or a woman?" Notley wanted to know.

McGuire shrugged. "I couldn't tell from the voice."

"Did she leave with this person?" Will broke in.

"Who knows? I guess she probably did. I didn't stay around to see." McGuire was getting restless. "Look, can I go? I've told you all I know."

"Just one more thing," Notley said. "What were you wearing that night?"

McGuire frowned. "Why do you need to know that?" He waited a moment, but no one said anything so he sighed and answered. "Wind pants, a tee shirt, and a windbreaker."

"Did the windbreaker have a hood?"

"Sure, yeah, it did, but I didn't have the hood on. That's just for when I ride. If it rains, you know."

Will waited while Notley wrote that down. "We'll need contact information so we can find you again if we need to," he warned the American finally. "A list of where you'll be for the next couple of weeks, at least."

"I can do that, but I'll have to make plans with the other guys first because we're just kind of going with whatever strikes our fancy," McGuire agreed. "Maybe I could email a list to you when we get it figured out? I don't have anything to hide."

"When do you plan to return to the U.S.?" Notley reached across the table and handed McGuire a sheet of paper and a pen.

"Not for three more weeks," he said. "We've got a return flight out of Heathrow on May 18th."

"Give us your flight information, as well," Notley instructed him.

They waited while McGuire wrote down the necessary information and then saw him out the door.

"A blonde man," Will commented as they drove across the bridge toward the A470, thinking of the anonymous phone calls they'd received.

"But not tall," Notley pointed out. "And no hood on."

"Still..." Will said, "there might be something there."

Notley looked at him, annoyed. "What was that about what he was drinking? How's that relevant?"

Will increased speed, ignoring Notley for a moment as he eased onto the highway. He'd have to tell him sooner or later. "I got a tip last night," he said finally. "Anonymous. "It led me to a possible attack site, and there was a wine bottle there, Glyndwr sparkling wine. They carry it at the Tanat and probably at the New Inn, as well. Forensics is checking it out."

Notley's mouth fell open as he stared at Will. "When were you going to tell me about this anonymous tip?"

Will swallowed, summoning courage. "I was waiting for the right moment."

Incredulous, Notley stammered, "The right moment? Like maybe before we interview a potential suspect?"

"Like right now," Will said firmly. "I told you, didn't I? It might be nothing. Let's wait and see what forensics says about it, okay?"

"No, it's not okay," Notley went off. "Nothing you do is just okay. You ignore the rules, ignore procedure, ignore everything."

"Ignore you?" Will couldn't stop himself.

Notley's balding spot turned red. "You'd better not ignore me," he sputtered. "I didn't ask to work with you, Cooper. If I think you're leaving me out of the loop, I'll have a little talk with Chief Superintendent Bowers; see what he thinks. I'm telling you, you won't last long in the department unless you learn to mind the rules."

Will bit his lip and stared at the roadway ahead in silence. He could hear Notley fuming beside him, breathing hard and waiting for Will to counterattack.

"Where did you find the bottle?" Notley asked at last. "Or is that a secret?"

"It's not a secret," Will snapped. "It was alongside the footpath, in a place we'd missed when we walked it. Forensics missed it, as well."

"But your tipster found it," Notley said.

"Yes," Will conceded.

"Man or woman?" Notley wanted to know.

Will thought fast. "Woman." *I have to admit that much, but I'm not going to give her up to you, Notley.*

Notley glowered beside him. "And you went there and found it?"

"I did," Will admitted. "Last night, just before dusk."

"You could have called me, or we might have gone up there today."

"It was after hours. I assumed you'd have plans. And today we were coming down here to Dolgellau. I didn't want to leave it any longer than necessary, especially considering the rain we had yesterday." Will knew they sounded like excuses, but maybe they'd be good enough to allow Notley to save face.

They were. "Next time, you tell me," he warned Will as they climbed out of the Volvo in Caernarfon.

"Sure," Will agreed, not looking at Notley. "I'll keep you informed." *If it's something I want to share,* he added mentally. He was wondering if he could see Bronwyn again, maybe on the weekend when he was off-duty. So far nearly all their information had come from her, so it stood to reason that she did have sources they couldn't access. Maybe if he could put her at ease, get her talking more, he could solve the case much faster than he and Notley could, working at odds with each other.

It was worth a try. It might buy him some peace from Notley's bullying if he came in with some useful information. At the very least, he would have the company of a pretty young woman to enjoy.

Chapter 12

Bronwyn turned her face to the sun and closed her eyes, breathing in the scents of wet soil and blooming bluebells, woodruff, lavender, and herbs. It was her lunch break, and she'd chosen to take her egg salad sandwich outside to the sensory garden. She had spread a towel on the wooden bench to protect her bum from the previous day's rain and sat enjoying the rare sunshine, the sandwich disappearing more quickly than the half hour she had free from her tasks.

It was the right thing to do, calling the detective and showing him where Glynnis had been attacked, she told herself firmly. *I'll deal with the fingerprint problem later, if it comes to that.*

She thought about him. Casually-tossed light brown hair spoke of recklessness, she imagined, and those brilliant blue eyes said intelligence. But there was something else, something not as easy to put a finger on. He seemed almost disdainful toward his partner at times and casual in his approach to the case. *Why?* She wondered. *What's made him so callous?* It didn't seem fitting for a detective to be like that. He must have been curious about where her information came from, but she appreciated that he hadn't pressed her on it. She certainly had no intention of telling him about the Twlwyth Teg or Pysgotwr or the pool of water in the forest. She'd had enough of counseling for a lifetime already.

She glanced at her watch and sighed. Only five more minutes, and she'd have to be back to work. St. Melangell's feast day was May 27th, and this year they planned to celebrate it with an organized walk and a mountain bike ride, complete with tee shirts for the participants and lunch after in the area between the church and the centre. She was praying for a nice day, as the lunch would be picnic-style, outdoors, and it'd be a shame to try to herd people into the small conference room instead. Although she'd started the sketch for the advertisement posters before Glynnis' death, she'd procrastinated too long now and ended up rushing the design. She was still dissatisfied with the result. With the event only a couple of weeks away, she needed to finish the artwork that afternoon and get it to the printers so that the advertisements could be posted in the next day or two. Even at that, it was a short deadline for registrants, shorter than it should have been, even though most of the participants would be last-minute hikers on holiday anyway. They'd need registrations a week before the event in order to get the tee shirts made in time. She sighed. Deadlines were not something that worked well for her, especially when something else was on her mind.

She stood, stretched, and picked up her towel from the bench. There were days, and this was one, when she wished she didn't have to work at all.

She walked back to the counseling centre's door, noting several official-looking vehicles parked alongside the roadway. Obviously Detective Cooper had shared the information about the attack spot, then, and people had been sent to examine the area and gather evidence. She hoped he hadn't told them that the information had come from her, although how he could have avoided doing so was beyond her imagination. Perhaps someone was already waiting in her small office to talk with her and to get her prints to compare to those on the bottle.

But when she got there, the office was empty, and no one seemed to be looking for her, so she sat down at her desk, leaving the door open, and pulled out her art materials.

Rash Boon, she mused as she worked on the poster. *Someone made a promise, a rash promise, that somehow led to Glynnis' death. But who?* That was the question, wasn't it? Bronwyn wished she knew more about what the investigation had found so far, but she knew she shouldn't ask, nor would she be told if she did. She wondered who besides her was on the suspect list. *Davyyd? Surely not.* With his easygoing manner, she couldn't imagine him that angry at anyone, no matter how sad he'd looked in the pub that night. *That protestor? Maybe.* She couldn't think who else might be on the list. *Who made the promise? What kind of promise could it be?*

Was it Glynnis who made a promise that brought about her own death?

She held her drawing out at arm's length and studied it critically. *The wording needs to be more colorful,* she criticized herself. She picked up an orange-red oil crayon and began to color. *Thick.* Her mind changed topics. *What was that all about?* She had first heard the Twlwyth Teg shouting it about the time of Granny Powers' death. *Thick. Thick? THICK!* Nothing made sense to her, neither Granny Powers' words nor Glynnis' death, nothing.

There was a light tap on her open door, and Janice Hatcher stuck her head in. "Almost finished?" she asked.

"Close," Bronwyn told her, holding up the poster for her approval.

"Oh, Bronwyn, it's lovely," Janice blurted. "It's perfect!"

Bronwyn blushed. "Not perfect, but I think it'll do."

"Why don't you take the afternoon off and drive it to the shop in Llangolen?" Janis suggested. "Clarence Randall is volunteering this afternoon, and you know he'd prefer to handle the entire site on his own if he's allowed. Your group from St. Giles has gone home for the day. There's no need to stay on such a beautiful afternoon."

Bronwyn smiled. Clarence Randall was a 92-year-old man whose mind was still as sharp as it had been when he was a young miner in the area. Although he walked with a cane, he delighted in showing people around the grounds, spouting details of history and a love for the place. He certainly could handle any foot traffic that came in unannounced, and her office work could wait for the next day. "Why not?" she agreed.

Janice hesitated in the doorway. "How are you doing, Bronwyn?"

Bronwyn met her gaze. "I'm fine, Janice. I'll be better once the crime's solved, but I'm holding on for now."

"They're saying Hal Corse has been questioned," Janice mentioned. "The protestor? He lives just down the valley."

"I hadn't heard," Bronwyn told her as she filed the information in her memory. "I know they talked to Glynnis' parents and her husband, as well."

Janice nodded. "They'll get to the bottom of it, the sooner the better, I'm thinking. I worry about people walking that footpath."

"As long as people stay in groups, it should be fine," Bronwyn reassured her.

"Well, then, you're not doing it alone, are you?"

"I…" Bronwyn paused, caught off guard, "I haven't walked the footpath alone since the murder." She could be truthful about that much, she thought, as she'd only walked a bit of it down to Pwyll Iago.

"Well, that's okay, then," Janice smiled, the concern vanishing from her face.

Bronwyn loaded her sketch into the Volvo, cranked the engine, and eased out of the car park and onto the little B4391, narrowly avoiding a rental car full of tourists as she pulled out. The sun shining in the window forced her to lower the visor, and she pulled into the first lay-by she came to in order to search for the sunglasses she hadn't worn in months.

Thick, thick? THICK! She thought as she drove slowly down the roadway, but nothing came to her that made any sense. Maybe she'd mistranslated their words? She frowned. It was possible. It was amazing she'd learned to understand them at all, considering how infrequently she'd overheard them.

Another oncoming car forced her to pull into the next lay-by, as well, and when she pulled back to the roadway and looked in both directions, the first thing she saw was a fisherman walking alongside the fence line separating roadway from pasture with his fishing pole slung casually over his shoulder. *Pysgotwr!*

Abandoning the car, she scampered across the lay-by and onto the grassy area beside it with a welcoming smile on her face.

He waited for her. "Bronwyn! How good to see you!"

"I could hardly believe my eyes," she answered.

He glanced around. "Come, walk with me a bit," he suggested. "It's more open here than I prefer."

People certainly might find it strange to see a huge man with leaves in his hair and beard standing at the side of the road, Bronwyn thought. She had always wondered if others saw Pysgotwr as she did, or if he, like the fairies and the Cwn Annwn, were generally invisible. *Invisible?* She wondered with sudden insight. *Or maybe they just blend in so well that most people don't notice them, like the faces in my paintings.*

Pysgotwr interrupted her thoughts. "You have the sight, Bronwyn."

"Is that why I see you when others don't seem to?" They'd stopped in a small grove of fir trees, and the shadows fell across his face as she looked at him, making him look like a sapling, bending slightly in the breeze. He'd propped his fishing pole against a tree, and he watched to make sure his spaniel Michelangelo didn't knock it to the ground as he ran around them.

He leaned towards her. "I blend with the forest. Surely you can see that? I am part of it, not separate from it, as are you." The oak leaves around his face had deepened into an emerald green, and the earlier tendrils of green vines had become thicker with early hints of fruit to follow as summer developed.

Bronwyn frowned. "What do you mean? So, I'm separate, but I can see you and the others? How?"

"Many children are born with the ability to see, but nearly all lose it as they grow and become aware of their own world."

"Why didn't I lose it, then?"

"Another piece of the puzzle, dear Bronwyn."

She sighed. Why did Pysgotwr always have to talk in riddles? "Can you tell me who murdered Glynnis?" She'd might as well get right to the point before he wandered off again.

"No, I cannot," Pysgotwr said, "for I do not know the answer."

Bronwyn blinked in amazement. "You don't?"

"I believe the Twlwyth Teg know, but I cannot be certain." His cheerful face loomed above her. "I do not think it matters much in the whole of time."

Bronwyn shook her head. *The whole of time?* "It matters to me, because I am a suspect."

"Yes," Pysgotwr agreed, "that is a concern for the time that is now."

She thought for a moment. "Can you at least tell me if Glynnis' murder is linked to Granny Powers' death?"

Pysgotwr waved toward the distant mountains. "All things are connected, Bronwyn. We are all a part of a great whole, and so everything is connected, some in ways we cannot fathom."

She shook her head. "You know that's not what I meant. I want to know if Granny Powers' death caused Glynnis' death in some way?" She held her breath, waiting.

Pysgotwr picked up his fishing pole. "That is a complex question, and there is not one simple answer to it. Again, I must remind you that all things are connected, Bronwyn, and so yes, there is a connection between the two deaths in Pennant Melangell, although what it is may not be the type of connection you're thinking of." He looked at her thoughtfully. "I think it will be all made clear to you in time."

"If the Twlwyth Teg are talking to me, they are aware of something I need to know."

"Most likely."

"I'll find out what it is in their time, not mine. Not today?"

He smiled and shook his head, the leaves whispering against his face. "Not today."

She watched as he continued on his way until he entered a grove of trees and was lost to sight, blending with the forest completely within seconds of entering it. As always, Pysgotwr's words to her created more questions than answers. *I should have asked about "thick,"* she chided herself, but it was too late and there was nothing that could be done about it now.

On Friday night, Bronwyn's dad had made a plan to meet her mum when she got off work at the shop in Llanrhaedr and take her out for a meal at the Greenbank Hotel in Llangollen, so Bronwyn decided to treat herself to a meal at the Tanat Inn.

The pub was filling up fast by the time Bronwyn walked through the door and chose a corner table on the "meals" side of the establishment. She sat down, asked for a ginger beer from Mai who was serving, and then decided to order the vegetarian lasagna, with fried mushrooms and horseradish mayonnaise as a starter. Waiting for her meal, she settled back into her corner and watched the crowd.

Local farmers staked out their favorite tables to discuss lambing and the weather, three village councilmen carried on a lively discussion about funding for restoration of the village hall, and tourists jostled each other for the remaining few tables, timid about calling out their orders as the locals did. A fire burned in the stone fireplace, adding the desired atmosphere but forcing those sitting closest to move their tables as far away as possible. Mai ran back and forth with orders, assisted by Cecil Lumly who had yet to find a replacement for Glynnis. A scent of Guinness draft and Scotch whiskey competed with roasted meat and fried fish, making Bronwyn's stomach rumble in anticipation.

She saw Glynnis' husband, Davyyd Paisley, sitting alone at another table nearly hidden in the far corner. She found herself watching him as he ate his steak and potatoes in solitude. He looked pale in the reflection of the flickering fire, and his eyes seemed dulled and sad.

On impulse, she got up and walked over to his table. "It looks like you could use a friend." She pulled out the chair across from him. "May I?"

He looked up at her, frowning. "Miss Bagley, right?"

"Bronwyn," she said with a smile.

He hesitated, setting down his fork, and then nodded. "Sure, I could use some company. You're the one that found Glynnis."

"I am," she agreed. "And again, I am so sorry for what happened."

There was an awkward moment when he said nothing while she sat down, and then he nodded toward the other side of the inn. "I've already got one."

"Excuse me?"

"A friend."

"Well, then, why aren't you sitting together?" Bronwyn wondered, stretching to see the person he'd indicated.

Davyyd sighed, a slight shudder running along his arms and down to where his hands cupped his Guinness. "I didn't think it proper for Rhonda and I to be sitting here together so soon after Glynnis....well, you know, especially here in Llangynog."

"Rhonda's your ex-girlfriend?" Now Bronwyn could see her better as the woman turned toward them, watching. Straight blonde hair framed a rounded face with a pert upturned nose and a generous mouth that was turned downward in a contemplative frown at the moment.

"Rhonda was my best friend for years and then my girlfriend after." Davyyd's eyes filled with tears. "I loved her, and I still love her, God forgive me." He glanced at Bronwyn and dashed a napkin at his eyes. "I shouldn't be telling you all of this, should I?"

"I've a good listening ear," she told him. "I'm not the police."

He nodded. "It just about kills me every time I think about what I did to her."

Bronwyn hesitated. "Then why did you marry Glynnis, if I may ask?"

Davyyd stared off into the distance, his eyes blank. "Glynnis and Rhonda met at university. They were flatmates; that's where I met Glynnis. She was always there, and there was that charm of hers." He turned to look at Bronwyn. "She had amazing charm, did

Glynnis – charm for the men. But women…sometimes I think now that it was just the idea of competition, just to find out if she could take me away from Rhonda. And she did." A tear rolled down his cheek. He didn't seem to notice. "I am so sorry for hurting her, so very, very sorry."

Bronwyn waited, not sure what to say. When he hiccupped and began dabbing at his face again with the napkin, she decided to go on. "You did love Glynnys, though, too?

"I did, or I thought I did. She was so awfully proud of me, you see – the idea that I was an engineer and all. It made me proud, as well. And when she told me she was pregnant…"

"I didn't know about that," Bronwyn murmured.

"I wanted to marry her by then anyway," he insisted.

"But…?" Bronwyn prompted him.

"But then there were always other men, blokes like that American here that night. You were with him, yeah? Glynnis would take a shine to someone like that, especially if he was with another girl, and then she'd flirt with him, try to lure him away." He hesitated. "I don't know if it ever went further than that, but it seemed she just had to see how far she could get, you know?"

"That must have been hard for you," she sympathized.

"Yeah," he agreed, "it was hard, all right."

Bronwyn squinted off toward the bar area. "And Rhonda has come to offer her sympathy," she surmised.

"Oh, here you are!" called a voice from a few feet away, and Bronwyn looked up at Mai, who was balancing a tray that bore Bronwyn's ginger beer and mushrooms, among other things. "You moved tables."

"I thought Davyyd looked lonely," Bronwyn told her, nodding toward him. "He was Glynnis' husband. This is my sister-in-law Mai."

"Hello," he greeted her politely.

Mai nodded hurriedly before dashing off to deliver the rest of her orders. "Have a nice chat then," she called back over her shoulder.

"You've stayed here in Llangynog," Bronwyn observed. "I didn't expect that. I thought you'd want to get away from here."

"I'd like to," Davyyd confessed, "but the detectives asked me to stay in the area, and my job won't be ending for another few weeks, so I've told them I'd stay on. Most days I've been dashing off for

Oswestry as soon as the day's work ends, but today I thought I might avoid Rhonda by eating here instead."

"And Rhonda followed you here?" Bronwyn probed.

Davyyd looked at her warily. "It's nothing. She wants to talk, to help me through this, she said, but I've been avoiding her successfully, for the most part. It's not that I wouldn't want to move on again sometime, but not with Rhonda. We've too much of a past, I think, too many skeletons in the closet, as they say."

Bronwyn reached for a mushroom and dipped it in the mayonnaise, pushing the plate toward Davyyd. "Help yourself. They're amazing," she said. She hesitated, unsure how much to push him. "How long has Rhonda been here?"

Davyyd pushed tousled brown hair away from his eyes. "She came to the memorial and stayed on in Oswestry." He looked at Bronwyn. "Not in the hotel I'm in, of course. I didn't ask her to stay."

"No, of course not," she soothed him as Mai put her plate of lasagna on the table.

He watched her eat, seeming comfortable with their silence for a few minutes. "It must have been horrible for you, finding Glynnis like that. Were you friends?"

Bronwyn sighed. "Not really. You just told me how she was. Well, she seemed to take a special delight in bullying me even more than others." She choked on a bite of lasagna, chagrined. *My gosh, what have I said? He was her husband, after all, and he's just lost her.* "I didn't mean any offense," she mumbled.

"No, it's okay. I've no illusions where Glynnis was concerned," Davyyd assured her.

Bronwyn smiled at him and thought that he was looking a bit happier than he had when she'd first seen him. "You're going to be fine," she told him.

"I know," he agreed. "Once I can get away from Llangynog and from Glynnis' family, it'll be better."

"Is Glynnis' family giving you a hard time?" Bronwyn thought about Glynnis' mother, a fierce competitor whose daughter had scored a major prize in marrying this man. She would not be taking the death lightly, Bronwyn suspected.

"Her mum seems to be undecided about me now," Davyyd admitted. "Having the police question me didn't do me any favors. And her dad drinks far more than he should, and sometimes he says things he shouldn't when he's had a few too many." He shrugged.

"You know how it is. Glynnis was their only child. If I even glance at another girl, all of a sudden I'm a disloyal husband and probably had a hand in her death."

"Then you shouldn't be sitting here with me," Bronwyn observed.

"For more than one reason," Davyyd agreed, nodding toward the bar.

Rhonda was watching them with such hopelessness on her face that Bronwyn closed her eyes in shame. "I've got to go," she blurted. "I've got an early day tomorrow, a group coming into the counseling centre for the second day of their conference."

Davyyd's face, relaxed into an inviting casualness, fell. "It being a Saturday tomorrow, I hoped we might have lunch together somewhere," he said. "I've felt rather shunned here until you sat down, and weekends are especially hard to be alone."

Bronwyn blinked in surprise. But perhaps it was just friendship he was needing, after all, she reminded herself. She was the one who had sat down with him and told him he looked as if he needed a friend. "Perhaps another time?"

"Give me your number and I'll call," he promised.

Finding a pen in her purse, she scribbled her mobile number on a napkin and then added her name, just in case he forgot whose number it was. She'd like to meet him again, she thought. He had such a friendly, open manner. Glynnis had not deserved him, that much was certain. *How mad would Glynnis be if she knew that her husband was asking to have lunch with me?* Bronwyn grinned to herself. She should have more reverence for the dead, but this was Glynnis she was thinking of.

Still glowing from the attention Davyyd had given her, Bronwyn set off for the walk home through the village. Darkness had fallen, and this time there was no full moon to light her way. Still, there were the few streetlights and light spilling from cottage windows, and Bronwyn certainly knew the path home.

A breeze tossed her hair forward into her face, and she lifted a hand to brush it away. She could hear the wind in the trees alongside the roadway, but as she cocked her head to listen, she could hear the bleat of a faraway lamb, as well, and then the hoot of a night owl.

Suddenly a rustling sound behind her caught her attention, and her heart quickened. She strained to listen, glancing over her shoulder into the darkness. It sounded like running feet, and it was approaching fast. She quickened her pace, feeling very alone and vulnerable, and all of a sudden, she wondered if she'd look a fool if she stopped by one of the cottages and asked for a ride home.

Maybe it was the Twlwyth Teg? But they had never approached her so noisily and so quickly before; generally, it was more as if she'd just stumbled onto them and they were suddenly there. This was something else, then.

The rustling became a galloping noise, and despite herself, Bronwyn broke into a run. Now her heart was pounding, but she couldn't risk another look behind her. There was no time. She raced across the dark pavement toward the nearest lit cottage, praying that she wouldn't stumble and fall before she could get there.

The galloping noise raced toward her, faster, faster. It couldn't be more than a few paces away, getting louder as it approached. The wind had picked up at her back, thankfully propelling her forward, but it seemed she could hear nothing but those galloping feet and her own thumping heart.

Suddenly Bronwyn knew she wasn't going to make it to the cottage door. Whatever it was, it was just a few feet behind her and would be upon her in moments. She stopped, swerved to one side, and turned to face her attacker.

The wind gusted as a dead gorse bush tumbled past her, carried on the wind from wherever it had been hiding through the winter and down the roadway. Bronwyn gasped as it passed, and then she saw it for what it was, and she laughed aloud. *My God, Bronwyn, now it's shrubbery you're frightened of?* She chided herself. What if she'd reached the cottage door? What a fool she'd have looked then. She shook her head. *I've got to put this behind me, or this time I'll end up in the loony bin for sure.*

But putting it behind her wasn't so easy. That night Bronwyn slept little, tormented by vivid dreams that left her shaking and sleepless as she awoke and tried to relax back into rest again. The Twlwyth Teg were there in her dreams, and so were Glynnis's husband Davyyd and the detective Will Cooper, all mixed up in a hodgepodge of fantastical events that seemed completely real until she woke and knew they weren't.

In the morning she could remember none of it, except for the Twlwyth Teg's words, repeated over and over throughout the dream. "Thick!" they'd shouted. And then there'd been something new. "It's you, it's you, it's you."

She went to work, exhausted and with a nagging headache made worse by the fact that the words kept running over and over in her mind on a seemingly endless loop. *Thick,* she mused. *That seems to be their obsession lately, but what does it mean? Thick can mean stupid. Am I being stupid about Glynnis' death, or something associated with it?* And then she shivered. *It's me, they said. It's me....* She refused to think of it more, despite the words running over and over in her head. Trying to get a meaning from a dream was crazy. *It will only lead me down false paths,* she told herself.

But however firmly she tried to put the words out of her head, they remained, and she couldn't help but wonder if they were true. "It's you!" they'd said, and what else could they mean than that it was her that was the murderer? Maybe she was crazy, after all. If she could imagine Pysgotwr and the Twlwyth Teg, maybe she could have killed Glynnis and only her subconscious was aware of her deed.

She got the group from St. Giles settled in and shut herself up in her office to work on the feast day promotion, leaving the door just slightly ajar so that someone from the group could find her if they had an unexpected need. There were two volunteers working at the centre that day, as well – Brianne Baker and Nesta Barton - both able to handle drop-in pilgrims easily enough.

She forced her dreams to the back of her mind and concentrated on her computer screen. Surprisingly, she moved along quickly, managing to assign tasks to various volunteers, make a timeline for the event, and even to estimate a budget that she thought would fit into their meager surplus.

A tentative knock on the door startled her, and she looked up to find Reverend Wicklyff standing with his head in the doorway. "I thought I'd check to see how the feast day planning is coming along," he explained.

"Come in," she welcomed him with a smile. "I'm just working on it now." Turning the computer screen toward him, she showed him what she'd accomplished. "I think the budget will be close," she told him, aware of how little they managed to take in, "but perhaps some of the participants will be moved to donate a bit once they're here."

"They never seem to realize what it costs to keep a place like this up," Reverend Wicklyff lamented. He paused and then abruptly changed the subject. "How is the investigation getting along, Bronwyn? I assume you are being kept informed?"

"Not really," she told him. "I think I'm still a suspect, so they aren't telling me anything."

"You? A suspect?" he protested, but she could see from his eyes that he'd known it. "I told that young detective that you were innocent. I guess he didn't listen very well."

"Thank you for that. I appreciate your trust in me, especially when you don't really know if it's true."

His eyes widened. "What are you saying?"

"Nothing," she hurried to add, hoping he believed her. *Why did I just create doubt in the one person who believes in me?* "I was just surprised. You couldn't know for sure."

He relaxed. "Surely you must realize that a person in my position gets pretty good at reading people."

"I suppose that's true," she agreed, needing to hear more, especially after the doubts the dreams had given her.

"I knew from the first time I met you that you were a person of peace. You have that air about you, accepting, calm, and spiritual."

"But I was angry with Glynnis," Bronwyn protested. "I wasn't peaceful and accepting when she was around. I really didn't like her." She looked up at him. "But I didn't kill her."

"We all have our moments of weakness, life's little annoyances," the reverend went on, "but I'm sure your nature would not be to act on your anger." He shrugged. "Sometimes there are things one can't explain. Perhaps this is one of them. But, no matter what turns up in their investigation, I will always remain steadfast in my conviction of your innocence."

Bronwyn sighed. "Thank you. That means more than you could possibly know. I think there are others who are not so sure about me."

He nodded. "There are. But time will prove you innocent, I'm sure.

Bronwyn was still basking in his unfounded, but welcome, faith in her that afternoon when she drove through Llangynog on her way home, crawling along at a snail's pace in order to avoid running over the protestors who'd occupied the village and filled the streets, blocking traffic long enough to hand their brochures to passing drivers. *It was only dreams, not visions,* she told herself, thinking of the nightmares she had suffered. *Not true, any of it, just my unconscious mind panicking, that's all.*

Her mobile phone chimed as she came into a service area, and she picked it up to glance at the number. Missed call, one voice-mail said the screen. The number was unfamiliar.

She punched the button for voice mail and held the phone up to her ear as she negotiated around the parked cars lining the village streets. Another beautiful day had brought hikers and mountain bikers out in droves.

She played the message, sitting up in her seat as the voice came on. "This is Inspector Cooper calling. I'd like to talk with you some more without my partner, if it's possible. How about lunch tomorrow? I could pick you up and we could go to one of the nearby villages. Call me back and let me know." He had left a number, which he repeated twice before ending the call.

She felt a flush run from the top of her head down her face and onto her neck. *What does he want?* She thought frantically. *Didn't he say that his partner wanted to question me some more? Can't he wait for that?*

But maybe it was something else. He had seemed reluctant to include his partner when he'd talked to her before and he'd even helped her out when he distracted his partner so that she didn't have to meet him in the churchyard that one time. Was it that he and his partner didn't get along? Maybe he wanted to solve the crime on his own. Maybe he thought that, between them, he and Bronwyn could figure out a solution to the crime without going through the normal police channels. Maybe he was just after keeping all the glory for himself.

But I have nothing more to tell him. Her panic returned. She couldn't tell him about the dreams, and there was no possibility of revealing her sources. She could do nothing more to help him along in the investigation unless she stumbled upon something more from the Twlwyth Teg or Pysgotwr. If she agreed to meet with him, she might slip and say something she'd regret. But if she refused to meet with him, he'd have to assume that she had something to hide.

But, even if she had no more information she could share with him, Detective Will Cooper certainly had information he might share with her. If she knew who the other suspects were, wouldn't it help direct her questions when she did meet Pysgotwr again? Wouldn't it help the next time the Twlwyth Teg spoke to her?

She mulled it over through dinner with her mum and dad, eating little and getting worried looks from her mum in return. After the meal, she took old Nan and wandered out into the pasture with her dad, checking on the new lambs and feeding Hobbs a handful of carrots. While her dad carried the newest of the lambs into the barn for its inoculations, she lagged behind, thinking of the careless way Detective Cooper seemed to work, at odds with the intelligence in his eyes.

Later she pulled out her mobile phone and called the number he had left. When he answered, he sounded pleased she had called.

"I'll meet you, but not in Oswestry," she told him. "How about Welshpool? It's bigger, so we'll have more choices for lunch." *And it's large enough for us not to be noticed, not on a Sunday anyway when most of the villagers from Llangynog would stay at home.* Oswestry would have plenty of inns and pubs, as well, but in addition she didn't want to take the chance of running into Davyyd Paisley at the moment.

"Sure," he agreed without hesitation. "Shall I pick you up?"

She took a moment to think about it. Small villages were notorious for gossip, and someone would surely notice. "Will you be driving your own car or the unmarked police car?"

"My own," he told her. "I can't use an official vehicle when I'm not on duty."

His own vehicle had to be less recognizable than the police car. Surely no one would know who was driving. "Okay," she agreed.

'I'll be at your house just at noon, if that suits you," he offered.

Her parents would object, she knew, but wouldn't protest too loudly. She wouldn't let them. After all, wasn't it better for her to be socializing with the police than with someone who might turn out to be the killer? They could have no argument with that. "I'll be ready."

She closed her phone and sat down on her bed, patting the quilt beside her so as to entice old Nan to jump up. Detective Cooper seemed nice enough, a lot better than his partner. She'd have to be careful, though. He'd surely want to know now where her information came from, and she couldn't tell him. Nor could she tell him how worried she was that, somehow, she was to blame for Glynnis' death. *It's you, it's you, it's you...* the words played over and over in her mind. They must mean something, and it couldn't be good.

I hope I've done the right thing, she worried. *What if I help him, and then the trail leads back to me?*

Chapter 13

Bronwyn changed her clothes three times before settling on a pair of dark brown trousers and a silky cream blouse with a brown lamb's wool cardigan over it. She put sensible walking shoes on her feet and stood up to brush off the bits of old Nan's hair that had stuck to the trousers in the few moments she'd sat on the bed. Her choice of outfit wasn't glamorous, but it would have to do, she told herself firmly. It wasn't as if it were a date, after all, just an opportunity for Detective Cooper and herself to try to coax information from each other. She stood in front of her mirror and brushed her hair, adding a pair of gold hoop earrings at the last minute. Then, satisfied, she walked downstairs and watched for Detective Cooper out the window.

"You're sure about this?" her mum had asked at breakfast before leaving for the church service earlier that morning. "He may not have your best interests at heart, you know."

"I know," Bronwyn agreed, "but I want to try to find out where the investigation's going, and this is the only way I know to do it."

"He's a detective," her mother objected. "He knows how not to tell you anything at all, while he'll be trying to get any bit of information out of you that he can."

Bronwyn sighed, looking down at the poached eggs cooling on her plate. "I want to do this, mum. And I've nothing to hide anyway."

"I don't think this young man means any harm to Bronwyn," her dad put in quietly. "I was watching him when they came to talk to her that first night. He seemed to be on her side, as much as he could be."

Bronwyn shot him a tentative smile. "I thought the same thing." *And he was nice when I took him to Pwll Iago. I don't think he gave me up when the forensics people asked how he'd discovered the attack site.*

"Bronwyn's not had much of a social life since she came back home," her dad went on with a smile in her direction. "Maybe she just wants to have a nice lunch out with a good-looking young man."

Her mum looked up at that. "Is that it, Bronwyn? Are you thinking he's interested in you that way?"

Bronwyn blushed. "No, of course not. I just want to find out about the investigation, that's all. I don't imagine he's interested in anything but the same."

But she wondered as she waited if, perhaps, she was wrong about that. She pictured him, the tousled hair and those intelligent blue eyes, his easy manner of talking to her, even the hint of rebellion as he got between his partner and her, sought her out on his own. Admittedly, she sometimes felt desperate for a relationship with someone, her protestations to Maddock aside. Maybe the nervousness she felt with him was more than just fear about being a suspect in the case.

At precisely noon, a small car turned up the driveway toward the farm house, and Bronwyn let herself out the front door, calling off the two sheepdogs that had come bounding from the barn to greet the visitor.

Inspector Cooper put on the parking brake and got out of the car, leaving the motor running. "Hi," he greeted Bronwyn. "Am I on time?"

"Exactly on time, Inspector," she said, eying him shyly. He had on jeans and a blue denim shirt, making him look more American than British. He'd put the top down on the car, and the breeze had tossed his hair into wild array.

He stood beside the driver's side of the car. "You'd better call me Will since I'm buying you lunch." He smiled easily. "Shall I put the top up? It'll blow your hair all over otherwise."

She looked at the car, some kind of little sports car, but not a new one. "I think I'd like the wind," she told him. "I'll pull my hair into a ponytail."

He grinned at her, looking pleased. "We'll leave it down for a while then. I've heard clouds are expected later in the afternoon. Are you ready?"

She nodded. "It's nice of you to take me to lunch." She stepped toward the car, and Will hurried to open the door for her.

"I've an ulterior motive, I'm afraid," he told her. "There are some things we need to talk about before my partner schedules another interview."

Her smile faded. So, it was to be a business lunch, after all. "I thought as much." She pulled a band from her purse and gathered her hair into a ponytail low on her neck.

Will hurried around the car and got in on the driver's side. "Do you mind if we go for a bit of a drive before lunch?"

"A drive would be nice," she said, "and besides, the village is full of protestors again, so it's better if we go the round-about way." *That way no one will see us together,* she assured herself. *Somehow she'd rather no one know she was going to lunch with one of the detectives on Glynnis' murder case.*

Will eased the car down the driveway, being careful not to hit the two sheepdogs that escorted them. "The protesters haven't given up then?"

"Not at all," she explained. "Apparently they've been gathering signatures, hoping to get a review in the courts before it's final."

"How do you feel about it?"

The car gathered speed, and Bronwyn felt the words being torn from her mouth. She raised her voice. "I'd not like to see it any more than anyone else here would."

Will turned from the B4391 onto the A494 and turned south. It would be a circuitous route to Welshpool, but Bronwyn guessed that he'd chosen it so that they would avoid all of the small villages where they might be recognized by anyone they didn't want to have to explain their meeting to. He must feel the same way she did, then. They fell into silence as the car picked up speed and the wind battered at them.

Bronwyn relaxed into the seat and closed her eyes against the sun. She could smell the grass and the occasional patch of wildflower, and the acrid scent of a sheep pasture filled her nose as they passed it by. Once she heard the shrill cry of a hawk hunting in a field, and a constant chatter of birds grew and then receded away as the car flew past groves of trees where they gathered. It seemed nice having a car without a top, she thought, closer to nature. It also postponed the tension of having to talk, and she was happy to do so now that she'd put herself into the situation at hand.

At Bala, the car slowed and Will turned onto a small lane, the B4403. They crossed a bridge over the River Dee and then bumped along at a much slower speed, watching for oncoming traffic on the narrow roadway.

"This way we'll avoid the congestion in Dolgellau," Will explained, and Bronwyn remembered that there was a police station there. She eyed him curiously from her seat beside him, trying not to be obvious. Why would he not want anyone to know he was meeting her?

The silence between them grew awkward, and Bronwyn tried to think of a way to start a conversation. Why had she agreed to this? She shifted in her seat, turning her head to look out at the countryside passing by.

"Am I making you nervous?" Will asked, causing Bronwyn to startle. She turned to look at him. "Because I don't mean to," he went on. "I'm not out to find evidence against you or anything. I just thought that maybe we could work together a bit, try to put together what you know and what I know and maybe come up with a result."

"I don't know anything more," she protested more quickly than she meant to. *Now he'll be suspicious.* "I already showed you everything I knew about."

He glanced at her. "Well, then, the worst thing that can happen is that we'll have a nice lunch."

She smiled at that, and afterward she felt easier with him.

As they drove slowly along the narrow roadway, he began telling her about his orphaned niece Lark. "She's smart," he told her, "and she's interested in practically everything, but at the moment, she's really interested in rabbits."

Bronwyn laughed. "Rabbits! I hope you told her all about St. Melangell then." She liked that he was sharing some of his personal life with her; it took the pressure off to discuss the case.

Will shook his head, pulling into a lay-by to let an oncoming car pass by. "I didn't know much about the legend when I talked to her this past week, but I did buy her a book about it and a pottery garden rabbit for the next time I see her."

"Do you see her often?"

"Not as often as I'd like," he explained. "I go to Gloucester on a weekend sometimes if I'm not working, and last summer she spent a week with me in Caernarfon when I had the time off."

He obviously loved her, Bronwyn could tell that much, and knowing that reinforced her impression that he was a nice man. "You're important to her, then. She's lucky to have you." She paused, wondering if it would be too bold to ask. "What happened to her parents?"

He waited a few moments before answering, and Bronwyn thought she had ventured into something she shouldn't have. "Her mum died of a drug overdose, and if she ever had a father, no one knows who he is."

"I'm sorry." Bronwyn thought for a moment and then tried to change the subject. "I have a niece and a nephew, too."

"In Llangynog?"

"Yes, they're my brother's children. He married his school sweetheart and stayed in the village."

"Do a lot of young people stay here?"

Bronwyn shook her head. "No, most leave after school. Everyone in the village is either really old or young and married. Except for me, of course."

"I remember you went to university in Wrexham. Why did you come back after?"

She bit her lip. It was none of his business really, but he'd asked so she supposed she'd have to come up with a plausible answer. "I missed it, the village," she said at last. She wasn't going to tell him that she didn't finish at the university, that she was so homesick she just quit and went back to live with her parents.

But he was apt at reading between the lines. "Homesick then?" he grinned.

Her heart sank. *What must he be thinking of me?* "That's it," she agreed because it was the easy thing to do and she couldn't think of a comeback that wouldn't make things worse.

He must have sensed her discomfort, then, because he fell silent, and she scooted over against the window and let the air blow in her face, a coward when it came to explaining herself to him.

At Dinas-Mawddwy he stopped at the stop sign and then merged onto the A458 which would take them the rest of the way to Welshpool. Their mutual silence continued as the car picked up speed again, and Bronwyn sat back, grateful for the fact that the road noise made the lack of conversation less awkward. *What was I thinking, accepting his offer of lunch?* She chided herself again. It had been foolish of her to think he wouldn't see right through her half-lies and evasions. What did she have to gain from this?

In Welshpool, they drove around the city centre twice before finding an empty space alongside the roadway to park in. Will put the top up on the MGF, locked it, and then walked with Bronwyn on the sidewalks, glancing into the shop windows and searching for a welcoming place for lunch. He'd taken to chatting again, keeping the conversation to non-personal topics, and she tried to relax, breathing slowly and answering him, trying to keep up her side of things without looking as self-conscious as she felt.

They decided on the Royal Oak, which Bronwyn thought was probably more expensive than Will had planned but offered a quiet atmosphere where they could talk. He asked for a corner table, away from the other diners as she tried to steel herself for what lay ahead.

Bronwyn excused herself to the restroom so that she could try to get a comb through her wind-snarled hair. Despite the ponytail, wisps had blown away from the band and whipped around her face until she felt a total mess. Combing it helped, but not as much as she'd hoped. Perhaps Will Cooper was used to girls whose hair had been tossed about in his little convertible.

When she rejoined him, Will was studying the menu. He ordered salmon with jacket potatoes, and Bronwyn was too nervous to do anything but order the same. Didn't a lot of vegetarians eat fish? She thought so. Anyway, Pysgotwr was a fisherman, and he was a guardian of the land, so it must be okay. And truthfully, she liked salmon.

"Would you like a glass of wine?" Will offered as the waiter hovered.

Did he hope that would loosen her tongue? Well, if it did, so be it. Her hands were quaking so hard she'd probably not be able to hold onto her fork, and maybe a glass of wine was just what she needed. "That would be nice."

"Red or white?"

"Red," Bronwyn replied automatically, and then a jolt of impropriety hit her. "Or must we have white with fish? I usually ignore that rule because I never drink white."

Will nodded at her. "We'll have a bottle of the Sugarloaf Vineyards Deri Coch" he told the waiter, who raised his eyebrows, obviously impressed.

"I've not had that one," Bronwyn told him. "Judging from his reaction, it must be good."

"One of the few Welsh reds worth drinking," Will said.

She smiled, and then realization struck her. "What if I'd ordered the Glyndwr sparkling wine?"

He grinned back. "Then I'd have been suspicious."

He's good, Bronwyn thought.

She expected that, now that the business of ordering their lunch had been taken care of, he would get down to the matter of prying more information from her. She realized that he would still wonder why she'd hiked the footpath to Pennant Melangell so quickly on the Sunday morning she'd found Glynnis' body, and certainly he'd want to know more about how she'd found the place where Glynnis was attacked. Maybe telling him that she heard and saw things that others didn't wasn't such a great idea, after all. She felt her stomach clench as she prepared for the interrogation to come, and suddenly salmon didn't sound so good.

But Will Cooper surprised her by asking a question she felt took them off in another direction entirely, one that left her wondering what he was up to. "What do they mean when they say Pennant Melangell is a 'thin place'?"

She thought for a moment and decided that a short explanation wouldn't convey what she wanted it to. "Have you ever sat and made yourself really still, perhaps in a garden or by the seashore?"

"Sure," he said, but she knew he didn't realize yet what she meant.

"Your mind is empty, and you are experiencing the world through your senses. It's a little like meditating, except you're alert to what you're experiencing. Maybe you hear a bird singing in the tree above you or a bee buzzing as it passes or even the whisper of the leaves in a breeze. You smell the earth, the dirt, maybe a subtle sweet scent of a flower or two. You feel the sun on your face or a cool breeze or even the damp mist if you're out early enough. And suddenly, you feel yourself a part of it all rather than a separate being. You feel a connection to all of creation."

She looked at Will and saw that he was watching her intently. "That's what happens at Pennant Melangell more often than at other places. The boundaries between worlds are thinner there because it's a sanctuary and has been a sanctuary for thousands of years. People come to Pennant Melangell because of that connection, because it makes them feel at peace, protected, safe."

"Like Stonehenge?" Will asked.

"Yes, I think it's sort of the same," Bronwyn agreed, "but there aren't so many of those places now. Civilization changes things. That's why the gas pipeline is such a big deal. People will say it's because of the danger to us or to wildlife, but really, it's just another intrusion of civilization on a place that's already seen more than its share from mining and the quarries."

The waiter interrupted them with the bottle of wine. Will tasted it, nodded his approval, and their glasses were poured.

Bronwyn watched nervously, trying to think about where he was going with his asking about Pennant Melangell. Would he guess that her information came through the mystical elements allowed by the thin lines between worlds? But how could he?

She took a sip of her wine and then decided to go on the offensive. There was no need to sit there worrying about what she was revealing, after all. "Who are you suspecting in Glynnis' death?"

Will's eyes widened, and he hid an amused grin. "You thought you'd try to get some information out of me rather than wait for me trying to do the same to you," he accused her.

"And why not?" she shot back, mortified that he'd seen through her so easily. "It only seems fair that you tell me a bit of what's going on since I've given you all the evidence you probably have so far."

"That's true, but I am still wondering about how you knew that evidence was there."

"I went for a walk and found it," Bronwyn reminded him. "I told you that."

"But why not turn around at the farm? Why go on past it? I know you had to be back to work that morning, so you didn't have time to go far."

She felt herself blush. He'd managed to turn things toward her again, very neatly. "I...I overheard something, so that's why I went to Pwll Iago."

He set down his glass of wine and stared at her thoughtfully. "Where were you when you overheard it?"

"I..." Bronwyn started, but just then the waiter interrupted them with their meals, so she took the chance to think it out more fully. *Why did I tell him I'd overheard something?* She chided herself. *Now he'll badger me about it, and I can't tell him the truth. I was afraid of this, that he would push me into a corner.* She sighed and picked up her fork, poking at the salmon.

"You were where?" Will reminded her.

She sighed. "I was in the forest south of Llangynog." That much was true, at least. "I was in a little clearing, doing a sketch."

He chewed a mouthful of salmon. "I've seen some of your art in the gift shop at the church."

She blushed again. "Then you know I'm telling the truth." She took a forkful of salmon, savoring the buttery flavor. It was very, very good. Maybe she should re-think this vegetarian thing.

"Who did you overhear?" Will persisted, interrupting her enjoyment.

"Who?" She hesitated, looking up at him. The intelligence in his eyes was still there, but now the recklessness she'd thought she'd seen before was gone, replaced by an intensity that intimidated her. Maybe she had imagined the earlier recklessness. If so, she might be in trouble. "I don't know. I overheard a voice, someone else out walking. I didn't want to be seen, so I hid and just listened."

"Just a voice?" Will sounded skeptical. "One voice, not a conversation?"

"Just the one," she said, thinking furiously. "Talking out loud to himself or herself., or maybe on a mobile. If it was a conversation, I only heard the one side." *God, what a stupid thing to say. I am thick!*

He was frowning. "What did this voice say?"

I can't say "rash boon" and "stirk" and "lynchett" and "cantir." She closed her eyes, feeling trapped. "There was nothing about Glynnis specifically. It said something about a place where an earthen wall met a cattle pasture. There was something about a rash promise, as well, but I didn't understand that part. I just assumed it was something to do with Glynnis' death." She looked over at him pleadingly. "I couldn't exactly ask questions, could I?"

"No, I guess not," he admitted. "You assumed it had to do with the murder. Why? The things you overheard could have been about anything."

She bit her lip. "The murder was on my mind, and I guessed that…that, well…I knew a place like that, there by Pwll Iago, and it was near to where the murder had to have happened, so I just thought it might be connected."

196

"So, you put it together and figured out whoever you overheard was talking about the farm alongside the footpath? It was that easy?"

"I thought about it and I couldn't think of another place that fit the description."

He considered, taking a bite of his potato. "Man's voice or woman's?"

"I couldn't tell," she lied. *Are the Twlwyth Teg male and female?*

"Okay," he watched her thoughtfully. "Whoever you're protecting, you're doing a bang-up job of it."

"I'm not protecting anyone," she protested. *Except myself.*

He waited, watching her closely, and when she didn't offer any further elaboration, he took a breath. "Look, Bronwyn…can I call you by your first name?"

"If you want me to call you Will, you'd better call me Bronwyn."

"Okay, Bronwyn, you have to know you're a main suspect in this case." His voice was firm, but still calm, as he watched her face. "I don't think you did it, but my partner is pretty sure you did."

Tears sprung to her eyes, unbidden. She blinked at them angrily.

"I need to hear the truth from you. That's all I ask. Tell me the truth, and I'll believe you and do what I can to help you. Okay?"

She bit her lip. "I am telling you the truth."

He hesitated, then shook his head a little and changed subjects with a rueful smile. "Okay, a rash promise, then. Let's talk about that. Was that it exactly?"

She nodded. *Close enough.*

"Would you consider your source to be reliable?"

"I don't have a source. Really, I just overheard it. That's the truth." *Please believe me.*

He frowned. "Then the 'voice' you overheard. You thought it reliable?"

"Why wouldn't it be? People don't just tell lies when they're talking aloud to themselves."

His eyebrows shot up as he looked at her doubtfully.

"Okay, I think it would be reliable then. if that's what you need to hear." She thought about the Twlwyth Teg, which might not be trustworthy under normal circumstances, but so far, they had led her in the right direction in this case. It'd be better to avoid talking about a source at all, though. Time to switch topics. "Can you tell me anything about the investigation? Considering that I found Glynnis, I think I should know what's going on. That might help us figure out what the promise was."

. "You know I can't tell you anything. I'd be in trouble if I did."

"But isn't there a bit you could say? I told you what I knew," she begged. The wine was making her dizzy. She felt bolder than she had earlier.

He frowned again, taking another sip of his wine. "Not until I forced it out of you," he reminded her, and then he relented. "Okay, we've interviewed quite a few people, and I don't think it'll hurt to tell you who. Not that all of them are suspects," he warned her.

"Of course not," she agreed, looking at him eagerly.

"We started with you," he grinned, "and then there was Glynnis' family – her parents and her husband. We talked to the protestor she had the run-in with at the pub the night she died, and we just recently found the American you were with that night."

"He's a suspect? Or did you want to verify my whereabouts?" she ventured.

Will gave a little laugh. "He was a person who'd had contact with Glynnis that night, so we needed to talk to him."

"Who else?"

"We tried to find Glynnis' old flatmate, the girl Davyyd Paisley was dating before Glynnis, but she seems to have disappeared for the moment. We talked to her new flatmate and a neighbor."

Bronwyn's heart fluttered. "I know where she is."

"Who? The flatmate?"

"I saw her at the Tanat Inn on Friday night."

He stared at her, and she shifted uncomfortably. "What was she doing there?"

Bronwyn set down her fork and pushed a strand of hair away from her face. "She was following Davyyd Paisley around."

"Stalking him?"

"Oh, no." Bronwyn didn't want to give the wrong impression. "They weren't even together. She had come to the memorial and stayed on to try to help him cope, that's all. They were sitting on opposite sides of the room, and he told me he wasn't interested in her anymore."

"Yet there she was," Will mused. "That's interesting."

"Is she a suspect then?" Bronwyn wanted to know.

Will shook his head. "I'm not sure."

"Shall I try to talk to her?"

His answer was quick and vehement. "No."

She waited for a moment, but he didn't seem to want to offer any more information. Taking another large sip of her wine – and noting that the glass was nearly empty – she took her chance. "Look, we both want this investigation to end. At least, I want to know my name is clear, and I assume you want to solve it. Right?"

"Right," he said warily.

"So why can't I talk to Rhonda if I have the chance? A sympathetic ear might get more information from her than a copper would."

"Because it's not done like that," Will insisted. "I appreciate your contacting me when you overhear something useful, but you know I can't let you put yourself at risk by encouraging you to talk to a possible suspect in the crime. That's my job; let me do it."

"I can be discrete," Bronwyn wheedled.

He shook his head, but caught her eye. "Listen, if you keep telling me when you hear or see something, I'll try not to ask you things like why you walked that footpath in an hour and a half that morning. We know you did it, because there are witnesses who saw you at both ends. But the question is, why?"

Bronwyn lowered her eyes. "Would you believe another anonymous voice?"

"No," Will said shortly. "And that's another reason why we can't work together on this. I need the truth, not anonymous voices."

"I told you it was the truth," she insisted.

"No, you didn't." Will's voice rose, and she could see that he made a conscious effort to lower it. "Look, I said I believe you're innocent, Bronwyn, and I do. No matter what went on between you and Glynnis Paisley, I can't see you killing her over it. But I know you aren't telling me everything you know." He paused and then laughed shortly. "You aren't a very good liar."

Feeling like a schoolgirl caught out and unwilling to give up her secrets, Bronwyn took a deep breath. "Okay, it's true there are things I can't tell you. No matter what you say, I can't and I won't. But I do want to help you solve the crime." She thought for a moment and then lowered her voice. "And I am innocent, no matter that some of the evidence points toward me." *At least, I think am,* she reminded herself, thinking of the dreams. *It's you, it's you, it's you...*

He set his fork down, too, and signaled the waiter for the bill. "What do you say we find somewhere quieter where we can talk more?"

She looked up sharply. "I've told you all I can."

He sighed. "I thought we'd talk about the "rash promise" bit, and I'd rather the other diners at the Royal Oak didn't overhear us, that's all."

"Okay, then." No matter how much she wished he'd take her back home, she guessed now that he wouldn't until he he'd gotten everything from her he'd wanted.

"Can you try to trust me, Bronwyn?" He ran a hand through his tousled hair, watching her intently.

She nodded. "I'm trying to."

They drove back up the A458 toward the coast. A few light clouds had appeared to drift lazily across the sky, and Bronwyn found herself chilled in the open car. *Only May,* she told herself. *Maybe it's a bit early in the year for a drive in a convertible.*

Will either noticed her discomfort or was cold himself because he reached down and cranked up the heat, which billowed out in waves and warmed them quickly. "Good heater," he called over to Bronwyn, raising his eyebrows. "You warm enough?"

"I am now," she shouted back over the noise of the wind.

At Mallwyd he turned south, drove just a few miles, and then exited onto the B4104. "I thought we'd try Aberdyfi," he told her over the noise of the road. She could smell the sea more strongly as they neared the coast, and she nodded, feeling a little insecure again so far from the inland forestland she loved.

The clouds thickened as they merged onto the A493, and Bronwyn was glad when they finally drove into Aberdyfi, a beautiful little village on the coast of mid-Wales.

"I've not been here before, but I thought we could find a shop, maybe get another bottle of wine, and take it to the beach," Will suggested.

Bronwyn glanced at him. *More wine?* She was still unsure of his motive in inviting her out. *I like him,* she admitted, b*ut I don't really trust him, even if I said I'd try to.* Suddenly she wished she'd had more experience with men, at least enough so she could interpret his actions.

In the shop he studied the wine selection, finally choosing a Kendall Jackson reserve pinot noir from the United States – a medium-priced wine that he told Bronwyn he'd had before and enjoyed. He added a sleeve of plastic cups and a corkscrew to his basket before heading for the cashier.

"We could go to a pub alongside the river Dyfi, if you'd rather," he offered as they waited their turn in line, "but I thought we'd have more privacy if we took this down to the beach." He grimaced a little. "It's just that I can't take a chance on someone finding out that I'm telling you things I shouldn't."

Of course! "The beach is fine," Bronwyn agreed. "I've not been to the beach often so it's a bit of a treat for me."

They parked the MGF in a public car park near the marina and walked down onto the sand, where they stopped to take off their shoes. The sand was coarse and cold on Bronwyn's feet, and she found herself floundering in it alongside Will as he walked away from the marina and the congestion of people and cars. Dark clouds were moving in from the west, and the gulls shrieked loudly overhead.

He reached out to take her arm. "It'll be better when we get down to the waterline."

She let him steady her, grateful for his hand on her arm. "Are we going far?"

He nodded up the beach. "Just to the picnic area."

She saw then that a few picnic tables had been set up in a grassy area on a bluff separated from the beach by a bank of grass made pale from the salt coating its leaves and stalks. Sitting up there so close to the sea, she understood that the roar of the waves would effectively mask their conversation from the other brave souls who'd ventured out for a May picnic before the season's warmth had truly set in. It was a good choice for holding a private conversation.

He released her arm as they climbed a short trail up the bank and found a table just being vacated by a family of four – mother, father, and two little boys – who had decided that enough was enough and were heading home for the rest of the afternoon.

Bronwyn sat and put her socks and shoes back on while Will opened the bottle of wine and poured some into the two plastic cups he had brought in his jacket pocket. The roaring of the waves pounded in her ears, the salty tang in the air filled her nostrils, and she let the peace of the sea's vastness calm her. The earlier wine they'd shared with lunch had mellowed her. She'd have to be careful not to drink too much more or she'd lose whatever wariness she had left and tell Detective Cooper everything.

"Let's talk about the rash promise," Will said as he sat down across from her on the picnic table's rough gray bench. "That's a good clue, gives us something to work on." He raised his glass of wine in a salute.

Despite herself, Bronwyn felt a flood of pleasure at his words. The little picnic area was an intimate setting, Bronwyn thought, one that invited confidences. "I've thought about it a lot, but I can't think what it might mean," she confessed.

Will cocked his head to one side, thinking. "Let's start with her husband. "What kind of promise might they make to each other, do you think?"

"Not an ordinary promise, like to love each other forever, but a rash promise," she reminded him. "I can't imagine Davyyd Paisley doing anything rash, so it must have been Glynnis herself that made the promise in that situation."

"She might have promised to stop flirting with other men," Will said thoughtfully, "and then when she wasn't willing to keep her promise, he killed her for breaking it."

"He seemed pretty sad that night at the pub," Bronwyn agreed.

"Sad enough to kill her?"

Bronwyn thought about it. "I don't know him well enough to say. He seems nice, though, more bewildered than angry."

"Still, jealousy can be a powerful motive."

"Maybe the marriage itself was the rash promise." A picture of a flummoxed Davyyd floated in Bronwyn's imagination. "I got the idea there wasn't much of a courtship, just Glynnis telling him she was pregnant and then a quick wedding."

Will laughed. "So Davyyd found himself in a bit of difficulty and rashly promised to love and cherish to the end of his days before he found out what he'd have to put up with from Glynnis?"

Bronwyn grinned. "Makes sense to me."

"Okay, that's a good start. How about the flatmate?" Will sounded happy, relaxed. "What rash promises could have been made between her and Glynnis?"

Bronwyn thought about it, gazing out at the water. She took a sip of her wine, which was good. It might be hard not to drink too much. "It would be something to do with Davyyd," she suggested. "They'd been friends, and then enemies after. Maybe Glynnis promised not to hurt him, but she hurt him anyway when she kept up her flirting. If the other girl truly loved him, she probably wouldn't want him hurt."

"Or she might, if she thought it might bring him back to her," Will pointed out. "Maybe the promise came earlier. What if Glynnis had promised not to try to take Davyyd away from her, and then she did it anyway?"

"That's good," Bronwyn conceded, "very possible."

"My partner and I really need to talk to her," Will said. "Let's move on to someone else. How about the American, Mark McGuire? I'm having a bit of trouble seeing him as a suspect."

"Well, it's easy enough to see what kind of promise Glynnis might have made to him," Bronwyn pointed out. "She was flirting with him, and he was liking it."

"So, she might have led him to expect he'd be meeting her after she got off work, and then maybe she put him off, said no…"

"After leading him on some more, getting him to walk with her up the footpath in the moonlight."

"Interesting idea," Will nodded at Bronwyn. "Very romantic." He picked up the bottle of wine and refilled their cups. "It'd be a classic story, wouldn't it?"

Bronwyn giggled. "And Glynnis would be exactly the type to lead him on for a bit. That's her."

"You'd known her from childhood?" Will asked.

"Sure, and some of my earliest memories are of her bullying me. We were never friends, Glynnis and I. I think I was terrified of her, actually."

Will watched her, and Bronwyn blushed. *I probably shouldn't be harping along on how much I hated her,* she criticized herself. *Too much wine.*

"Anyway…" Bronwyn thought it was time to change subjects again, "how about the protester? Hal Corse?"

"Do you know him?" Will was still studying her, his face serious.

She shook her head and picked up her wine cup for another sip. *Slow down, Bronwyn,* she told herself. "I've heard his name, but I don't know him. All I know is that he lives down the valley, has a farm there. My dad and brother probably know him, though."

Will blinked and glanced away toward the water, watching the waves roll in for a moment. "I can't imagine what promise either Glynnis or Corse could have made to each other that would have drawn her out onto that footpath," he confessed. "It didn't sound as if there was any love lost between them that night."

Suddenly a wave of the futility of it all rolled over Bronwyn. "We're getting nowhere, Will. Neither of us has any idea of what happened really."

He looked at her again. "My old partner and I used to do this kind of thing a lot." He spoke slowly, his voice gentle. "It may not seem helpful at the moment, but then something else will line up with our guesses, and then maybe it'll all fall into place."

"You think so?"

He nodded. "I do."

She looked at him speculatively. "You said your old partner. Not the one you have now?"

"God, no. Notley's an idiot." Will grinned ruefully. "Fancies himself a real Sherlock Holmes. He even uses a cane and has a calabash pipe he smokes in the car."

"He does? Really? Sherlock Notley," she giggled. "When he interviews me again, I'll not be able to keep a straight face. He'll be asking me questions, and I'll be wanting to answer, 'Elementary, my dear Notley."

Will roared with laughter. "Come, Notley, come! The game's afoot."

Bronwyn felt the giggles overwhelm her and she looked away, trying to stop them. After a moment she sneaked a look at Will, though, and both of them dissolved into uncontrollable laughter.

It was a few minutes before either of them were able to speak again, but then Will turned serious. "Notley will be questioning you again this week, you know."

Bronwyn swallowed a giggle and tried to look solemn. "Are you warning me?"

"He'll be wanting to know why you hurried up that footpath on the Sunday morning you found Glynnis."

The giggles disappeared. "You said you wouldn't ask," she implored him, disappointed that he would use a moment when she was feeling easy with him to challenge her again.

"I won't. Notley will." His face brightened. "Was it something Cecil Lumley said to you?"

"Cecil?" she repeated. "No, of course not."

He studied her for a moment longer, then reached out to gather the empty wine bottle and the cups into his hands. "One more question then, before we go? Why was Glynnis' wedding ring missing?"

"Her ring?" Bronwyn repeated. "I hadn't heard about that."

Will grimaced. "I should probably have kept that to myself, but I thought you might have some ideas about it."

Bronwyn shivered. The clouds had thickened and a wind had come up as they'd been sitting there, and she felt suddenly chilled. "I suppose she and Davyyd could have had a fight, and she'd taken it off to tell him she was done with the marriage."

"Or he took it off her finger after he killed her," Will pointed out. "Or she might have taken it off so that whoever she was meeting wouldn't realize she was married."

"Mark McGuire knew she was married. I told him."

"But Glynnis wouldn't have known that, would she?"

"No, I suppose not." Bronwyn pulled her sweater closer around her.

Will stood up. "You're freezing, and it looks like it's going to pour rain any minute. We'd better go."

Bronwyn got to her feet, noting that her head was swimming a little dizzily. "I had a good time, Will," she blurted, mortified as soon as the words were out of her mouth. "Knowing about the ring is good. Now I have something I can try to find out."

"Be careful," he warned her. She could tell by the way he was looking at her that he was intentionally ignoring her words about 'having a good time.' "Don't ask around about the ring, and don't talk to Rhonda Morris, either. Promise me?"

"I won't take any chances," she assured him, not wanting to give him the actual promise.

They dumped the garbage in the bin and then struggled back down the beach through the deep sand. By the time they reached the smooth, wet sand at waves' edge, Bronwyn's feet were numb from the cold, although her head had cleared a little. Will walked close beside her in silence, and she wished their picnic could have gone on longer. She had enjoyed his company in the end, or perhaps she'd simply enjoyed the challenge of discussing the case without revealing anything she meant to keep secret. Either way, she was reluctant to see the day's adventure end.

Rain began to spatter on the roadway as they climbed back into the MGF, so they left the top up and chatted casually as they headed back toward Llangynog. Neither of them ventured into anything serious, keeping their talk about the spring weather and explorations of North Wales they had in common, and beneath their conversation lurked a current of wariness that had returned as soon as they'd left the isolation of the beach.

The rain had cleared inland by the time he saw her to the door of the farmhouse.

"Thank you," he said as the sheepdogs circled them and Bronwyn tried to fend them off so that they didn't muddy their clothes. "Could we do this again sometime?"

Her heart fluttered. *It's only a case to him,* she reminded herself. "I'd like that."

"I'll call," he promised her, "but we'll have to meet on the sly, you know."

"I know," she grinned, "so Sherlock Notley doesn't find out."

"Right," he agreed, but then he looked down at her with a frown. "Call me if you hear anything else. Don't try to solve this case yourself, okay?"

"I won't," she promised him, and she didn't think she would now that she'd found an ally she felt she could trust.

Her dad came to stand beside her at the window as she watched him drive away. "Nice man, then?" he asked gently.

"Yeah, he was," she told him, wondering what would happen if Will Cooper thought about it later and decided that she might have made that rash promise to Glynnis herself after all those years of bullying.

I like you, Will Cooper. Please help me figure out how to prove my innocence, to myself and to you.

Chapter Fourteen

Filled with an exuberance he didn't want to analyze, Will stopped at the junction of the B4391 and the A470 to put the MGF's top back down before driving on west toward Caernarfon. The rain had stopped, and even the sky toward the coast looked clearer. He let out a whoop as the car picked up speed, reveling in the cold wind blowing in his face and allowing his sudden unexplained happiness to run unchecked. It had been a great weekend, even if he had ignored both Lark and Lesley in the end.

At least the joy ran unchecked for the hour or so it took to approach Caernarfon. It wasn't until he drove past the city walls that reality hit him like a wall. *I should not have told her about Notley,* he chided himself then, feeling the contentment fade to a feeling very much like a hangover. *An information hangover,* he thought. *I said too much, and now I am going to be regretting it until it passes. If it does.* Whatever had possessed him to tell her about the missing ring? That, at least, was information that should have been held back, information that would help identify the killer since it hadn't ever been made public. What if Bronwyn mentioned the ring when Notley was questioning her? Will's heart sank. That would put the suspicion squarely back on her, that was certain. And it hadn't been very professional to call Notley an idiot, even if he was one.

Once back home again in his flat, Will poured himself a measure of Famous Grouse and sat in his chair to think. *It was the wine,* he told himself. He'd thought it might loosen Bronwyn's tongue, and it had loosened his instead. He shook his head at his stupidity.

What did it matter? Will tried to put his blunder into perspective. So what if Notley found out that he'd told Bronwyn about the ring? He didn't think Bronwyn would let it slip that they'd met behind Notley's back, but if it came down to it and she mentioned the ring, he might have to admit to it just to divert suspicion away from her again. That meant he'd have to endure a tongue-lashing from Notley and probably face Chief Superintendent Bowers' disappointment, as well. He supposed he might even lose his job over it if Notley had his way. But did he really care?

No, what bothered him more was whether the information he'd shared with Bronwyn would put her in danger. He closed his eyes and sipped his drink. He'd listed the suspects for her. What if she decided to interview them herself, hoping to clear her name on her own? *God, what if she were to be murdered because of something he'd done, some lapse he'd made? It would be Julia all over again, wouldn't it?* It would kill him if it happened again.

I should call her, he thought after a while. *Warn her about mentioning the ring.* He glanced at the time on his mobile phone. *No, too late.* Her parents would think there was something amiss if he called this late at night. *I'll call in the morning,* he promised himself.

But in the morning, he woke late and had to skip breakfast, dashing into the office nearly a half hour late.

"Nice weekend?" Notley asked sarcastically.

Will ran his hand through his unkempt hair. He'd had time for a shower, but not much else. "Fabulous," he mumbled.

"Bowers wants to meet with us this morning," Notley informed him. "Actually, he wanted to meet with us at nine, but half the team was still missing at that time."

Will shrugged. "Sorry about that. Something came up."

"Yeah, I bet," Notley snorted. "I'll call and let him know we're ready."

"Are we?"

"Are we what?"

"Ready?" Will growled. "Maybe we should go over notes again before we talk to him?"

"We'll have to do that later." Notley reached out to pick up his phone. "Can't keep the gov waiting too much longer or he'll think we're scrambling for something to tell him."

Chief Superintendent Bowers glowered at them when they joined him in the conference room. "You're late. It's no wonder you've not made any progress on the case."

"It's my fault, sir," Will spoke up. Why not admit it? Bowers had already spoken to Notley and knew it was Will who was late.

"Maybe a new alarm clock then?" Bowers grumbled, but he had apparently been mollified because he let the matter drop and picked up his dry erase marker. "Where are we?"

Notley glanced sideways at Will and spoke up. "We found the American and talked to him this week."

"Remind me," Bowers barked.

He'd been flirting with Glynnis Paisley in the pub that night she was killed," Notley reviewed it for him. "He'd been there with Bronwyn Bagley, and she took off in a huff afterwards. We thought it might be motive."

"You think Bronwyn Bagley killed her over this man?" Bowers' eyebrows rose an inch. "Isn't that a bit of a stretch?"

"They had a history," Notley explained. "Glynnis bullied her for years. This might have been the thing that put her over."

Bowers nodded. "Or this American met the victim after and, when she wouldn't go along with what he had planned, he killed her."

"We thought of that angle and asked him about it, but he says no. He says he waited for her outside the pub and she put him off, wouldn't have naught to do with him then, so he gave up and went off to the hotel."

"In Llangynog?"

Will consulted his notes. "Llangollen."

"You believe him?"

"We have no evidence to the contrary," Will pointed out.

Bowers thought for a moment and then wrote on the whiteboard. "So, he saw her off when she finished work that night? Is that correct? Did he see her into her car?"

"He said someone called from the car park and she headed over that way." Notley glanced again at Will. "He claims he didn't pay much attention to who it was that called her, as she obviously wasn't interested in him."

"Shame," Bowers said, "so no clues as to an identification."

"It matches up with what our two anonymous callers said."

"Okay, there is that," Bowers said thoughtfully. "Still, check with the hotel in Llangollen to see if anyone can confirm what time he got there that night. Did he have a room to himself, or was he sharing with a mate? Can anyone alibi him?"

"He said he was sharing a room with another of the men. We'll check with him, sir."

"Okay, what else do we have?"

"We walked the footpath from Llangynog to Pennant Melangell ourselves to see how long it takes."

"And?"

"It took us more than four hours," Notley said. "Bronwyn Bagley walked it in less than two hours that morning she found the body. Seems suspicious to me."

"Interesting," Bowers commented. "Have you asked her about it?"

"We didn't push her too much that first time, it being the same day she found the body, but we plan to get back to her again."

"She would walk it faster than we did," Will interjected, feeling self-conscious. "She's used to the route and probably doesn't have to stop and catch her breath as often as we did."

"Still, for her to do it in half the time it took us is odd. We're still going to question her more about it," Notley grumbled, with an annoyed look at Will. "Can't let a contradiction like that go unanswered, not with all the other evidence pointing to her."

"Good. Do it soon., and I expect you to be thorough this time." Bowers wrote on the whiteboard. "What else?"

"We got another tip," Notley told him. "Anonymous, of course."

"Remind me about the others. Two phone calls, weren't they? About the Paisley woman meeting someone after she left the pub?"

"Yes, two to my phone," Notley answered, and Will smirked. He couldn't help it. The important tip had come to his phone, not Notley's. "Both called to say they'd seen Mrs. Paisley after she left the pub. One said she was talking to someone, a taller blonde man, just outside after the bus had gone, and the other said she'd met someone in the car park, someone wearing a hoodie. Medium height, couldn't tell if it was a man or a woman."

"The first caller said definitely a man?"

"He thought a man," Notley supplied. "Taller than Mrs. Paisley."

"So that leaves it open to either a man or a woman," Bowers commented. "She wasn't taller than average, so a woman might have been taller. And it might be anyone calling. Maybe even the killer himself, calling to throw you off the track."

"We thought of that, too," admitted Notley.

"Male or female?"

"Both male voices," Notley told him.

"Quigley's trying to trace them?"

"Yes, he's working on it."

"What about the new call?" Notley waited, his foot tapping lightly on the floor.

"I got that one," Will said, "and it was a good tip. The caller said there was a spot where the hedge had been torn and the fencing broken alongside the footpath to Pennant Melangell just at a farm called Pyll Iago. I got the call after hours, so I went alone to check it out, and I found what looks like the place where Mrs. Paisley was first attacked. It was off the path; not something our people might have seen earlier."

Bowers was standing straighter now, pen poised to write. "Why did you think it was the attack site?"

"Once I walked away from the trail over the hedge, the grass was all mashed down, and it looked like some blood there on the ground, although we'd had quite a bit of rain since the murder. There was a wine bottle, as well – something that might have been what she was clubbed with."

"What does forensics say?"

"We haven't gotten the report yet, but it should be to us today."

"Good work," Bowers complimented him, and Will saw Notley stiffen beside him. "What else?"

Will waited for Notley to speak, hoping to mollify by letting him suggest the plan for the week.

"I thought today we'd spend going over the forensics report, get their take on the wine bottle and the site, and review our notes from the interviews," Notley finally said. "Then I'd like to get back to Llangynog and interview Bronwyn Bagley again."

Bowers nodded. "The parents have been calling, so I'd like you to check in with them, as well. They'll need a bit of an update, just the basics though, of course. We've got to keep them happy."

"Done," Notley said. "We might check with the owners of the pubs to see if they sell the type of wine in the bottle, as well."

"Any other ideas?" Bowers watched them expectantly.

"I've a thought," Will offered. "We've still been unable to locate Rhonda Morris, the girl Davyyd Paisley jilted to marry Glynnis. We talked to her flatmate this week, and she said Miss Morris went to the memorial service and never returned to Cardiff after. I'm thinking we should talk to Davyyd Paisley, see if he knows where she might be found." He'd thought long and hard about how to explain knowing that Rhonda Morris was following Davyyd Paisley around, and he hoped that he'd come up with the right way to lead straight to her without involving Bronwyn or pretending he'd gotten another anonymous phone call. If that kept up, sooner or later someone was going to check his phone records to see if they could trace the calls, and he'd have to explain the fact that there weren't any.

"You didn't ask him about it before?"

"We didn't know she'd gone missing before."

"Good then. It sounds as if you'll have another day or two in Llangynog this week."

"We can't seem to escape the place," Notley agreed as they walked back to their office.

Will spent the morning at his desk, trying to focus on the notes he'd taken during the interviews and jotting down questions he thought of as he did so. Just before midday, the forensics report arrived on their desks.

"No prints on the bottle," Notley reported with a grimace.

I did a good job of wiping it before I turned it in then, Will congratulated himself. Of course, he'd also erased any useable prints that would lead them to the murderer, but it had been the only thing he could think of that would take suspicions off Bronwyn – and himself, he admitted mentally. *If Bowers ever found out, though, that would be the end of my career for sure. Tampering with evidence would not – could not – be tolerated.*

"They found traces of Glynnis Paisley's blood in the grass at the scene," Notley went on, "and a bit on the bottle, just beneath the label where it wouldn't have come off if the bottle was cleaned."

"Then someone did club her over the head with the bottle." Will sorted through the paperwork on his desk and found the earlier forensics report. "A blow to the back of the head," he read aloud.

"Which didn't kill her," Notley added.

"No, but whoever it was dragged her up the path afterward, so it must have done some damage."

Notley was looking at his own copy of the forensics report, frowning. "Didn't Davyyd Paisley say Glynnis was pregnant?"

Will blinked at him. "Yes, he did. Why?"

Notley tapped his finger on the papers. "There's nothing here about it."

Will thought for a moment. "The medical examiner would have made a note of that, wouldn't he?"

"Definitely."

"Maybe he skipped it, not thinking it pertained to the case?"

Notley picked up his phone. "I'll just check on it and see what he says."

Will's mind spun as he waited, watching Notley's face for a sign of what he was hearing from Dr. Francis Roark. Davyyd Paisley had, indeed, said he'd married Glynnis when she'd told him she was pregnant, and – he checked over his notes – Glynnis' flatmate Emma Smith had mentioned it, as well, although she'd said, "apparently Glynnis told him she was pregnant," so in her case it was probably just an educated guess, surmised from something Rhonda Morris had told her in passing. Was it possible that Glynnis had lied about it? Or perhaps she'd suffered a miscarriage early on? In either case, might it not be a reason for both Davyyd Paisley and Rhonda Morris to be angry with Glynnis? Angry enough to kill?

A rash promise? He wondered about that. Perhaps there had been a matter of Glynnis making a rash promise to lure Davyyd Paisley away from Rhonda Morris when they were having a spat and then having to lie to carry it out, or a promise of...

His thoughts were interrupted by Notley's exclamation of excitement. "What one man can invent, another can discover, my dear Cooper. The game's afoot – again!"

"Then she wasn't pregnant?"

Notley shook his head firmly. "Never had been."

"An interesting turn of events, then," Will observed.

"Very much so," Notley agreed with a smug grin.

By the end of the afternoon, Will and Notley had put together a good list of people to talk to a second time, along with nagging questions to ask. The list did include Bronwyn, of course, but Will thought he had managed to keep Notley's pre-planned questions for her to subjects she'd be prepared to answer, unless Notley ventured beyond them, which was likely. He wondered if he should call her and tell her what questions to be ready for. That would be a serious breach of conduct, but it was something he wanted to think about. He'd also be curious to hear what Davyyd Paisley had to say about Glynnis' obvious lie about a pregnancy, though, and if Paisley came through with information about Rhonda Morris' whereabouts, that should also prove an interesting interview.

He stopped by a market on the way home and bought a steak for his dinner, thinking it would be a welcome change from his usual fare of tinned beans on toast and omelets. He'd fry up some chips to go with it and feel more satisfied with his day.

After he'd enjoyed his supper – and it had been a treat – he went out for an evening walk inside the city walls. The castle was beautifully lit at night, dominating the town, and even if the chatter of voices emerging from the open doors of restaurants and pubs drowned the voice of the sea, the salty smell was still on the air in a damp mist that felt appropriately mysterious to Will as he pondered the day's discovery.

At the least, attention had been deflected away from Bronwyn, he thought. *Why am I so set on her being innocent?* He thought about it, not for the first time. There'd been something about her from the start, a sort of combination of vulnerability and strength, that intrigued him. That she had secrets he had no doubt, but he didn't think that whatever she was hiding had much to do with what happened to Glynnis.

Glynnis' mother calls her fey, bewitched, he recalled. *Bewitched, and she works at a 'thin place'...what does all of that mean?* He smiled to himself. *Does she have the second sight then? Is that how she 'hears and sees more than most'?* He shook his head. *Superstition, that's all it is. No one has second sight.*

After a while he sat down on a bench beneath a streetlight and watched the fog swirl in the air around him. He pulled out his mobile phone and scrolled down to Lesley's number. He hesitated, and then he sighed and punched the call button. He'd thought he might take the risk of telling Bowers he had family issues to deal with and would be going to Gloucestershire on the weekend, so it'd be stupid not to make plans before she had something else on her agenda. He could always back out on his plans if Bowers told him no.

She answered on the first ring. "My caller ID says it's Will. How are you, stranger?"

"Good," he replied. "I thought I'd give you a call and see if you were free this Saturday?"

"Saturday I am totally free, especially since it's you asking," she responded quickly. "Did you solve the case?"

"No, and that's why it's just a Saturday," he explained, inexplicably thankful that he had only the weekend free. Bowers had said no weekend work. They might be on rotation to be on call again, but that didn't mean much to Will. "The investigation's been limited to weekdays only, so I thought that unless something urgent comes up, I could see you on Saturday and then get to Gloucester to spend some time with Lark on Sunday."

"Oh, so I'm to share you with Lark then?" Lesley teased. "No romantic weekend in the Lake District?"

He grinned. "Not this time. I've promised her I'd see her soon, and I've been putting her off for too long while we try to solve this case."

"You've been putting me off, too," she reminded him.

"It's been busy," he admitted. "You think of what you want to do, and I'll get there early so we'll have the whole day. Should I call Edward, too?"

"No, this time I want you all to myself," she informed him.

"Okay, then. I'll pick you up at ten."

"I can't wait," she laughed as he rang off.

He glanced at the time. Nearly 10 p.m. He hesitated over the numbers, thinking about that second call, and then he shoved the phone back into his pocket, annoyed with himself for even considering pre-warning Bronwyn about the interview. *What are you thinking, Cooper?* he murmured aloud. No matter how vulnerable she seemed, it wasn't worth the risk of his entire career. She wasn't anything to him, after all.

It was too late to call his parents, but he'd arrange with them to spend Sunday with Lark. If the weather was good, he thought he might take her to Folly Farm. He'd never been there, but he'd seen the advertisements and knew they had plenty of farm animals, including rabbits, that he knew she would love. They could grab some bacon rolls or pastries to eat on the road, spend several hours on the farm, and he'd still have enough time to return her back home and get to Caernarfon at a decent hour. He thought of her, red blonde curls escaping her braids, bright blue eyes alight with curiosity, that sweet way her mouth turned up in a smile at the slightest provocation. Sunday would be a good day.

Tuesday morning found Will and Notley driving west toward Llangynog once again. Notley had called ahead and arranged meeting times with Glynnis' parents Edwirt and Gwnn Newberry, the owner of the Tanat, Cecil Lumley, and most importantly, Davyyd Paisley. Although Notley was anxious to get back to Bronwyn again, the discovery of the previous day made it imperative that they speak with Davyyd Paisley as soon as possible, so they planned a second trip to Llangynog on Wednesday to speak with her.

By then we'll have found Rhonda Morris, Will assured himself. They could interview her on Wednesday, as well, and then the rest of the week would be free to follow up on what they'd found.

Glynnis' parents met them at the door of their cottage.

"It's about time," Gwnn Newberry complained, while her husband watched silently from behind her. "Come in and tell us what you've found. I hope you're making better progress than it appears."

Will followed Notley into the room, choosing to sit on a chintz-upholstered chair in a bright corner near the window. The room's furnishings overwhelmed him. A brightly-patterned sofa competed with checked chairs in bright green and red, all covered in busy floral pillows. The mantel and end tables were crowded with vases of silk flowers, statuettes, and a collection of antique porcelain sheepdog figurines. Heavy floral draperies blocked out some of the sunshine streaming through the windows, but not enough to dampen the cacophony of riotous color.

"We aren't able to tell you much," Notley began apologetically. "We've had several good tips, and we're following some excellent leads, but so far most of what we know we need to keep to ourselves."

"Gobbletygook," snorted Mrs. Newberry. "I want to know what you're really doing. They say if you don't solve a case in the first 48 hours, it probably won't be solved. This has been going on for more than two weeks, and I want to know just what you've accomplished."

Notley sighed, chastened, and Will decided to try his hand at mollifying her.

"As my partner said, we can't tell you everything about the investigation," he began, "but we can tell you a few things."

She was watching him avidly. "Such as?"

Will glanced at Mr. Newberry, who had yet to say a word. "Several eyewitnesses have come forward to say that Glynnis met someone in the car park after she was done at the Tanat Inn the night she was murdered," he continued. "This was after the final bus had left, incidentally. Would you have any idea who she'd be meeting?"

Mrs. Newberry snorted. "If it wasn't Davyyd, it's hard to tell who it might be. Do you have a description?"

"We don't have a reliable one," Will admitted. "Did you see anyone she might have met after work that night, Mr. Newberry? You were at the Tanat Inn earlier in the evening, I understand."

Glynnis' father looked down at his feet, which were clad in well-worn boots. He thought for a long moment, and then shook his head. "It could have been Davyyd, waiting for her to get off. We've only his word he left Llangynog earlier, after all."

"How about the protester, Hal Corse?"

"Suppose it could have been him, too."

"Or the American she was flirting with? Will persisted.

"Don't know anything about that," he insisted, glancing at his wife.

Will nodded at Notley, who took over the questioning. "Glynnis wasn't wearing a wedding ring when she was found. Did she have one on earlier in the evening?"

Mrs. Newberry glared at him. "Of course, she was wearing her ring. What do you think, she'd take it off? I'd say whoever killed her stole it afterward."

Notley met her look. "You're sure?"

"Of course, I'm sure," she snapped.

He turned to Mr. Newberry. "Was she wearing it while she was working that night?"

The man's shoulders slumped. "Guess she was," he mumbled. "Didn't see for sure, but then, I wasn't noticing things like that, was I?"

"No, sir, there's no reason you would," Will assured him. He exchanged a look with Notley, and then took the plunge. "Was Glynnis pregnant?"

Mrs. Newberry's eyes flew open in shock at the baldness of the question, but her husband simply slouched further down in his seat. "What's that got to do with anything?" she demanded, her face reddening.

"Maybe nothing, but you never know what's important until you're done with an investigation," Will soothed her.

"Can you answer the question, ma'am?" Notley pushed her.

"Said she was," mumbled Mr. Newberry, to Will's surprise. He hadn't expected the man to speak when his wife was clearly the one in charge.

"And was she?" Notley demanded.

The man eyed him. "Don't think so," he replied carefully.

"Of course, she was!" Mrs. Newberry rounded on her husband viciously. "If Glynnis said it was so, then it was true."

The man shrugged. "Guess so, then," he conceded.

"Clearly Mr. Newberry knows more than his wife's willing to let him say," Notley observed as they walked back toward the centre of the village.

"They were both a bit bothered by that line of questioning," Will agreed. "What one man can invent, another can discover."

"You're getting pretty good with the quotes," Notley told him. As if it had reminded him of something, he reached into his pocket and pulled out his pipe and tobacco pouch. He stopped to push some tobacco into the pipe's bowl, and then sealed the packet up again and put it back into his pocket. "Do you think Glynnis invented the idea that she was pregnant?"

"I think everyone thought Davyyd Paisley was a good catch for Glynnis, and it might have proved embarrassing to think that she'd won him through lies and deceit."

Notley puffed on his pipe and nodded. "It's a wicked thing to tell fibs."

Will grinned. "Is that a quote, too?"

"Sherlock Holmes," Notley assured him.

They'd timed their visit with Cecil Lumley before the lunch rush so that he would be able to talk with them while serving the day's few early patrons.

"Course we carry Glyndwr sparkling wine," he blustered as he nodded toward a couple of men who'd just entered the pub. "Get to you in a minute," he called to them before he turned back to Will and Notley. "We try to carry a good selection of local wines. Tourists like them."

"Can you tell us how many bottles were sold the night Glynnis Paisley was killed?" Notley asked him.

"If you can wait a minute," he answered, "while I get these men their drinks, then I'll check on it."

They waited, watching him pull the pints the men had ordered and deliver them to the table. He returned, red-faced and blustering, and sat down on a bar stool, pulling a laptop computer sitting on the counter closer to him.

"We only sell it by the bottle," he explained as he scrolled through his records, "so the sale would be marked in the inventory for tax purposes. Ah, here's the night. Let's see…" They watched him count to himself as he scanned the page. "It looks like six bottles, four paid for in cash and the other two by credit card."

"Can we get the cardholders' names?" Notley asked.

Lumley tore off a piece of a napkin and scribbled. "Here you go."

The owner of the New Inn across the road told them he did not stock many local wines, but the Glyndwr sparkling white was among the few they carried. Unfortunately, he did not keep as thorough records as Cecil Lumley did and could not say if any had been sold the night Glynnis was murdered. "Sorry," he told them cheerfully. "How's the case coming along?"

"We're getting close," Notley assured him as they left the New Inn and headed back to the car park.

"We can put Quigley on tracking down the people who bought the wine with credit cards," Will suggested.

"My idea exactly," Notley agreed.

They had arranged to meet Davyyd Paisley on his lunch break on site of the future gas pipeline along the Tanat Valley floor. They stopped by the car park in order to retrieve their wellies from the boot of the Volvo, having learned on their previous excursion up the footpath that it was better to come prepared than to destroy a pair of shoes along the way.

He had obviously been watching out for them, Will noted, as he set down his laptop computer and came to meet them when they approached.

"How's the investigation coming along?" he greeted them, calling out in a friendly voice that made Will wince, knowing what was to come.

"We're making good progress," Notley assured him, coming to stand facing him in the tall spring grass. The river flowed quietly beside them, burbling contentedly as it made its quiet way down the valley.

"I'd offer you a seat," Davyyd Paisley said, "but there are none to be had."

"It looks like a good fishing stream, though," Will observed.

The man smiled, an easy smile that came naturally to his good-natured face. "Plenty of dark pools where the trout can hide," he agreed.

Notley was watching him. "We won't keep you long from your work," he broke in with a glance at Will that said he was irritated with the idle chatter.

"Whatever I can do to help, I'm happy to do."

"Okay, then," Notley peered at his notepad as if reading something written on it, although Will knew for a fact that it was a blank page he stared at. "You told us earlier that you'd married Glynnis because she told you she was pregnant. Is that right?"

The smile faded from Davyyd Paisley's face. "It's true. She did tell me she was pregnant, and that's when I decided we'd better get married."

"You'd not have been in such a hurry otherwise?" Notley inquired.

The man frowned at him. "What are you getting at?"

Notley sighed. "Let's go at this a different way, then. You were dating her flatmate, and then you had an affair with her, she said she was pregnant, and then you asked her to marry you. Do I have all of that right?"

"That's right."

"And was it true?" Notley watched him carefully now.

"Was what true?"

"Was she pregnant, or did she just tell you she was?"

Davyyd Paisley's face told them the truth before he said it. "She lied to me," he admitted. "She told me a month or so ago that she'd miscarried, but I knew better by then. It was all a lie."

Will spoke up. "You must have been pretty angry with her."

Glynnis' husband looked at him, his eyes empty. "What could I do? All I could think of was what a mess I'd made of it all, and just because of that day when Glynnis was home alone in the flat and Rhonda wasn't." He gazed toward the river. "I couldn't put all the blame on Glynnis; I was at fault as much as she was."

"You were trapped," Notley surmised.

Davyyd Paisley turned to stare at him. "I loved Glynnis. I did." But there was no strength in his voice to back it up.

"A lie like that would be hard to forgive considering that you'd left a longtime girlfriend suffering as a result," Will supplied.

"It would," the man admitted. "It would."

"So, your relationship with her changed after that, didn't it?" Notley went on. "You didn't trust her anymore. You wondered how else she'd duped you? And then that night at the Tanat Inn, there she was flirting with that American. You couldn't help but be angry."

Davyyd Paisley reached up to run a hand through his already-tousled hair. "That's why I left her there. I couldn't watch her anymore."

"But you waited for her after?" Notley suggested.

"No, I didn't. What are you suggesting? That I killed Glynnis because of a lie?" He shook his head decisively. "No, you've got that wrong. I just didn't want to wait around to see who she'd come out of the Tanat with at the end of the evening."

Notley smiled like a Cheshire cat. "Okay, then, let's go on to something else."

Now Davyyd Paisley watched him warily. "What is that?"

"We're still looking for your former girlfriend, Rhonda Morris. Her flatmate told us she'd come to the memorial service and then never returned to Cardiff."

The man's face paled. "She did come to the service," he muttered. Will could see that he was leaving out the rest.

"Do you know where she is now?" Notley asked.

Will watched Davyyd Paisley struggle with what to say. *He's already hurt her by marrying Glynnis,* he thought. *Now he'd like to protect her if he can.* But if he lied, they'd soon find out, and he knew that. He was neatly trapped.

"She's....she's in Oswestry," he stammered at last.

"Seeing you." Notley did not make it a question.

"No," Davyyd Paisley protested. "We're not seeing each other."

"Then why is she there?" Notley asked softly.

He knows the man is trapped, Will thought, wanting to help, but unable to.

"She thought she could help me through this," Davyyd Paisley told them carefully. His shoulders drooped, and he looked as if he were going to cry. "I've been avoiding her as much as I can."

"Why?" Notley's voice rose. "Why not fall back into her arms, as they say?"

"I...there's too much that's wrong between us now," Davyyd Paisley stuttered. "I messed up, and no matter what Rhonda says, there'd always be a wall between us."

"So, you aren't interested in renewing your affair with Miss Morris?" Notley pushed him.

"No, I'm not. I'll move on eventually, but not with Rhonda. Not with her."

Notley paused, and Will decided to end the man's torture. "Where could we reach Miss Morris, sir? We've been looking for her, need to ask her a few questions."

Davyyd Paisley's affable face had crumbled. "She's at the Wynnstay Hotel in Oswestry, last time I heard anyway."

"Thanks for that," Will said. "We'll just have a little chat with her then."

"Thanks for your cooperation," Notley added needlessly, for both of them knew that Davyyd Paisley's cooperation had been forced, at best.

As they strolled the footpath back toward Llangynog, Notley swung his cane triumphantly. "We've made great progress today, Cooper."

"I'm not sure what it all means, though," Will warned him. "We may be on the wrong path entirely."

"We may be," Notley agreed, "but we're getting closer, and I've a feeling we're on the verge of pushing the villain out into the open."

But that was not to be....not yet.

Chapter Fifteen

Wednesday morning found Will and Notley cruising along the A470 toward Llangynog, hopeful of locating Rhonda Morris somewhere in either Llangynog or Oswestry early in the day and then meeting Bronwyn for a scheduled interview at three that afternoon. Glynnis' former flatmate still had not contacted them, but they told themselves that could mean that neither her current flatmate nor her neighbor had informed her that they wanted to talk to her as easily as it could mean she was avoiding them. Of course, it also meant she was ignoring their voice mail messages. Will just hoped that it didn't mean she had taken the fact that they were looking for her as an alert and decided to go into hiding. Quigley had managed a photo from her family, so at least they had that to go on as they maneuvered through the village streets looking for her. It wasn't the most efficient way to locate a person of interest in a case, but sometimes things had to be done the hard way.

The sun had come out again, dissipating some early fog on the coast and becoming brilliant as they had driven inland past forested hills and rolling hillsides. Lines of thick trees marked the boundaries of fields where cattle and sheep grazed, and twice they had glimpsed thousand-year-old ruins in the distance. It had been a peaceful drive, thanks to Notley's contemplative silence.

"Davyyd Paisley would have told Rhonda Morris we're looking for her." Will broke the silence as he maneuvered around a cluster of bicyclists in his lane. "It looks bad for her that she hasn't bothered to contact us."

"Doesn't mean much," Notley disagreed. "Surely in drugs and alcohol you had lots of people you were trying to talk to who didn't return calls. Most of the time it just means that people these days would rather avoid us than help us out."

Will thought about that. He'd concentrated more on Rhonda Morris – and Davyyd Paisley – since his lunch with Bronwyn on Sunday, and if the 'rash promise' idea that Bronwyn said she'd overheard meant anything, he liked how it connected to one – or both - of them. "She has motive," he said at last. "Glynnis stole the love of her life from her, and she did it under false pretenses. Once she found that out, she would have been furious, I would think. It would explain the viciousness of the knife wounds and the missing wedding ring."

Notley shrugged. "Love triangles happen more often than we think. Usually, they don't lead to murder."

Will sighed. *We'll find out soon enough,* he told himself as he lapsed back into silence and his own thoughts.

He had thoroughly enjoyed meeting with Bronwyn on Sunday once he'd managed to put her at ease. He couldn't think of her as Miss Bagley any longer; she was Bronwyn in his mind, not a good thing when she was one of their major suspects, but there it was. He couldn't help it. Not only was she lovely to look at and charming to talk to, but the play of words as they tried to give each other a minimum of information while extracting as much as possible from the other had been entertaining, a game of sorts. While he had tried to be on his guard, he had found himself relaxing into an exchange very much like the ones he used to share with Edward, his former partner, as they brainstormed the possibilities from evidence they had gathered. He had felt alive again, engaged in the chase as it were. It had been a welcome feeling and, despite the information hangover he had suffered afterward, it had left him exhilarated.

They arrived in Oswestry mid-morning, and Will drove through the village slowly and found a parking space on the first pass through. A mix of multi-story brick and half-timbered buildings lined the streets, many with street-level shops. Cobblestone streets added to the charm, and Will noticed several areas where benches and flower boxes had been set for pedestrians to rest or enjoy a lunch outdoors.

They walked past the shops, listening to the chatter of tourists and watching for the Wynnstay Hotel. They found it on Church Street, a tall brick building with gleaming white columns supporting the covered entranceway and small flower boxes filled with petunias hanging from each side.

Inside, they approached the check-in desk and showed the attendant their warrant cards.

"We're looking for a Miss Rhonda Morris," Notley told him.

The man consulted his computer. "We have her staying here, room 236."

"Do you know if she's in at the moment?"

The clerk glanced up at him. "She went out earlier. Miss Morris has been staying with us for over two weeks now, so I'm familiar with her. She generally goes out after breakfast and returns in the evening."

"Does she eat breakfast here at the hotel?"

The man nodded. "Most of the time." He hesitated, giving them a distrustful look. "What did she do, may I ask?"

Notley returned his distrust with superiority. "She did nothing that we know of. We had some questions for her about a case we've been working on, that's all."

"Because," the clerk went on as if Notley had not spoken, "she's a lovely girl, very nice, friendly. I heard she might have some connection to that murder up in Pennant Melangell. Is that why you're here?"

"We really can't say," Notley insisted.

"Does she dine alone?" Will broke in, trying to ease the tension apparent between the two.

"She's always alone at breakfast," the man sniffed. "I wouldn't know about her other meals, as I'm not here on the evening shift."

Notley nodded. "Have you seen her with a man, tall, brown hair?"

"No, not at all." The man turned to his computer and began to type. "If you'll excuse me, I have work to do."

Notley watched him for a moment. "Okay, then, thanks for your time."

"It looks like Rhonda Morris made a conquest," Will observed as they emerged onto the street.

"He did seem a bit smitten," Notley agreed. "Where do you suppose she goes every day?"

"Stalking Davyyd Paisley," Will supplied what seemed to him the obvious answer. "She's probably in Llangynog keeping a watch on him right now."

Notley sighed and pulled his pipe and tobacco pouch from his pocket. "I wish she'd call us. I hate wasting time searching for someone who's probably not even in the picture for this crime."

"Should we check at the Smithfield before we leave town? Maybe someone saw her there with Davyyd Paisley, not that it matters that much since they obviously have a past together. Still, if they were spotted enjoying a candlelight dinner, we might have something."

Notley waved up the street with his pipe in hand. "Lead on, Cooper. It can't hurt to check."

Their unplanned stop at the Smithfield Hotel proved much more successful than their planned chat with the clerk at the Wynnstay.

They went into the hotel's restaurant, Will glancing at his watch and wondering if it was too early for lunch as he remembered the seafood pancakes he'd enjoyed when they'd met Davyyd Paisley there.

The hostess greeted them and directed them to one of the waiters who usually worked the evening shift but had taken an extra shift that day to cover someone who was ill.

Notley showed him the picture they had of Rhonda Morris.

"Sure, I've seen her," the man said. "She's been in several times to have dinner with one of our guests."

"That would be Davyyd Paisley," Notley told him.

"I don't know. His check goes on his tab, so I don't see his name."

"Tall man, dark hair, friendly sort of face?"

"Could be," the man allowed. He gestured toward the photo. "I remember her because she was so pretty, and he didn't seem that interested. You know? Here's this gorgeous girl trying her best to be the girl of his dreams, and he's got a look on his face like the last place on earth he wants to be is sitting at a table with her."

"When were they here last?"

The man frowned, thinking. "Not last night, but maybe the night before? He's been staying here awhile, maybe two or three weeks, and he comes in to eat alone about half the time. I heard he's working on the pipeline down the Tanet Valley, but he doesn't seem to hang out with the other engineers on the project. It was his wife was murdered there, wasn't it? I think I saw him with that other woman on Monday night, but not on Tuesday."

They thanked him for the information and, with a final longing glance at an empty table, Will followed Notley from the restaurant and the hotel.

"On to Llangynog?" he asked as Notley stood on the sidewalk looking up and down the street.

"We've plenty of time before our interview with Bronwyn Bagley. Maybe we should have a stroll around town, see if we spot her by chance?"

"Sure." Will wasn't going to argue. He'd had enough of sitting around Llangynog's pubs to last him a long time, and surely there was more chance of Rhonda Morris hanging around in Oswestry, where there were at least a few shops to entertain her, than of her lurking around Llangynog waiting for Davyyd Paisley to finish his work for the day.

They walked up Church Street as far as it went, glancing into the shop windows and doors, and then they crossed the roadway and started back down. They were nearly to the village centre when Notley's mobile phone rang.

Will waited while Notley swiped the phone and turned away to talk. Oswestry was a pretty village, he thought, with plenty of shops and pubs. Maybe he should bring Lesley here sometime. She would enjoy the shops at least, and it wasn't such a long drive from Caernarfon if she were to come for a weekend. There must be a castle in the area they could visit, as well, this being Wales where castles were found every few miles. The English had been very determined to subdue their enemies those many years ago.

He turned at Notley's exclamation of triumph. "Guess what, Cooper? That was Rhonda Morris calling. She's going to meet us in an hour at the restaurant in the Wynnstay Hotel. We're buying her lunch."

Will looked at his partner in amazement. "She called?"

"She called," Notley grinned. "We can interview her, have some lunch, and still be in Llangynog early for our meeting with Bronwyn Bagley. Is there anyone else we should talk to again while we're in the area?"

"Hal Corse?" Will wondered.

"If there's time, we could look him up, see if he's still involved with the protesters."

They wandered back up Castle Street to one of the small pedestrian areas where they found a free bench to sit on while they waited.

Notley leaned his cane against a corner of the bench, filled his pipe and lit it, taking a puff and sitting back with pleasure. "There's nothing like a pipe to comfort you on a spring day."

Will glanced sideways at him, remembering how Bronwyn had laughed when he'd told her about Notley. "It's bad for your health," he said sourly, regretting the words as soon as he'd said them. There was no need to antagonize Notley; he was caustic enough toward Will when they were getting on nicely.

But Notley wasn't in the mood to take offense. "Who's it down to then, Cooper?"

Will considered. "I'm liking the American, Mark McGuire."

Notley's eyebrows went up in surprise. "Why?"

Because the idea of a rash promise fits, Will thought. "Glynnis was flirting with him earlier in the evening. Maybe when she finished up at the pub, he talked her into a moonlight hike up the footpath. She took off her ring, hoping he wouldn't know she was married, encouraged him. And then for some reason she decided not to go through with it, put him off, and he was mad enough to hurt her."

"Possible, but not likely," Notley told him, puffing on his pipe from the side of his mouth. "Why would he be mad enough to kill her? Murder is a big leap for someone who's just a rejected lover, and this one was particularly savage. Someone was in a real rage. You think this American goes around murdering every girl who agrees to a date and then backs out?"

"He's a solicitor," Will reminded him. "Maybe he thinks he knows enough to get away with it."

Notley pulled the pipe out of his mouth. "I think you're wrong."

"You can't see him as an American serial killer? Okay then, who do you like for it?"

Notley pondered, and then took the pipe and tapped it alongside the bench. "Since you don't want me to say Bronwyn Bagley, I'll go with Rhonda Morris and Davyyd Paisley together. Former lovers, torn apart by Glynnis' lie. Why wouldn't they want their revenge? They lured her out onto the footpath that night, killed her, and threw the wedding ring away as a sort of statement."

"A way of shouting out that the marriage was over?" Will agreed, liking the idea. "But why not just a divorce? Why kill her?"

"Maybe she had something else she could hold over them," Notley suggested.

"Bleeding them for settlement money or something," Will agreed. "Or they were just that angry that they needed revenge."

"That's the way I see it," Notley said. "We'll have to hope one of them makes a mistake, says something out of turn."

"We still don't have a murder weapon, other than the bottle, and that didn't kill her," Will reminded him. "Maybe when we find it, we'll have a fingerprint that will point to whoever it is."

Notley nodded. "The case is far from over," he said.

They waited forty-five minutes and then decided to go to the restaurant and wait for Rhonda Morris to arrive.

They had been seated and were settling into chaste glasses of iced tea when she was shown to their table. They stood to greet her.

She was lovely, Will thought immediately. Fresh-faced and healthy, she was of above-average height and willowy slender, graceful in her movements. Her blonde hair showed just a touch of dark at the roots, and Will wondered if she'd dyed it in order to look more like her rival, Glynnis Paisley, as she attempted to reconnect with Davyyd Paisley. Brilliant green eyes lit her face, and a smattering of pale freckles kept her looking like the girl next door rather than some conceited movie star. *Rhonda Morris would have presented quite a challenge to Glynnis,* he thought. *It wouldn't be easy to steal a boyfriend from someone who looks like this, especially when they'd been together for some time.*

"I'm sorry I didn't call you earlier," she apologized to them once she was seated and had ordered her own glass of iced tea. "I got your messages on my mobile, but I ...well, I was intimidated at the thought of contacting you. I guess I thought if I just waited a bit, you'd find whoever did this to Glynnis, and then I'd be able to avoid it entirely."

"The case is carrying on longer than we hoped," Will told her, "and we've been anxious to talk with you."

"I don't know how I can be of any help."

Notley smiled at her reassuringly. "You never know what you might say that would lead us to the killer."

Will glanced at him, remembering their conversation from earlier, and suppressed the instinct to go easy on this girl. She was high on his list of suspects, just as she was on Notley's, and it wouldn't do to enable her avoidance of the sensitive topics they would have to broach with her just because she looked innocent.

"We already know you and Glynnis had a major falling out a couple of months ago," Will began once their meals had been delivered, beating Notley to the punch. He looked at Notley out of the corner of his eye to see if he objected, but Notley simply picked up his sandwich and took a bite.

"We weren't on the best of terms," she admitted, picking at her salad with a fork. She seemed nervous now that they were down to it, and Will suspected that most of the salad would go uneaten.

"Did the two of you get on well before that?" Will thought he'd move away from the confrontation for the moment and try for a more complete picture of their relationship first.

Rhonda Morris bit her lip, staring down at her plate. It took a moment before she answered. "I think we got on well enough at first. We were both busy with classes, and I had a job then, as well, to help pay for my schooling. We went out together in the evenings sometimes."

"Where did you go?"

"To films or out for a bite to eat, sometimes to a pub."

Will watched her. *Nervous. She doesn't want to look me in the eye. Why?* "Did Davyyd go with you when you went out together?"

She looked up at that and then away. "No, we only went out together when Davyyd was busy."

"So, the three of you never went to get something to eat together or out for a casual drink?"

"No."

Will waited, watching her, hoping for her to become uncomfortable enough to elaborate.

She did. "I...Glynnis tended to be more friendly with Davyyd than I was comfortable with, even from the beginning. That's why I wouldn't have invited her along when he took me out somewhere."

"You didn't trust her?"

"I trusted her well enough, I think. But she had this thing about her. She seemed to enjoy the challenge of taking girls' boyfriends away from them." She glanced up and then down again, again picking absently at her salad with her fork. "She'd do it when we'd go out for a drink. Pick someone out, some couple, and then I'd watch while she'd happen to bump into the guy or something, chat him up, see if she could steal him away. It was like a game for her, you know?"

"So Glynnis had enemies, and she didn't mind making more?"

Rhonda Morris swallowed, nodding. "I guess you could say that. No girl wants to think her man can be so easily led astray."

Including you, Will thought. "Then you disapproved of what Glynnis was doing?"

She blushed, color spreading from her neck up into her hairline. "Not at first. I thought it intriguing, funny, if truth be known. We'd laugh about it after...how mad the girls were, how easy the men were to distract."

"When did you first suspect she might intend to do this to you?" Notley had finished his sandwich and crisps and decided to take over.

She sighed, thinking. "Glynnis always flirted with Davyyd. I never did like that. And then after I saw how much she enjoyed stealing other girls' boyfriends, I tried to keep him away from her as much as I could. I guess you could say I realized what she was capable of, and it wasn't funny any longer."

She must have been something, Glynnis, to be able to lure Davyyd away from this girl and not let her conscience bother her. "And then there was that day she was alone in the flat when he came to visit."

She looked up again at that, and her face was desolate. "I didn't know he was coming to visit."

"He didn't know your schedule?"

"I'd taken an extra shift at the shop. I had a class cancelled at the last minute and then they called and asked, and I said okay, I'd do it. I didn't know Davyyd was coming to see me." Tears filled her eyes, and she dabbed at them with her napkin. "I'm sorry. It still hurts me so."

"I can imagine," Will broke back into the conversation, wondering how to make it easier on her. Despite himself, he had to feel compassion for this lovely girl. "Did you find out right away they'd been together?"

She sniffled, rubbed at her eyes and then offered an embarrassed half-grin. "I'm sorry. I should be over it by now. It was just so hard.

I thought Davyyd and I were a couple for life, that we would be married when we both finished school. I felt so betrayed."

She hadn't answered his question, Will realized, wondering if it was important enough to ask again. "How did you find out about their affair?"

"That's the other embarrassing part. I didn't. I had no idea. Davyyd had left by the time I got home that evening, and of course Glynnis said nothing. It wasn't until...until they told me she was pregnant, that they were getting married..." She trailed off, catching a sob in her throat.

"They told you together?" Will said as gently as he could.

She struggled to contain tears. "No....it was Davyyd. He came one day when Glynnis was gone out and sat on my sofa and told me."

"How did you react?"

She looked at him, and he felt she was being genuine. No one could put on an act like this one. "I was devastated, thought my world had come to an end. I cried and I...I guess I screamed. I was so angry, you see...so mad at Glynnis for doing that to me. And I was so hurt. Davyyd....I loved him so." She stopped, seeming unable to continue.

Will sat back in his chair, waiting for her to regain some of her composure. After a few moments, he asked, "Did you see either of them after that?"

She shook her head. "Glynnis had moved her stuff out before Davyyd told me. I realized that later, after he'd left. I didn't want to see them after that."

Notley leaned toward her. "Where were you the night she was murdered, if I may ask?"

Will winced at the bald question. "We have to ask that of everyone who had a possible conflict with Glynnis."

She looked from Will to Notley. "I knew you'd ask for an alibi, and I'm afraid I don't have one. I was home alone in the flat. My flatmate, Emma, had gone home for the weekend to see her mum."

"She didn't come back that Sunday night?"

Rhonda chewed on her lip. "She had no classes on Mondays, so she usually stayed over."

Notley consulted the notes he had been scribbling as she talked. "So, let me see if I've got this right. You never saw Glynnis or Davyyd again until after Glynnis died. And then you saw Davyyd at the memorial service. Is that right?"

She nodded, silent.

Will watched her, alert to changes in her demeanor. She was hard to read, being already upset, but he thought he saw a wariness come over her.

"Can you tell us about seeing him there, what you said to each other?"

"I...it was awkward. I tried to stay in the background, but I wanted to let him know I was there if he needed me." She looked at Will pleadingly. "Who else would he have to turn to? Who would know how to help him get over it?"

He nodded at her encouragingly. "You waited a bit before approaching him?"

She brightened. "Exactly. I waited until after the service, when they were out in front of the church greeting everyone, and when I saw him alone for a moment, I went over to him."

"What was his reaction?"

"He...he didn't seem to want me there, but I'm sure it was just because Glynnis' parents were there and he didn't want them to think anything bad of him. I hugged him and told him I was staying in Oswestry at the Wynnstay Hotel if he wanted to meet and talk later."

"And then what did you do?"

"I left. I came back to Oswestry and sat in my room and waited for him to call."

"What about your classes? Your job?"

"Neither mattered to me as much as Davyyd did." Rhonda seemed unembarrassed at the admission.

Notley took over again. "And he did call?"

She looked at him with a slight smile lighting her tear-stained face. "The next day."

"You've been seeing each other again?" Notley concluded.

"No, not really," she elaborated. "We've met for dinner a few times, talked a bit, but it wouldn't be appropriate for us to get back together so quickly, would it?"

"Does Davyyd seem to want to get back together with you?" Notley asked a crucial question, and Will listened carefully for her response.

She hesitated. "Not right now, of course." Despite her efforts, tears formed again in her eyes, and she blinked rapidly. "And he's right. It's too soon. He doesn't want people to think badly of him, which they might if he moved on too fast." She eyed them. "Even you might think it wasn't right."

"But he's indicated that he wants the two of you to be together again once all this is past?" Notley persisted.

She took a moment to gather herself before answering. "Right now, he says he doesn't see us getting back together ever, but I know once he's had time to get over this thing with Glynnis, he'll change his mind. I want to be there when he does. I'm the one he needs. I was always the one he deserved because he's a really good person. I love him with all my heart, and I won't let anyone else hurt him like Glynnis did. He'll see that once things settle down again. I'm not sorry Glynnis died."

She calls it 'this thing with Glynnis,' not his marriage, Will mused, trying to keep his expression neutral. All of a sudden, she was sounding rather desperate.

"What are you doing here in Oswestry," Notley asked her, "if Davyyd isn't interested in renewing your relationship right now?"

She blushed again, wiping at the tears. "I probably shouldn't be here," she admitted, "but I want to be close by in case he needs me."

Notley nodded at that, smiling at her, a feral smile.

His crocodile smile, Will thought, *luring her into a false sense of security before springing the trap.*

He was right. "When did you find out Glynnis had lied about being pregnant?" Notley blurted, startling both Will and Rhonda Morris.

She stared at him, face mottled with tears. It took another long moment before she composed herself enough to speak. "It was Glynnis who told me, Glynnis herself. She ran into me in a shop, stopped to....I guess you'd say she taunted me. Told me how easy it was to steal Davyyd away, how easy it had been for him to believe the lie." She looked up at them, her eyes huge in her face. "She told me she'd lied, just like that."

"How did you react?"

Her voice quaked. "I didn't know what to say. I think I just backed away, just wanted to get away from her so I could think."

"No shouting match in the shop then?" Notley asked cruelly.

She swallowed, reached for her iced tea. "No, that's not my style." She thought for a moment and then gave them a glimpse of the nice girl the hotel clerk had been smitten with. "I'd have forgiven her, you know. I hated her for hurting Davyyd because I still love him. But I would have forgiven her if she'd let him go after."

They let her compose herself again before feeling they could leave her alone to try to finish her meal. She picked at her salad in silence, eating little. Finally, she looked up at them and tried to smile. "I know this wasn't a very good interview. I knew I'd be emotional; that's why I didn't call you back sooner. But I hope it helped somehow."

"It's been very helpful," Notley assured her as they paid the check and left.

"Now, that was something," Notley commented as they walked toward the Volvo waiting alongside the roadway in front of a "Pins and Needles" shop.

Will nodded agreement. "She's a mess, completely devastated by what happened."

"Do you think she's capable of murder?"

Will pictured her face, happy light freckles and a natural tendency to smile washed out by the streaking of tears. "I think Glynnis' thoughtlessness ruined some lives, and Rhonda's clearly not thinking logically about it all."

"And that Glynnis got joy from it," Notley concluded in disgust. "Still, Miss Morris seems a nice enough girl. I can't picture her attacking someone as viciously as Glynnis was attacked."

"Desperation pushes us beyond what we think we're capable of," Will said. "I don't think we'd be wise to rule her out just yet."

Will had been dreading the interview with Bronwyn all morning, but now that the time was fast approaching, he felt inexplicably more at ease. Maybe it was the result of their questioning of Rhonda Morris that put his mind at rest, for however their meeting with Bronwyn went, he thought it had to pale in comparison with Rhonda's emotional distress.

Their lunch with Rhonda Morris had taken longer than expected so that there was no time to look up Hal Corse before they met with Bronwyn.

"I can't think of what we'd have asked him anyway," Will confessed.

"Sometimes you just ask the same questions as before and hope their story changes," Notley informed him.

Don't change your story, Bronwyn, Will thought, mentally telegraphing a warning.

Bronwyn had arranged to meet them in her office at the counseling centre. "It's the middle of my workday," she'd explained when Notley called, "so it's easier for me if you can meet me here." Will wondered, though, if she simply wanted to spare her parents any further worry that might arise from knowing that a second interview had been scheduled.

She'd pushed an extra chair into the small office so that everyone could sit, despite the crowded conditions. Her desk was overflowing with loose papers. "St. Melangell's feast day," she explained. "May 27th. We're having an organized walk and mountain bike ride. I'm a bit overwhelmed, I'm afraid." She glanced at Will, and the ghost of a smile curved her lips. "Please, sit down."

"This won't take long," Notley said, and Will hesitantly let him take the lead.

Bronwyn sat back in her office chair, keeping her eyes on Notley, a fact for which Will was extremely grateful. *Please don't give me away,* he pleaded mentally. *Don't let on that you know about the ring. Don't mention the rash promise.*

"I'm not sure that there's anything more I haven't told you," Bronwyn said. "I was late for church services in the village, so I walked to Pennant Melangell for the afternoon service there, and I found Glynnis in the churchyard. That's all."

"But it's not quite all, is it?" Notley contradicted her softly. "We walked that footpath. So did our forensics people. And we checked the blogs on the internet. Two hours – or less – is a far shorter time than it takes to do that hike, isn't it?"

"It is if you're new to the footpath, if you're stopping to look at the views or to take photos," she argued, obviously having anticipating the question and prepared an answer. "But I've walked that path a hundred times. I could do it in my sleep."

No! Be careful, Bronwyn. Will's mind took the same leap he knew Notley's would. *If she could walk it in her sleep, she could walk it in moonlight.*

"Have you ever walked the footpath at night?" Notley asked.

A confused look suffused Bronwyn's face. "At night?"

Notley nodded. "In the dark."

She shook her head. "Why would I? That would be a foolish thing to do. Even if you know the path, there are stiles to climb over, turf bogs to wade through..."

"But you could do it, if you wanted to?"

Bronwyn hesitated, and then nodded slowly. "I suppose I could."

Having won that concession, Notley changed his attack. "See, the way we think it happened," he went on, "is that you started up that footpath at a normal pace, but something happened along the way that made you speed up. Somehow you learned that Glynnis had been attacked, and that made you run up the footpath so that you got to the churchyard in far less time than you would have otherwise."

"No," she protested.

Notley cut her off. "It's the only thing that makes sense, Bronwyn. May I call you Bronwyn?" At her nod, he continued, "Someone told you about Glynnis, and you ran to try to save her, or to find her body, something." He paused, letting that sink in, and then concluded. "Who was it?"

Panic had filled her eyes, and Will's heart sank. Notley would see that as surely as he did.

"No one told me about Glynnis. I told you that. I just walked up the footpath, and then I found Glynnis in the churchyard. Wouldn't I tell you if I knew who'd killed her? Don't you think I want you to know I'm innocent?"

Notley stared at her for a long time, waiting to see if she'd break. Will knew the technique, knew that silences were often as important as questions in an interrogation.

When the silence had stretched on long enough that Will thought he'd have to break in and smooth things over, Notley grunted and then smiled. "I guess we can always schedule you for a polygraph, can't we?"

The color drained from Bronwyn's face. *Who are you protecting?* Will thought. *Why are you keeping secrets?*

Her chin went up. "That's okay then," she defied him in a shaky voice.

Notley nodded and stood up. "You'll have to come over to Caernarfon. We'll let you know when it is."

They showed themselves out of the building, got into the Volvo in silence, and started down the lane toward Llangynog.

"She knows a lot more than she's saying," Notley said finally. He reached over to roll down his window and pulled his pipe from his pocket. "If she didn't commit the murder herself, she knows who the murderer is."

Will shook his head, watching the roadway ahead for oncoming cars. "I don't think so," he disagreed. "She obviously knows something, but I don't think she knows who did it. Like she said, why wouldn't she tell us if she knew, just to get herself off the hook for it?"

"Then how do you explain her record-breaking speed on that footpath? She had to learn somewhere along the walk that Glynnis had been attacked. How would she learn that unless the murderer told her?"

Will thought about it, watching Notley puff on his pipe out of the corner of his eye, wondering how much he dared say. It wasn't just Bronwyn he would protect, after all; his own reputation might suffer if he voiced his suspicions aloud. "Glynnis' mother said Bronwyn was bewitched," he mumbled after a moment, taking the chance. "Maybe she had a vision."

Notley snorted. "God, Cooper, that's all fairy tales!"

"Maybe," Will said noncommittally. If Notley spread the word that he'd even said something like that, he'd might as well resign from the department now.

And then Notley slapped the dashboard with his free hand, hard. "She's your informant, isn't she?" he sputtered. "She showed you where to find the attack site."

"What?" Will stalled for time. "What are you talking about?"

"You've been meeting her behind my back, haven't you, Cooper?" Notley shouted. "It was her on the phone that day, the day you said it was a girlfriend. You met her, and she showed you that place. You knew where it was the next day."

"You're crazy," Will sputtered. "Why would I meet her behind your back?"

"Why, indeed?" Notley's face had turned red with rage. He slammed his pipe against the outside of the car, knocking live cinders out that flew in sparks behind them and probably denting the car door in the process. "I knew I couldn't trust you. I told Bowers you didn't have what it takes for major crimes. Maybe now he'll believe me."

Will gripped the steering wheel and swallowed hard. "Notley, listen to what you're saying. Would I do that? Why would I keep information from you, if I had it? Would I risk my career, my reputation, meeting a suspect in a murder investigation behind your back? I'm not stupid, Sean. You're jumping to conclusions here. You need to calm down and think it through."

"I am thinking it through," Notley growled. "You've protected her from the first, Cooper, and you're still protecting her. I have to ask myself why, and the only thing I can come up with is that you know something about her that I don't."

"I don't know any more than you do," Will lied as smoothly as he could. He slowed, entering Llangynog, and then stepped on the brake, ready to crawl through the crowd of protesters who still lined the village roadways. "I want to solve this case as much as you do, Notley. Don't you believe that?"

Notley glared at him. "Maybe you want it too much, Cooper."

"Maybe I do," Will agreed with him, and then he pointed. "There's Hal Corse, holding a sign."

"Then he's still protesting," Notley muttered, still glaring at Will.

"He is," Will agreed, hoping that Notley's attention had been successfully diverted.

That evening, Will poured his customary glass of Famous Grouse, adding a bit extra to help him cope with the stress of the day's events. Before he sat down in his chair to drink it, though, he picked up his mobile and scrolled down to his parents' number.

His mother sounded delighted to hear from him, raising his suspicions at once. "There's a charity lunch at the Cheltenham Art Museum on Sunday. I was going to have to find Lark a play date, but if you're going to be here, that'll make it easier."

Will remembered those play dates, often set up with schoolmates he didn't even like. "What about father?" he asked, knowing the answer but wanting to force her to say it.

"Working again," his mother sighed, but not unhappily. Will guessed that much of the success of their marriage had been due to the fact that they spent little time together.

"I'll pick her up around half eight, then," he said. "We'll get some breakfast out and then spend the day together."

"You won't have her home before six, will you?" his mother asked.

"I'll keep her out until then," he promised. "I want to take her to Folly Farm. I think she'll like the animals. Don't tell her, though. I want it to be a surprise."

When Lark came on the line, she chattered excitedly. "Did you solve the case, Uncle Will?"

"No, not yet, but we're getting close."

"I was telling Graham about it," she informed him.

"That's Graham with the rabbits?"

"Yeah, that one. I told him you're the best murder detective in all of Wales."

Will smiled. "It sounds like you exaggerated a bit."

"But you are the best," Lark protested, and he couldn't help feeling a little puffed up by it.

Later, he sat in his leather chair, sipped his scotch, and thought. *I lied to Notley today,* he reminded himself. *I outright lied to him, and it was all I could think of to do.* And he thought he knew why. It came down to Julia again. Somehow, Bronwyn reminded him of Julia. Oh, not the drugs – not that. But there was vulnerability there somehow, a secret life both had held within that they'd not shared until it was too late.

Too late for Julia, he corrected himself. *But not too late for Bronwyn, not yet.*

He'd committed himself to being gone all weekend now. He thought he might regret having done that before the weekend was done. *I'll call her next week, see if I can see her again,* he told himself, knowing even as he thought it that he wouldn't dare meet her again in secret. Every time he met Bronwyn, he took a chance on someone finding out. Notley was right. What he was doing was something that rightfully should cost him his job.

He studied the sketch he'd bought at the gift shop in Pennant Melangell. Bronwyn was a talented artist, one who put a lot of detail into her work that captured the magic of the place, at least in his eyes although he was no art expert. He admired the lacy leaves seeming to flutter in an unseen breeze, the rough-barked tree trunks, the intricate moss on half-toppled stones. Then something caught his eye, and he looked closer. There – etched into one of the gravestones in the foreground of the sketch – was what appeared to be a face. He stood up, walked over, and picked up the sketch, holding it up to the light. Yes, it was definitely a face, now that he saw it better.

But not a human face. *Fey,* he told himself.

I wish I could see you again, Bronwyn, he thought, *but I can't – not without ending my career, and I don't think I can do that even to prove you innocent.* Was she truly innocent, though? Unless she really did have visions or something, she offered them a lot of unanswered questions that remained to be resolved. He had to admit to himself that he had yet to make up his mind about her, much as he wanted to believe that she couldn't have murdered her childhood schoolmate.

It would be good to distance himself from the case this weekend – let things settle. Maybe then when he came back to it, he'd come up with a clearer picture of just who was guilty and who wasn't. Sometimes it just took a bit of time away to bring things into focus, and at the moment the thoughts swirling in his head were only confusing him. Surely by Monday when he got back to business something would stand out that would bring the solve they needed so badly.

Chapter Sixteen

Bronwyn no longer harbored doubts that the first St. Melangell Feast Day celebration was going to be a huge success, despite her inability to meet deadlines. The counseling centre had been flooded with applications for both the organized walk and the mountain bike ride, so many that Bronwyn wondered how the tee shirt shop would be able to produce enough shirts in time. Suddenly volunteers and co-workers who had avoided her for the most part since Glynnis' murder deluged her office with constant questions and requests, unable to handle the planning any longer without her. She found she barely had a moment free for lunch in the midst of planning, meetings, and last-minute dilemmas, and she guessed that free weekends would be a thing of the past until at least the first of June.

All of this activity meant that she had little time to spare a thought for Glynnis' murder investigation, and that was a good thing, she told herself. Maybe it was time to put it all behind her, if she could. The murderer might never be identified, after all. Months would pass and then years, and eventually it would become a bit of village lore, nothing more.

But she couldn't just dismiss it completely; not yet.

The interview with Will Cooper and the other detective she thought of now as Sherlock Notley had shocked her. She'd thought herself ready for it, with answers prepared and defense solid. That Notley would so baldly attack her had not occurred to her, and she thought her answers to his direct assault had probably incriminated her more than if she'd just closed her mouth and said nothing. *What if he does schedule a polygraph for me?* she worried. *I'd be the laughing stock of all Wales if they knew who I met alongside the footpath that morning.* She'd be back to counseling at the least, and maybe more. If word reached Reverend Wicklyff, she'd almost certainly lose her job. She'd be left with a choice: leave Llangynog and go somewhere where no one knew her name or become Granny Powers reincarnated.

More than that, she didn't want Will Cooper to know, she realized with a jolt. Somehow, for reasons she didn't want to think about, his opinion of her mattered more than she wanted to admit. *Even though he didn't come to my defense,* she reminded herself. Nor had he called in the days since their meeting on Sunday. Oh, she knew he shouldn't be seen in her company, him being on the same case she was a suspect in, but despite knowing that, she'd still hoped for a phone call at the least. That wasn't asking much, was it? True, she'd been nervous about him, but she'd thought they'd worked together rather nicely brainstorming answers to the case once she'd relaxed a bit. She knew it was foolish to hope he might find her attractive, but she couldn't help hoping that had something to do with the way the day went. After all, he'd only invited her for lunch, and the trip to the beach was an added and unexpected bonus that she thought might have meant he was enjoying their day out together as much as she had in the end.

It was that disappointment in his failure to call her that led her into trouble again.

After the two detectives had left her office, she tried to busy herself with entering the race applicants' information into the spreadsheet she had created to keep track of them all. She worked mindlessly for two hours as she tried to ignore the niggling worry in the back of her mind and then, with back aching from hunching over the computer and eyes strained from trying to decipher often illegible hand writing, she abandoned the effort and decided to call it a day.

Glancing toward the sensory garden beckoning in the fading sunlight, she considered stopping there for a few minutes to try to let the tranquility of the setting dispel the feeling of impending doom the thought of the polygraph had created. But, seeing several hikers wandering inside the garden enclosure, she shook her head at the foolishness of worrying about something that might not even happen and squeezed into her dilapidated old car for the short drive into Llangynog.

The little B4391 was quiet that sunny afternoon. She pulled into a lay-by once to allow an oncoming car to pass and then continued on into the village without even noticing the beauty alongside the roadway, overwhelmed with the same thoughts she had been trying hard to banish.

The village, by contrast, was congested with pedestrians returning from day hikes and mountain bikers willing to lean their bikes up against the pub walls while they went inside for a pint or a bite of supper. Summer season had begun early with the nice spring weather, and if these early crowds were any sign of what was to come, by mid-summer they'd be awash in visitors.

Protesters continued to block the roadway, as they had now for a couple of weeks, although on weekdays they tended to congregate only in the early evening in order to catch returning hikers and bikers at a time when they would be most concentrated in one place. She supposed they all had regular jobs that required their attention during the rest of the time and felt a little guilt at not offering to join them in their quest to preserve the Tanat Valley from a future environmental crisis. *I love this valley,* she reminded herself, making a pledge then and there that, once the feast day celebration was over, she would at least write letters in support of the protest.

As Bronwyn inched the Volvo through the crowd, a man waved his sign at her and signaled for her to roll down her window.

She complied with a guilty roll of her eyes. "Good job, doing this. I wish I had the time to join you."

He nodded at her. "It's a good cause, but that's not why I stopped you."

She arched her eyebrows at him. He looked to be in his late 30s, strong and fit in the way that someone who did physical labor for a living might be. His dark hair and even darker eyes seemed to imply an intensity that would push him toward the sort of activity he was engaged in – attempting to block something that threatened environmental disaster in the face of modern-day profits.

"You're Bronwyn Bagley, aren't you?" the man asked, staring at her as if daring her to deny it.

She felt a flutter of fear in her chest. "Yes, I am."

He stuck his free hand through the window. "Hal Corse. Nice to meet you."

"Mr. Corse," she stuttered, taken off guard. She stared at him. Yes, she might recognize him from that night in the Tanat Inn, she thought. She didn't shake his hand.

"Call me Hal," he told her when it became clear she wasn't going to respond.

A car horn sounded behind her, and Bronwyn glanced reflexively in the mirror, seeing a line of cars stopped in the lane behind her. "I've got to go," she murmured, feeling the blood pounding in her temples.

"Could we talk sometime?" he persisted, leaving his hand on the car window so that she couldn't drive away without the possibility of hurting him. "We both want to clear our names on this murder. I thought we might discuss what we can do to accomplish that."

She sucked in a breath, holding it as she eased her foot off the gas pedal so that the Volvo rolled forward a few slow inches.

"Tonight, maybe? I'll be done here in another half hour or so," he insisted, gripping the car window. He glanced toward the rest of the group.

Bronwyn instinctively recoiled from the man's forwardness. Not that he'd have any reason to harm her, but with what happened to Glynnis, it made sense to play it safe. Still, if she put him off now, he'd probably persist in his demands to meet her anyway. She'd might as well get it over with. "At the Tanat?"

"I wouldn't want my wife to think I was meeting lovely young girls in the pub," Hal Corse said firmly. "Besides, I'm not welcome there any longer, not since the night Glynnis Paisley spilled the beer on me. Wish I'd never heard her name." He looked at the growing line of cars behind Bronwyn's Volvo as another horn sounded. "I won't hurt you. I just want to talk. If you hiked down along the river a bit to that second grove of trees, we could talk without my wife or anyone else hearing about it. Please?"

Bronwyn really didn't like the idea of meeting him in a solitary spot down alongside the river at dusk without anyone knowing about it. "Maybe we could meet another time, then? Earlier in the day? Maybe at the counseling centre?" She eased the car forward another couple of inches in order to appease the car behind her. "Plenty of people come up there. It wouldn't look odd for us to meet at my office."

He let out his breath in impatience. "Look, I saw you with that detective. You drove right past my place with the top down, and me out in the pasture with the sheep right by the roadway. Couldn't help but recognize the two of you. So, I know you're helping him, working with him. And I want to talk. It's either you meet me tonight, or other people hear about you driving around the countryside with him, and I don't think that would be good for his career, do you?" He leaned on the window as Bronwyn drew back toward the centre of the car. "What's it to be?"

Another horn blared at her from behind as her heart thudded. They'd tried to be so careful not to be seen, she and Will, both of them working at avoiding places where they'd be recognized without seeming obvious about it to each other. But maybe she could still do some damage control about that, now that she knew they'd been spotted. She nodded reluctantly. "Okay, I'll meet you there in half an hour, but you'll say what you have to say fast. I need to be back here in the village twenty minutes after we meet. I'll have someone waiting for me." She'd made that part up, but he couldn't know that.

"You'll not tell anyone we're meeting each other," he warned her.

She shook her head, mute.

"Agreed," he said, and he tossed a protest brochure into the car, lifted his hand off her window at last, and watched as she rolled the car through the rest of the protesters and then picked up speed again after.

It's crazy to meet with him, Bronwyn chided herself as she drove up to her parents' stone farmhouse. She wondered for a minute whether she should call Will Cooper and tell him about the meeting. *No, it's better to wait until I see what he has to say,* she told herself. How would it look if she called Will Cooper every time she felt a little uncomfortable? God, he'd think she was stalking him, making things up just to talk to him. Anyway, she was too shy to do it. It had been hard enough to work up the courage to call him about the murder site, and that was a lot bigger deal than this was. If he wasn't going to call her, she wasn't going to call him.

She parked her car in the driveway, changed into jeans, a tee shirt, and her favorite brown cardigan, and went into the kitchen where she chose a stout butcher knife that would squeeze into her purse. *I can protect myself if it comes to it,* she assured herself, knowing it was a lie. She walked out to the barn to tell her dad she'd be missing supper. She could pick something up in the pub after her little talk with Hal Corse; sit and eat and think about what he'd had to say.

She found her dad with Maddock, mucking out the lamb pens. She wrinkled her nose at the acid scent, wishing she'd come just a few minutes later when fresh straw would sweeten the air for a short time at least.

"Not going out walking on your own?" her dad asked, giving her a worried glance.

"I am, but I thought if I walked alongside the river near the village it would be within shouting distance should anything happen." She smiled, trying to make it genuine so as to ease his concern. "This feast day celebration has me up to the eyeballs in work, and if I don't get out and get at least a short stroll in, I'll probably not manage it much longer. I won't go far, and I'll be careful, I promise."

Maddock forked a load of dirty straw into an overflowing wheelbarrow. "There's a lot of talk about you in the village, you know. People wondering how it was you hurried up the footpath and found Glynnis' body that morning."

She blew out an exasperated breath. "I hope you're defending me?"

Maddock grinned. "Sure I am. I just tell them the Twlwyth Teg told you about it."

"You wouldn't!"

Her dad shook his head at Maddock warningly. "You know he's just teasing, Bronwyn."

She narrowed her eyes at Maddock, suspicious. "Maddock?"

He laughed. "You used to believe they were real, Bronwyn, until Mum and Dad got you counseling. I think you still do, but now you just keep quieter about it."

Her face flushed with heat. *Am I that transparent? Maybe I shouldn't sneak them into my sketches, after all.* She lifted her chin, going on the offensive. "Maybe they did tell me then. Maybe they still talk to me, tell me things. What would you say to that?"

Maddock's laughter faded. "You don't mean that, Bron, so don't even say it or you'll turn into another Granny Powers. The whole village will think you're mental."

"What do you mean?" She glared at him.

"He means," her dad broke in softly, "that you'd hear and see things no one else does, and people would listen even if they did think you a bit crazy." He gave Maddock another look. "Just ignore them, Bronwyn. It doesn't do to listen to village gossip."

Bronwyn glanced at the time on her mobile phone as she marched up the roadway through the village and toward the bridge.

She was going to be late meeting Hal Corse, and the sky was growing darker even as she hurried along. *This is stupid,* she scolded herself. *I don't know this man, and he's a suspect in Glynnis' murder. Why does he need to meet me in secret anyway? Can't he just tell his wife why he's meeting me?*

She crossed the bridge and veered off onto the footpath that followed the river as it meandered peacefully down the valley. Soft grass brushed against her legs as she strode down the narrow trail, and in places the water gurgled and bubbled when it fell shallow over stony narrows. A lark trilled from a fence post across a field, and she saw something big scurry across the path ahead, perhaps a badger.

She found Hal Corse waiting in the shadows beneath a grove of willows, ash, and birch. He'd been smoking a cigarette, and he flicked the stub into the river when she came close.

"I thought you were all about the environment," she chided him, deciding to take the offensive from the start in the hope of hiding her nervousness.

"A cig's not going to kill off all the life in the area," he responded curtly, "like a gas pipeline might." He stepped out of the shadows and looked back up the trail as if to check that no one else was coming along behind her.

She faced him, squaring her shoulders and standing as tall as she could. "What's so important that you had to blackmail me to get me out here?"

He shrugged. "I want this murder investigation to go away, that's all. I don't like having my neighbors looking at me, wondering if I'm a murderer, and I don't like not being welcome at the pubs."

"Well, neither do I, but there's nothing I can do to help either of us."

"Oh, I think there's plenty you can do," he sneered. "It's obvious you've got inside information about things, isn't it?"

"I don't know anything more than you do."

"Sure, you do." He watched her, his eyes boring into hers until she flinched. "You and that detective seem to be great friends, after all."

"He doesn't tell me anything," she insisted, taking a step backward. "And we're not great friends."

"Then why are you out driving around with him on a Sunday afternoon?" he persisted, stepping closer. "I bet the two of you are comparing notes on the investigation. Can you deny it?"

"Yes, I can." She raised her chin and glared at him.

"Then what else would you be doing with him?"

She closed her eyes. "Maybe we're seeing each other." *Not good! Not good! But what else could she say?*

Hal Corse grunted. "Well, then, there are other ways to end the investigation, I guess, if you refuse to help me."

"What do you mean?"

He stepped closer to her, and she backed away another step in response, despite her best efforts to look as if she weren't afraid. He gave a little laugh, amused. "Afraid of me then? Guess that takes you off the suspect list. You'd not be worried about me if you'd murdered her yourself, would you?"

"I'm not afraid of you," she mumbled, grasping her purse where the knife hid. "Tell me what you meant by ending the investigation."

Hal Corse laughed again, a humorless sound that clashed with the quiet burbling of the river. "Wonder what the chief superintendent would say if he knew his detective was dating one of the suspects in a murder case?" He shook his head. "Anything that detective said would be suspect then, wouldn't it, because he'd be...what's the word? Prejudiced. Yeah, that's it. Prejudiced."

Bronwyn stared at him in silence.

"This is what I want you to do, right? I want you to tell him you know I wasn't involved." He stepped closer again, looming over her, and she knew the fear would show on her face. "You came out of that pub after I left that night. Did you see me anywhere? Was my car still in the car park? A Renault Laguna, black with plenty of mud spattered on it? No, because I had gone home. You need to tell him that. Tell him my wife told you I was home early. It's true, and he'd better believe you. Because if he doesn't, if he comes to see me again or talks to anyone about me, that's when the chief superintendent will get an earful. Got it?"

Bronwyn nodded, mute.

He glared down at her for a long moment, and then gestured abruptly. "Go on, then. You'd better get back to the village, or your twenty minutes will be long gone."

She took a shaky breath. "I...I don't know why he'd believe me."

"He'd better," Hal Corse glowered at her, "because if he doesn't, you're going to be sorrier than you know."

She was still shaking when she climbed up the few steps from the riverbank to the edge of the bridge and came out onto the roadway. *Oh, God! Why did I say that?* A flood of panic threatened to turn her fear into tears. She stood still for a moment, trying to gather her courage. *I'll have to call Will now. Tell him about it.* The last thing on earth she wanted to do, though, was to tell him she'd said they were dating when it wasn't true. He'd think she was imagining things that weren't true, making up a relationship like a desperate teenager. How could she tell him what she'd done? She couldn't, that was the bottom line. But she was well and truly trapped. She'd have to tell him, wouldn't she?

Maybe she could plead ignorance, hope he'd think Hal Corse had seen them together and made an assumption?

Or she could simply do as Hal Corse wished.

God, how could she have been so stupid? She never should have met Hal Corse, and she'd have been better off. *Dumb! Dumb! Dumb!*

She thought back to the night of the murder. There had been a few cars in the car park when she'd left, four of them she thought. They hadn't been familiar to her, cars she'd seen in the area frequently enough to recognize them. She wasn't sure what a Renault Laguna looked like, and mud spattering would be a common thing to find in the spring in Wales. Still, if she concentrated, she thought she could picture the cars there, and she didn't think there'd been a black one. Two reds maybe, a white, and something silver or gray, maybe a Kia, she thought.

She sighed and shook her head. She'd have to think it over before doing anything.

She walked to the Tanat Inn, hoping her face wouldn't betray her agitation. Thankfully, dusk had fallen quickly so that no one seemed to notice anything amiss as she walked through the open doors and found a small table hidden in a shadowy corner.

Mai came to take her order, looking at her inquisitively as she did so.

Bronwyn ignored the look and ordered a vegetarian curry and a glass of wine. She made sure it was red.

She had her glass of wine and was picking at the curry when a voice woke her from her thoughts.

"You look like you could use a friend."

She looked up at Davyyd Paisley, who was holding a pint of Guinness in his hand and grinning at her. "I think I've heard that line before."

"It does seem familiar, now you mention it." He sat down in the chair across from her without waiting for her invitation. "I never called you, did I?"

She gave him a rueful glance. "It's only been a week."

"Is that all? It feels like weeks last forever these days. I can't wait to be done with this job so I can go back home to Cardiff."

"I thought you were to remain in the area until the case is solved."

"Cardiff's not so far, when you think of it. I'm sure they'd let me go as long as they have all my contact information. It's not as if the case is being solved quickly, after all. It might be years at this rate." He sipped at his pint. "What do you think? This Saturday? Maybe dinner, a movie? Just as friends, of course. Glynnis' mum would have my hide if she thought I was dating again so soon after losing her."

She thought quickly. With the feast day celebration coming so soon, she really should be spending weekends at the counseling centre working, but everyone deserved at least one evening a week off, didn't they? Why pass up a chance at someone with both a friendly face and a good-paying job? Plus, there was the bonus of thinking she'd gotten one over on Glynnis, God rest her soul, who would be mortified to know that her husband was seeing Bronwyn, even casually. Still, why would Davyyd be interested in her? Why did he want to spend time with her? "You aren't doing this just to avoid Rhonda, are you?"

"No, I promise you, I am not asking you out to put Rhonda off."

A trace of guilt on his face told her otherwise, but she chose to ignore it. "Saturday will be fine," she told him. "But it'll have to be in the evening. I have a ton of work to get done for the feast day, so I'll be working until at least five."

"Then would six o'clock be good?" he asked.

"It would," she agreed, ignoring the happiness that she felt in the pit of her stomach. Her social life had definitely improved, even if it all revolved around Glynnis' death. "Will you pick me up at home?"

He frowned, and then offered a wry smile. "Would you mind very much meeting me in Oswestry? That way I can avoid Glynnis' parents seeing us together, if possible?"

"Oh, of course." She should have thought of that.

"At the Smithfield," he told her, "at six. We can drive somewhere from there, maybe get dinner in another village, explore the countryside a bit."

"That sounds great," she agreed, smiling up at him. First Will Cooper and now Davyyd Paisley. Maybe she wouldn't end up a lonely old Granny Powers, after all.

She hoped he'd sit and chat while she ate, but he got up quickly again and, with a murmured apology, made his way through the evening crowd. She watched him set his empty Guinness glass on the bar, pay his tab, and walk out. *A good-looking man,* she thought to herself. *And nice, as well. Glynnis didn't deserve him. But I might, when he's ready.*

She finished her meal in solitude, busying herself with watching the other patrons of the bar, listening in on their conversations and grinning at the jokes that flew from one table to another among the locals. It gave her a comfortable feeling to watch her neighbors and friends this way. *I was right to come back home to Llangynog,* she thought, enjoying the feeling of belonging to a place as much as to a family. She thought of her dad, his peacefulness, his intelligence, and his wisdom. Roots make a big difference in the way a person fits into his community, his world, she thought. *I'm glad I will have that sense of belonging.*

Later she sipped the last of her wine and stood up, feeling much more relaxed than she had when she'd arrived. With a wave at Mai, she pushed her way through the crowd and out the doors onto the roadway, checked for traffic, and began the stroll home in the warm May evening.

She'd only gotten a short way before a woman's voice called her name from behind her, startling her and setting her heart to pounding once again. She was going to die of fright one of these days if they didn't solve the murder soon, she thought.

She stopped, turned, and squinted in the light from the car park as the other woman approached. Tall, with blonde hair glinting in the streetlight..."It's Rhonda Morris, isn't it?"

The woman smiled and touched her on the arm. "Yes, how did you know?"

Her blonde hair didn't look quite natural now that she was close enough to see, which of course it wasn't since you could see the dark roots beneath, but she was still very pretty. *Not glamorous,* Bronwyn thought, *but the sort of lovely girl a man would want to marry.* Now that she could see her close up, Bronwy could see that she had a kind face, too, much like Davyyd Paisley's. They would have made a nice couple, she thought idly. "Davyyd Paisley pointed you out to me last week when he was here," she said, hoping she hadn't made it sound as if she were spying on the woman.

Rhonda nodded. "I saw you talking with him just now and thought you must be old friends."

"Not old friends," Bronwyn corrected her, "new ones. I was the one who found Glynnis' body that morning, so that's what brings us together." She hoped she wasn't making it sound as if she were after a relationship with Davyyd Paisley. Although she was thrilled that he'd asked her out, she didn't especially want to taunt this poor woman with the fact, not after she'd lost him already to Glynnis. "I knew Glynnis from the time we were in nursery school together, but I only met Davyyd after her murder."

The woman's eyes darkened. "I heard about the American that night in the pub, how Glynnis flirted with him and you walked out."

Bronwyn reached out to touch the other woman's hand. "Yes, it's true. I didn't know Davyyd at that point, but Glynnis had talked about him to me and I guessed who he was when I saw him with her dad. I felt bad for him, watching Glynnis flirt with another man. Glynnis did that to both of us, didn't she, taking a man we liked away from us? It'd be something we'd have in common."

"She was rather horrible," Rhonda observed, "and I'm not sorry she's dead."

Bronwyn thought for a moment. "Neither am I, truthfully."

Rhonda smiled at that. After a moment she took a step closer to Bronwyn. "Can I ask you something?"

"Sure." The glass of wine was taking effect, and Bronwyn was feeling mellow. "What is it?"

"What was it like finding Glynnis like that in the churchyard?"

Bronwyn looked at her. Her pretty face was rapt with interest, but she didn't seem ghoulish about it, just curious. "It was awful, of course. Glynnis was lying against the church wall, and I knew right away she was dead, but, somehow, I wanted to...well, to comfort her, I guess. It was silly, I know." Bronwyn shrugged and shook her head. "But sometimes we do things without thinking about it, and that's how it was up there. It was sad and terrible, even if I didn't especially like Glynnis."

Rhonda nodded. "I thought it would be that way. You didn't hate her anymore then, once she was dead." It was a statement rather than a question, and Bronwyn thought she understood the curiosity she had noted earlier.

"I guess that's when we forgive people whatever hurt they've caused us."

Rhonda frowned. "I don't think I could ever forgive her, but maybe I don't hate her so much anymore. I think now I feel she got what she deserved."

Bronwyn watched her. She couldn't see this woman hurting Glynnis, any more than she could see Davyyd Paisley doing it. She just seemed too nice, too honest. "What will you do now?"

Rhonda looked at her, seeming to come out of some sort of private reverie. "Life will get back to where it was before Glynnis, I hope." She paused, her eyes flat. "Davyyd and I are getting back together, you know. He doesn't think it's proper yet, but I'll be there waiting for him for as long as it takes, and then he'll come back to me. I love him. He and I would have had such a lovely life together. I'd never have hurt him like Glynnis did."

"I'm sure you wouldn't have," Bronwyn murmured, watching Rhonda's face.

"She lied to him," Rhonda went on softly. "Told him she was pregnant, but she wasn't." She looked closely at Bronwyn. "How could someone do that to a man she loved?"

"She obviously didn't love him," Bronwyn told her, "not really. I'm not sure Glynnis ever understood what love meant."

"No," Rhonda agreed, "no, she had no idea. But I do." She studied Bronwyn's face with eyes that had gone suddenly fierce. "I do, and I will have him back."

Later, at home in her attic bedroom, Bronwyn thought about the evening. Who would have thought she'd have a chance to talk to three of the suspects in Glynnis' murder all in one night?

Hal Corse she did not like at all. He was pushy and arrogant, sure that he could bully his way out of the investigation, if it came to that. Could he have murdered Glynnis, though? It seemed rather an overreaction to murder someone over a few pints of spilled beer, even if he did feel strongly about the pipeline. And didn't they all feel that way about it? None of the village would be happy to see that pipeline mar the beauty of the Tanat Valley, that was a given.

As for Davyyd Paisley and Rhonda Morris, they both seemed simply too nice to have murdered anyone. It was true that Glynnis had done something unpardonable to the two of them, something that, no matter what Rhonda thought, had probably ruined any chance the two of them had at happiness together. But would they murder her over it? Bronwyn wished she knew. Despite her open, friendly face, Rhonda had given her a glimpse of something else, an obsession with Davyyd and an intense hatred for Glynnis that even her death had not eased. It made her wonder. And it made her uneasy. She was sure Rhonda had an ulterior motive in approaching her; she'd wanted to warn Bronwyn away from Davyyd, to make clear her claim to him. If she was aware that Davyyd had asked her for a date, and if she was Glynnis' murderer, would that put Bronwyn at risk? *Yeah, it would.*

Beside her old Nan sighed and stretched, and she laid back on her pillow and tried to calm her mind so that she'd be able to sleep. Davyyd...she smiled at the thought of him. How nice to have a date with someone she might actually have a future with, once things had settled, despite poor Rhonda's possessiveness. Then there was Will Cooper. She knew it was foolish to dream about a detective who was most definitely interested in her only as far as she could help him solve a crime. But truthfully, she'd love to have a real date with him, not just an inquisition of sorts. She'd enjoyed their day out in the end, and she thought him attractive in a sort of roguish way. Safe at home in her bed, she was finally willing to admit that she was terribly disappointed he hadn't called her all week. There it was, then. She'd been longing for a catalyst to change her dull but safe life in Llangynog, and now it seemed that Glynnis' death had brought more opportunities than she had time for.

What was needed, she mused, was some final answer to the case. The murder weapon would be the thing that would solve it, she thought, or perhaps the missing wedding ring, if it could be found in the possession of whoever had stolen it. Perhaps the Twlwyth Teg would give her more clues if she gave them the opportunity. What would Will Cooper think of her if she solved the case for him? Would he be grateful or resent her for it?

But what if it led back to her? She'd found Glynnis. It was her fingerprints on the churchyard gate, her bloody shoeprints on the pathway, her fingerprints on the wine bottle. It was her who knew the pathway to Pennant Melangell so well she could do it in moonlight. It was her who Glynnnis had insulted that night. And it was her the Twlwyth Teg pointed their fingers at. *It's you, it's you, it's you...*

Maybe she *was* mental, as Maddock had said. Maybe the Twlwyth Teg were a creation of her imagination, a way for her crazed mind to explain how she knew things about Glynnis' death. Could it be possible? Could all the things in her past – the Twlwyth Teg, Pysgotwr the Green Man, the faces in her sketches, even her homesickness while at university in Wrexham – could all of that be signs that she was as crazy as Granny Powers had been thought to be? Was that her legacy from Granny Powers? Did she somehow know it to be true?

She tried not to give in to panic as she shoved all these thoughts into the back of her mind, where they would not rest no matter how hard she tried to dismiss them. *Wait and see what tomorrow brings,* she told herself to little avail. *If it really was me, as the Twlwyth Teg say, I will know sooner or later.* In the end that thought did not comfort her, though.

When she finally slept, she slept soundly, and she managed to keep herself so busy the rest of the week that there was little time to allow her self-doubts to nag her, disturbing as they were.

It wasn't until early Saturday morning as she walked in the morning's mist through the empty sensory garden toward the doors of the counseling centre that she glanced through the gateway to the churchyard and saw movement among the gravestones. Then she knew that at least some answers would be given to her, whether she welcomed them or not. She only hoped that she'd understand what they gave her this time.

She slipped through the archway and stood on the misty path, waiting, her heart thudding in anticipation.

Silently they surrounded her, large and small, beautiful and hideous, bright and dull. The mist swirled around them as they circled her so that the faces appeared formed of imagination, and a chill of fear ran down her spine. *Are they real?*

"The aetheling fails." Even though she was expecting it, the voice drifting out of the mist startled her.

"Dog companion carries the chaffer," boomed another, echoing off the church wall and into the distance.

"Common profit must be considered," demanded a third voice. "The guardian must live."

"Thick!" whispered a fourth voice, a single voice that became many as it grew like a wind through the muzzling mist. "Thick! Thick!"

Then there was silence for a full minute, two, three.

"Tell me what to do," Bronwyn whispered into the fog when she could stand it no longer. She knew they were still there, although she couldn't see them. She felt their presence, felt their bated breath in the swirling mists of the churchyard.

"It's you," they whispered back finally.

Chapter Seventeen

Bronwyn stumbled into her office, her shaking legs barely holding her up. *It's me, it's me, it's me....* The words rolled around in her head, roaring in her thoughts until she felt her head would explode with the pain of it.

How can it be me? she cried silently. *How? I am NOT a murderer, I know I'm not. Yet...*

There was a knock on her closed office door. She looked at it, wondering when she'd closed it. She didn't remember, even though it had been just a few seconds ago that she'd come in.

She drew a shaky breath, trying to compose herself, and squared her shoulders, though inside she was still quaking and she felt like throwing up. She wouldn't, though. Somehow, she'd have to get through the next few days until the feast day celebration was over, and then maybe she could take some time off work. It would be good to pull away and relax, to wander in the forest again, maybe indulge in some sketches, maybe even get away from Llangynog a bit, see something else.

She forced a smile onto her face and opened the door.

Janis Hatcher stood there, a smile etched on her own comfortable face. "I saw you come in, Bronwyn. Are you okay?"

She decided on a half-truth. "I walked through the sensory garden on my way in, and I guess my senses overwhelmed me," she confessed. "The mist swirling around made it feel haunted. It frightened me, that's all." She didn't want to sound too crazy; Janis was a psychologist, after all.

Janis watched her for a moment, studying her face. "I'm guessing that you're still getting over the fright of finding Glynnis Paisley. You look terrified."

"I am," Bronwyn took a steadying breath. "I was, at least, but I'm fine now that I'm inside. What is it you needed?"

"I thought we should go over a few things before the meeting with the volunteers this morning," Janis said briskly. "This is the last time we'll have them in a group before the big day, and I wanted to be sure we didn't leave out anything, this being our first time for this celebration."

Ah! The volunteers' meeting. She'd nearly forgotten it. Since many of them worked during the week at other jobs, they'd scheduled this meeting for a Saturday so they could all attend. It all came flooding back – the meeting this morning, her planned afternoon making up the schedule after they'd assigned tasks to everyone... and then her date with Davyyd Paisley.

How was she going to get through the day? She straightened, meeting Janis' concerned eyes. "Okay, then, let's talk about it now. Do you have the list we made up?"

They spent the next forty minutes planning their meeting with the volunteers, and after she managed to push the Twlwyth Teg into the far back corner of her mind, Bronwyn found she could concentrate, after all, and even manage to sound professional about it all. Her two years of university had not really prepared her for all the duties of a counseling centre manager, but with the help of people like Janis, Reverend Wicklyff, and even the volunteers like Caderyn Baker in the gift shop and old Clarence Randall with his enthusiastic tours, she felt like she was able to at least cope, if not a little bit more.

The mist had burned off and sun was streaming through the windows as they met with the group of some twenty volunteers, all from the surrounding area. After giving an overview of what the day's events entailed and how they could help, she sat at a table and signed people up for tasks like checking the participants in, handing out race numbers, setting up water stations at strategic points along the pathway, and organizing lunch for those finishing the course. More volunteers would be on hand at Pennant Melangell itself to provide tours of the church and the sensory garden, and Reverend

Wicklyff would be in charge of telling the legend of St. Melangell and the hare every half hour outside the church doors. They hoped for a festive, celebratory day, when all was said and done and, while it seemed overwhelming at times now, Bronwyn did feel that the day would be a success in the end.

By the time the meeting broke up, it was nearly two o'clock, and many of the volunteers were still meeting in smaller groups. Bronwyn had planned to take the sign-up sheets into her office and make a master list of who was to work where, and then to begin on the name tags and reminders for the volunteers. She'd thought that she might be able to sneak in a few minutes for searching out the Twlwyth Teg's latest words to her, as well, knowing that she wouldn't be able to concentrate on her chores unless she had given herself the opportunity to figure out their latest message. But just as she headed toward her office, a wail echoed from the front of the conference room.

She hurried toward the commotion. "What's wrong?"

Nesta Baker, one of the volunteers in charge of sensory garden tours, caught at her arm. "Dera just told me that Padrig can't be here today. His sister's in hospital in Swansea, may be there for a while. Heart trouble, apparently. But then who's going to teach us about the garden, what to say to the people?" She looked at Bronwyn anxiously.

With an internal roll of the eyes, Bronwyn smiled. "Surely you know all about the flowers, Nesta? You, who always have great entries for the flower show in August?" She suspected that Nesta was trying to back out of her commitment, but her method of doing so was putting the other two garden volunteers off, as well.

"I know about flowers, all right," Nesta puffed, "but not how it's all to fit in a garden like this one, not without Padrig to tell me about how it was planned and what it's meant to do."

Bronwyn took in the fact that the other two volunteers were slowly backing away, distancing themselves. "How about if I tell you about the garden then? I've studied it quite a bit, could probably tell you the things you don't already know. I'll just fill in for Padrig for now."

In the end, that was just the first crisis of three that afternoon, and not only did Bronwyn not get the master list of volunteers typed up, but she didn't manage to turn her computer on at all. When, finally, she had a moment to catch her breath, she was startled to find that it was already nearly half-four, so with a longing look at the sleeping computer, she closed her office door, waved goodbye to a few of the volunteers who were working in the conference room, and hurried out of the counseling centre.

The Twlwyth Teg's words will have to wait, she told herself firmly. She'd probably be able to better enjoy her time with Davyyd Paisley if she had an inkling what their next clues would reveal, but that luxury was not available to her now, even after the day she'd suffered through, unless she was willing to be late for her dinner with him, and she was not. But she could research it when she got home that night, she promised herself. *Maybe I'll even find that it wasn't me; that they mean something else when they say that.*

Once home, she threw off her clothes and changed into a flowered skirt and short-sleeved pink blouse, taking time to brush out her dark hair and put on a pair of silver earrings. She smiled at herself in the mirror. It would have to do, she told herself. She didn't think she looked as tired as she deserved to be.

She searched for her brown cardigan, thinking that it would be welcome as the evening cooled, even though the sun had been brilliant all day once the mist burned away. Not finding it in her bedroom, she clattered down the stairs and saw it at once, draped over the back of the sofa.

"Oops!" she told her mum, who had poked her head out of the kitchen when she heard the footsteps. "I thought I put this away last time I wore it."

Her mum raised her eyebrows. "It's been there a couple of days, at least. I thought you were so busy, though, that I'd just take it upstairs when I remembered it."

"Beat you to it," Bronwyn grinned, grabbing it. "Don't wait up for me, mum. I'll be fine."

Her mother gave her a look that held so much affection Bronwyn felt guilty. "Be careful, love. He's just lost his young wife, and I think he must be a suspect in the case himself."

"Don't worry about me, mum. He's a really nice man, a lot nicer than Glynnis ever deserved," she reassured her. She was a bit worried herself, though. She didn't just think he might be a suspect; she knew from her outing with Will Cooper that he was one of the most likely suspects. *I've still got the knife in my bag if I need it,* she reassured herself. *He'll not bop me over the head with a wine bottle without a fight.* Besides, she didn't intend to wander off on a lonely footpath with him, and surely, she was safe if they stayed in public places?

Her mother smiled, though her eyes were still concerned. "Come in to say goodnight when you get in, will you?"

"I'll do that, mum," she agreed, and then she gathered up the sweater, car keys, and bag and went out into a beautiful May evening for a meeting she was both excited and apprehensive about.

The Volvo gave her no trouble as she drove down the B4391 past Pennant Melangell to Llanrhaeadr-ym-Mochnant, where she turned onto the B4580 toward Oswestry. There were better roads leading that direction, but none as direct as the little lanes, and she enjoyed the slower pace of them and the scenery more than she enjoyed the ease of driving on roads where the necessity of lay-bys for oncoming traffic wasn't required. The road followed the river some of the way and was bounded by pastures full of sheep, groves of trees, and rough, rocky hillsides with the sun-tipped Berwyn Mountains looming in the distance. It had to be one of the most beautiful places in the world, she thought, and she felt the stress of the day fading away.

She found a parking space in the car park for the Smithfield Hotel and phoned Davyyd Paisley on her mobile to let him know she'd arrived. Grabbing her jumper and bag, she slipped out of the car and locked it, hearing as she did so a ping on the paving at her feet as something fell from the pocket of the cardigan she carried.

She looked down and froze. A ring lay at her feet, a gleaming silver wedding ring, one that was gleaming because it was still new, having belonged to the only newlywed Bronwyn was aware of – Glynnis Paisley. She had never seen Glynnis' wedding ring, or never noticed it at least, but she had no doubt who this ring belonged to.

Her heart pounded in her ears, and she thought for an instant that she might faint. Then she squatted down and picked up the ring, looked around to see if anyone had noticed, opened her bag, and dropped it in.

I did not put it there. I didn't. I didn't! she told herself firmly. She saw Davyyd Paisley come out of the hotel's front doors and turn toward the car park. *I didn't!*

But did she? She was no longer sure.

She wore that cardigan a lot, she told herself. Anyone could have dropped it into her pocket.

Anyone? She had worn the jumper on her excursion with Will Cooper. She had also worn it a few days before when she met Hal Corse down by the Tanat River. *And I met Davyyd Paisley in the pub that same night,* she remembered, finding that more frightening. *And Rhonda Morris, too. Did one of them put it there? Or did I put it there myself?* In any case, it meant that she had been in close proximity to the murderer in the past few days, whether it was one of them or – she couldn't let her thoughts go there – herself. No, not her. One of the others had to have put that ring in her pocket. Which one?

Suddenly she felt vulnerable. She wished she had time to call Will Cooper. He would protect her if he could, wouldn't he?

But there was no time, for suddenly Davyyd Paisley was there in front of her, smiling his easy smile and with a warm welcome in his brown eyes.

She smiled back, said hello, and wished fervently she'd not agreed to this dinner out with him so she'd have had time to translate the Twlwyth Teg's words, think about what finding the ring meant, and not feel quite so in danger as she felt at that moment.

They got into his car, a white Toyota Camry several years old, and Davyyd pulled out onto the A5 toward Shrewsbury. "There are a lot of restaurants to choose from there," he told her, and she was simply glad they were heading somewhere that would be congested with people so that she wouldn't be alone with him.

He seemed to sense her agitation and occupied her with light chatter and little jokes, so it wasn't long before she began to relax, despite the memory of what was in the bottom of her bag. *Two things, really,* she reminded herself, *the ring and the knife.* But then she laughed at one of Davyyd's nonsense jokes and thought that she might enjoy herself that night, despite it all. He really did seem a very nice man. *If he did kill Glynnis, it must have been for a very good reason.*

I must be suffering from hysteria, she thought, letting herself settle into his very pleasant company.

They parked the car near the Quarry in downtown Shrewsbury and spent a half-hour strolling through the gardens, enjoying the beautifully blooming formal beds of marigolds, petunias, pansies, and other annuals framed by fragrant green alpine borders. Fountains splashed gaily, birds swooped overhead, and the awkwardness of being with Davyyd faded away as they walked, chatting quietly. Afterwards, they wandered into the medieval old town area, admiring the whitewash and dark timbered buildings and finally choosing a restaurant called "Renaissance" for dinner.

Davyyd ordered the variety menu, and Bronwyn the vegetarian variety, a six-course dinner where items on offer would be chosen by the cooking staff, giving them a surprise with each course.

"This is fun," Bronwyn told Davyyd as they waited for their first course.

He nodded. "I did this one before, and everything was delicious," he assured her. Then he picked up his glass of wine, took a sip, looked at her, and turned serious. "Thank you for coming out with me tonight. I...I didn't mean it so much as a date as just a chance to spend an evening out with someone." He grinned ruefully. "Since Glynnis died, my co-workers have more or less shunned me. I don't know if they think I murdered her myself, or if they see me as bad luck somehow and want to keep their distance." He waved his glass at her. "I figured you must be a suspect, as well, so the two of us could keep each other company."

She smiled at that. "It's true. My co-workers have been the same way, so I know exactly what you're talking about."

"Not that I don't think you're someone I'd like to date someday," he told her, "but at this point I'm not even ready to consider the idea of seeing someone again."

"Of course, you aren't. It's only been a few weeks. You're still in mourning."

"But I'm not sure I ever really felt married to Glynnis," he admitted softly. "It was such a whirlwind of activity - her telling me she was pregnant, having to tell Rhonda, the little wedding ceremony we had, and then living in our flat together until I was sent to work in Llangynog. Now that I think of it, it seems like a dream I had, or..." he grimaced, "maybe a nightmare."

She looked up at him sharply. "Then you weren't happy together?"

"How could we be?" he shrugged. "She lied to me, you know. She was never pregnant." He stopped talking, and then swiped at his eyes with a free hand. "God, I felt horrible when I figured that out, knowing what I'd done to Rhonda, and it was all because of a lie."

"You must have been really angry with her," Bronwyn suggested, holding her breath.

But he didn't confess. "I felt more sad than anything else. But I'd committed to her so I was going to try to make it work, stay with her and be a good husband to her."

"That would have been hard," she told him. "I knew Glynnis, you know."

"I thought she was with that American that night when she didn't come back to the hotel," he confided in response. "I watched her flirting with him, watched you leave, knew I had to leave, as well, or I was going to explode."

"So, you went on ahead to Oswestry, thinking she'd take the bus back."

"She'd done that several times before. But when she didn't come in on the bus, I just knew she was with him, the one she'd been flirting with." He hesitated. "I thought then that our marriage would be over."

Bronwyn considered that. "Well, it is, I guess."

"But not for the reason I thought." Davyyd concluded.

After that, they talked about their childhoods. Davyyd had been born in Chepstow, where he'd grown up picnicking on the castle grounds and listening to his father's obsession with Welsh history. "I'm named after Llewelyn Fawr's son," he told her. "They probably discussed naming me Llewelyn, but decided Davyyd was a more modern name. Thank God. Can you imagine how I'd have been teased with a name like Llewelyn?" He'd played cricket and football, excelled in school, and followed his two older sisters to university in Cardiff, where he'd met Rhonda. "She was the only girl I'd really ever dated," he confessed. "We went out for three years." He seemed startled at what had happened with Glynnis, and Bronwyn felt sad for how his life had been destroyed in an instant with a simple, horrible lie.

She told him a little about herself, about growing up on the farm in Llangynog, about her sketches, and about her abortive attempt at university in Wrexham. "I missed home too much," she said, not mentioning the Twlwyth Teg or Pysgotwr.

"Then you'd not consider moving away?" Davyyd asked.

"I just couldn't," she answered truthfully.

She described her job at Pennant Melangell. "I'm sort of a jack-of-all-trades, but I have to be the one in charge, the one who makes sure everything gets done." She went on about the feast day celebration, confessing that she felt overwhelmed by it and sometimes wished she hadn't thought it up at all. "When the idea came to me, it was before Glynnis died. There wasn't as much on my mind then as there is now."

"I'd like to come to the churchyard sometime, to see where it happened," Davyyd said, "but so far I haven't been able to make myself do it."

"It's beautiful there," Bronwyn empathized, "and the tranquility of the place would help you heal, I'm sure."

When the conversation turned naturally to Rhonda Morris, Davyyd was defensive. "She was the most wonderful, kind girl, the kind of girl every man wants to marry in the end," he said, guilt clouding his face. "But I guess I was complacent with our relationship, wanted a bit of excitement. You know how it is? She was the only serious girlfriend I'd ever had, and Glynnis offered a bit of adventure, something different from what I had with Rhonda."

"She wants you back," Bronwyn murmured. "She's forgiven you."

"She deserves someone better," he retorted. "She's too good for me."

When they'd finished their dinner, they walked along the River Severn and through the cobbled streets of the old town centre, wandering into several art exhibits along the way. Bronwyn was pleased to find a few sketches among the watercolors, oils, pottery, and craft pieces. Music spilled out of the open doorways of pubs and clubs, and once they listened for a few minutes as a tour guide stopped nearby to point at the 17th century Rowley's House across the street and describe its ghosts to the fascinated tourists following him. "Shrewsbury is the most haunted county in England," he proclaimed.

"A haunted town!" laughed Bronwyn after they'd moved on.

"Imagine!" Davyyd joked back. "A place in England that's haunted!"

By the time they got back to Davyyd's car and turned onto the A5 toward Oswestry, Bronwyn was feeling relaxed, content, and very tired. *So what if I haven't had time to figure out the Twlwyth Teg's latest message or to think about how Glynnis' wedding ring got into my pocket?* she comforted herself. It had been a wonderful evening, and she couldn't help hoping that Davyyd Paisley would call her again.

They parted in Oswestry, Davyyd walking her to her car and giving her a kiss on the cheek. "I had a lovely evening," she murmured, not sure what was appropriate.

"So did I," he answered, and she believed him.

She drove west out of Oswestry, taking the longer route on the "A" roads as far as Llanfyllin so as to avoid the dark and lonely "B" roads as long as possible. She wasn't a fool, after all. There was no sense in taking chances she didn't have to.

As she drove, she thought reluctantly about the Twlwyth Teg, not wanting to disturb the mood of the evening with a return to the panic she'd felt earlier that day. *Atheling*...She'd heard that word before somewhere. Sure, it was a medieval term, but maybe she'd read it in a book? *Atheling*...She thought it meant a prince or a lord of some kind. *Atheling fails*...There were no more princes in Wales, unless you counted the Prince of Wales, which couldn't be right in this case. Maybe a lord? But again, she didn't know of anyone who would fit the puzzle. Whoever it was, he had failed, or he was going to fail, if the words of the Welsh fairies were correct.

She had no idea at all of the next words. *Dog companion carries the chaffer*...She didn't know what a dog companion was, nor a chaffer either. *I could be a dog companion, though,* she realized, thinking of old Nan. But was that what it meant? Maybe in medieval days a dog companion was someone who led the hunt, who controlled the hounds. Didn't they have something called "dog boys," who even slept with the hounds in their kennel? *Oh, my. I must be tired,* she thought. *None of that has anything to do with Glynnis' murder, that's for sure.* That was one for Google.

Common profit must be considered...Common profit must be what profited everyone, rich and poor alike. Who was acting in the name of common profit, though? And what acts had they committed, or were they going to commit? Were they suggesting that she act for the common profit, whatever that was? Or were they doing it?

And who was the guardian? They'd mentioned a guardian twice now, and she still had no idea who it was, nor did she understand it when they shouted "Thick!" at her. She did understand their final words, though. *It's me...*

Maybe I should stop by the counseling centre to use the computer, she thought suddenly. She'd be driving right past. *It'd be deserted this time of night.* She wondered if she was brave enough. After finding Glynnis' body, she'd been jumpy even if she arrived an hour earlier than everyone else in the daylight. Now, in the middle of the night, it would be worse.

Still, maybe she'd sleep better if she looked the words up, and the computer was far faster and easier than her mobile when it came to that. It would be safer to wait and do it on her phone, of course, but not only was it easier on the computer with its bigger screen, but it was also less likely that anyone would discover what she'd been up to. Medieval words recorded in a search on a computer in a medieval church wouldn't call attention to themselves. A search for medieval phrases on her phone would be a different story entirely, should someone look. At the least, they would raise questions about her sources again. If for some reason she became the major suspect, someone might access her phone to check her calls and search history. Maybe knowing what they meant would help her figure out how Glynnis' wedding ring got into her pocket, but that would have to wait. *Patience,* she told herself. But when she had doubts about her own involvement in Glynnis' murder, patience was hard to come by.

Her thoughts were interrupted by the chiming of her mobile phone just as she turned onto the B4391 toward Pennant Melangell and Llangynog. She must have just driven into a service area, being near Llanfyllin.

She picked up the phone and managed to hit the keys for her recorded messages.

The single message was short and concise. "This is Will Cooper. Call me when you can."

Her heart skipped a beat. *Finally!* She took a deep breath and hit the re-dial key, holding the phone to her ear while she drove.

He picked up almost immediately. "Hey, thanks for calling me back."

"I just came into a service area and saw that you called," she told him. "When did you call?"

"Just a few minutes ago." His voice was soft. "I was wondering if you'd seen or heard anything else since we've talked." Now she could hear a grin in his voice and couldn't decide whether to be offended or not.

"I see and hear a lot of things," she evaded him, thinking of the ring and trying to decide whether to mention it or not. *I could just toss it into the shrubbery alongside the footpath, pretend I never found it.* "You chose a late hour to call and check." *I shouldn't have said that.* What did it matter when he called? She was just happy that he had.

He didn't seem offended. "Not that late. You must be driving. You said you just came into a service area."

"And I'll be driving out of it in a minute," she said.

"Where are you, then?" The question was casual, even if the intent might not have been.

"Driving home from Oswestry." She'd might as well tell him. "I had a dinner with Davyyd Paisley tonight."

Silence stretched to an uncomfortable conclusion. "Why would you do that? Do you have a death wish? What if he's the killer?"

"He can't be. He's too nice," she retorted. *It's me, it's me, it's me...*

Silence returned for a minute, two. She glanced at her phone, wondering if she'd lost the signal. Finally, Will spoke. "I feel I've involved you in this, and if something happened to you now, it'd be my fault. I couldn't handle that. Not again. Please, promise me you'll be careful."

"I was involved in this long before I met you," Bronwyn informed him. "We didn't even meet until after I'd discovered Glynnis' body. Remember?"

"Of course, I know that." He sounded exasperated now, and Bronwyn regretted her flippancy. "Please promise me you won't take any more chances? I know you want to clear your name, but this isn't the way to go about it."

"I'll be careful," she hedged. "I didn't,,," she stopped herself. He didn't need to know why she'd gone to dinner with Davyyd.

But he'd caught it. "Didn't what?"

"I didn't do it to clear my name." There went the chance of seeing Davyyd again.

There was a moment of silence. "You won't meet anyone else who's a suspect in the case? Because it really wasn't a safe decision to meet Davyyd Paisley, even if he does seem too nice to murder someone."

You can't tell me what to do with my personal life, she thought defiantly, but she was too timid to say it aloud. She was glad he didn't know about Hal Corse. "I'll try to avoid the obvious suspects," she mumbled.

"Call me if you need me for anything, okay? I mean it. If anything seems off to you, don't go checking it out on your own. Let me do it."

"I will."

"You have my number?"

"I just called you back," she reminded him. "It's in my messages."

"Put it on speed dial. Just in case."

Maybe he did care, after all. "Where are you?"

"Gloucester. I came to see my niece."

"That's a long way to come if I need to call for help," she pointed out.

"I can drive fast," he assured her back just before the phone went dead.

She bypassed Pennant Melangell and met no other vehicles until she drove through Llangynog, where several vehicles remained in the car park despite the late hour. She crept through the village, mindful of pedestrians, and then sped up toward home.

Once inside, she stopped by her parents' bedroom to let them know she'd arrived home safely. *I've got to get my own place,* she told herself as she climbed the stairs to her bedroom. *24 years old, and I still have to check in when I get home from a date.*

In her bedroom, she closed the door and sat on the bed, pushing old Nan to one side. She opened her bag and took out the shining wedding ring. Silver bands twined together to spotlight a small but brilliant pear-cut diamond. She held it up to the light from the lamp on the nightstand to see it more closely.

There was no doubt that it belonged to Glynnis. But how had she ended up with it?

She twisted it in her fingers, staring at it, trying to will it to reveal its secrets.

Could I have put it in my pocket that morning when I found Glynnis? She tried to remember what she'd done in the churchyard. She'd not been thinking straight, or she'd not have picked Glynnis up and held onto her, ruining the crime scene. But why would she take the ring from Glynnis' finger and put it in her pocket? It made no sense.

Had she murdered Glynnis? Surely the Twlwyth Teg wouldn't keep saying *"it's you"* unless it was true. Would they have any reason for trying to make her believe she was crazy? Maybe they'd killed Glynnis themselves and then wanted Bronwyn to think she'd done it for some reason. But why? Somehow, she felt that whatever was going on with them was connected to Granny Powers in some way. But how? She shook her head. *If I'd killed Glynnis Saturday night, I'd have found myself with bloody clothes. Wouldn't I have done?* That was something she could cling to, anyway. *No bloody clothes; no murder.* Right?

So, if she didn't put the ring in her pocket, who did and for what reason? The moment that thought had formed, another followed on its heels. *Someone must be trying to frame me. I've got to get rid of the ring. Just in case....in case someone else put it in my pocket and not me.*

She wished she'd thrown it out the car window as she'd driven home that evening. Who would find it alongside the roadway between Pennant Melangell and Oswestry? No one, at least not for a long time.

But she hadn't thrown it out the car window, so now what was she to do with it? She thought about it. She could creep out of the house; take old Nan with her and cross the pasture into the woods until she got to her secret pool of water and throw it in there. She glanced at the window. It was dark of the moon, so there'd be no moonlight to travel by, but she could take a torch, manage it in the dark.

She almost pushed herself up off the bed before she realized that she couldn't do it. The pasture and woods that had always seemed to envelope her in safety no longer felt quite so safe. She'd be terrified to walk out there in the dark.

What else could she do with it? She couldn't simply hide it among her clothes or under the mattress. She pushed old Nan aside and slid to the edge of the bed, looking around the small room. In her desk? Too obvious. Amongst her sketching materials? Taped to the back of one of her sketches?

She stood up and walked to the window, pushing it open wide. In the barn? Maybe. Or out in the pasture. She could go out the next morning early on the pretext of taking Hobbs a carrot and then bury it beneath the apple tree in the pasture while her dad was having his breakfast or was off to church. No one would notice disturbed earth in a pasture where animals churned the ground into mud every spring day. Yes, that was it.

She laid the ring on the window sill, wishing there was moonlight to light its beauty before it went into the earth, perhaps never to be re-discovered and admired again. After a moment's thought, she left it there and went back to her bed. If there was a heaven, maybe Glynnis would look down and see it glimmering there when the morning sun's rays fell upon the window. The thought gave her a bit of peace.

She tried to think of the good time she'd had with Davyyd and the fact that Will had called to check on her as she drifted into a restless sleep. It had been a good day, all in all. And the next morning she would be up early, take care of the ring, and get up to Pennant Melangell to use the computer. Maybe then she could figure out the puzzles once and for all.

But as her consciousness left her to the emptiness of sleep, the Twlwyth Teg's words still haunted the fringes of her mind – "*It's you.*"

Chapter Eighteen

Will had tried to deal with his guilt the rest of the week. He'd not thought that Notley would threaten Bronwyn with a lie detector assessment, and he could see from her face that she'd been both shocked and mortified at the idea. Clearly there were things she wasn't telling them; she'd admitted as much to him when they were at the beach that last Sunday. But he couldn't fathom what she was so frantic to keep secret, nor why. Surely, she must be protecting someone. Who? Why was she so desperate to protect her secrets? Could it be a family member she didn't want discovered? He couldn't, for the life of himself, think how it could be otherwise, either a family member or herself.

Unless she really did have visions or something, like ancient druids who claimed to have the second sight. He shook his head and grunted at the idea. *God, I hope she doesn't believe she's one of those.* He didn't see her as being mental, but you sometimes couldn't tell. People looked normal and even acted normal, until they didn't.

He'd thought they'd connected well that day, that she'd finally relaxed a bit with him. He'd enjoyed spending the time with her, sparing with her over how much each was willing to reveal, and he had to admit to himself that he was attracted to her, and not just for the information she could give him. She was different from other girls he'd known, and he thought if this murder case wasn't standing between them that perhaps she would lose that wariness she always seemed to have and they might have fun together. Whatever the case, he was finding her harder to shake from his mind than he liked, and he was tempted to try to see her again.

But not until the case was solved. Spending the one day with her had been a mistake he was not about to repeat. Notley had gotten too close to the truth after their second interview with her, and he didn't dare risk his place on the force with what he had to admit was a whim. Yes, he found her attractive, but wanting to spend time with her, to brainstorm with her about the case, even to wrangle with her over what she wouldn't tell him –none of that was worth the risking his career.

He would have to distance himself from her, and that was really what this weekend away was meant for. He'd spend Saturday with Lesley, which would most certainly take his mind off Bronwyn. Lesley, although he didn't see her often these days, was a link to a past that he continued to hold onto strongly despite knowing deep down that it was lost to him. Lesley was lovely, intelligent, sophisticated, and great fun. He told himself it would be great to see her again.

Then why am I not looking forward to the weekend? He ignored the question. Once he was with Lesley, thoughts of Bronwyn would retreat to the back of his mind, he was sure. It was just the case that kept him focused on her. *It's gone on too long, and I can't think of anything else,* he assured himself.

Until he thought of Lark. He smiled at the thought of her. Spending Sunday with her would be a treat, and he was grateful that his parents already had plans for the day so that the awkwardness of spending time with them could be avoided.

He and Notley had stopped in Llangynog on their way home, their destination the Tanat Inn where Notley hoped to catch a moment with Cecil Lumley to ask about Bronwyn's demeanor on that Sunday morning he had seen her walking the footpath to where she would discover Glynnis Paisley's body. They put the car in the car park and then walked past a group of young men playing five-a-side football pitch and another group of elderly men on the bowling green. Children shrieked joyfully in the play park as they continued on, making Will smile.

"What's so funny, Cooper?" Notley growled, still irritated after his unsuccessful bullying of Bronwyn.

"Nothing's funny. It's the kids. They make me smile."

Notley looked sideways at him and rapped his cane on the sidewalk a bit harder. "Don't find them amusing myself."

"No kids, then?" Will asked him casually.

"Of course not. You?"

"Not yet, but someday I'd like one, I think," Will admitted. *One like Lark, intelligent and curious and entertaining.*

"Kids don't fit into the lifestyle of a murder detective," Notley grumbled. "You've got your head in the clouds if you think otherwise."

They found Cecil Lumley pulling pints behind the bar, with two barmaids on hand to deliver them to the tables.

"Guess Glynnis Paisley has been replaced," Notley noted.

"Summer business is just getting started," Lumley explained. "I needed someone right away." He gave Notley an annoyed look. "Bet you didn't come in to ask about my workers, though, did you?"

"We came in to ask about Bronwyn Bagley," Notley agreed.

"Told you already, I saw her on the footpath near eleven or half-eleven."

"What we wanted to know is how did she seem to you?" Notley told him.

Lumley sloshed a beer on the counter as he handed it over to the new barmaid, spattering some on Notley's jacket. "Normal. She seemed completely normal. Just a girl out for a walk on a rainy Sunday morning."

"Not in a hurry?"

Lumley shook his head.

"Did she stop and talk to you?"

"Said good morning and asked about the fishing."

"Did she look agitated?"

Lumley let out an exasperated breath. "You're wrong if you think she killed Glynnis. She didn't have the look of a murderer that morning, I can tell you."

Will and Notley spent the rest of the week working in the office in Caernarfon, typing out notes and transcripts of their interviews, tracking the whereabouts of the American Mark McGuire, and debating who they should re-interview in the hope that eventually someone's story would change or someone would slip up and reveal something only the murderer would know.

In their Friday meeting with Chief Superintendent Bowers, he informed them that this would be their last free weekend before being put back into the rotation.

"The case has gone on nearly three weeks. If it hasn't solved itself by now, chances are you have free time on your hands for a new case if one turns up."

"Then we're classifying it as unsolved?" Will asked.

Notley shot him an annoyed look. "He didn't say we're giving up, Cooper. You're still stuck with me on this one, like it or not."

Chief Superintendent Bowers nodded. "Sean's right. You'll keep working the case as long as new leads develop, but it can be secondary to whatever new case comes up."

"Right," Will said, thinking that the weekend couldn't get there fast enough.

On Friday night he debated whether to drive down to Cardiff, where Lesley lived, or whether to wait for the morning, deciding at last that he didn't want to put Lesley in the position of deciding whether to invite him to spend the night at her flat or not. *I told her I'd see her on Saturday,* he reminded himself, *so showing up on a Friday night might not be such a great idea.* He wondered idly if she dated other men during the long weeks when he didn't call her and decided that he'd be surprised if she didn't. One of these days she'd probably tell him she was moving in with someone who actually saw her on a regular basis. It would be no more than he deserved.

He considered calling Bronwyn, but resisted the urge. It was probably better to keep his distance, even on the phone. He wondered, though, if he was just being a coward. He hadn't defended her at all when Notley interrogated her the second time, not like he had tried to on that first afternoon after she'd just found the body. Maybe she wasn't thinking too highly of him now. He'd do well to avoid her, most likely.

He ended up spending most of the evening straightening up his flat, which had begun to look rather too lived in. He washed up the dishes that had piled up in the sink, put clean sheets on the bed, and even polished the floor. It was near midnight when he finally sat down in his chair with his allotted portion of Famous Grouse and relaxed.

All the housework seemed to have done the trick for taking his mind off things, because he slept in later than he'd intended the next morning. He showered and dressed, then threw a change of clothes into his overnight bag and caught the A437 south. He would drive the major roadways through central Wales, which would put him in Cardiff near the noon hour that he'd arranged with Lesley.

As it happened, there was quite a lot of traffic, it being a sunny Saturday nearing the end of May when the temperature could be counted on to allow for excursions to the seashore, picnics on castle grounds, and other outdoor activities. Weaving in and out of traffic in his little MGF, Will nearly slammed into stopped traffic ahead as he neared Builth Wells.

Must be an accident somewhere, he groaned internally. Late already for his date with Lesley, he knew he'd now be later still. He pulled out his mobile and rang her.

"Lorry accident," she informed him. "I was afraid you'd get stuck in that mess."

"I'll be there as soon as I can find a detour around it," he promised her, thinking that so far, the day had not gotten off to a great start and hoping fervently that it would improve.

He was nearly an hour late by the time traffic had been diverted away from the crash. Crawling along behind a long line of cars, Will fumed about the slowness of the pace, but could do nothing to improve his circumstances. He knew he needed to get over his foul mood before meeting Lesley, but couldn't manage to dispel it as the frustration of the slow traffic melded with the frustration over Notley's methodical slowness in solving the case and filled him with a despair he'd hoped he could put behind him, if only for the weekend. But if he were honest, it wasn't just Notley or the traffic. He could hardly remember a time when he hadn't felt irritated in the past two years. He fretted about the unwanted transfer, he worried about exposing people like Bronwyn to danger, he antagonized Notley when he probably deserved better. *Julia,* he thought, *why is it that you affect me more in your death than in your life?* He knew he needed to put her death behind him, but how could he when it seemed to haunt every aspect of his life?

Lesley met him at the door of her flat, grinning and shaking short dark curls that startled him.

"Weren't you a redhead last time I saw you?" he asked, amused.

"I was," she laughed, "but as you'll recall, that was some time ago."

"Only three weeks," he protested. *Has it really been only three weeks since our weekend at the Cheltenham races?* It seemed a lifetime.

"Three long and trying weeks," she agreed merrily. "Where are we off to then? I wasn't sure how to dress."

He looked at her moss green blouse and short cream skirt, with ruffles of all things. "I was hoping you'd have some ideas."

"As it happens, I do. There's a crafts fair down at the bay that I'd really love to wander through. After, I thought maybe we'd do a bit of wine tasting downtown and then dinner somewhere."

He nodded. "That sounds fine, if that's what you want."

"Come in then, while I get a jumper. It might be cool down by the water."

He stepped into the flat and looked around while he waited. He'd forgotten how artistic it was, or maybe he'd just not noticed before. Nearly every wall was painted a different brilliant color, but somehow it all tied together with the cubist art she was partial to, along with a good collection of interesting pottery pieces. There were fresh flowers on the small dining table, he noticed, wondering if she'd bought them or they'd been given to her. The room smelled clean with opened windows allowing a light breeze to stir gauzy draperies.

She flounced out of the bedroom, carrying a multi-colored cotton jumper. "Hey, I almost forgot to ask. Lila, my neighbor, has extra tickets for Rhydian tonight in the arena, if you're interested. They're not cheap, but I'd love the chance to see him. We could split the cost."

"That would go late, wouldn't it? Until midnight or after?"

"Yeah, but so what? You're not driving back to Caernarfon tonight anyway." A frown replaced the cheeky grin she'd worn earlier, and suddenly the freckles stood out across her cheeks and nose.

"No, but I have to pick Lark up early, before breakfast," he explained. "Mum's off to a charity event in Cheltenham, and Dad's going in to work."

"And you need your beauty sleep?" she teased, but he could tell he'd disrupted her jovial mood.

"You could go anyway, if you wanted to, with your friend."

"Maybe I'll check with her later, after I've had the day to change your mind." She was smiling again, and Will thought he'd made it through that hump, at least. That grin had promise in it, and he didn't feel averse to being persuaded.

They spent several hours wandering through the arts and crafts booths, Lesley taking time to examine the offerings carefully while Will stood waiting on the promenade. When they were halfway through the lines of booths, they bought paper boats of fish and chips to eat standing up while looking out over the harbor. Lesley pointed out some of the famous buildings edging the bay.

"St. David's Hotel is there," she pointed, "and just down below us is the Celtic ring."

Will leaned down to look and nodded. "I never took much time for sightseeing when I was working here, I guess."

"No, you were more involved in the night life, doing what you did."

He sighed. "I still miss it."

"Then murder's not your thing?"

He considered it for a moment. "It's learning something new all over again, when I was good at what I did before. It'll probably be okay with time."

"Then they'll not be sending you back here soon?"

"No, there's no possibility of that."

"You're sure?"

"Absolutely. My days here are over."

After a few minutes of quiet contemplation of that fact, Lesley seemed to gather herself, and then she talked about the art they had seen, her infectious smile and determined upbeat attitude attracting looks from several passing men. "I've enjoyed decorating my flat so much."

"It looks great." Will's compliment was sincere. "I hadn't remembered it being so colorful before."

"No, color is my new passion," she said, and indeed, she did look great in her brilliant and colorful cotton jumper and new dark hair. She had always been stylish, a girl to flaunt when she was at his side.

After their brief lunch, Lesley found a primitive-looking pitcher in a brilliant sapphire blue color, along with two tiny Asian-style clay cups to buy.

While he was waiting for her to make her purchase, Will wandered into a booth filled with nature sketches, examining them with interest. Although they seemed skillfully done, he objected to the artist's tendency to add detail that seemed designed to create an impression of charm, rather than realism. *Bronwyn's art is more truthful,* he thought. *She draws exactly what she sees.* Then he cocked his head to the side to consider another thought. *Does that mean she saw the face she put into the sketch I bought?*

Lesley interrupted his thoughts, taking his hand and pulling him from the booth. "These are so perfect! Won't they look great sitting on my coffee table?" She glanced at him and frowned. "Did you even see what I was buying?"

"Blue pitcher and cups," he managed, "right?"

"Have you suddenly developed an interest in art?"

"Art? No, it's just those sketches caught my eye, is all." He wasn't going to admit to more than that.

"Sketches, huh? And what exactly did you like about them?"

He smiled. "I didn't like them. That's the thing. I bought a sketch recently in a gift shop at the church where the murder we're working on took place. I think it's a lot better than these."

"Good for you, then," she cheered him. "That's the first step in art appreciation."

Later in the afternoon they locked her purchases in the boot of the car and walked along the downtown streets, looking for shops offering wine-tasting and finding fewer than they'd hoped for.

"We could drive out to Llanerch and Rutherford Hill," Will offered. "They're close enough."

"No, let's not." Lesley shook her head. "If we go driving around the countryside, we'll never be back in time for dinner."

For the concert, you mean, Will thought stubbornly, although he didn't say it aloud.

They'd had a nice day, Will had to admit as they sat down to penne spezzatino at Bellinis Restaurant in Mermaid Quay. The case had disappeared from his mind almost entirely for the time being. By the time they ordered a decent bottle of Llanerch winery's Celtic Dry White wine to accompany their meal, he'd spent a bit more than he'd budgeted for the day's entertainment, but being with Lesley was worth it, he told himself. He hadn't missed the admiring looks other men had shot her way, and it felt good to be out with a girl who most men would consider a catch. If they wanted to sit in a nice restaurant with a good meal and a view of Cardiff Bay out the window beside them, surely it was worth the few extra pounds. Besides, he was feeling a little guilty about neglecting her the past three weeks and even more so that he was deserting her for the Rhydian concert later that night.

She chose a time as they were finishing their meal to press him about the concert, but her mistake was to begin by asking about the case.

"I can't say much, you know," he told her, hoping she'd drop the subject.

"But surely you could say who the suspects are? I know it was a young woman who was killed. Stabbed, wasn't she?"

"Stabbed and clubbed over the head." He hated relating the grizzly details while they were still finishing their dinner.

"And you have no leads?"

He shook his head at her, grinning despite himself. "You're going to get it out of me one way or another, aren't you?"

She winked at him. "Is it working?"

He nodded. "We have a few things. We've found where she was first attacked alongside a footpath that runs from Llangynog to Pennant Melangell. We found a wine bottle she was hit with there."

"No fingerprints?"

"No. It had been cleaned." *By me.*

"So, what's kept you so busy that you couldn't call me more than once in the past three weeks?"

Will's eyes met hers. "There were a lot of people to interview, some of whom we had to track down, and Llangynog isn't exactly close to Caernarfon. They wouldn't spring for a temporary office there, so we had to drive back and forth, which amounted to lots of time on the road, which I had to spend with Notley, so you should feel sorry for me. There's a lot of paperwork, office work – that sort of thing, as well." It sounded like excuses, and he knew Lesley would realize that. "It's not like drug work, where you can make plans ahead of time. It's more a matter of being ready to run off somewhere when something turns up that might mean something."

She was watching him. "Who did you interview?"

Bronwyn, he thought. *Bronwyn who's not as sophisticated as you, who may not turn heads the way you do, but who has something about her that makes me think about her more than I should.* "The usual suspects. The woman's husband, family, her flatmate, employer, a couple of people she was seen with that night….the woman who found her body."

Lesley digested that. "And it took three entire weeks to do that?"

"Like I said, we had to track people down, and nothing's near to Caernarfon when the murder's happened on the far side of our district."

Lesley sat back and picked up her wine glass. She took a sip, leaving a lipstick print on the glass. "You aren't going to the concert with me tonight, are you?"

Will picked up his own wine glass, holding it in his hand, but not drinking. "I told you it would be too late. I have to pick Lark up by half-eight at the latest, and it's a bit of a drive to Gloucester."

"Nine o'clock wouldn't do?"

"No." The stubbornness was back. He didn't like being pushed. "No, it won't. I promised her breakfast, and a day at Folly Farm. She's just a little girl. I'm sure she's used to eating early, and we'd want to get there in time to see it all."

Lesley sipped her drink, studying him with serious eyes. "Lark isn't Julia, Will," she said softly. "You can't make up for what happened to Julia by doting on her daughter."

Will stared at her. "Is that what you think I'm doing?"

"It's obvious, isn't it? You always put her needs ahead of your own. Ahead of mine, too, truth be told. I wanted to spend the evening with you, and most likely the night, as well. Why can't you see that?" She paused, taking a deep breath. "You can't change what happened by spending time with Julia's daughter, Will. Nothing you do with Lark will make up for whatever guilt you feel about Julia's death. Lark has her own life. She's probably not going to follow in Julia's footsteps, whether you spend time with her or not."

Will set his wine glass on the table. "I spend time with Lark," he blurted furiously, "because I enjoy her. She's funny, she's smart, and she's curious about everything. We have fun together. It has nothing whatsoever to do with Julia." As the words flowed from his mouth, he knew they were true. Julia was past. Whatever guilt he had felt over her death needed to be past, as well. He wasn't trying to atone for that guilt by spending time with Lark. He spent time with Lark because he loved her.

Across the table, Lesley was silent. Her face had gone pale at his outburst, her freckles standing out more in the candlelight than they had in the sun earlier. "And what about us, Will?" she asked at last. "Because I want more than we have together. A phone conversation once every three weeks and a visit once a month isn't enough for me any longer."

He let out a breath he hadn't know he was holding and bit back his anger. *So, this is it, then,* he thought, surprised that he didn't feel any stronger emotion than a vague relief. "What kind of relationship can we have, Lesley, with me living in Caernarfon and you here in Cardiff?"

"I thought maybe, since you are so resentful about your re-assignment, you'd quit the force and find something else to do." She blushed, obviously not having anticipated the need to say it so blatantly. "I like my job; you don't."

"So you'd have me quit the force and come here to do....what?"

She shrugged. "I don't know. What else would interest you? Didn't your father want you to follow in his footsteps?"

"Yeah," he said bitterly, "but it's not what I want."

"Then what do you want, Will?" Lesley narrowed her eyes. "What do you want?"

He looked away, out toward the bay and the boats drifting in to see the lights of the city. "I don't know what I want. I only know what I don't want, and I don't want to quit the force and move here to Cardiff and become a workaholic solicitor like my father."

"You'd be closer to Lark here," Lesley pointed out.

Will turned to look at her. "No, Lesley, that's not going to work. You just said I spend too much time with Lark. I have no intention of quitting the force and moving back here, so let it drop, okay?"

"Then that's it? We're done?"

"If you want it that way." He gestured toward her wine glass. "Finish that up and I'll take you home."

"I can make my own way, thanks." She stood up. "I'll just get my pottery out of the car and be off."

He opened the boot for her and lifted her parcels out, handing them to her carefully.

She reached out and gave him a one-armed hug, awkward with the packages in her other hand. "Listen, Will, if you're sitting in your hotel room all alone tonight, and all of a sudden you regret the choice you just made, you can call me and I'll take you back, okay?"

Guilt flooded him. *God, she really cares.* He lifted a hand and raked it through his unruly hair. "I'll be doing some thinking."

She smiled at him, blinking at tears. "Take care of yourself, Will."

He nodded mutely, and then he watched her walk away from the car, away from him, away from his life. *She was a bloody beautiful girl,* he thought. *What have I done?*

After that, he knew he needed to leave Cardiff behind, to drive away so that he wouldn't be tempted to look back. *It's for the best,* he assured himself, even as he wondered if he should take her up on her offer and call her before it was really too late.

He drove across the Severn Bridge into England and checked into a hotel in downtown Gloucester, thinking that he could sleep late and still pick Lark up on time. Once settled into his room, he sat down on a chair by the window, screwed open the stopper on the flask he'd brought along, and watched the city relax into night. In the distance, long boats tethered to docks on the river twinkled with lights as their occupants relaxed for the evening before allowing themselves to be rocked into sleep. Closer, he could see couples walking on the sidewalks below, chatting, holding hands, laughing into the night. If he looked out the corner of the window, he could just glimpse the magnificence of Gloucester Cathedral on the nearby hill.

He felt lonely. Of course, Lesley's suggestion that he leave the force and move to Cardiff had been ridiculous; he was still in shock that she would think of it. But that didn't ease the emptiness he felt knowing that he might never see her again.

He'd forgotten in the time he'd lived in Caernarfon how sophisticated Lesley was. Her brilliant flat, her expensive clothing, even her stylish hairstyle spoke of a confidence he wasn't sure he could match, particularly as a disgraced police detective. Truly, it was a wonder she'd hung on with him as long as she had. What she wanted was someone with more prestige, a solicitor like his father, someone who earned a top salary and who carried some weight in the community. Certainly, she hadn't wanted someone who only called her on occasion and saw her even less.

He sipped his whiskey, enjoying the warmth of it, letting it settle into his stomach. What had she said? She'd said that Lark was not Julia, and the minute she'd said it, something inside him had changed.

No, Lark was not Julia. Lark was lively, curious, outgoing, and confident, whereas Julia...Julia had shut herself off from the world from the time she was only a baby. Julia had never been outgoing; she had seemed to live in an isolated world of her own with her singing to herself, playing at dress-up, and shutting herself up in her room. Even if he'd tried, Will would not have been a part of Julia's world. Might he have noticed the drug use then? Suddenly he didn't think he would have, even if he'd been looking for it. Julia had always been unusual, with her pale, dreamy eyes and tendency to keep herself secret. Even if he'd tried to be close to her, he'd probably have thought that her behavior was just Julia being Julia, nothing more.

And with that realization, all the guilt he'd felt for the past two years fled, to be replaced by anger. How dare Notley use his feeling of guilt - indeed, encourage it – to put Will on guard, thinking that he walked a narrow line between keeping his job on the force and being fired? How dare he intimate that Chief Superintendent Bowers found him lacking somehow? How dare he run this case the way he wanted to, which had produced nothing of value, instead of allowing Will to make some of the decisions and take the lead, at least some of the time?

He pounded a fist on the table in frustration as defiance flooded him. Well, damn Notley! He'd do what he needed to do, and if Notley complained to Bowers, he'd defend himself. Surely Bowers would understand what drove him to seek information behind Notley's back if he understood that Notley's Sherlock Holmes imitation and overbearing interrogation tactics pushed witnesses into silence rather than eloquence? And if not, he didn't really care.

He strode across the room and fumbled in the pockets of the jacket he'd thrown onto the bed, finding his mobile phone. Sitting down by the window again, he pushed the numbers he'd memorized in the past week.

There was no answer.

He hesitated and when her voice mail answered, he left a quick message. "This is Will Cooper. Call me when you can." He closed his phone and leaned back in the chair, letting the disappointment he felt at her not answering to blend with the defiance and anger he'd felt earlier and knowing that all of it would end by producing a languid acceptance as the emotions fizzled.

He was lying on his bed watching the BBC news when his mobile rang a short time later. "Hey, thanks for calling me back," he told Bronwyn, grinning and hoping she knew it. "I was wondering if you'd seen or heard anything else since we've talked?"

Afterward, he wished the conversation had gone better. She hadn't seemed to catch that he was just teasing her, sounding a little offended as she answered his intended lighthearted question. When she confessed that she'd been out with Davyyd Paisley, he'd nearly gone off on her. What was she playing at anyway? She knew Paisley was one of their most likely suspects; surely, she realized that going off on a date with him was a foolish risk? He'd hung up feeling angry and frustrated with her, a feeling that hung with him far into the night. It wasn't jealousy, he told himself. He didn't care if she dated other men, had no right to care. But, really...Davyyd Paisley?

I'll call her tomorrow, he promised himself. *I'll ask if she'll see me after hours on Monday, make sure she sees the risks in what she's doing.* If he could just convince her to trust him to solve the case instead of involving herself in it, it would be better for them all. He turned over restlessly, trying to relax.

Hours later he finally drifted off into a dreamless sleep, unaware that Monday would be too late to make the call he'd planned.

Chapter Nineteen

Will felt more cheerful the next morning after his frustration with Bronwyn faded overnight. She'd been on her way home when he'd talked to her, after all, and she'd been safe. He'd talk to her on Monday and make it clear she was to leave the investigation to him. That was all he could do, truth be told. She was an adult who made her own choices in the end.

As he drank his morning cup of tea, Will marveled that the burden of guilt he'd felt over Julia's death for so long could be dismissed with that simple, casual remark from Lesley. Yet it had happened. He found he could think neutrally about Julia for the first time in two years and see her for the way she actually was. He saw with clarity he had not possessed before that he could not be blamed for failing to see the downward spiral that led to her death. The truth was that there was nothing that would have created a closer bond between them; they had been vastly different people. The age difference meant he'd been gone from family life when she was just a child, and there had been no inclination on his part to spend time with parents or a young sister who he scarcely knew. How had he ever come to blame himself so deeply for her death?

Humming under his breath and looking forward to his day with Lark, he checked out of the hotel before eight o'clock, stopped by a nearby bakery to pick up pastries, filled the car up with petrol, and was knocking on the front door of his parents' home by half-eight.

Lark flung the door open and hugged Will around the waist, which was as high as she could reach. "Where are we going? Grandmother said somewhere special!"

He leaned down to hug her back. "We are going somewhere special." He straightened to see his mother hovering behind Lark near the staircase. She was dressed in a lilac suit, with a flowered silk scarf around her neck, her hair dyed chestnut brown and neatly coifed.

"She's been waiting for nearly an hour," she reported, a frown furrowing her brows.

"I said half-eight," Will reminded her, reaching out to tousle Lark's reddish blonde curls. *She could have said hello before criticizing me.* Ignoring his resentment, he squatted down to Lark's level. "Hey, I like the haircut. It looks good, short and curly."

She glanced sideways at her grandmother. "Grandmother thought it would be easier."

"Well, I like it. You're a lovely lady," Will assured her. He stood up and faced his mother, stepping into the foyer even though he hadn't heard an invitation to do so. "We're off to Folly Farm, so it'll be a full day. I'll hope to have her back by half-six or seven, if that's okay."

His mother nodded. She looked tired to Will, pale and drawn, the wrinkles lining her face at odds with the bright chestnut hair. "I'll be at the charity event in Cheltenham all day. Your father is joining me in the afternoon, and the two of us will plan to be home by six at the latest then."

Lark fidgeted, her eyes shining. "Folly Farm? Oh, Uncle Will, that's my favorite place in the whole world! Do you think they have rabbits there? Can we stay all day?"

A rush of love swelled Will's heart. "I'm sure they have rabbits there, and we'll stay as long as we can, love. I do have to drive back to Caernarfon tonight, you know."

"I've always wanted to go. Graham says it's the best."

"Then it'll be a treat, won't it?"

He glanced up at his mother and saw she was watching them with a curious look he couldn't read on her face. It disturbed him. "Has father left for work already?"

His mother's pensive look faded into a shrug. "You know how he is – he couldn't be bothered to wait around and say hello when he had pressing concerns at the office."

"On a Sunday," Will observed.

"I'm not sure he even realizes it's a Sunday," she murmured.

Will grabbed Lark's little lavender backpack and put it in the boot of his car, and then they drove off, leaving his mother standing in the open doorway waving at them. He watched in the rearview mirror as the brick Georgian-style house grew distant and noted that she hadn't yet moved inside by the time he turned the corner onto the next street.

"Is Grandmother feeling okay?" he asked Lark as an irrational concern nagged him.

Lark shrugged. "Same as always."

Will pulled out the bag of pastries, and Lark sorted through them before unfolding two napkins and placing one on each of their laps. "Powdered sugar," she said wisely, and then she used another napkin to wrap a butter and jam scone and handed it to him, keeping a second one for herself. "Grandmother doesn't let me eat pastries."

"It'll be our secret then," Will responded, and he was gratified when his comment brought an answering giggle.

He got onto the M5 south as soon as he could and then relaxed into the drive, listening to Lark's excited chatter and glad he'd decided to spend the day with her. His break-up with Lesley notwithstanding, it had been a good idea to get away from Caernarfon and the case for a couple of days. Indeed, he felt nearly as light-hearted as Lark as they flew down the freeway exchanging jokes and stories, looking forward to their day's adventure.

Just north of Bristol, they took the turnoff for the M5 and crossed the Severn Bridge. Will smiled as he watched Lark with her forehead pressed against the window to see the spectacular drop to the wide river delta below them. "It's a big bridge, isn't it?"

Eyes glued to the window, she nodded. "Are we in Wales now?"

"Sure, we are. Don't you remember when you came to visit me last summer? We came across this bridge then, too."

"I forgot how big it was," she told him. "Are there lots of castles in Wales, Uncle Will?"

"You know it. Remember how King Edward I decided to end the Welsh uprisings once and for all?"

"He built castles," Lark agreed. "I remember Caernarfon Castle. This summer are we going to another one?

"Conwy," he said, enjoying re-connecting with her. "And some others, if you want. They're everywhere, you know."

"Can I stay the whole summer?"

Will laughed, pleased. "I have to work, love. I get two weeks free, but that's as long as I can manage at this point."

Once they'd crossed into Wales, Will engaged Lark in watching the road signs, encouraging her to look at the unwieldy Welsh words with their many letters and lack of vowels as they hurried toward their destination. Lark, just beginning to read, found them overwhelming, but it entertained her for a bit trying. It was lucky Wales was a small country, Will thought. Even on the M4 it would strain Lark's six-year-old patience waiting the two-plus hours the journey would take when such a destination was at hand.

Lark spotted the first signs for Folly Farm midway across south Wales, and she proved a good navigator as she directed Will to the necessary turnoffs to take them there. She was bouncing on the seat as they took the final turn and crawled up the dirt lane bordered by wood and wire fences toward a rusty red barn ahead.

They parked the car and hurried together to the entryway where enormous posters announced the special events of the day: K9 Capers and Keeper Talks.

"What are we doing first?" Lark blurted the moment after Will had paid their admission and received a map and brochure in return.

He laughed and steered her toward a cluster of straw bales where they could sit. "Let's sit down a minute and make a plan."

She looked up at him, unbelieving. "We can't sit down. We've been sitting in the car for more than two hours."

She's more logical than a lot of adults I know, Will conceded. "Okay, then we're off to Jolly Barn?"

"Are the rabbits there?"

Will consulted the brochure. "It says there are rabbits there."

They spent a happy hour in the barn, hurrying from pen to pen to see kid-friendly goats, pigs, sheep, donkeys, miniature horses, and chickens. After Lark had tried her hand at milking the life-size plastic cow and Will had helped her to hold a bottle of milk for an eager kid goat, they admired Henry the Horse and Lily the Lemur and then found the pet handling area, where Lark at last got to hold a miniature lop eared rabbit.

The adoring smile on her face as she cuddled the tiny creature in her arms melted Will's heart. *Why can't mother and father let her have a little rabbit?* he wondered. It would live outside and cause them no trouble, other than maybe eating a few of his mother's flowers in the garden. *Aren't a few flowers a good sacrifice for a child's happiness?* If they kept it in a pen, it wouldn't even do that. He considered for a moment buying Lark a rabbit himself, along with the pen, food, and other necessities. What would they do – make him take it back? He sighed. Yes, they probably would do exactly that. And he could hardly keep it in his flat for the few times she got to visit him.

Later, they made their way to the Fun Fair, where they rode together on the vintage big wheel and the dodgems, Lark shrieking with excitement. It wasn't until Lark was in line for the giant helter skelter that Will's mobile phone rang for the first of many calls that would come that day.

He waved her on and swiped his phone, watching her as he answered, "Will Cooper."

"Will?" quavered the voice, and he recognized a distressed Bronwyn Bagley on the other end.

"What's going on? Are you alright?"

"I'm...I'm fine," she whispered, "but why didn't you tell me they were coming with a search warrant this morning? I could have done with a bit of a warning. I thought...well, I thought you'd do that much, at least."

"A...a search warrant? I didn't know," he stammered, cursing Notley silently at the same time. "I'm down in South Wales with my niece. What did it say they were searching for?"

"Glynnis' ring." Bronwyn's voice was quiet, and he could hear fear.

He swallowed hard. He had to ask. "Do you have Glynnis' ring?" As soon as the words left his mouth, he wished he could take them back.

There was a hesitation, just long enough that he knew something was wrong. "No."

"You're sure?"

"Yes, of course, I'm sure." She raised her voice a little. "I said I don't have it."

In for a penny, in for a pound. "Do you know where it is?"

Again, the hesitation alerted him to something unsaid. "If you think I do, then perhaps I shouldn't have bothered calling."

What aren't you telling me, Bronwyn? He wished he could push her, but didn't want to chase away any more of the trust she might feel for him. "Did they say why they got the warrant?" It wouldn't have been issued unless there'd been a good reason for it, Will knew. The laws were very strict on that. There must have been an informant. But why hadn't Notley called him about it?

"They said someone called and told them I had it." Her voice broke, and Will could picture the distress reddening her cheeks, tears in her eyes. "Why would someone do that?"

Because they're trying to frame you for the murder. "I'll check on it and see what's going on," he told her. "I'll call you right back."

He fumed while he took the time to wait for Lark at the helter skelter and to see her into the line for the chair-o-planes before opening his phone and dialing Notley's mobile. *Damn Notley, ruining my day,* he thought. *Can't I be free of him even on my weekend off?*

Notley took his time answering. "Where are you, Cooper?"

"What do you mean, where am I? What are you playing at, Notley?" Will's voice shook with anger.

"I drove by your flat, saw your car was gone, so I had to do this without you." Will could hear the nonchalance in Notley's voice.

"Why didn't you call me?"

"To what end, Cooper? So you could call and warn her we were coming?"

"Because I'm your partner, Notley. Remember? Because we work together on this case. You accused me of going behind your back, but what are you doing now if not going behind mine?"

"I did what I thought I needed to do," Notley insisted. "You've always wanted the Bagley woman to be innocent, never mind the evidence. I thought the investigation might go better if I went ahead with the search warrant without you along to bugger things up."

Will took a deep breath, trying to control his fury. "Did Bowers know about this?"

"He knew about the search warrant and approved it."

"Did he know you deliberately left me out of the loop on it?"

"I didn't deliberately leave you out, Cooper. I told you, I drove by your flat and saw your car was gone."

"But you didn't call."

"No, I didn't call. I assumed you'd left the area for the weekend, as you usually do even when you're on call and not supposed to. I called a team of investigators and went ahead on my own. It's not as if I'm here without official support."

"On your own," Will repeated, trying to think if there was a way to handle the situation to his advantage. "Bowers gave me permission to leave the area. Family business."

"Hmph! I'm surprised he didn't see through that ruse."

"Not a ruse," Will growled.

"The Bagley woman must have called you, or else how would you have found out we're here?" Notley's voice was silky, self-satisfied. "Friends now, are you? Or maybe more?"

Will wasn't going to give him the satisfaction of an answer. "On what grounds was the warrant issued?"

"An unidentified female called me and said she'd seen Miss Bagley put the ring in her jumper pocket."

"When?"

"What do you mean, when? When did she see her do it, or when did she call me?"

"Both," Will nearly shouted. Lark had finished with the chair-o-planes and skipped up to him. She glanced up at his face and fell quiet, watching him. He gestured toward the golden gallopers, but she shook her head.

"She saw her put it in her pocket on Friday night, and she called me yesterday morning."

"A whole day, and you didn't bother to inform me," Will concluded bitterly. "And Bowers approved of that?" He reached down with his free hand to caress Lark's curls.

"Bowers wasn't concerned with who knew what; his only worry was getting the warrant and doing the search before she disposed of it somewhere."

"But you didn't find it, did you?"

For the first time in the conversation, Will heard uncertainty. "No, we didn't. We pretty much tore apart the house looking for it, and now my people are outside with metal sweepers searching the grounds, the barn, the pasture, all of it."

"How long have you been there?"

"About three hours so far, and we'll probably be another couple of hours before we're done, unless we find it before then."

"No idea who the informant was?"

"Female, that's all."

"Maybe she put the ring in Bronwyn's pocket," Will seethed viciously. "Maybe she set her up."

"And if that happened, either the ring should be in the jumper pocket or Miss Bagley should have called and told us she'd found it," Notley retorted. "How else would you explain it, Cooper? If she wasn't guilty and she found it, why wouldn't she call and report it?"

"Maybe she's frightened. She's already too involved in the case, having found the victim in the churchyard." *And she knew about the attack site.* He glanced down at Lark, who was staring at him with huge eyes. *How long would it take to get to Llangynog? Three hours?* They'd be done by the time he got there. "Listen, Notley, I'm in South Wales, too far away to get there by the time you're finished. Call me if anything turns up, okay?"

"Sure, of course I'll do that." Will didn't miss the satisfaction in Notley's voice.

"And treat her nicely," Will warned him.

"It's a wicked world," Notley said, "but things must be done decently and in order."

Sherlock Holmes again. "Then I have your promise?"

Notley grunted. "I'll do my best to ignore her. How's that suit you?"

Will closed his mobile before he said something he knew he'd regret and squatted down beside Lark. "I have one more call to make, love. It won't take long. Do you want to go on the golden gallopers while I'm busy?"

"Did they find the man who killed the lady?" Lark's solemn look melted Will's anger.

He softened his voice, tried to make it sound teasing. "Hey, do you think they could find him without me there to help?"

She bit her lip while she considered his question with a disarming seriousness. "No," she decided after a moment, "because you're the best detective in North Wales."

"That's right." He grinned and then decided on a partial truth. "It was my partner, love. He's not a very good detective, and he's done something behind my back that's made me mad, that's all. It won't ruin our day out, I promise."

"Sure?"

"I'm sure. Now run along and get in line for the gallopers, and after that we'll go on the land train in Folly Wood, okay?"

"Where the ponies are?"

"Where the ponies are," he agreed.

He watched her skip to the line, her smile restored, and sighed. He'd make this call to Bronwyn and then try to forget the case again for the rest of the day. Lark deserved his full attention, and he deserved a day away from the frustration he felt with Notley.

Bronwyn answered before the ring sounded on his phone. "Will?"

"I talked to my partner just now. I didn't know anything about this, Bronwyn. Do you believe me?"

"Yes, of course." But she didn't sound as if she did.

"They'll be searching the farm, I'm afraid, but there's nothing to worry about, okay? The caller said the ring was in your jumper pocket, and if it's not, then you're fine. Can you trust me on that?"

"Do I need to stay here while they search?"

"Yes, I'm afraid you do. Did you have plans today?" *Please don't say you were spending it with Davyyd Paisley.*

"I....I just had some work to take care of up at the centre," she murmured.

Again, he felt a vague doubt. *She's keeping something from me.* "Notley said they'd be another couple of hours, is all. You'll be able to go to the centre later." He hesitated. "I'm too far away to make it up there before they're done. Otherwise, I'd come and make sure Notley's doing it properly."

"It's okay." He thought he could hear disappointment in her voice. "I'll be fine."

He took a deep breath. "Nothing else you want to tell me?"

There was a long silence. "What do you mean?"

He glanced over to see that Lark had finished with the golden gallopers and was heading his way. "Nothing. You sounded as if there was something else you might want to say, that's all. Listen, I'll call later and you can tell me how it went, okay?"

"Okay, "she agreed, but she sounded nervous, and that made Will nervous, too. He closed his phone, knocked his knuckles on a wooden fence rail for luck, and stepped forward to meet a grinning Lark.

As they walked toward the waiting area for the train, Will tried to think about his options. Something nagged at him, some premonition or emotion he couldn't identify, something which pushed him back toward Llangynog. But he couldn't take Lark back to Gloucester early. His parents had made it very clear that they wouldn't be home until after six, and it was only just a bit before one. Besides, he couldn't – and wouldn't – disappoint her, he thought as she tugged on his hand, urging him to walk faster. *This day is for Lark. Tomorrow I'll get back to business dealing with Notley and the case. Bronwyn is safe enough with police all over the property, after all.*

They rode the train, a brilliantly colored choo-choo with four cars and an engine. Lark seemed quieter than she had been earlier as Will pointed out deer, llamas, and sheep grazing on the slopes of the green parkway. In the distance, people hiked along a footpath that ran through the parkland.

"Can we do that later?" Lark wanted to know.

"After lunch," Will promised her, remembering that all they'd eaten so far had been those butter and jam scones.

Trying to recapture her earlier exuberant mood, Will bet her a pound she wouldn't find a horse or pony before he did, and to his delight she saw one almost immediately, a huge Shire horse standing beneath a willow tree.

"I won!" she sang out, holding her empty hand toward him.

He dug for a pound coin in his pocket. "Are you buying me lunch, then?" he teased.

"No! I'm buying a stuffed rabbit," she retorted primly.

"Then I have to buy lunch? We're having whatever I choose then," Will told her. "Mashed turnips and porridge. You must have something healthy to eat."

"I must have a sausage and chips," Lark chimed in, and they laughed together as the little train rounded a bend and a small herd of Shetland ponies appeared just beside the train.

They had eaten lunch and were watching the K9 Capers when Will's phone rang again. He answered it, shouting to be heard over the noise of the crowd as they cheered a collie named the Artful Dodger through a tunnel of tubes, over a hurdle, and toward the finish line.

"She's clear." Will had to strain to hear Notley's voice on the other end. "We went over the place from top to bottom, inside and out. There's no ring."

A flush of relief brought a smile to Will's lips. "Then your tipster was wrong."

"Or she got rid of it before we got there. She's hiding something, Cooper. You should have seen her face when we showed up at the door."

"Maybe she's just tired of you harassing her," Will suggested before he jabbered a farewell at Notley and went back to cheering for the next dog, this one another collie named Film Star dressed in a purple silk dress and sunglasses.

He waited to call Bronwyn back until later while Lark was in the restroom, hoping to hide the fact that he was semi-working on their day away together despite his best intentions.

"I hear they didn't find anything," he reported quickly when she answered.

"They searched everywhere, but there was nothing to find." He could hear the relief in her voice. "I'm driving up to the counseling centre now to get my work done. Better late than never, I guess."

"Don't do anything risky, okay?" Will's earlier feeling of apprehension hadn't faded with Notley's report.

"I'm just going to use the computer, that's all."

"No walking down the footpath, right?"

"Right," she agreed.

"Is anyone else going to be there?"

"The Sunday service will have ended an hour ago, and everyone will be headed back home by now. Of course, there are always some hikers and mountain bikers stopping by."

"Lock yourself in, then," Will advised her, "and be watchful when you walk to your car."

"You're lovely to worry so about me."

"I worry about everyone," Will told her, wishing he'd said something else the moment the words came from his mouth. He saw Lark walk out the restroom door. "Call me if you need anything."

"Mobile service is spotty up there," Bronwyn replied, "but I'll be fine. Don't worry." She sounded upbeat now and eager to get to her work.

Will relaxed after the call and followed Lark contentedly as she led him toward the footpath through the park. "Oh, it's a walk now, is it?" he teased. "You're going to be tired tonight."

"No, I won't," Lark retorted. "I have lots of energy. Grandmother says so."

"I bet she does," Will joked. "I bet she does."

"Are your phone calls done now?" Lark eyed him like a school master would a wayward student.

"All done," he said. "Business concluded. I am free to enjoy the rest of the day with my favorite niece." And, indeed, they managed an entire hour of peace strolling at leisure through the daisy-dotted fields. Many of the animals were friendly, allowing Lark to pet them. She pulled fistfuls of grass up to feed to the ponies, who happily nibbled it from her fingers with a gentleness he found relaxing, and even the huge shire horse stood patiently and let Lark pet his shoulder as he gazed off into the distance.

By four o'clock, Will was exhausted. Lark, unfortunately, was not. "Let's go to the Carousel Woods!" she sang out as they emerged from the zoo area.

"How about we go over there," he pointed to an outdoor play area, "and I sit on a bale of straw and watch you while you do the dragon adventure?"

"After that can we go to the Carousel Woods?" she wondered.

"What's wrong with the play area outside?"

"I want to pan for gold," she told him. "Then we'll get rich, and you can quit working and come live with us."

Why do all the women in my life want me to quit my job? Will wondered wearily. But he put a smile on his face and followed her into the Carousel Woods area, where they stood in line for their pans and learned how to slosh the water around to find tiny specks of gold that disappointed Lark, but didn't surprise Will in the least.

It was while he was sitting in the outdoor play area watching Lark threaten a much larger boy with a plastic sword on the pirate ship that his mobile rang for the last time that day.

"Cooper here," he answered mechanically.

"Can you come to Pennant Melangell?"

He sat up on the straw bale. "Bronwyn? What's wrong?"

He strained to hear her whispered voice through the static on his phone. "I'm frightened. She's here, and now my car won't start."

He thought of the ancient Volvo. No surprise there. "Who's there?"

"I…can you please just come?" Her confession came in a rush then, relief apparent as she opened up to him. "I don't know how I know the things I know. I don't know if I imagine them or if I really do hear someone talking about it. I'm not mental, though, really I'm not."

What? "But who is it you're frightened of?"

She paused for a long moment while he held his breath waiting for her to finish. "It's Rhonda. She's here, and it doesn't feel right. I'm afraid to go outside. I don't know what to do."

"Call 999," he instructed her immediately. "I'm three hours away, Bronwyn. That's too long to wait. Where are you now?"

"I'm in my office. I locked the doors." Her voice faded away.

"Bronwyn? You have to call for help. You can't stay there alone."

"I already called 999. They don't think it's an emergency, and they said it'd be a few hours before someone could get here. I'm afraid…what if she's gone when they get here? They won't believe me that she was here. They'll think I'm paranoid, wasting police resources. Please, can you come?" she whispered. "You must be far away, too, but can't you just come and check for me?"

"I want you to be safe. Is there someone else you can call? Your dad, maybe, or your brother?"

"No, I can't. They left after the detectives finished searching our farm to go to a meeting in Welshpool. Something about the sheep. They won't have their phones on."

He tried to contain his temper. Why the hell was she so stubborn? "Call 999 back. I'm too far away."

"Please come," she begged, her voice trembling. "I'll wait here in my office. No one knows I'm here."

But there was the matter of her car in the car park. "She must know you're there. She'll have seen your car."

"It's…it might be just my imagination." He could hear the panic in her voice. "Maybe I saw someone else, and it wasn't Rhonda at all."

"But you thought it was?"

"She was wearing a hoodie, but it looked like her. And she was watching for me, I'm sure she was."

"You've got to call 999 again," he insisted. "Bronwyn? Promise me you'll call right now." He waited, but dead silence filled the other end of the line. Their call had been cut off.

He hit redial and waited. Nothing. Surely Bronwyn would answer. Had the phone line been disabled?

Agitated and angry, he thought what to do. The responsible thing would be to call 999 again and impress on them that the emergency might actually be real. Bronwyn was right: maybe Rhonda wasn't Glynnis' murderer. Maybe Rhonda wasn't a threat to Bronwyn. Hell, maybe she wasn't even at Pennant Melangell. Bronwyn herself said she wasn't sure if it was her imagination or what. But what if the threat was actually real? Could he take a chance? He'd worked to build a degree of trust with her, and now it came boomeranging right back at him. What was with her? Maybe she did murder Glynnis, after all. Something wasn't right with her, that was for sure.

In addition, there was the case to solve. It was a selfish thought, but if he summoned 999 again and Rhonda was there and threatening Bronwyn, she'd be safe but he'd be cheated of the satisfaction of solving the case, without Notley. How badly did he want credit for that? Bad enough to race to the rescue and hope she'd be okay in the meantime? He'd really like to stick it to Notley after he'd gone and gotten the search warrant without telling him. And if he called 999, they'd know Bronwyn had called him. The game would be up, and Bowers would not be happy to know that he'd developed a relationship, no matter how innocent he tried to make it sound, with a murder suspect behind his partner's back.

He took a deep breath. Okay, he thought, irrational anger surging despite knowing he had to go. It was probably a mistake, but he'd honor her wishes and race off in his little MGF, if that's what she wanted so badly. It was crazy, but okay, he could probably get there in two hours if he really pushed it. It'd be a major nuisance figuring out what to do with Lark, but if emergency services didn't think Bronwyn's problem serious enough to hurry someone out to check, then it was up to him to do it instead. Unlike them, his conscience wouldn't let him just ignore her. Not after Julia.

He stood up and looked for Lark, spotting her as she raced from the pirate ship to the giant purple dragon across the play park. "Lark!" he called out. "Lark!"

She heard him and stopped in her tracks, the plastic sword swishing in an arc over her head. "Over here, Uncle Will!"

He ran toward her. "Lark, love, we've got to go." What was he going to do with her? He couldn't take the extra time to drive her home to Gloucester, and knowing his parents, they wouldn't be home on time to take her off his hands anyway. "Come on, sweetheart. I've got an emergency, and I need you to come with me fast."

"But what about my rabbit?" She pulled the pound she'd won in their bet from the pocket of her turquoise overalls. "I need to buy my rabbit first."

Will knelt down in front of her. "There's no time, Lark. I promise you we'll get you a stuffed rabbit. I promise, okay? But right now, I need you to help me with my case. And the first thing we need to do is to run to the car and get going."

"To Caernarfon?" Lark wondered as he stood and she took his hand, pulling him toward the exit.

"To Llangynog," he corrected her, "or actually, to Pennant Melangell."

"Where the princess and the hare were?"

He glanced at her in wonder as she hurried him along. "The very place."

"Is it the murderer, Uncle Will?"

"I don't know, Lark, sweetie. I have to go and investigate." He swung her to a stop and unlocked the car.

"I'll help you." She looked up at him. "I'll be brave."

"You'll stay in the car and be safe," he told her, lifting her onto the seat. "I need you to do exactly what I tell you to do and no arguing about it."

"But..."

"Lark, you need to do this for me, okay? I can't do my job if I'm worrying about you."

She snapped her seatbelt closed. "Okay. I'll do what you say. But if you need help, I might have to call 999."

"That's a good thought, love. That's exactly what I'll need you to do."

He tried to call Bronwyn back again once they were in the car and had bumped down the dirt lane to the nearest main road, but there was no answer. He knew she'd called from her office phone, there being scanty mobile service at Pennant Melangell, so her failure to answer his call worried him. But if she stayed locked inside her office, she'd be okay.

He turned west, hoping that whatever roads he took would lead quickly to the A 487 that ran up the coast. Once on that highway, he could push the little MGF to top speed, but even at best, it would take him at least two hours to get to her.

I wish she'd call 999 again, he thought as he drove. Why did Rhonda Morris frighten her so much when she'd been meeting with the other suspects all along without feeling threatened? Maybe it was all about her mental health. If she really didn't know where the information she'd shared with him had come from, what did that mean? Was she crazy? Should he call despite his promise and have someone go out there and check on her? But what if it was nothing? He'd be giving his relationship with her up to Bowers for no good reason if that was the case. Surely, she would call someone besides him if she really felt threatened, wouldn't she?

Whichever way it went, chances were that the case would be solved in the next few hours. He glanced sideways at Lark.

Losing Julia had been devastating; it had taken him two years to get beyond his guilt and anger over her death. Putting Lark in danger now was unthinkable.

Yet wasn't that exactly what he was speeding north to do?

Chapter Twenty

Bronwyn's first reaction upon discovering the ring gone that Sunday morning was annoyance. Supposing that it had somehow fallen off the windowsill, she got down on her hands and knees and made a hasty search of the floor in the vicinity of the window.

Finding nothing, she sighed, dressed in a pair of jeans and a baggy sweater, and slipped outside unnoticed so that she could search the lawn directly beneath her window.

When she again found nothing, she began to worry.

A more thorough search of both areas still turned up no trace of the ring so that, by the time she had gone inside and joined her parents for breakfast, her mind was on anything but the eggs, toast, mushrooms, and grilled tomato her mother set in front of her.

"What's up for you today?" her mother inquired, unaware of her distress. "Coming to church with us?"

"I have work to do up at the centre," Bronwyn mumbled, wondering if she'd imagined the whole thing. *Maybe I am crazy,* she thought with a shudder. *Maybe I am turning into someone like Granny Powers.* But she didn't think Granny Powers had imagined things like a dead woman's wedding ring in her pocket.

"You're always working," observed her father. "Got enough saved to replace that old car yet?"

Bronwyn shook her head. "I'm on salary, so I don't get paid extra when I work weekends." She cut into the broiled tomato with her knife. "Once the feast day celebration is over, I won't be so busy. Maybe I can take a few days for myself."

"That'll be good," her mother concluded. "Maybe then you can have more of a social life. It's been nice seeing you going out a bit lately."

Bronwyn rolled her eyes. "Don't get excited, Mum. I've only been asked out so Detective Cooper and Davyyd Paisley can grill me about what I know."

"Surely that's not true," her mum protested.

"Of course, it's not." Her dad reached for the butter. "You're an attractive girl, Bronwyn. The case may have served as an excuse, but if they're honest with you those two men asked you out for reasons that had nothing to do with Glynnis' death."

Detective Inspector Sean Notley and his crew of technicians turned up at the door before they'd finished breakfast, preventing Bronwyn from conducting a more thorough search for the ring and sending her into an irrational panic that they'd find it before she could hide it.

The only thing she could think to do was to phone Will Cooper, who hadn't turned up with Notley and the technicians for reasons unknown to her. The reason for his absence, however, was made clear once she'd reached him on his mobile: he hadn't been told about the search warrant. That made her feel better about him, but did nothing to dispel what had now turned into something close to terror.

She and her parents followed the technicians around the house as they tore through drawers, searched closets, felt beneath mattresses and furniture, and even screened through the ashes in the fireplace in their quest to find Glynnis' wedding ring. She held her breath when they found her brown cardigan and turned the pockets inside out, only releasing it when no hidden ring clanged to the floor at their feet.

When they headed outside to search the farm's grounds, she watched them from the kitchen window, having been firmly admonished to stay indoors.

"Do you have Glynnis' wedding ring?" her dad whispered, keeping an eye on the constable who'd been assigned to watch them.

She shook her head, mute, knowing he would guess there was something she wouldn't – or couldn't – say.

He continued to study her for a long minute and then reached out to take her hand. "Someone obviously set you up, sweetheart. That means you're too involved in this whole thing."

"I'll stay safe, Dad," she murmured, with a sidelong glance at the constable. "I won't take any chances."

The search took long hours, hours that began in agony as Bronwyn feared discovery and then turned to bemused curiosity as nothing was found. Wherever the ring had gone, it was definitely not anywhere in the house or on the farm, not after that thorough search, Bronwyn told herself.

"Can we at least know who it was told you Bronwyn had the ring?" her dad asked as Notley stood in the doorway when they were finished.

"Anonymous tip," Notley grunted, his dissatisfaction obvious on his face.

"Obviously a false one," her dad observed.

Notley stared at him. "Or we were too late."

"I don't think you can assume that was the case," her dad argued. "You didn't find anything to incriminate Bronwyn, did you?"

Notley sighed and shook his head. "Not here."

"You're not going up to my office?" Bronwyn blurted before she could stop herself.

Notley's eyes flew to her face. "Should we?"

"Of course not. You would be wasting your time," she snapped and, although she could see suspicion in his eyes, she suspected the search warrant covered only the farm, leaving him helpless. In any case, he'd not have found anything there, either, unless a search of medieval phrases meant something to him.

When the technicians finally left, it was after three o'clock. The Sunday church service at Pennant Melangell would have finished by then, the church would be locked up, and other than a few lingering souls, the church grounds would soon be deserted except for passing hikers and mountain bikers stopping by for a look.

Although she felt nervous at being in the counseling centre when no one else was nearby, she was determined to use her computer to look up what the Twlwyth Teg had told her before the day was out, despite the delay Detective Notley and his crew had caused. Thus, she ignored her parents' concerned looks, climbed into the Volvo, and drove through Llangynog, thinking that she would just lock herself into the counseling centre, use the computer, and then hurry back home. *I'll be safe there,* she assured herself. *It's me…it's me…it's me.* If she did, indeed, murder Glynnis, then her fear was for naught, she thought. And if it was someone else? Then it was certain that whoever that person was, he or she had tried to frame Bronwyn with the ring, and that would mean she did have something to fear. *I'll be careful,* she promised herself. *I'll be in and out in a hurry, before dark.*

The singing of her mobile phone startled her in the quiet of her car just as she crossed the bridge and she wriggled in her car seat until she was able to pull it from her pocket and see that it was Will Cooper calling.

Happy that he'd called her back, she answered, hearing the relief in his voice as he told her that Notley had found nothing in his search, followed by concern when he reminded her to be careful.

"You're lovely to worry so about me," she said, immediately wishing she could take the words back.

His impersonal response eased her mind. "I worry about everyone."

As the Volvo bumped its way up the narrow road, she found herself wishing she felt safe enough to confide in him. While Detective Notley made her feel guilty and resentful, Will Cooper made her feel protected, as if he truly wanted her to be innocent and was determined to help her prove it. But how could she tell him she saw fairy creatures that surrounded her and told her things in medieval English, things that demonstrated an intimate knowledge of Glynnis' death? How could she say that these same creatures told her, "It's you," as they circled her? How could she tell him that she feared Granny Powers' gift to her was only her legacy of mental imbalance? Most of all, how could she tell him that she feared she had killed Glynnis herself?

307

The car park was empty when Bronwyn pulled into her favorite spot closest to the walkway to the counseling centre's front door, but there were still two people wandering through the sensory garden and the churchyard. The church and the counseling centre would be locked.

She kept an eye on the people as she walked to the door and unlocked it. She slipped inside quickly and then re-locked the door, glancing around to assure herself that the entrance and halls were empty. She gripped her purse tightly in her hands, comforted by the memory of the large knife she'd kept inside since her meeting with Hal Corse. No one was going to hit her over the head with a wine bottle if she could help it.

She scurried down the hallway to her office, closing and locking the door behind her after glancing into the shadows in the corners to reassure herself that she was alone. Only then did she begin to breathe normally, although it took a few moments for her heart to stop skipping.

She woke the sleeping computer and logged on, listening to its whirring in the silence of the empty room. As she connected to the internet, she mumbled the Twlwyth Teg's words under her breath. *Atheling fails. Dog companion carries the chaffer. Common profit must be considered. The guardian must live.* There was no need to recall the end of the Twlwyth Teg's message: *"Thick"* and *"It's you"* were burned into her memory, where they played over and over despite her efforts to ignore them. She should probably have settled for searching on her mobile rather than risking the counseling centre, but it seemed worth the risk to have the ease and anonymity of using the computer.

It took only a few minutes to find the first word. "Atheling: a nobleman, prince, hero, or man." *Well, that's vague enough,* she sighed. So, basically anyone who was male was an atheling? How helpful was that?

Frustrated, she nevertheless took a few minutes to think about the message before moving on. How many "athelings" were connected with the case? Davyyd Paisley, Hal Corse, and Mark McGuire were the ones who came immediately to mind, but there could be others, she supposed, that Will Cooper had successfully kept from her.

Maybe Davyyd had been a failure as a husband. Was it possible that he'd threatened to leave her once he found out she'd lied about being pregnant? Or maybe when he left her that evening at the Tanat

Inn, he'd failed to protect her from her murderer? She nodded, pleased with her thinking. She liked that idea.

How about Hal Corse then? It was harder to think of a way he might have failed. But the Twlwyth Teg had used present tense, not past: "fails," not "failed." Could it mean the protest would fail, opening the way for the gas pipeline to be built? What would that have to do with Glynnis' death? Or was their message intended to relay something else, something about Bronwyn and Granny Powers and....

Suddenly a thought flew into her head, and she straightened in wonder. Why hadn't she seen it before? "Thick! Thick! Thick!" the Twlwyth Teg had shouted at her for the past month or more. And what was "thick" but the opposite of "thin"? Pennant Melangell was known as a thin place, one of those few places in the world where the lines between the worlds might be crossed. Although it was often assumed that the other world referred to was the spiritual world, was it not also possible that it referred to the enchanted world that had always been such a vibrant part of Celtic folklore? If so, then could it not follow that the Twlwyth Teg were frantic with worry about the gas pipeline, an intrusion into one of the few remaining fragile environments that could still be called thin places?

So, if Hal Corse was the "atheling" who fails, how did that relate to Glynnis' death and Bronwyn herself? Was she supposed to somehow involve herself with the protest so that it would succeed instead of fail? How could she make a difference? And how did it connect with Glynnis?

She shook her head. Maybe she was wrong about the protest. But she knew she wasn't wrong about "Thick!" It made perfect sense.

Drawing herself back into her task, she thought about the American, Mark McGuire. How could he fail? She waited long minutes for an idea to come to her, but finally had to give up. She had nothing that pointed to where he might have failed in something, unless it was his failure on their casual date, which seemed totally unconnected to anything else that had happened.

What other men might be going to fail? A picture of Will Cooper drifted into her mind, his tousled hair, brilliant eyes, and easy laugh echoing in her memory. He could fail to solve the case. Would that be a bad thing? If those vague suspicions were right and she was guilty of the murder herself, then his failure to solve the case would be to her benefit. Maybe that was what the Twlwyth Teg wanted.

When she could think about it no more, she put the first phrase behind her and began to search for the next: "Dog companion carries the chaffer." This entry took longer to find, in part because she had to search for both "dog companion" and "chaffer."

She found "chaffer" first, and felt her heart lurch in her chest as a rush of fear flooded her. A "chaffer" was a large knife, a knife like the one she'd put in her purse when she'd met Hal Corse and had carried with her ever since. If keeping old Nan at her side meant she was a "dog companion," then it appeared that this reference was to her.

She stood up and looked blindly out the little window in her office toward the parking lot. *How could I have murdered Glynnis without knowing I'd done it?* she wondered. She thought of the visions she'd seen, the clues she'd received. What if she'd imagined the Twlwyth Teg and Pysgotwr, as well as the visions themselves? What if she'd only thought others had given her messages, when in reality she'd known what they'd supposedly told her because she'd done it herself? *I can't be crazy!* she cried, but could she ignore the other words that ran endlessly in her head? *It's you...It's you...It's you...*

Shaking her head in denial, she forced herself back into the chair and into her task, scrolling through the information with shaking hands as she tried to find a meaning for "dog companion." When she found one at last, she blinked in surprise. "Dog Companion: a lovers' mediator or go-between; a person carrying messages; a person who consoles grief." Once she realized that the phrase's meaning had nothing to do with her relationship with old Nan, she found she could gather herself together again as she pondered new choices.

As far as she could see, none of the suspects in the case could have served as a lovers' go-between, as no one except Glynnis herself wanted her and Davyyd to be together. There had been no messages that anyone had discovered. But who had consoled grief? That was much easier. The obvious person was Rhonda Morris, the ex-girlfriend who had been practically stalking Davyyd Paisley the past few weeks. She'd made it plain that her motive was to reconcile with him, but how far had she gone to make that happen?

Bronwyn sat back in thought. Did Rhonda Morris carry a knife in her purse?

Chilled, she glanced around her little office once again, assuring herself that no one could come in through the locked door and tiny window. She stood and looked out the window again, checking to see if anyone was out there in the dwindling daylight.

A white car parked next to hers caught her eye. The car park had been empty when she'd arrived at the counseling centre. It was an odd time for a visitor to arrive at Pennant Melangell, too late for the Sunday service and nearing dusk. Stretching to look past the car park, she could see that a few tourists still talked in a group near the entrance to the sensory garden.

Perhaps she should leave while other people were still about?

She took a deep breath. There was only one more phrase to check on; surely, she could do that quickly. Then she would hurry out to her car and drive toward home and safety as quickly as she could.

"Common profit" she typed on the keyboard, and she scrolled through the findings until she found exactly what she'd expected to find: "for the good of the realm, family, nation, or humankind." Whatever Glynnis had been doing, then, it had not been for the good of the many and had therefore brought about her death. But how?

She could think about it at home, she decided, shutting down her computer. Grabbing her keys and purse, she paused for one last look out the little window and then hurried out her office door.

As she locked the front doors of the counseling centre, a figure standing alone in the sensory garden caught her eye. Huddled in the shadows, the person wore a hooded jacket that hid his or her face and seemed to be looking in her direction. Her fingers shaking, Bronwyn managed to lock the door, and then she hurried down the walkway and to her car.

She unlocked it and slipped inside, pushing the button for the locks as soon as the door swung shut. Not bothering with her seatbelt, she pushed the key into the ignition and turned it. Silence greeted her efforts.

With an exasperated oath, she tried again and again, four times, checking to make sure the transmission was in park and jiggling the steering wheel in case it had locked up. Not even a weak grinding answered her efforts. Finally, she pounded her fist on the dashboard in frustration. The car's engine was dead.

She looked out the car's windows, but she couldn't see much as the second car parked beside hers blocked her view. She got her mobile phone out of her pocket and swiped it. No service.

Trying to think past the beating of her heart, Bronwyn considered her options. She could wait in the car and hope someone would happen by that she could summon for help. She could wait and hope that her parents would come looking for her at some point in time. Or she could try to get back inside her office and use the land phone to call for help.

The last option seemed to Bronwyn the best. Taking a deep breath, she opened the car door, slipped out, slammed it shut, and ran toward the counseling centre's doors.

From the corner of her eye, she saw the figure beside the garden entrance start to move toward her. She scrambled in her purse, pulling out her set of keys, and slammed the proper one into the front door.

She jerked it open, went inside, and locked it firmly behind her. Then she hurried back up the hall to her office and carefully locked that door, as well.

She crossed to the window and looked out. The person in the hooded jacket had reached the car park and stood leaning casually against the second car. The hood shadowed the face beneath so that from a distance Bronwyn was nearly unable to see who it was.

Nearly, but not quite. As Bronwyn pressed her face to the small window to get a better view, the figure turned to look toward her, and she caught a glimpse of light hair beneath the hood. *Rhonda!*

Bronwyn backed away from the window, ducking to make sure she couldn't be seen. Heart pounding, she eased the office phone off its charger and sat down on the floor beneath the window, hoping she couldn't be seen if Rhonda should approach and try to look inside. With shaking fingers, she dialed 999.

The operator answered immediately. "999. What's your emergency?"

How to explain without sounding like she'd lost her mind? "I'm alone at Pennant Melangell, and there's someone here who I think is threatening my safety."

"Are you safe now?"

"Yes, I've locked myself in my office. I work here."

"Why do you think this person intends to hurt you?"

"There was a murder here a couple of weeks ago, and I think she's the one who did it."

"Do you have any evidence of that?"

Bronwyn blew out an exasperated breath. "No, but I'm afraid to try to leave. My car won't start, and I'd have to walk home."

"Okay. Is there anyone you can call to help you?"

"No, just you." *No way am I calling my parents or Maddock. They'd have me back in counseling for sure.* "Can you send someone?"

"I can have a couple of constables check on you, but it'll be a couple of hours. Pennant Melangell is at a fair distance from anyone I have available, and I have other emergencies that are more pressing. Can you stay locked in for now? And call back if things change so we don't send someone out needlessly."

"I…yes, I'll do that," Bronwyn huffed, hanging up. What good were emergency services if they dismissed people as easily as that?

She hesitated, thinking what to do, and then scrolled to find Will Cooper's number on her mobile. She punched it dark again before dialing the numbers on the office phone, hating that it lit up as she did so. She'd rather sit in the dark in case Rhonda was watching the window.

When he answered, she took a thankful breath. "Can you come to Pennant Melangell?"

"What's wrong?" he asked. She could hear noise in the background, as if he were at a carnival or sports event.

She couldn't speak aloud. If Rhonda was outside the window, she might be overheard. "I'm frightened," she whispered. "She's here, and now my car won't start."

"Who's there?"

Where should I start? she thought. *How much can I say?* "I…Can you please just come?" She raked her free hand through her hair and plunged into a confession she didn't want to make. "I don't know how I know the things I know. I don't know if I imagine them or if I really do hear someone talking about it. I didn't lie to you." There, it was out. Now he knew, and she hated that he did. "I'm not mental, though, really I'm not."

"But who is it you're frightened of?"

Wasn't it obvious? Or maybe it was just to her. "It's Rhonda. She's here and it doesn't feel right. I've been watching her out the window, and she's acting like she's waiting for me to come out. I'm afraid to go outside. I don't know what to do."

"Call 999," he instructed her immediately. "I'm three hours away, Bronwyn. That's too long to wait. You're inside now?"

Three hours? But she'd already tried 999, and they were reluctant to come. What if they showed up and then Rhonda was gone? They'd think she was crazy for sure and that, along with what she'd just told Will Cooper, would surely be enough for them to lock her up for a long, long time. "I'm in my office. I locked the doors."

"Bronwyn? You have to call for help. You can't stay there alone."

"I already called 999," she whispered fiercely. "They don't think it's an emergency, and Pennant Melangell is so far from anything, it'll take hours for them to get here. I'm afraid of her...and what if she's gone when they get here? They won't believe me that she was here." Will might not believe her either, if he came all that way and Rhonda was gone. "I can stay locked in here and be safe, but I can't leave if I think she's gone. I tried that already. My car won't start." She didn't think she was crazy, but no one else saw Welsh fairies or visions in pools of water. She really couldn't ask Will to drive all that way, either, though, now that she thought of it. *Why did I call him?* He seemed to like her, that was why, and that made her trust him, but it wasn't right to ask him to come that far for what might well turn out to be a false alarm, just her imagination running amok. "Never mind," she told him. "I forgot you were so far away." She hadn't, of course. That's why he didn't show up earlier when they were searching for the ring. "I'm sure it's okay. Even if it is Rhonda, she won't mean me any harm. I've never done anything to her to make her want to hurt me."

But Will wasn't ready to give up. "I want you to be safe. Is there someone else you can call? Your dad or your brother?"

No, she thought. *Not even them. They know what's in my past, and they'd think I was crazy now for sure.* "No, I can't. They left after the detectives finished searching our farm to go to a meeting in Welshpool. Something about the sheep," she lied. "They won't have their phones on. I'll wait here in my office until she leaves or the constables show up."

"She must know you're there. She'll have seen your car."

"It's...it might be just my imagination. Maybe I saw someone else and it wasn't Rhonda at all. I'd feel a fool if there's a big fuss, and nothing was wrong. I feel foolish enough calling you and asking you to drive all the way here just to help me get home." And she did. "Please forget I called, will you?"

"But you thought it was her?" He almost sounded angry.

In for a penny, in for a pound. "She was wearing a hoodie, but it looked like her. And she was watching for me." A chill ran down her spine. There could be a perfectly reasonable explanation for

Rhonda's presence, but her actions said otherwise, and that was what frightened Bronwyn so much.

"You've got to call 999 again. Bronwyn? Promise me you'll call…"

But she couldn't, could she? "I won't take any chances."

She waited for a response that didn't come. "Will?" she whispered, but the phone was dead.

After that, she cringed on the floor beneath the window for what seemed like hours, but was probably much less. She was afraid to open her mobile phone to check the time, and when she picked up the office phone to check if it was working, it remained dead. Why had she called Will Cooper for help? What a fool she'd been. Like anyone else, he'd think her mental when he arrived and found her hiding from nothing. Would he come anyway? And if he did, then what?

The worst that could happen, she told herself, was that some constables would eventually show up to check on her, and they'd get her home. Will hadn't sounded like he would come, and now she hoped he wouldn't. He'd be raging at her if he drove all that way for nothing, and what could he do that the constables, who would eventually come to check it out, couldn't?

Maybe Rhonda would think she'd sneaked out another way and was gone. She really hoped now that Will wouldn't make the effort to come to her rescue. She'd over reacted, and he'd think the worst of her. That thought scared her almost more than Rhonda did.

After a while, as she sat on the floor and watched the room grow darker, she pushed her mind in other directions and thought about everything that had happened since Granny Powers died. "I'm passin' it all over to you," Granny Powers had said, and then Pysgotwr had answered Bronwyn's questions about it with, "An ancient presence has been stilled."

What ancient presence had he been speaking of? Although he might have referred to some fairy creature like the Twlwyth Teg, he had said it as if there were only one – and that single presence, the one who'd made Pennant Melangell what it was, had to be Saint Melangell herself.

She thought about the legend. St. Melangell had established a sanctuary for women and wild creatures after her encounter with the Irish prince, a sanctuary which had then been preserved and protected by the prince's descendants for hundreds of years after his death. What if their protection still existed? What if someone, a guardian, continued to protect Pennant Melangell and provide sanctuary not just for humans, but for everyone and everything that lived in its protective circle? "The guardian comes," the Twlwyth Teg had also said, and "The guardian must live." What if their terror came from knowing that a guardian had died just before the valley was threatened in a way that might end their very ability to exist?

Had Saint Melangell's ancient presence been preserved in Granny Powers' uncanny abilities? And, if so, had Granny Powers passed it on to Bronwyn with her whispered words on that long ago afternoon?

"It's you...It's you...It's you..." the Twlwyth Teg had told her. She felt her stomach quake in response. What if they hadn't meant that she was the murderer; what if instead they meant that she was the guardian?

All of a sudden, she had to stand up, to pace the room as her thoughts overwhelmed her. *Could it be?* Could she have misinterpreted their words as they mixed clues about Glynnis' murder with the revelation that she was now to take on the mantle of that ancient presence that had preserved Pennant Melangell through all these hundreds of years? *Could it be?*

And with that thought came another. *Do I want it to be true?*

Granny Powers had been thought of as mentally deficient throughout the long years of her life. She'd made predictions that had come true; she'd watched the comings and goings of the village with a benevolent eye. But had she been happy?

I can't do it, Bronwyn thought with dismay. *I can't give up hope of a normal life, a life that includes a husband someday and children and my job. It's not what I want for myself, not in the least. I can't do it!*

A sound outside the window forced her to the floor again, cowering behind the desk and hoping she wasn't visible from above.

What if she were the guardian? What did that mean as far as Glynnis' death was concerned?

First, she thought with relief, it meant that she wasn't Glynnis' murderer. And second, she thought with dismay, it probably meant she was responsible for helping to solve the crime, for bringing peace back to the sanctuary established so long ago.

Gathering her courage, Bronwyn stood up and walked to the window. It was getting close to dark now, the car park in shadows. She gazed out, examining everything she could see. The white car still occupied the space next to her Volvo, but she didn't see anyone near it or anywhere else within her view.

She lit her mobile phone to check the time. It was half-six, nearly two hours since she'd called Will Cooper. She knew he'd drive fast, if he'd decided to come to her rescue. And the police, too; surely, they'd get around to checking on her now before long. Maybe someone would be there soon, if she needed help.

She could sneak out the back exit for the centre and run for the footpath. She suspected that, if she could reach the path, she would then have the advantage over Rhonda or whoever was out there waiting for her, as she'd walked it all her life and could probably do it in the dark, should it come to that. But it wouldn't help solve the case if she ran away and hid.

Surely her duty as guardian, whatever that meant, included trying to help Rhonda find peace? St. Melangell wouldn't have fled if someone had been in need, would she?

Resolute now, even if she was shaking inside, she unlocked her office door and strode down the hallway toward the front entrance, ears straining for every tiny sound. Nothing seemed off. Perhaps whoever had been out there earlier had been just a tourist, after all, and the thought of Rhonda existed only in her imagination. She'd only caught a glimpse, after all. She braced herself mentally. She'd be mortally embarrassed if Will Cooper came racing up to save her from nothing more than her imagination.

She opened the front doors, stepped outside, and locked them again behind her. She stood and studied her surroundings, quaking inside at every moving shadow, but seeing nothing out of place. Clutching her purse tightly, she wondered if she should remove the knife and have it in her hand and ready if it should be needed. *No, she told herself, it's better not to look threatening.*

She walked toward the sensory garden, every sense alert. The slight breeze had faded with the coming of dusk, creating the stillness that lies between light and dark. No hooting of owls or stirring of bats disturbed that silence, for the night creatures had not yet emerged, although creatures of the day had already gone to nest or den or forest glen. A small fountain splashed lazily in the distance, but other than that, it was silent. The church loomed white in the graying light, the yews surrounding it a dark background.

Bronwyn stopped at the wooden bench that was her favorite perch. She sat down, trying to calm her fluttering stomach. She relaxed her shoulders, trying to breathe in and out in long, calming breaths. *Where are you?* she called out silently to the Twlwyth Teg, but no fairy face appeared in the twilight garden. *Where are you?*

And then something stirred in the shadows among the gravestones, and Bronwyn heard the hushed rustle of grass, stood up, and turned.

The figure she had seen earlier stepped closer to the bench that separated them and then reached up to push back the hood that covered her fair hair. "Hello, Bronwyn," Rhonda said. "Will you show me the churchyard now, the place where Glynnis died?"

Chapter Twenty-One

Bronwyn eyed Rhonda carefully, noting her unkempt hair and the resigned look in her green eyes. She had not previously noticed the big black purse Rhonda clutched beneath one arm, but now she wondered if she carried anything that could be used as a weapon in her bag. If her instincts were right, it was Rhonda that was the "dog companion," after all.

The wooden bench still separated them, offering Bronwyn a small bit of safety. She didn't need to look around to know that the garden would give her little chance of escape should she try to run, but at the moment Rhonda didn't seem threatening. *Maybe,* thought Bronwyn, *she just wants to talk.* There had been no Cyn Annwn hanging around recently, after all. The thought made her suppress a giggle. *I must be hysterical.* Surely the absence of a Cyn Annwn was a good sign, though? *Would it appear to me if it foretold my own death?*

Bronwyn planted a smile on her face, hoping it didn't look as false as it felt. "I'm surprised to see you here this time of day. It'd be easier to see the churchyard in the daylight, and then you could see the church itself, too. It's quite interesting, you know. It's lovely inside, very old, and Saint Melangell's shrine has been rebuilt into the chancel walls."

Rhonda stared at her, frowning a little. "I didn't want to be in the churchyard when other people were here." She grimaced, her frown deepening. "But I did want to come when you were here."

Bronwyn nodded. "You seemed to be waiting for me. How did you know I was here?"

"I saw your car."

"You didn't need me to show you the churchyard. It's always open, even when the church is locked up."

"But you know where it happened, where she died," Rhonda mumbled, her eyes taking on a dazed look. "You were there with her."

"Yes, that's true," Bronwyn gripped her purse in her left hand, wondering if she could get the knife out quickly enough if she needed it. She tried to ease the zipper open with her fingers, but couldn't manage it.

"I was the one he needed," Rhonda cried out suddenly, and Bronwyn took an involuntary step backwards. "It was always me. I loved him, and I was good to him."

"I know," Bronwyn soothed her. "Glynnis was all wrong for him, selfish and bullying."

Rhonda focused on Bronwyn. "Me, not you," she clarified. She shifted her purse to her other hand, fingering it unconsciously. "I love him more than life itself."

Bronwyn tried to suppress a shiver. "He just invited me out so he could talk about things. It wasn't a date, but just two friends talking. Davyyd feels bad about what happened. He needs friends, but not a girlfriend yet. He told me that."

Rhonda glared at her. "I know what it was. You were taking over just like Glynnis did before. But you knew that Davyyd and I were together again. I told you. You shouldn't have been with him."

Bronwyn watched her in silence. Somewhere to her left a bird trilled in the dusk. She could smell the clover trampled beneath her feet, and the bits of nature calmed her and gave her courage.

Rhonda seemed uncomfortable under her gaze. "Show me the place," she demanded after a moment's pause, her voice quavering in the silence of the garden.

"Why?" Bronwyn defied her. "Why do you really want to see it, Rhonda?" She had no intention of taking Rhonda further into the churchyard. She'd be even more vulnerable there if Rhonda attacked her, with the gravestones and uneven ground to try to run across.

Now it was Rhonda who was caught off guard. "I just want to see it, that's all."

"Why?"

"I want you to show me where it happened. I need to see it."

"Is that what Davyyd would want, Rhonda? Is that helping him heal? What would he think if he knew you were here? Shall I call him?" But her mobile wouldn't work at Pennant Melangell. Davyyd Paisley couldn't come to intercede with Rhonda.

Rhonda's eyes darkened. "Let's leave Davyyd out of this."

Bronwyn watched her, trying to stay calm. "But it's Davyyd at the centre of it all, isn't it?" she murmured. "Tell me what happened, Rhonda. It's okay. I can see you need to talk to someone about it."

Rhonda hesitated, clutching her purse close to her chest. "If you show me where she died, I'll talk to you there."

"And if I won't go there with you, what then? I think you already know where it happened, Rhonda, don't you? I don't need to show you."

Rhonda's eyes filled with tears as she fumbled with the clasp on her bag. "You'll go," she blurted, "or I'll hurt you."

"Like you hurt Glynnis?"

Rhonda looked at her with empty, hopeless eyes and gestured toward the church wall.

Bronwyn liked having the bench between her and Rhonda, but as she watched, Rhonda reached into her bag and pulled out a huge knife. *Dog companion carries the chaffer,* she thought frantically. *So, it was Rhonda.* Her heart beat a desperate rhythm against her ribs. *Not me! Not me!*

She had to give it one last try. "Look what Glynnis did with her deceit, Rhonda. She took Davyyd away from you, but she also destroyed both of your lives. Where does it stop? How many lives have to be destroyed before it ends?"

"She didn't destroy my life or Davyyd's," Rhonda retorted, her face twisted with anger. "I can still have him back, once you're out of the way. I won't let anyone else take him away. He deserves better. He deserves someone who loves him with all her heart." She waved the knife. "Walk that way."

Bronwyn took a deep, steadying breath. Okay, her efforts to make peace with Rhonda were paltry, at best. It was probably time to admit failure and change course. Maybe once she was clear of the sensory garden, she could make a run for it? And then there was the knife in her purse. Rhonda didn't know about that. Once her back was to Rhonda, she could open the bag and get the knife out while they walked. But what good would that do? Could she bring herself to hurt Rhonda if that was necessary?

Obediently, not knowing any alternatives, she turned and began to stroll through the garden. The shadows edging the stone walls had turned darker now, and she heard a nightingale trill from the distance, perhaps from one of the yews. Carefully she pulled the zipper on her purse open and felt inside for the knife as she walked, drawing it out slowly and pressing it against her stomach, out of sight.

When she had gathered all the courage she could manage, she flung her purse behind her back and sprinted toward the signpost to the footpath. She tried to hold the knife blade down as she raced across the car park. All she needed now was to trip and fall and stab herself. She strained to hear running footsteps behind her and knew she couldn't waste the second it would take to look over her shoulder to see if she was being followed.

She reached the footpath and started up it. She'd run nearly fifty feet when something hit her hard, taking her feet out from under her. The knife flew off into the bushes alongside the path as she fell and skidded on her face in the dirt.

Rhonda had tackled her, but then had fallen away to the side of the path as they tumbled to the ground. She jumped up quickly, recovering fast. Bronwyn scrambled to her hands and knees, crawling desperately away from Rhonda in the dusky twilight, the gravel on the path scraping her hands.

Suddenly Rhonda loomed over her, holding the knife out as she stepped closer, and Bronwyn froze, crouching in the dirt. "Why did you run?" Rhonda spat angrily.

"Why do you think?" Bronwyn retorted. She caught the glint of her own knife lying in the shrubbery behind Rhonda and knew she couldn't get to it.

Rhonda glared, eyes malevolent in her angry face. "Glynnis ran, too."

"But you don't have a wine bottle this time, do you?" Bronwyn taunted her.

"Get up!" Rhonda demanded. "And don't run again, or this time I'll stab you wherever you land."

"I'm not going to the churchyard," Bronwyn told her defiantly. She eyed the knife warily. "I'll fight you here before I'll walk back to the churchyard in front of you again."

"Whatever you want," Rhonda screeched, and she lunged at Bronwyn with the knife.

Bronwyn threw herself backward, tumbling across the pathway and into the bushes. Frantically. she reached out to block Rhonda's knife thrust, and she felt a sharp pain as the knife stabbed into her palm and skittered down her wrist.

Screaming, she tried to roll away from Rhonda, aiming toward the spot where her knife had fallen, but Rhonda stabbed down with the knife again, and Bronwyn had to twist away so that the knife just grazed her side. She kicked out toward Rhonda, landing a blow to her arm that spun her away across the path.

Bronwyn scrambled to her knees as Rhonda leapt to her feet, leaning down to swoop up the knife where it had fallen beside her. She stood slowly and waved the knife at Bronwyn, eyes glazed.

Bronwyn saw a slight movement in the bushes behind Rhonda and, keeping a wary eye on her as she advanced, squinted to try to see what had made it.

"Get up," Rhonda spat. "Why are you making this so hard?"

"Why do we need to go to the churchyard, Rhonda?" Bronwyn stalled. The bushes were moving more now, and she thought she could see a tiny face peeking through. *The Twlwyth Teg!* "Why can't we just settle things out here instead?"

A swarm of tiny fairies emerged from the bushes, as tiny as pebbles. Behind them other, taller faces watched to see what would happen and she could hear a murmuring as they whispered in unison over and over. "The guardian must live."

"It needs to be in the churchyard," Rhonda spat, apparently unaware of the sounds behind her. "Holy land, so I can be forgiven."

Bronwyn watched the little fairies gather around Rhonda's feet. One, tiny and deep purple in the shadows, began to climb up her leg like an insect, creeping upward quickly.

She swatted at it as Bronwyn gasped in alarm. "Get up!" she commanded again. "The insects are coming out. We need to finish this."

Bronwyn cringed further away across the path, cowering in the shadows. "Rhonda...can't you see them?"

Now two larger fairies had emerged from the shrubbery and stood in front of Rhonda, blocking her path. Just as she was about to step on them, they took a simultaneous leap that carried them midway up her thigh. She screamed, pushing at them, the knife forgotten as she dropped it and pried at them with her hands. "Get it off! Get it away from me!"

Bronwyn watched in silence, too shocked to speak.

"Get it off!" Rhonda screamed again, pushing at the fairy that clung to her, both arms wrapped around her leg so that it could not be dislodged. Rhonda squirmed and wriggled, twirling on the path in a macabre dance as she tried to push it off. Then another fairy, this one mottled dark and darker in the dim light, flew up to light on Rhonda's shoulders, and she twisted violently as she tried to escape it. "What are you doing? Help me!"

Bronwyn stood and backed away hastily as the struggle brought them closer. She felt helpless, wanting to call the Twlwyth Teg away, but too afraid to try it. She had no idea whether they would listen to her or obey her if she did call out to them, and in any case, her fear of Rhonda kept her silent.

Then Rhonda dove to the ground and scrabbled in the dirt for the knife that still lay near her feet. Her grasping fingers swirled in the dirt as she panted and cried, still trying to shake the Twlwyth Teg free as more surrounded her. Her fingers found their target, and the knife came up from the ground and stabbed toward the mottled fairy on her back. It leapt away when it saw the knife blade, but not quickly enough. With a shriek of pain, it fell from her back with a spray of dark blood.

The others reacted immediately, diving off her body and toward the bushes, fleeing both their enemy and their responsibility.

Rhonda gasped, looking around desperately. "Where are they?" she demanded, waving the knife again.

"I don't know," Bronwyn told her, edging toward the spot where her own knife had fallen.

Rhonda stepped closer, stopping her in her tracks. "What were they?" she choked, her voice barely under control.

Bronwyn shook her head again. "Your imagination, I guess, Rhonda. You're not well. Let me get you some help, okay?"

Rhonda glared at her and then abruptly whirled and ran back up the trail toward the church.

It didn't take long for her to disappear in the near total darkness. Bronwyn knelt by the side of the footpath and felt in the grass until she found her knife. She picked it up, tucked it in her hand with the blade downward, and began to follow Rhonda, seeing the dim shapes of shrubbery and fence beside the trail that guided her. Her other hand dripped wetly, blood flowing freely from the knife wound. How Rhonda could run puzzled her. *Maybe she'll run into a tree and knock herself out*, Bronwyn thought irrationally. *Maybe she just ran a little way and is waiting for me ahead.*

She didn't know what else to do but to return to the centre. It was too dark with no moon to walk the footpath all the way to the village and too cold to just hide and wait for morning. The counseling centre would be safe enough if she could get inside and lock the doors, and surely someone would be there soon. They hadn't come far down the trail before Rhonda had tackled her. Even in the dark, it should take just a short time to walk back out again.

She walked carefully and quietly, ignoring the urge to run. Her cut hand and wrist throbbed, and when she felt the wounds with her other hand, she felt the slick wetness of blood. She listened for rustling in the grass and bushes, stopping when she thought she heard something and then continuing on when no one emerged to threaten her. An owl hooted in the distance, a steady voice that came at regular intervals. When crickets and frogs began to join it in a nighttime chorus a short time later, Bronwyn felt she could scream. *How can I hear Rhonda through all that noise?*

She had only walked a short way when a torch lit the night, sweeping from side to side across her path. She froze in place, wondering if she should hide behind something or crouch beside the trail. *Rhonda didn't have a torch,* she reminded herself. *Or did she? Who knows what was in that big bag besides a knife?*

Then the torchlight found her and stopped, fixing her in its bright glare. "Bronwyn?"

"Will!" she shouted as relief flooded her and made her legs weak. She took a stumbling step toward the torch and stopped, nearly falling. "Will you put that down? I can't see."

"Sorry," he said, and the torch's beam lowered to the pathway beneath her feet. She knew where she was once she saw the landmarks in its light, almost to the car park. "What are you doing out here?"

She could hear something odd in his voice, a tentative note. *He thinks I've gone mental.* "It's Rhonda, Will. She's here, and she's the one who killed Glynnis. She told me so."

"You're sure she's here? I didn't see her." Alarm in his voice frightened her, but still that note of hesitation remained.

He doesn't believe me. "She waited for me in the sensory garden." She started walking toward him slowly, although what she really wanted was to run to him and feel the safety he brought with him. "She was mad because I'd had dinner with Davyyd. She said she wanted me to show her where Glynnis died, but when I wouldn't go with her, she attacked me."

"Where is she now?"

She could see him now, could see the doubt and fear combined in his face. "I don't know. She ran away, back toward the car park." She held out her wounded hand. "She stabbed me with a knife when she tackled me."

He looked at her and then raised the light to flash it on her hand. She held it out, blood still dripping from the open wound. She could see the cut in her palm now, a deep cut but in the fleshy part where she supposed it would do little damage. The cut trailed down her wrist, fortunately shallower but still bleeding.

He reached out with his free hand to take hers and held it palm up, examining the cut in the light. "Looks deep, but I think it'll be fine," he said, and then he suddenly dropped her hand and took a step backward, swinging the torch to light her other hand. "What's that?"

Bronwyn stood very still. "It's a knife, Will. I had one, too. I put it in my purse when I went to meet Hal Corse, and I still had it with me."

It was hard to see against the glare of the torch, but there was no mistaking the alarm in Will's voice. "Give it to me, Bronwyn."

She held it out, handle up and blade down.

He reached out with his free hand and snatched it from her, stepping back again. "What's this really about, Bronwyn?"

"I told you…" she started, but then they both turned toward the car park as a scream cut through the quiet of the night.

"Lark!" blurted Will, and he turned and ran, holding the torch in front of him like a spotlight to light the way.

Bronwyn ran after him, trying to keep up with his longer stride. She didn't want to lose the light, nor did she want to lose his protection. Who was screaming?

Then the scream was cut off, ending abruptly as they raced from the pathway's entrance and into the car park. Will kept running, his torch now lighting the third car that occupied a space across from Bronwyn's and the white car – his MGF. As they approached, Bronwyn could see gashes in the soft convertible top and an opened door that gaped to show no one inside.

"Lark!" Will shouted, stopping beside the car and flashing the light inside.

Lark? Who…? Bronwyn ran up behind him and stopped. "You brought your niece?"

"I had to bring her along," he panted before calling out again. "Lark!"

"Rhonda has her," Bronwyn moaned.

"I didn't know whether to believe you or not," he cried. The torchlight gleamed on the edges of the car park, the yews, the church, the counseling centre as he used it to search. "I left her locked in the car." He paced a few feet one way, and then another. "Lark!"

"It wouldn't have been hard for Rhonda to cut through the top." Bronwyn caught a sob. "We have to find her before anything happens."

Will swung the torch in an arc. "Not you," he said, already moving toward the churchyard. "You go inside and call 999. I can't think why you didn't insist they come when you called earlier. Then lock yourself in and watch for us out the window. If I come back with Lark, you can unlock the door, but not before. Understand?"

"No," Bronwyn protested. "I can help you search. It's me she wants, not Lark."

He turned to her, grabbing her arms. "I don't have time to argue with you, Bronwyn," he snapped. "You go inside and stay there. I have enough to worry about with Lark. I don't need another person out there distracting me."

"But I can help…" *The Twlwyth Teg might help again if I'm there to call them.* "I left my keys in my purse, and I threw it at Rhonda. I don't have them. And the phone is dead anyway."

"What?" he asked incredulously.

"I don't have the keys, and the phone stopped working right after I called you."

"Then go find somewhere where you can hide." His voice was impatient. "I don't have time for this, Bronwyn." He reached into his pocket and pulled out his keys. "Here, I have another idea. Take my car and drive into town so you can call 999 again. And tell them to hurry!"

She resisted. "Over there," she pointed. "Shine it over there and I'll see if I can find my purse. My phone's inside."

"Just get in the car. My phone's in there. Go!"

"What if you get hurt? Who's going to help Lark then?"

He whipped around to face her. "You can't help me. Get that through your thick head. The best thing you can do is to drive somewhere where you can get real help."

She could see the sense in summoning help, and she knew she'd tried his patience to the limit. "Okay, it's not far to where your mobile will work. I'll be right back."

He swung the torch in a broad arc. "I'm going to look in the churchyard. You stay somewhere safe if you come back. Or better, go on home. That way I don't have to worry."

But what about Lark? Bronwyn ran toward the car park as he swung the torch to light the churchyard. A lump lay almost directly in the path, her purse; it was a wonder they hadn't stumbled over it. She followed him just long enough to pick it up, and then ran to his car.

The little car rumbled to life, and she backed up quickly and pulled out of the car park and onto the lane. She drove faster than she should have, watching for wildlife in her headlamps, and within a few minutes, she hit the brakes and skidded to a stop. She had a signal.

The call took only a minute, the operator assuring her that the help she'd called for earlier was already on the way.

When she'd finished, she maneuvered the car into a U-turn and drove back toward Pennant Melangell. There was no sign of Will's torch as she pulled into the car park as close to the counselling centre as possible, got out, and ran to unlock the door. Once safely inside, she took a minute to turn on all the lights in the building, reasoning that the light shining from the windows would make it easier to find Rhonda. Then, ignoring Will's instructions, she hurried back out the door and into the night, listening for any sound that might tell her where to find Will and Lark – or their enemy.

There were no voices, but she saw a light in the churchyard that she assumed was Will's torch, so she headed that way. Walking carefully but quickly, she managed to get to the arch that served as the churchyard gate without stumbling and falling.

Across the churchyard, against the church wall where she had found Glynnis' body those three weeks before, stood Rhonda. Hair wild now and eyes bright with agitation, she held a struggling young girl against her chest who Bronwyn assumed was Will's niece Lark. Rhonda held the knife in one of her hands, and it grazed the child's clothing as she tried to wriggle away from her captor.

Will stood facing them, with his torch fixed on Rhonda's face. "Easy now," he was murmuring. "It's time to let her go, Rhonda."

Rhonda saw Bronwyn stepping up behind Will and tightened her hold on the girl. "It was me," she mumbled, "me that loved Davyyd."

"I know," Will soothed her, "I know it was. And you love him still, don't you? Do you love him enough to end this now, Rhonda? It would hurt him to know that people died because of a bad decision he made with Glynnis."

"It was the only thing I could do," Rhonda moaned. "I never could have gotten him back as long as she was there. He needed me."

"And now she's gone. There's no need to hurt anyone else. Davyyd wouldn't like to think anything that happens here tonight was his fault, would he?"

"No!" Rhonda shouted, nearly strangling her captive as her anger flared. "It was never Davyyd's fault. It was Glynnis! And now Bronwyn, too." She began to cry then, a thin crooning wail that echoed eerily in the night.

Bronwyn stood behind Will, watching Rhonda. She remembered the sad look on Rhonda's face that night she'd first met Davyyd at the Tanat Inn. *Why did I ever meet him for dinner?* she wondered now. *I knew how she felt. It makes me nearly as much a beast as Glynnis was, doesn't it?*

She saw Will tense as Rhonda let out another keening sob. "Rhonda, please…let her go," he begged. Bronwyn could see the torch trembling in his hand.

Rhonda looked up at him, blinking away tears. Her hands shook, the knife chafing across Lark's chest. "I can't now, can I? I'm so sorry." Suddenly the knife swung out and away, its point aimed directly at Lark.

"No! Not Lark!" As Rhonda swung the knife back toward Lark, Will leapt forward with a frantic cry. He landed hard, knocking both Rhonda and Lark to the ground. His aim had been crooked, designed to deflect the knife away from the little girl, and it was dead on. With a scream and some frantic scrambling, Lark rolled away and scuttled to her feet.

Will struggled with Rhonda on the ground. Like a wild animal, she clawed at him with one hand while trying to swing the knife toward him with the other. He battled the hand holding the knife, ignoring the pummeling fist while holding onto her arm with both hands, shaking and pounding the arm into the ground in an attempt to free the knife while ignoring the blows to his face and chest.

But the knife found a mark as Rhonda's desperation gave her strength. As he turned his face away from a blow, her knife arm broke free and she stabbed at him wildly, connecting with his left arm and shoulder. He cried out in pain and lunged lopsidedly at the knife, but she gathered herself quickly to her knees and then plowed into him hard, head-butting him in a sprawling blow.

Will fell backward with a sickening thud as his head connected with one of the crumbling slate headstones. He slumped to the ground with a moan and lay still.

The torch had fallen to the ground when Will attacked Rhonda, its light flaring on the grass to illuminate the very spot on the church wall where Glynnis had died. Lark ran toward Will, but Bronwyn reached out and grabbed her overalls strap, swinging her around behind her with a sharp, "Stay here!"

Rhonda took a shaky breath and rose, still brandishing the knife. She didn't look at Will, but kept her gaze on Bronwyn, chin raised defiantly.

"Give me the knife, Rhonda. It's over now," Bronwyn said, her voice quiet in the still churchyard.

"It's far from over," Rhonda cried. "When all of you are dead, then it'll be over. No one will know it was me. That's the only way Davyyd and I can be together again now."

Bronwyn swallowed, trying to think. "I called 999. The police know it's you, Rhonda. It's best if you give me the knife and let me tend to Will before….before he bleeds too much." *Before he dies,* she thought, hoping the blow to his head hadn't killed him already. She couldn't say that, though, with his little niece standing behind her.

With a savage scream Rhonda lunged at her, knife swinging wildly so that Bronwyn didn't know how to avoid it. Shrieking, she leapt to one side, pulling Lark with her, to dodge the attack. "Run, Lark!" she screamed. "Get out of the churchyard! Hide!"

Rhonda came at her furiously, slashing with the knife and bellowing out her anger and frustration. Wildly, Bronwyn tried to evade her blows, seeking a chance to knock the knife from Rhonda's tight-fisted hold, but finding none. She darted toward a headstone to her left and managed to use it as a shield against a vicious thrust of the knife.

"Rhonda!" she cried, hearing the terror in her own voice. "Drop the knife!"

A hysterical laugh and another lunge with the knife answered her as Rhonda darted around the headstone and came at her, slashing hard with the knife.

It connected, tearing a gash in Bronwyn's jumper and nicking her shoulder as she leapt away behind another gravestone. "Help me!" she screamed. "Help!" *Where are the Twlwyth Teg?*

"What's that?" Lark's voice came from somewhere behind her near the churchyard gate.

Bronwyn risked a glance toward the shadows of the gravestones. Movement there suggested that they were no longer alone.

Rhonda had seen them, too. "What are they?" she demanded, waving the knife toward Bronwyn. "Tell me what they are!"

"You know what they are," Bronwyn told her, reluctant to name them with Lark there. *She'll tell Will. How will I explain that away?* "You met them before down on the footpath."

Rhonda widened the arc of the knife. Bronwyn couldn't see her eyes, but she felt fear emanating from her. "Tell them to go away."

"Or what, Rhonda? You're already trying to kill us. The only thing keeping you from hurting us is them."

"I...I'll let the little girl go if you tell them to go away," Rhonda tried to bargain.

"They won't touch you if you give me the knife and sit down on the ground." Bronwyn was guessing, but thought she was right. The Twlwyth Teg were there to save the guardian – *her!* – and wouldn't do anything to give themselves away unless they were forced to.

Rhonda swung the knife around once more, turning in a half-circle, and then with a despairing cry she flung the knife away from her. She began to sob, gasps of misery coming from her in great gulps.

"Give me your shoelaces," Bronwyn called out to Lark. She watched Rhonda while she waited for the little girl to take off and unlace her trainers, glancing now and then at the shadows where she knew the Twlwyth Teg waited and watched.

It seemed to take a long time for Lark to remove a shoe and unlace it, but it was probably only a minute or two. Bronwyn was aching to run to Will, to check if he had a pulse. *Where is the emergency crew?* she wondered, knowing that it had been only a short time since she'd called, even if it did seem hours.

But it had been long enough. Just as Lark freed a shoelace from one trainer, lights swept the roadway outside the churchyard, blue and red swirling in the darkness of the moonless night.

Rhonda had seen them, as well. With a howl of fury, she launched herself toward the churchyard gate, nearly tripping over Lark as she fled out and across to the car park and into the darkness of the night.

Bronwyn ran to Will and knelt beside him, reaching out a tentative finger to try to feel a pulse in his neck. Blood streamed from his wounded shoulder across his upper arm and into the grass beneath, pooling darkly. Limp and gray, he lay still in the dim light from the torch, still glaring weakly against the church wall. She could feel nothing. She bent to his open mouth, listening for a breath.

"Stand up and hold your hands in the air," commanded a voice behind her.

She ignored it. Bending lower, she closed her eyes and tried to feel a hint of his breath on her cheek. "Will," she whispered. "Please, please..." She couldn't finish the thought.

Footsteps approached, and suddenly Bronwyn was aware of Lark yelling in the background. A hand came down tentatively on her shoulder. "Let us take care of him," someone said, and the hand slipped to her elbow to guide her up and away from Will.

She watched paramedics move in and kneel around Will, while Lark still cried out behind her and the man who had moved her away kept his hand tight on her arm. "Come on," he said. "We have a lot of questions for you."

She resisted when he tried to pull her away. "Please let me stay with him!" she cried, giving way to sobs that shook her to her very core. "Please. He saved our lives. I have to stay with him." Her voice shook, and she could hardly force the words out.

"We'll let you know as soon as the paramedics have something to tell us," the man soothed her. "But now you have to come with us."

Numbly, she let him lead her across the churchyard and into the car park, where he helped her into the back seat of a panda car and shut the door. She slumped on the seat, her body quaking with sobs as she held both hands to her face.

The front doors of the patrol car opened, and a man and a woman got in. Turning sideways in their seats, they waited for her to regain control. She didn't hurry.

It was after the ambulance left, siren blaring, that her sobs changed into hiccups and the woman handed her a box of tissues. The two officers waited while she blew her nose and dabbed at her eyes. Her face felt swollen and she knew she looked awful.

"You're hurt," the woman said. "There's blood on your face. We need to get a paramedic to look at you."

"It's just my hand." She held it out, palm up. Blood still trickled from the deep cut. "I've gotten it on my face."

"It looks like you've cut your face, as well," the woman persisted.

Bronwyn took a shuddering breath. "Tell me about Will."

"Inspector Cooper is being taken to hospital," the woman said after a minute. "He had a nasty blow to his head and lost a lot of blood from his shoulder. It may be touch and go for tonight, but if he's stabilized by tomorrow morning, he should recover fully." She hesitated, and then added, "You can't really tell with a bad head wound until he's had an MRI. Sometimes they're not as bad as they seem, or sometimes they're worse."

Bronwyn sat in silence, her shoulders still heaving occasionally with suppressed tears. She sniffled.

The man sighed. "I'm Constable Henry Richards, and this is Constable Mary Tappan. Do you want to tell us what happened here tonight?"

First things first. "The little girl who was with us...what happened to her? Is she okay?"

"She's fine." Constable Tappan seemed to be the one to give Bronwyn information, while her partner asked the questions. "Child services has been called and will meet us in Caernarfon to take her on until someone else can be located."

"Can you start by giving us your name?" Constable Richards asked impatiently.

"Bronwyn Bagley. I'm the one who found Glynnis Paisley murdered here three weeks ago." Once she'd begun, she found the story flowed from her quickly. She told them everything – about finding Glynnis, about meeting with Will Cooper, about finding where Glynnis had been attacked, about meeting with Davyyd Paisley, Hal Corse, and Rhonda Morris. She even told them about finding the wedding ring in her pocket. The only thing she didn't tell them was about the Twlwyth Teg and the Cyn Annwn, but she thought she could be forgiven that omission. "Did you find Rhonda?" she asked at last.

"The little girl said there was someone else here tonight," Constable Tappan told her, "but we didn't find her."

"She ran across the car park just as you arrived," Bronwyn told them. "You had to see her in the headlights."

"Apparently not," Constable Richards informed her. His eyes met hers. "You're sure there was someone else?"

"Yes, of course there was," Bronwyn sputtered. "If you'd come faster, you've have seen what happened. You...you don't think I attacked Will, do you? And Lark?"

"We don't think anything, miss. We just gather the facts."

"But...but Lark told you about Rhonda."

"She said a woman slashed the top of Detective Cooper's car with a knife and took her hostage."

"And you think that was me?"

"We're looking for someone else, miss. We haven't found anyone yet."

"Her car is here. The white car." Bronwyn twisted in the seat and pointed. "There."

"We're checking on that."

Bronwyn thought for a moment. "What happens now?"

Constable Tappan smiled at her. "Now that we have your statement, we'll take you to hospital to get your hand and wrist looked at. The forensics people will be here all night, looking at the scene." She stopped talking and glanced at her partner. "Then, if Detective Cooper wakes up and corroborates your story, you can go home."

Bronwyn stared at her, her mind thick with confusion. She felt lightheaded, unable to breathe. "I may be charged with assault?"

Constable Richards turned away and started the car. "It may be even more than that, Miss Bagley. At this point, it looks like it could be attempted murder, at the least."

Chapter Twenty-Two

Will's first awareness was of sound: the steady beeping of a machine, the snap of a blood pressure cuff on his forearm, the murmur of voices above him. None of this lasted long, however, as he faded away again into blackness.

When he next drifted into wakefulness, sensation had come to join the sounds and, though muffled by something that blurred his mind and refused to allow his eyes to open, the pain throbbed in his head and his shoulder. He felt something enclosing his finger, and probing hands that turned his head this way and that, examining and tut-tutting at what was found. If the voice accompanying the hands said anything to him, he didn't manage to catch it.

Later, when real consciousness began to return, he found himself longing for the oblivion that had accompanied those earlier periods of semi-awareness. Blank white walls, an array of machines, and constant attention from nurses and doctors told him that he was in hospital and most probably in a critical care unit. He lay still on his narrow bed, trying to formulate thoughts that would not become images. He fought to keep his eyes open, failing most of the time. He wondered if his injury was permanent, if he'd ever be fully awake again.

The night passed and some of the next day, though Will was largely unaware of it. Finally, though, came a moment when he was able to listen to a doctor and understand what was said to him. He struggled to focus on the face looking down at him, fighting to stave off the sleep that held him hostage.

"Can you understand me, Mr. Cooper?"

Will labored to speak, but words would not form. He tried to nod instead.

"Good." The doctor's manner was brisk and businesslike. "You've had a serious head injury, but the good news is that you should recover completely. Most of what you're experiencing now is due to the combinations of the pain meds and anti-seizure drugs we've given you. Now that you're conscious, we'll be weaning you off those drugs in the next day or two. You'll be moving out of critical care and into a private room sometime tonight. Do you have questions?"

Will concentrated hard. "How long?"

"You've been here since last night. Do you remember what happened up at Pennant Melangell? It's Monday afternoon, so you've been here nearly a day already. You're at Gwynedd Hospital in Caernarfon. We'll see how you do once we get you off the meds. You may be here as long as another week."

It had seemed much longer that he'd been there. His wakeful moments must have been more frequent than he'd imagined. He tried to think about Pennant Melangell. He thought he'd gone there to help Bronwyn; he remembered that much. A stir of alarm formed in the fog. "Lark?" he managed.

"Once you're in a regular room, you can have visitors," the doctor answered, misunderstanding the question.

"No...Lark. My niece..."

"Was she with you up there?"

"Yes." Will's voice was a hiss competing with the beeping machines.

The doctor glanced at the machines and seemed satisfied with what he saw. "I haven't heard much about what happened. I'll try to find out and get back to you."

After that, Will alternated between worry for Lark and fitful sleep, shaking his head at the nurse when she came to put more meds in the IV bag. She watched him fight to keep his eyes open and said, "Okay then, tough guy. No more meds for now."

By the time they came to move him to a regular room, he felt he'd made great progress. Not only could he mostly keep his eyes open, but he could remember the majority of what had happened at Pennant Melangell. He used his good hand to feel the heavy bandages on his shoulder where Rhonda had stabbed him and ran his fingers along a series of un-bandaged cuts on his ribs. His head throbbed with the worst headache he had ever had, but that was the one injury he could remember nothing about. In fact, the last thing he could remember was leaping on Rhonda as she was about to stab Lark and then tussling around with her on the ground. Why hadn't emergency services sent someone to check when Bronwyn called? It'd have been down to them if someone had gotten killed up there, someone in addition to Glynnis Paisley.

As the medications wore off, Will found he was able to communicate more fluently. He was allowed Jello, broth, and a cup of tea, with the explanation that "head injuries sometimes manifest themselves in stomach upset." The doctor did not return with information for him about Lark, and once he'd been settled into his room, his nurses generally disappeared as well, frustrating him greatly. He decided that he needed to go home.

And then his situation improved. He woke from a light dozing to excited chatter and opened his eyes to see Lark peering through the doorway to his room. He tried to smile, working past the pain in his head to form a grimace that showed off his teeth, and held out his good hand. "Lark! You're alive!"

"No thanks to you," grumbled his mother who was following Lark through the doorway. Will could see his father right behind. "What were you thinking, putting a child into a situation like that?"

"He had to save Bronwyn, Grandmother," Lark babbled, "and he saved me, too." She reached out and took Will's hand, holding it in her own and squeezing his fingers. "I knew you'd catch the murderer, Uncle Will. She was the one who murdered the lady, right?"

"Right," Will said, squeezing back lightly on the fingers holding his. He looked up at his mother. "I had no choice, as you weren't home. I couldn't just leave her alone on the doorstep. That's one disadvantage to my job: I have to go when I'm called, even when it's not convenient."

"That's not really true, is it?" his father mumbled, frowning over the words. "That woman could have called someone else to help her. There are plenty of other people on the force, aren't there?"

"But she didn't. I'm the one she trusted. I worked hard to earn that, and it wouldn't have been right to pass it off at that point," Will told him. *Why can't they just be happy I'm alive?*

His mother seemed to read his thoughts. "We came as soon as they called. We've been staying just up the street at a hotel, waiting to make sure you're alright."

"Dangerous job this," grumbled his father, but he looked a bit proud in spite of it. "Guess you solved this one, didn't you?"

"Yeah, I guess so." *Without Notley,* he thought triumphantly. "Did you hear what happened up there?"

"Lark told us most of it. I gather this woman had murdered before, and then she chose this Bagley woman as her next target. What was her motive?"

"Jealousy." Will basked in a surge of pride. *I solved the case! Me, alone!*

"And she had Lark, got her from that flimsy little car of yours." His mother effectively punctured the bubble of self-satisfaction.

"I meant for her to be safe." Will glanced at Lark, who smiled at him. "She was really brave."

"But not as brave as you, Uncle Will. You tackled her so I could get away."

After they left, Will's mind had cleared enough for him to think about what had happened. It had been risky, admittedly, to race to Bronwyn's rescue from so far away and without backup. But that had happened at her insistence, and truthfully, he hadn't even known if she was in danger at all. Indeed, she may well have *been* the danger. She said she thought she might have murdered Glynnis. If that had turned out to be true, he had been foolish. It might well have been a trap, and there he would have been – putting both himself and Lark in a position where neither might have survived to tell the story. Why had he done it then? *Because my gut feeling was that Bronwyn was innocent and really in trouble.*

And it had ended well. While he didn't know if they'd caught Rhonda Morris yet, the case had been effectively solved. He knew who'd killed Glynnis Paisley, and why. Once they'd got that far in a case, it was all but over. *And I did it! Not Notley, me.* He felt pride returning. Surely this would prove to Bowers that he had what it took to be a homicide detective? Now his place on the force would be secure. And he found that he wanted it to be. Somehow the successful puzzling out of the clues and the triumph of solving the case created a triumph that matched what he'd always felt when he and Edward had managed a big drug bust. For the first time in nearly two years, Will felt that he'd found his place in the world.

Will knew there were questions that still needed answers. He'd forgotten to ask if Bronwyn was okay, but he assumed that since no one had told him otherwise, she must be. *What happened after I was knocked out?* he wondered. How had Bronwyn and Lark managed to escape Rhonda's threatening knife when he'd been disabled?

After a time, a knock tapped on the half-closed door, and Will got more of his answers.

"Hear you have a hard head," Notley commented as he strolled into the room, his cane tap-tapping on the shiny floor.

"That's what they tell me." Will grimaced, as much from seeing Notley as from his headache. He had the fleeting thought that maybe he'd made a bad choice, that the pain meds he had been refusing might have kept him asleep through Notley's visit, as well as relieved the pounding in his head. "Why are you here?"

"Bowers told me I had to come," Notley admitted. "He said it was protocol to visit my partner when he'd been wounded in the line of duty, even if that was down to his own stupidity."

"I'm thrilled." Will would rather have had Notley stay far away. He knew he couldn't be very happy with the way the case had turned out.

Notley pulled the one chair in the room around to the side of the bed. "I guess you're going to survive."

"Looks like it."

Notley studied him, a frown on his face. He seemed to think about his next words before blurting them out. "What were you playing at, Cooper? You went against every regulation in the book on this one."

"What do you mean? I solved the case, didn't I?"

Notley snorted. "Solved it? You were lucky, that's all. The way you handled it, three more people nearly got themselves killed, including you, and you didn't catch the murderer at all, having let yourself get knocked silly at the critical moment. You're lucky the constables got there when they did. That's the only thing that saved the lot of you."

Will blinked at him tiredly. He hated to ask, but his curiosity got the best of him. "Tell me what happened, Notley. As you say, I was knocked silly for the end of it. Rhonda broke into my car and kidnapped Lark. I remember that. Bronwyn and I followed her into the churchyard, and I tried to talk her into surrendering. Then she reached out with that knife, and I knew she was going to stab Lark. I threw myself at her, we tumbled on the ground, and then everything is blank after that. What happened?"

Notley laughed. "That's all you remember? You've got it right up to the point where you were knocked out of the picture, leaving a woman and a child to finish it up for you. Some hero, Cooper."

"Just tell me, will you?" Will's head throbbed, and his patience was wearing thin.

Notley shrugged. "All I know is that the constables got there and found Miss Bagley leaning over you, and you unconscious on the ground. They assumed the worst and took her into custody."

"They arrested Bronwyn?" Will couldn't grasp it.

"What else could they think? She was there; you were down and presumed dead. There was the matter of a large knife covered with her fingerprints. It was obvious she was the perpetrator."

"But it's straightened out now?" Will glanced at the machines at his side, impatient. "I need to talk to someone; to explain what happened."

"Oh, relax. It's all sorted now. They took Miss Bagley's statement, but your niece was the hero of the moment. She told them all about it – how you'd gotten a call from Miss Bagley, driven up from Folly Farm. That's way down south, isn't it?"

Will nodded. "I had permission from Bowers."

"And then you went out looking for Miss Bagley with your torch and left the kid in your car. A convertible!" He snorted. "How stupid could you be, Cooper?"

Will managed to stop himself from responding.

"So, Rhonda Morris slashed through the roof of the car. We verified that easily enough. You'll be buying a new rag top, I'm afraid. She got inside and pulled Lark out, then took her into the churchyard. Shortly after that, you and Miss Bagley arrived and confronted her."

"Bronwyn had called 999 again by then," Will defended himself. "I told her to lock herself inside."

"But she didn't. You tussled with Miss Morris on the ground and then she threw you off and you hit your head on one of the gravestones."

"That's what happened?"

"That's it. That old slate is hard stuff, but I guess your head is harder."

"And then the constables arrived?"

"A few minutes later. Miss Bagley had tried to talk Miss Morris into surrendering after you went down. The little girl says she was distracted, kept talking nonsense – something about making it stop, who were they, like that. Maybe she hit her head, as well? No? Well, apparently, she was frightened of Miss Bagley for some reason. Then she saw the lights from the cars and ran off."

"Did they catch her?"

"This afternoon. She was hiding out in one of the stone outbuildings at Pwl Iago."

"Has she confessed?"

Notley shrugged. "They found the knife on her. I think they're letting her sit for a while before getting to questioning her. Bowers told me I had to come talk to you before we got to it, tell you how thrilled I am you survived."

"I want to be there," Will said. So many unanswered questions...

Notley smirked. "That's not going to happen, Cooper. You're not likely to get out of here soon enough and, at any rate, you're off the case."

"What you do you mean, I'm off the case?"

Notley offered him a self-satisfied smile. "You're on official review. Nothing you did was done by the book, Cooper, and the department can't risk having rebels in the corps."

"But I solved the case."

"With great risk to your own life and others. I told you early on, you needed to learn to follow the rules or you'd be gone. You ignored my advice, and now you have to pay the price."

Will was suddenly aware that his heart was pounding in cadence with his head. "I don't believe you, Notley. I just did what I had to do, what anyone would have done."

"You met a suspect behind my back, Cooper. You failed to call for backup when it was required. You could have called me to go to Pennant Melangell, rather than making the long drive yourself. You risked lives and you nearly buggered up the investigation. You didn't even solve the case. Miss Bagley did. And you didn't save her, either. If the constables hadn't arrived when they did, the whole thing would still be a mystery, but a mystery with three additional bodies."

Will stared at him. "And it matters that much to you, Notley?"

"What do you think? You worked the entire case behind my back." Notley's face had turned red with barely-suppressed anger.

"What does it matter, as long as we solved it? Miss Bagley said she wouldn't talk to you, or even to me if you were there, as well. I did what I had to do to get the information we needed."

"The wages of sin, Cooper – the wages of sin! There's no excuse for what you did to me on this case."

"You're not Sherlock Holmes, Notley. The quotes, the cane, the pipe – they make you look a fool." It was all Will could think to say. "Anyway, you're guessing about most of it."

Notley nodded, his face twisted with malice. He stood up. "You look exhausted, Cooper. I'll let you get some rest. Maybe we'll let you know what we find out when we interview Miss Morris, if Bowers thinks it appropriate."

As he walked out, Will fumed with frustration. Was it true, or was Notley exaggerating, torturing him again? There was no way to know until he had a chance to talk to Bowers.

That chance didn't come until the next morning. The doctor had come in early. He'd been sympathetic to Will's pleas to be released and had promised that if a second MRI from that morning looked good, he could go home if he promised to take it easy and not drive for a few days.

Will was waiting for the results of his test when Chief Superintendent Bowers walked through his door.

"Are you still here?" Bowers asked jovially. "I thought by now you'd have found a way to sneak out."

Not quite sure how to take that statement, Will tried a grin. "I was about ready to look for the fire escape, but the doctor's going to release me in a few minutes anyway, so it didn't seem worth the effort."

Bowers returned the smile. "How are you feeling? I came in earlier, but you weren't conscious yet at that point."

Will decided on honesty. "My head hurts like hell, and I'm frustrated about being left out of the loop. Notley told me about the internal investigation."

Bowers nodded. "I thought he might. He didn't like being left out of things, and then when you solved the case behind his back, that marked you in his book."

"I didn't know how else to handle it. I was getting good information from Miss Bagley, and she refused to speak to me if Notley was there."

Bowers sighed. "No matter how pure your motives might have been, what you did not only put the investigation at risk; it also endangered innocent people. You know better than to take a suspect out for a day at the beach, at least. Rules are rules for a reason, Cooper. This time things worked out in your favor. But what if they hadn't?"

Will suppressed a protest.

"I know you're still working out some issues in your personal life," Bowers went on, walking toward the window and staring out. "Your instincts are good. You're personable enough that people talk to you when they might not talk to someone like Sean. You're aggressive and willing to take a risk. Sometimes that's a good quality." He looked back toward Will. "Still, there's no way you're getting out of this unscathed. There will be a price to pay."

Will nodded. "I understand." *Better to be humble at this point*, he thought. "Sir, I did tell Miss Bagley to call 999. I didn't intend to go in without backup. They didn't consider it enough of an emergency to send someone out, at least not fast enough to be of help."

"That's being investigated, as well. There was a possible terrorist threat in Conwy, of all places, and that was taken seriously enough that personnel were in short supply elsewhere."

"And the failure of the phone line?"

"It had been cut, something you don't see much of anymore now that everyone has a mobile. But Miss Morris must have known there was no mobile service there. If Miss Bagley had been able to tell the 999 operator that she had no phone, they would have sent someone out faster, but there was no way for her to communicate that. Still, several hours' delay in response isn't acceptable, no matter the circumstances."

Maybe, then the fault would be spread out, not all on him. "Can you tell me anything about your interrogation of Rhonda Morris?"

Bowers sat down in the chair, his face thoughtful. "I guess you've earned that much," he said. "I'm sure you've already guessed at why she killed Mrs. Paisley."

"A crime of passion," Will agreed. "Somewhat understandable, considering what Glynnis did to her and Davyyd, lying about her pregnancy and all."

"Nothing justifies murder," Bowers corrected him. "Apparently, though, she tried to accept it when Davyyd and Glynnis got married. She went on with her life, attended classes, never missed a day of work at her part-time job."

"And then she learned the truth."

"Yes," Bowers agreed. "She said she couldn't stop thinking of it then; it ate at her like a disease. She made several trips to their flat, spying on them in secret. That largely came to an end when Davyyd came to Llangynog to work; that is, until that night Glynnis was killed."

"Had she thought it out beforehand?"

Bowers shook his head. "According to her, it was a spur of the moment decision. She came out to Llangynog to confront Glynnis, that much she did plan. She sat in the Tanat Inn in a corner of the room and watched while Glynnis flirted with the patrons and Davyyd sat in his own corner in misery."

Will thought back. "Davyyd left early."

"That's right. And by that time, Rhonda was enraged. Not only had Glynnis trapped him with a lie, she'd treated him badly once they were married. When she saw Glynnis getting ready to leave work, she grabbed an empty wine bottle off a table and walked out behind her."

"So, there'd have been no way to track her down through the bottle, even if there'd been prints on it?" Will felt some relief at knowing his efforts hadn't hampered the investigation.

Bowers frowned. "Her prints were on it at some point, but no, we couldn't have identified her as the killer by finding out who'd bought the wine."

"Then she followed Glynnis out, but how did she get her to Pennant Melangell?"

She called out to her from the car park, and apparently Glynnis said goodbye to Mark McGuire, who'd also followed her out, and went over to Rhonda instead."

"Bold," Will observed.

"Yes, she was. This next bit was the tricky part. Rhonda told Glynnis she wanted to make peace with her. She told her that she wanted them both to go to the churchyard at Pennant Melangell to pray together and that, if Glynnis did that, there would be no more bad feelings between them."

The rash promise, Will realized. It was a promise Rhonda made to Glynnis, and Glynnis believed it enough to allow Rhonda to lead her to her death.

"They both got into Rhonda's car," Bowers continued, "and Rhonda drove to the church. They walked into the churchyard and then Rhonda pulled out that knife."

"The same one she attacked us with?"

"The same. We tested it and found residue of Glynnis' blood on it."

"But what about the wine bottle? Glynnis must have tried to get away."

"Yes," Bowers nodded. "She realized what was up and tried to run off. Rhonda had the longer legs, though, and she caught up with her near Pwl Iago, where you found the wine bottle. It was a full moon that night, so it was easier for her to see than it was this past weekend when it was you she was after. She tackled Glynnis and then chased her into the meadow. That's when she caught up and bashed her with the wine bottle. It knocked Glynnis out for a bit, and Rhonda dragged her over the hedge and onto the trail. When she came to, Rhonda forced her to walk back into the churchyard where she stabbed her."

"Why was she so set on the churchyard?" Will grimaced as a sudden pain shot through his wounded shoulder.

Bowers shrugged. "She wasn't thinking straight, remember. Somehow, she thought that if she killed Glynnis – and later Bronwyn – in the churchyard, she would be forgiven. That was how she managed to justify it in her own eyes. And she believed absolutely that she and Davyyd Paisley would be able to be together again."

Will thought about it for a moment. "I feel badly for her. She seemed a nice girl."

Bowers nodded his agreement. "I think she is a nice girl. She just couldn't stand having the man she loved hurt so badly."

"There was no problem with a confession?"

"She wanted to talk," Bowers told him. He offered Will a weak smile. "She still thinks there's some way she and Davyyd Paisley can have a life together."

"It'll be hard for him to move on after this."

"Yes, it will," Bowers agreed.

Me, too, Will thought. *If they decide I'm not fit to be a murder detective, where does that leave me?* Maybe he shouldn't have been so fast to break up with Lesley. If he had to find a new career, Cardiff offered more possibilities than Caernarfon did.

Not long after Bowers left, the doctor returned and told Will he could be released.

There was a moment of panic when Will realized that his release was conditional on him having a driver to take him home, but then he realized that his parents were probably still in Caernarfon, and they could manage to do that for him before they left for Gloucester. The doctor gave him a list of rules that he thought he'd probably ignore and then signed the papers.

Will called his mother's mobile and, to his relief, found that they were just arriving at the hospital to see him again before leaving for Gloucester. He summoned a nurse and was checked out quickly to his parents' custody.

"Maybe you should come home with us for a few days," his mother suggested with a meaningful glance at his father once she'd pulled out of the car park, "until you're better able to care for yourself."

Will wondered why she was driving, but didn't ask. "I'll be fine, Mother."

"William's a grown man," his father mumbled from the back seat. "He's probably got things he needs to do here."

"I've got a case to wrap up," Will mumbled. *What a joke,* he thought. *Even if they don't suspend me, the decision will never come in time for me to be part of the case again.* He felt a surge of anger toward Notley, but tried to push it away. If it were the other way around, he'd probably try to get Notley suspended, too.

"You see, he's busy." His father said.

"Which turn is it, Will?" his mother asked after a moment's silence.

"Two more on the left, just past the little café on the corner," Will told her. They didn't even know where he lived, never having visited him. He had to go get Lark when she came for a visit. *Good riddance to them,* he thought. I can struggle along on my own.

When they got to his flat, they walked him upstairs. His father stood in the doorway and his mother looked around distastefully at the secondhand décor while Will squatted down in front of Lark and took her hand.

"You were very brave," he complimented her. "I'm so very proud of you."

"You were brave, too, Uncle Will." Lark grinned at him hopefully. "Can I visit again soon?"

"I'll find out when I have some vacation time," he promised her, "and you can come for a whole week."

"After school is out," his mother interrupted. "She's already missed two days while we stayed and waited for you to get out of hospital."

"In the summer then." He winked at Lark behind his mother's back.

"It's almost summer, isn't it?" Lark giggled.

"Nearly," Will agreed. He hesitated. "I'm sorry for putting you in danger, Lark. I didn't mean for it to go the way it did."

"That's okay. I wasn't very scared." Lark glanced up at her grandmother. "I'll promise to be careful when I come this summer."

"William will not put you in danger again." His mother's impatience was obvious. "Come on, Lark. Time to let Uncle William get some rest. He'll need to sleep a lot over the next few days until he's well, and he can do that better once we're gone."

Will stood up reluctantly, fighting the dizziness that accompanied the movement. "Wait just a minute. I have something for you, Lark." He stumbled toward the side table next to his leather chair and picked up the little ceramic rabbit and the book about Pennant Melangell. He held them out toward Lark, not wanting to walk back across the room. "I got you these a couple of weeks ago at the gift shop up at the church."

"Where the lady tried to kill us?" Lark's expression was stark, her face solemn.

"Yeah," Will admitted reluctantly. "It's not a bad place, Lark. It's where the legend of the princess and the hare happened, sort of a magical place really. I'll take you back up there this summer and you can see the frescoes of the hares, okay? You'll see that it's a good place, after all. And until then, you can put this little rabbit out in the garden and read about the legend. It's not a real rabbit, but you could pretend it is." He shot a look at his mother, who glanced away.

"Thanks, Uncle Will." Lark's smile dazzled him.

"I'll call you, Lark." He looked at his parents. "Thank you."

Just like when he'd picked Lark up in Gloucester, his mother gave him a curious look that seemed more introspective than not, a look that made him wonder if something was going on he didn't know about. "We do care for you, Will," she managed.

Not "We love you," but it'll do, Will told himself as he closed the door behind them.

He did feel sleepy – the drugs still having an effect, he hoped – but there was one thing he had to do before he fell into bed. He hoped it wouldn't hurt his cause with the internal review, but he was willing to take the risk.

Picking up his mobile, he re-dialed the last number that had called his phone.

"Will!" Bronwyn sounded happy to hear his voice. "Are you still in hospital?"

"They let me out this morning," he told her, holding the phone to his ear as he sank into his favorite chair and put his feet up. "Are you okay?"

"You took the worst of it, I'm afraid." Bronwyn's voice was soft, but there was an edge to it that caught his attention. "I had stitches in my hand, but the cuts up my wrist were superficial, thank goodness, and the scrapes on my face from landing in the gravel when she tackled me look a lot worse than they are."

"Can I see you?" Will asked before he thought about it, and then he elaborated, "just for lunch or dinner. I've a lot of questions for you."

"Can it be after the feast day celebration this weekend?"

"Sure," he agreed, though he had to suppress a vague disappointment.

They agreed on a picnic lunch that next Monday, Bronwyn telling him that she would need a day off once the chaos of the weekend was over. "I'll make up the lunch," she offered, probably guessing that he had no imagination when it came to something like that. As he rang off, he wondered if he'd feel up to driving to Llangynog that weekend to take in the festivities. *I would if Lark were here to do it with me.*

The week passed slowly, with no word from Bowers as to his status in the department and little to do since he was not welcome at the station for the time being. Still feeling the effects of his head injury, Will found it easy to sleep through the major portion of each day, waking to the now-familiar headache and nausea that accompanied it. He forced himself to eat, relying on whatever he had in the cupboard, which wasn't a lot. During his waking hours he tried to watch the telly, but found himself quickly bored. His eyes wouldn't focus enough for him to read. He hated the wasting of the days.

At times he worried about what the result of the internal investigation would be. He'd felt elated when he'd known the case had been successfully solved, and he knew it was a feeling he'd crave now as much as he'd once craved the high of information obtained undercover. He didn't want his career as a homicide detective to end this way. He wondered if there would be a chance for an appeal should they decide against him.

When he felt well enough, he picked up Bronwyn's sketch and studied it, wondering who – or what – the face on the gravestone was. He still didn't know from whom Bronwyn got her information, nor was he sure she would trust him enough to tell him the truth about it. So, he sat and thought and wondered.

On Friday Chief Superintendent Bowers called to ask him to come in and answer questions relating to his possible suspension. That was how he'd worded it: "possible suspension." What did that mean? Was a suspension permanent? Was it a better term than "termination"?

He decided to take a chance and drive himself to the station, arriving safely. He was escorted to an office he'd not been in before. It was small, but big enough for the man who interviewed him and himself. The man asked questions, and Will answered them as truthfully as he could, watching the little cassette recorder as it made a record of his statement. When it was over, he felt he'd acquitted himself as well as he could have. The man had not seemed antagonistic toward him; indeed, as they'd shaken hands at the end, he'd made a joke about "Sherlock Notley" that made Will wonder if others in the department felt the same frustration with Notley that he did. Maybe having had Notley as his partner would work in his favor.

The weekend passed quietly. Will opened his windows wide to let in the sunshine and the noise of the streets below, thinking it might help to ease his restlessness. He imaged Bronwyn busy with her festival, arranging the races, solving problems that arose, laughing with her friends and neighbors. He envied her the roots she'd been born into. Few people these days had the close-knit family she did whose love for each other was obvious, nor did they have a tie to the land like she seemed to. He wondered if she realized how fortunate she was.

Monday came at last, and as if his body knew it, Will awoke feeling rested and eager to get out. His headache had faded, and his shoulder itched with stitches that needed to be removed, but he no longer felt dizzy or sleepy. He simply felt thankful that the worst was over.

Bronwyn met him at the door with a bright smile that created a flutter of confusion in his mind. He did a quick mental review. He had wanted to meet with her in order to get some answers to lingering questions, hadn't he? Or was his motive something more? Now that he was there with her, he wasn't sure.

They put the wicker hamper she carried into the boot and got into the MGF. Since he'd not been able to be out to get the rag top replaced, it was fortunate that it turned out to be a brilliantly sunny and unseasonably warm day.

"Where are we off to?" she asked cheerfully as he tried to avoid hitting the two sheepdogs who escorted them down the drive.

"I thought maybe Lake Vymwy," he suggested. He had chosen it because it was not too far away, it was beautiful, and it was somewhat isolated. They could talk there without the distraction of other people overhearing them.

"Not the seashore again then?"

He glanced at her. She didn't seem disappointed; maybe teasing? "Do you want to go to the seashore?"

She laughed. "I enjoyed seeing it, but today I think Lake Vymwy will be perfect."

350

As they turned onto the B4391, Will asked about the feast day celebration, and Bronwyn launched into a detailed summation of the events that carried them all the way down the roadway until they merged onto the A494, Will having decided to take the more circuitous main road rather than meandering along on the narrower roadways. He wasn't sure he wanted to be alone with Bronwyn quite yet.

The wind tore the conversation from their mouths as they picked up speed, giving Will a chance for some introspective thought. He glanced cautiously at Bronwyn. She had her eyes closed, wind battering her chocolate hair into wisps around her face, with a look of absolute peace on her face. *She's lovely,* Will thought suddenly, but the thought was quickly followed by a stern internal reprimand. *You've had enough of long-distance relationships, Cooper.* Bronwyn was tied to Llangynog, had been unwilling to leave even long enough for a university degree, while he would have to stay in Caernarfon, assuming he still had his job once the committee had made a decision. Even if they decided against him, though, there were no job opportunities waiting in the Tanat Valley unless he wanted to work in a shop, a pub, or hire out to a farmer.

The short stretch on the A494 lasted only to Dolgellau, where Will once again turned onto one of the narrow little roadways that criss-crossed Wales and led to the outlying areas and smaller villages.

"Did you find out why your car wouldn't start Sunday night?" he asked Bronwyn as she opened her eyes and glanced out the car windows.

"Dead battery." She shook her head. "Why would something like that happen just at the right moment for Rhonda to launch her attack? It makes no sense."

Will grinned. "Do you believe in fate?"

Bronwyn's eyes flicked toward him, snapping dark in the sunlight. "I do think there are connections between things that can't always be explained."

"Why didn't you just call your dad or someone else to come help you?"

She sighed, giving him an embarrassed smile. "After I'd found where Glynnis was attacked and then I found the ring in my pocket, I started to imagine that I was guilty, that I had killed Glynnis myself. I actually thought I might be losing my mind. I thought maybe I'd killed Glynnis and then forgotten that I'd done it." Her mouth twisted wryly. "I know it sounds crazy, but I just wasn't sure, and I didn't want just anyone to come up there and find out the truth."

Will was flattered. "You trusted me."

"More than anyone else at least."

"Bronwyn?" Will said after a moment. "I'm glad it turned out the way it did, that everyone was safe."

"But poor Rhonda," she said. "I didn't want it to be her."

When they arrived at the car park near Lake Vymwy, Will opened the boot and took out the hamper, along with a shawl he could throw on the ground for them to sit on. They set out on the footpath toward the lake, their footsteps muffled by a layer of fir needles and their way lit by brilliant sunbeams that forked through the trees.

As they emerged onto a viewpoint, Bronwyn stopped and caught her breath. "It's such a glorious lake," she told Will. "I'm glad they've left most of it primitive and not allowed holiday cottages built up all around it."

He stood beside her and took in the view. The brilliant lake sparkled in the sunlight as the water moved in the slight breeze. Although from this distance they could see the dam and its accompanying clutter of buildings on the one end of the lake, the rest remained nearly unscathed, with patches of evergreen forests reaching right to the water's edge. He gestured toward the dam. "Too bad about that."

"Yes, it seems we can't leave anything alone, can we? We always have to leave scars on the most beautiful places."

Will heard the wistfulness in her voice. "Like the gas pipeline would do."

"Yes, "she agreed, "like that." She looked at him shyly. "Did you know I'd joined the protestors?"

He raised his eyebrows. "You've joined Hal Corse and the others?"

She blushed. "Yes, well, it seemed like a good cause to me." She laughed when she said it, but Will thought there was something she was leaving unsaid, some echo in the air that spoke of a secret well-guarded. "I've gotten to know Hal Corse, and he's not a bad man. He's actually just determined not to see our valley misused again, like it was in our grandparents' day when they had the mines and the quarry. I guess you could call him an environmentalist."

"And now you've joined in, as well?"

She shrugged. "Pennant Melangell is one of the few thin places left in the world," she murmured. She seemed to speak with reluctance, and Will leaned closer to listen. "Places like that need to be protected now, or whatever it is that makes them mystical will vanish and we'll never get it back."

He thought about it. *The face in the sketch.* "Then you do believe there's some sort of magic at Pennant Melangell?"

"I think the Welsh prince's protection is still a force there, which explains the healing tranquility of the place. It's why we can be so successful with the counseling centre and why people are drawn to the shrine." She blushed again. "I can't explain it, but it's real. The mysticism exists."

"I believe you," Will told her.

They hiked to the water's edge and found a clearing with a picnic table as if it had been placed there for their pleasure. Bronwyn spread the shawl on the table and then opened the hamper.

"I'm afraid it's just an assortment of cheeses, bread, and fruit," she apologized. "I had to think of something vegetarian, which is something I'm still getting used to. But I did bring a nice bottle of wine." She peered at Will hopefully.

He looked at the offerings. "I'd say it's a real treat," he complimented her, "and all local, too, I'd venture."

"Well, there are a couple of English cheeses that are local and an Irish cheddar, as well," she said, "and I promise they're all nice."

He reached out for the bottle of wine. "It looks perfect." He saw Bronwyn relax and smiled to himself. Maybe the hour and a half drive between Caernarfon and Llangynog wasn't insurmountable, after all. But no…it would be close enough to date someone, but if he was thinking of a long-term relationship, it would never work out. *Leave her be, Cooper.*

It was while they ate their lunch that he was able to ask the questions that had nagged at him.

"Bronwyn...how did you really know?" He took a sip of the wine and looked at her, studying her face. "How did you really know where Glynnis was attacked? How did you find the wine bottle? How did you know about the rash promise?"

She blinked, suddenly thoughtful. "I told you I keep my eyes and ears more open than most."

"Yes, but...that doesn't tell me much," he said. "Somehow you found out that Glynnis had been attacked while you were walking up that footpath on that Sunday morning. Who did you meet? Who told you about it?"

"It wasn't Rhonda," she said, "so telling you wouldn't have helped you solve the crime, would it?"

Trust me, he thought. "No, it's just my curiosity that needs to be satisfied. There was someone, wasn't there?"

She bit her lip, considering. "Yes, there was someone," she said after a moment's thought, "but I can't tell you who it was. What I can tell you is that nothing could have been done to save Glynnis at that point, nothing I could have done or anyone else could have done, so it didn't make any difference what I was told or who told me."

"Then why tell you?"

"I don't know. I honestly don't."

"And the same person showed you where she was attacked."

She nodded. "Yes."

"Why not just tell you who'd murdered her then and have it done with?"

She looked surprised. "It's not..." she started and then corrected herself. "I'm not sure if my source even knew who'd done it."

Now it was Will who took a minute to let that digest. *Do I dare?* he wondered. *Can I tell her what I suspect?* "I saw some of your sketches at the gift shop in the church."

She seemed confused by the sudden change of topics. "I thought you might have."

"When I looked closely, I noticed something nearly hidden in one of them," he went on, watching as her face paled in the sunlight. *Hit a nerve there,* he thought. *I knew it!* "There's a face drawn onto one of the gravestones that you don't notice until you really study the sketch."

She looked at him, her eyes wary. "I do that sometimes." She tried to make her voice light, playful, but he could see that it was a strain. "Wales is a mystical country. I put the faces into some of my sketches to try to incorporate some of that magic. I always wonder if anyone will notice."

"I noticed." Will kept it short, waiting for her to become uncomfortable enough to elaborate.

She decided to go on the attack instead. "Are you saying you think something – a Welsh fairie maybe? – told me about Glynnis? Do you believe in the Twlwyth Teg, Will?"

"The....?" Will hadn't heard the name before and Welsh words always flustered him.

"The Twlwyth Teg. Welsh fairies. Is that what you think?" Her tone was still playful, but he could see the fear mixed with hope on her face. He knew that she wanted him to leave the topic alone.

He forced a laugh. "Of course not. I wasn't hinting at anything of the kind." *I guess I'll never know the truth. Oh, Bronwyn, why can't you trust me?* "But if you won't tell me your source, will you at least tell me about Glynnis' ring? You said you had it, didn't you?"

Now Bronwyn smiled at him, her relief apparent. "Yes, I had it. I found it in my jumper pocket. I had seen everyone connected with the case – Davyyd Paisley, Hal Corse, Rhonda – and I thought one of them must have put it there, but I didn't know who. I was in a total panic when Sherlock and his friends came to search."

Will grinned at the reference to Notley's nickname. "Where did you hide it?"

She shook her head. "That's the funny thing. I didn't. It had just disappeared from my bedroom sometime during the night. I never did find it again."

Will frowned. "Another strange coincidence?"

"I guess so," Bronwyn agreed. "I don't know how to explain it. Maybe the dog ate it."

They moved onto safer topics after that. Mark McGuire had gone back home to the United States, Will told her, having had that information from Constable Quigley on the day he'd gone in to meet with the man who was investigating his misbehavior on the case.

"And Davyyd Paisley has left the job and gone back to Cardiff," she offered her own tidbit of gossip. "Apparently Glynnis' mother was harassing him terribly, thinking that he was going back to Rhonda all along, and he could hardly wait to get away from her."

"Poor man. I wonder if he'll ever get back to a normal life again?"

"I hope so," Bronwyn said. "He was really nice."

"And Rhonda was a nice girl, as well," Will responded automatically. "She just couldn't face the idea that Glynnis would spend her life making Davyyd miserable."

"It's terrible," Bronwyn agreed, "what happened just because of Glynnis' bullying."

"That's often the way it is," Will told her. "It's often the victim who pushes the killer into doing something horrible. Everyone ends up losing something in the end."

Later they packed up the remains of the lunch and he drove her back home to Llangynog, taking the small back roads at a leisurely pace. The countryside had blossomed with late spring. Lush with knee-high grass, wildflowers, and luxuriant shrubbery, it lured them around bends in the road and through the small villages. They stopped in Oswestry for an ice cream and then finished the drive to Llangynog, though both seemed reluctant to finish the day's outing.

That evening back in his flat, Will received the phone call he'd been waiting for.

"Bowers here," said the brisk voice, and Will's heart thumped so strongly that he was afraid the chief superintendent would hear it over the phone.

"Yes?" Will held his breath, waiting for the verdict.

"You'll have two weeks' suspension without pay," Bowers informed him, "including last week. The report will go in your file, but as long as there aren't any further violations of department policy, you still have a job if you want it."

"Yes, sir, I do," Will managed. He felt like whooping with joy. "So, I can come back next week?"

"Actually, we'll be putting you on call this weekend as it's your turn in the rotation," Bowers told him passively. "That alright with you, or did you have a holiday planned?"

Will smiled at the sarcastic tone. "No, sir, no holidays. I'll be ready if I'm called."

"Yes, well," Bowers went on, "you won't be driving up from England or South Wales?"

"No, sir, I'll stay close by."

As he closed his phone, Will grinned. He reached for his bottle of Famous Grouse and poured himself a celebratory drink. *I did it,* he thought. *I solved the case, and I put Julia's death behind me.* Suddenly, life seemed full of possibilities.

And he hadn't totally eliminated Bronwyn Bagley as one of those possibilities...

Chapter Twenty-Three

That August day had begun with brilliant sunshine and a mugginess that kept the sheep dozing beneath the apple tree in the pasture. By afternoon when Bronwyn arrived home from the counseling centre, black clouds had appeared atop the mountains to the west. A feeling of nervous anticipation brought the collies begging at the kitchen door, and Bronwyn let them in as she let herself out.

She strolled across the yard, climbed the fence into the pasture, and waved at old Nan to join her as she headed toward the forested area on the other side. Perspiration matted the hair on her neck, but she kept walking as she had every evening that quiet summer.

The pool of water was still and dark when she arrived and looked into its secret depths. She sat on the flat rock and patted her side until old Nan jumped up and lay down beside her. After staring at the black water for a few minutes, Bronwyn closed her eyes and emptied her mind, letting her senses take over.

Now that the storm had moved closer, she could feel a slight rustle of wind on her cheek. Thunder rumbled in the distance, a quiet muttering that would grow as it came nearer. Unconsciously, she reached out to pull old Nan closer to her side. The old dog's deafness would protect her from the worst of the noise, but she would feel the impact if lightning struck nearby and be afraid.

A smell of moist earth filled her nostrils as rain began to patter lightly around her. She heard the ping of it hitting the water and opened her eyes to see the tiny splashes as it hit. The forest had grown dark, with shadows masking the edges of the pond. Droplets of rain sprinkled her bare arms and legs, and she reveled in the coolness.

She was so absorbed in the sounds and smells and feel of the storm that she didn't hear the footsteps approaching. It wasn't until she looked up and saw the face watching from the nearby trees that she knew she wasn't alone.

She smiled. "I haven't seen you in months."

Pysgotwr bent from the waist in a mockery of a bow. "You had no need of me." The leaves framing his face drooped with the heat of the day, limply framing his cheeks and chin. Berries now spotted the foliage, for it was high summer. He leaned his fishing pole carefully against a rowan tree.

Bronwyn tried to control her anger. "I had questions that needed answers."

"You know the answers already." Pysgotwr motioned to the spaniel, Michelangelo, who had begun to creep close to old Nan.

"When the Twlwyth Teg said, "It's you," they meant I was the new guardian of Pennant Melangell, didn't they?" Knowing Pysgotwr's habit of disappearing before she managed to get the answers she sought, she thought she'd better get right to it.

He bowed his head. "The ancient presence has been restored."

"Why didn't they just tell me who had murdered Glynnis? Why give me odd clues to figure out instead?"

"What do you think?"

Bronwyn frowned. "I've thought about it a lot, and all I can come up with is that maybe it was a test, a trial of some sort."

"To prove your worthiness?"

"I suppose so."

"The peace of Pennant Melangell had been disrupted," Pysgotwr told her. "Its protection had been diminished."

"That's why it wasn't a sanctuary for Glynnis."

"It was not," Pysgotwr agreed. "The ancient presence had been stilled. There was no guardian for a time. But the work of a guardian is not straightforward, Bronwyn. It is not a matter of simply taking on a problem; it is more often the manner of living a life that protects the sanctity of the site."

"And what if I don't want to be the guardian?"

Pysgotwr's eyebrows rose as his usual merry look changed to one of surprise. "Why would you refuse such an honor?"

A crash of thunder shook the ground beneath them, and the water stirred restlessly as the rain hissed down harder. "It's not the life I dreamed of."

"And what life is that?"

Bronwyn blushed, hoping the rain would mask it. "I'd like the same life as most girls my age dream of – a husband, children, a career."

"But why would you think you couldn't have those things?" Pysgotwr seemed truly puzzled.

"Granny Powers didn't have them. She lived alone, and everyone thought she was mental. That's not what I want for myself."

"No, certainly not," Pysgotwr murmured. "You are not Granny Powers."

"And the saint, too," Bronwyn persisted. "She lived a contemplative life as a hermit, more or less."

"Ah, and do you know of any of the other guardians besides the first and the last?" Pysgotwr questioned her softly.

"Well...no," Bronwyn admitted.

Pysgotwr looked as if he were ready to laugh. "Others have led quite ordinary lives, dear Bronwyn. They've served as healers, spiritual advisors, and leaders. Many are also wives and mothers. You, dear girl, have the ideal job in your career at the counseling centre, don't you? And love has always been a part of your life. I'm sure it will continue to be."

"Then I don't have to give up my dreams to be the guardian?"

"No, you don't have to give up your dreams," Pysgotwr assured her. "As long as you are committed to maintaining this place as a sanctuary, as a place of peace, you will be a successful guardian, no matter the complications you add to your life." He reached for his fishing pole. "Now I must find my fishing hole. The fish will be biting now that the storm brings a bit of coolness to the air, don't you think?"

"Just one more question, please?" Bronwyn begged, scrambling to her feet as a flash of light lit the forest and another clap of thunder boomed overhead.

Pysgotwr paused.

"Why did the Twlwyth Teg finally speak to me so that I could understand?"

Pysgotwr laughed cheerfully. "We can't have the answers to everything, dear Bronwyn! That's one of the mysteries you must always wonder about, I'm afraid. I don't believe it was easy for them, using language they are unfamiliar with." He whistled to the spaniel and turned away.

"Will you come back?" Bronwyn called after him.

"As long as there are thin places in the world, I will be there," his voice boomed in return as he disappeared into the trees.

In the Churchyard Spilled

Made in United States
Orlando, FL
03 May 2022

17453427R00221